I0692688

Crack the
Sky

Crack the Sky

The LEAP Conspiracy – Book 1

Fiona Kolodzy

Plum Drive Media
Reno, NV

Copyright © 2023 Fiona Kolodzy

All rights reserved

The characters and events portrayed in this book are fictitious. Any similarity to real persons, living or dead, is coincidental and not intended by the author.

No part of this book may be reproduced, or stored in a retrieval system, or transmitted in any form or by any means, electronic, mechanical, photocopying, recording, or otherwise, without express written permission of the publisher.

ISBN-13: 979-8-9871990-5-3

Library of Congress Control Number: 2023 - TBD

Please visit **fionakolodzy.com**

Cover design by: Naren Kelso

Printed in the United States of America

Dedication

This book is dedicated to my dear husband and partner in crime, Kevin Kolodzy, who also loves a good science fiction novel. Although I take full responsibility for any wonky science in this story, Kevin's knowledge of real geology, fluid dynamics, and orbital mechanics was indispensable.

Contents

Chapter 1: The Lost Colony

The odd thing about heroes is how often their selfless acts spring from rather unremarkable lives. Great deeds frequently emerge like unexpected pearls from the ooze of ordinary existence. They rise to the surface of that simmering stew, thick with poor choices, selfish dreams, petty resentments and weary surrender to societal pressures. Many heroes are born only on the day they are first reduced to dredging those mucky depths, hoping for a miracle.

A boxy little shuttle dropped from its mothership, then hurtled into the planet's troposphere with all the grace of a wet brick. Thickening gases shrieked past the battered vessel's hull as it cut deeper into the atmosphere. Sonic booms shattered the sky as its slashed a fiery wake across the heavens, yet not a single inhabitant on the planet below witnessed any signs of this intrusion. Only the three men enduring the bone-shaking descent inside the craft knew that for the first time in over three centuries, outsiders had returned to trouble this world.

Diplomat Devon Arkovic rode alone in the rear compartment of the shuttle, gripping the bare metal armrests of his seat and praying the ship could survive this punishment.

I've got a job to do if I can just make it down there in one piece.

He firmed his jaw, fixing all his thoughts on that awesome responsibility ahead of him, while the sky outside the viewport faded from black to blue.

There's no turning back now.

The shuttle creaked and groaned all around him, setting off a chorus of regrets in Devon's head.

I swear, if I get out of this, I'm going to kill Alistair Donahue. How in holy hogwash did he ever convince me to join this expedition in the first place?

Although, expedition was perhaps too grand a term for one lonely diplomat among a pack of fortune hunters in an aging freighter. Devon closed his eyes as the ship bounced through another patch of turbulence. Then, his first glimpse of the surface of the planet only turned up the volume on his howling pack of fears.

This whole thing is ridiculous. I can't do this mission alone, can I? It was never supposed to be this way.

All he could see were endless gray waves rolling across the face of the planet. No land. No people. No structures. Nothing anywhere on that globe-spanning ocean. The thought of sinking below the surface as millions of tons of water closed over his head made him want to wet himself.

Good thing I've got a p-suit on.

A pair of techs up on the mothership, *Osprey* had stuffed him into a slightly modified pressure suit for this journey. It was a clunky, uncomfortable garment, but one specifically designed to handle such accidents.

Of course, Devon had used p-suits before, and they had always seemed fine during EVAs in space. It gnawed at him, though, that he had never heard of them being used to sustain a man under water.

And water is all I can expect here on Marna. Ocean and more ocean.

There was no chance that today was going to resemble any of his past negotiations. Civilized discussions carried out in modern facilities featuring full accommodations for a standard human diplomat. Or, at a minimum, a tense mediation between warring parties on a battlefield.

But even that one was out in the open air.

The invisible hand that had recently clamped itself around his heart cinched a little tighter as he contemplated spending an entire day trapped inside this suit, buried alive under water. Raising a hand to ease the pull of the safety harness across his chest, Devon got another shock. The bulky gloves on his suit prevented him from getting even one finger under the suffocating strap.

Before he grew obsessed with accomplishing this simple task, it occurred to him that perhaps all the downsides of this awful p-suit were a distraction he could use right now. He set himself to composing a mental letter to the manufacturer telling them just what he thought of their inferior product.

It opened with several scathing comments regarding the cheap, stiff fabric they had chosen for the outer layer. Moving on, he gave them a full paragraph decrying the ridiculously undersized faceplate they had installed in the suit's floppy, one-size-fits-all headpiece.

Just as Devon got his runaway fear in check, the shuttle began banking downwards in a series of tight turns. His heart lurched up to join his stomach, somewhere up around his tonsils, as the ship bucked and rolled, helpfully adding a touch of nausea to his diversions.

"Damn hot shot pilot," he muttered, looking away from the dizzying view out the window. "What does he think this is, a combat drop?"

As if in answer to that rhetorical comment, a voice blared out into his earphones.

"Coming up on the drop site now," the pilot announced.

The view out the window looked no different from any other location: giant waves racing each other across the surface.

Devon gulped, at the sight before sternly reminding himself how privileged he was to be seeing this.

I ought to be thrilled to be seeing the fabled planet of Marna with my own eyes.

'Water World,' the crew on *Osprey* called this place in hushed tones. Home of the legendary 'Lost Colony.'

Devon sniffed.

What childish nonsense.

According to the LEAP Corporation records he'd studied, the colony here on Marna had never been lost at all. The entire operation had simply been callously written off, lock, stock and barrel, after the LEAP Corporation collapsed. Still, both legend and company records agreed that a final shipment of precious Glaeon had been left behind on Marna, along with the unfortunate colonists.

And now Alistair has roped us all into this reckless search for a legendary treasure.

He heaved a sigh of relief as the shuttle settled into a steady hover ten meters above the ocean. Once the ship was stationary, a hatch to the forward cabin popped open and Deck Chief Simmons ducked through.

"All right then, Mr. Arkovic, up you go," Simmons said, tugging away the strangling safety harness with a practiced hand, then offering an arm to help him stand. "Now, let me just look you over once more, and then we'll have you on your way to say how-de-do to them natives, okay?"

Panic lurked at the edges of Devon's mind now that the moment had come.

This whole thing is absurd. I can't go through with this crazy dive all by myself, can I?

The grizzled chief ran through some final checks on the suit while dispensing another round of technical advice. Devon struggled to pay attention.

"Remember," the chief said, pointing at his suit's locator beacon. "We'll be monitoring your position and any time we see you rising to the surface, we'll prep the shuttle for launch, in case you need immediate pickup. But your com won't work until you're about six meters from the surface. Your gas splitter will keep pulling oxygen out of the water as long as the power supply lasts. That gives you a full twenty-four hours of air, but try to check in before that. The captain will be waiting for your report, and I don't want him wearing out my deck plates pacing around."

"Okay, chief." He gave Simmons a falsely confident thumbs-up.

The old spacer led the way, while Devon plodded behind as they headed for the exterior hatch. Once the heavy door squealed aside, the surface of Marna glimmered up at him through the opening. His destination had the uninviting look of hammered metal.

Landing thrusters howled as the shuttle inched down as close as possible to the surface, stirring up a storm of mist and spray. A gale of crosscurrents plucked at him as he edged forward to join Simmons right on the lip of the open doorway.

He flinched to see that the surface below now appeared to be a spitting, steaming cauldron waiting to consume him.

Simmons cupped a hand around the microphone that rested next to his unshaven chin and a raspy chuckle filled Devon's ears.

"Do you want to jump for it, Mr. Arkovic, or shall I rig a sling to lower you down the rest of the way?"

Humiliation boiled in Devon's gut. He could see how much the chief was enjoying his dread as he eyed that miniature tempest covering the drop zone. It wasn't every day an old roughneck like Simmons got to watch a tenderfoot facing his first jump.

Maybe there is no way back for me anymore, but I do have a choice about how I go forward.

Ignoring the smirking Deck Chief, he closed his eyes and took in a big breath. With arms crossed over his chest and legs clamped together as he'd seen in the instruction vid, he bent his knees and counted to three. A moment later, Devon Arkovic plummeted the last few meters to breach the surface of Marna.

Chapter 2: Aliens on Approach

Devon's determination to stay calm and find some way to do this job died a quick death as he hit the water.

After his defiant leap from the shuttle, Devon landed feet first into a new set of troubles.

Much as he wanted to get on with finding the underwater city and making First Contact with the Marnians, there were a few other issues that demanded his attention first.

He sank down through the clear, bright water in a slow-motion glide, as his weight overcame the buoyancy of the gasses inside his suit. Although the surface was still visible in the upper corner of his faceplate, his breathing sounded loud and harsh in his ears, and the suit already stank of nervous sweat.

The garment clenched and mashed at him as he descended, first bulging, then constricting here and there, as it attempted to compensate for a changing pressure environment. According to the techs on *Osprey*, since the p-suits were designed for vacuum, they would never fully inflate in a pressured environment. They'd advised him to keep his fingers flexed during the descent, to prevent his gloves from slipping. There was no way to keep the faceplate on the shapeless headpiece from bobbling around, though. With every squeeze of the body portion of the suit, air burped up inside the headpiece. This sent the faceplate sliding from one side to the other, stealing away any steady view of his surroundings.

Half-blind and helpless, Devon drifted lower.

He wanted to scream with frustration.

How can I get my head in the game when I literally can't see out of this ridiculous excuse for a helmet?

It seemed odd that the techs hadn't fitted him with the normal type of bubble helmet that people typically wore with a p-suit. Then it hit him.

Were they trying to sabotage me? Is that why they put me in this awful equipment?

Lifting his arm, he rotated his wrist until he could see the control stud for the pair of thrusters attached to a belt around his waist. It was the second largest of the buttons on the panel, sitting right next to the vividly colored oxygen level display. He dabbed at the control, hoping to slow his descent and make the distracting spasms of his suit less painful.

There was a rippling sensation at his sides as the thrusters kicked in. Then, before he could do anything about it, the thrusters sent him rocketing back toward the surface.

Adrenaline sang in Devon's veins as he zoomed upwards. With an enormous effort, he raised his arm high enough to see the control panel with one eye. Another monumental feat brought his other hand over to the thruster control.

The little engines sputtered for a second, then cut off. Devon went limp as he coasted to a stop. The suit bobbled in place for a moment, then resumed its fall. Before he sank too far, Devon took a few minutes to run some cautious experiments on the unfamiliar thruster controls. Sweat poured off his brow by the time he'd mastered how to move up and down, glide forward, and achieve a steady hover.

Once he resumed his descent, the suit renewed its dreadful massage. This time, the connectors for his waste recycling systems also chimed in on the performance. Now, each time the suit spasmed, tubes in his nether regions went dancing about, molesting him in unspeakable ways.

The sensation was excruciating, but there was nothing he could do about it.

Could those damn techs have been ordered to give me this lousy suit? Is this torture some kind of payback from Captain Doyle for arguing with him over First Contact protocols? Would the captain really be that petty just because I was right all along?

As if in answer, the suit fabric drew in around his chest and puffed out around his legs, accentuating the abuse in his pants.

Devon gritted his teeth.

Blast Doyle and all his dirty tricks. Just let him watch me succeed in spite of this rotten suit.

***

"Please captain, we can't just send equipment down to the planet and start searching."

Devon kept up his best reasonable mediator manner as he explained, but so far, he'd made very little progress in changing Captain Doyle's views on how to make First Contact.

Perhaps it would have been smarter not to annoy the captain

while the man was eating. However, Devon's options were limited since between meals Doyle easily evaded him by keeping to the bridge where only officers and essential personnel were allowed. This was the third time he had button-holed the captain during the week while *Osprey* clawed her way out of the gravity well of the Alpha 896 system to prepare for the jump to hyper. If he didn't convince Doyle this time, Devon knew he might not get another chance before they reached Marna.

"Don't you think the Marnians will all be terrified if the first thing they see is some big scary machine in their waters, captain? An encounter like that could trigger mass hysteria among the aquatics."

"We don't have time for any diplomatic fol-de-rol," Captain Doyle sniffed. "And it won't be harming anyone for us to just go down and do our job, now will it?"

A small audience had formed around the area where the captain sat finishing his lunch at the officer's table. At least a dozen crewmen were resisting the allure of herbed roast chicken and warm bread from the serving tables in favor of clustering nearby to listen in while he tried to reason with the man. Seeing how they all nodded silent support for Captain Doyle's position, Devon switched to an argument that was more likely to engage everyone's self-interest.

"Well then, what about them harming us? You may not care about scaring the Marnians, but frightened people can often react violently."

"I'd like to see them try!"

Devon backed off a step at the captain's belligerent glare

10

before trying again.

"Fighting with them won't get us what we want, captain, and taking some time to make contact before we begin operations will pay off when it comes time for Phase II. We don't want to start out on the wrong foot and ruin any chance to gain their cooperation for that, do we?"

"Well, that's little to do with me," Doyle shrugged. "After this run, I'll never have to work again. Your fella Donahue and his lads at LEAP Corp can try to set up shop on Marna again, if they like. You won't catch me risking another trip out there."

Devon could almost feel the rush of greed that ran through the ring of crewmen at the mention of the profit every man hoped to earn from this venture. A film of sweat coated his brow as the men crowded nearer behind him.

"But making formal contact and opening negotiations for future trade is the whole reason I'm assigned to this mission. Please, captain, just give me some time to ease the Marnians into having us around. Remember, they've been isolated from contact with the rest of the galaxy for generations. Who knows what condition their society may be in after all this time?"

"What does it matter what state they're in?" Doyle growled, tossing his fork onto his tray. "Damn it, this isn't a research expedition for an anthropology journal, Mr. Arkovic. I've got a job to do and precious little time to do it."

"Don't you think those poor people have been through enough, being abandoned there for over three hundred years, without us frightening them to death?"

"All we want is the Glaeon in that harvester."

Murmurs of agreement came from the crewmen on all sides, and Devon nodded, trying not to flinch as the crowd pressed in around him.

"I realize that, captain," he said, trying not to smile nervously as the crowd jostled him. "But if we send our machines barging into their territory without permission, it will signal aggression. That could trigger an incident."

"We won't be hurting them if they keep out of our way."

"Standard Diplomatic Corps First Contact protocol is to send in one man to make an initial approach, captain. It's the tried-and-true method for introducing ourselves to an unfamiliar society. A single stranger is much less threatening. And taking time to learn about local customs helps avoid any misunderstandings that might lead to violence."

"We don't have time to waste sending someone down there to sip tea with the natives," the Captain said, thumping his own coffee cup down on the table and rising to his feet. "I've got to get on with my job, Mr. Arkovic."

"Of course, sir, and I want to see it go as smoothly as possible for all of us, as well as the Marnians." Devon gestured to include everyone in the compartment in that sentiment. "That's why Mr. Donahue sent me along, after all. I know you have your job to do, but can't you give me a chance to do mine first, for all our sakes?"

Doyle stalked off without replying, so there the matter stayed until the ship reached Marna and everyone on board woke from hyperspace hibernation.

Devon was dismayed to find that not only was he among the

last of the sleepers to be awakened, but that *Osprey* had been in orbit around Marna for a full day already by the time he woke. He noticed curious glances aimed his way in the corridors and lowered voices every time he entered a compartment, but none of the crew would answer his questions about what the captain had planned for the mission. All he could do was wait and see.

***

Early the next morning, Devon received a summons to attend a briefing in the captain's cabin. He reported as ordered, eager for details about the mission and perhaps one more chance to convince the captain to follow protocol. Instead of the full staff meeting he'd been expecting, he found only Captain Doyle, sitting in a chair behind a small desk with a wicked gleam in his eye.

"Well Mr. Arkovic, it seems we may have a use for you after all," Doyle said, by way of greeting.

Devon's questions burst out before he could stop them. "So, you've located the city? Is the harvester equipment intact? How many people are down there?"

Doyle only held up a hand, then pressed a stud on his desk before reading from the screen on his console in a flat, emotionless tone.

"Mission log: Day two in the Kappa Six system of the Larren cluster. As expected, there was no response to standard com hails when we arrived in-system, so we moved to a low orbit of the third planet, which conformed to the planetary parameters in the data provided by LEAP. We have performed all standard scans but found no trace of harvester equipment on the ocean surface. However, we have detected a large underwater settlement located in a warm zone between four underwater volcanoes. This also corresponds with the data provided by LEAP describing the site of their former colony. Based on these findings, we believe that this planet is indeed Marna, and that the settlement at the specified coordinates is Portbree, the primary population center that was attached to the Glaeon harvesting operation of their former colony. Since the harvester is not visible on scans of the surface, we are assuming that the equipment sank some time ago due to lack of maintenance. I have ordered preparations for a dive operation to search for the equipment and its cargo."

Doyle paused to glance his way, as if waiting for any comment.

Although this mass of information had him bubbling over with excitement, a prickling of caution warned Devon to contain any further sign of impatience.

"I see," he said, keeping his tone as neutral as possible.

He wasn't sure why the captain was sharing what must be his official mission report in this way, but Doyle only frowned up at him for another moment, then resumed his dictation. "We have scanned approximately thirty thousand life forms in the immediate vicinity of the city."

Devon gasped despite himself. "Thirty thousand? We never expected there would be so many."

Doyle only nodded and resumed reading aloud. "The size of the settlement will make operating a discreet search for the cargo from beyond the radius of Portbree impossible. Communication limitations will require us to stage our support vessel on the surface inside the boundaries of the city, which means we will inevitably encounter some of the local inhabitants during salvage operations. Therefore, I am formally adopting the recommendations of our diplomatic expert, Devon Arkovic, regarding initial contact and negotiation procedures."

Doyle pressed the stud on the console to end the recording and then turned to face him across the desk. It was obvious now why the captain had deliberately recorded this entire log entry to include the ship's diplomat voicing a few comments. It was a way to cover his own ass if the mission went awry after this point. But Devon didn't care. He was too relieved to be getting his way regarding First Contact.

"Well, thank you, captain," he said, "I appreciate your confidence in my recommendation."

He thought about adding something to the effect that Doyle's change of heart was better late than never, but that would be rubbing the man's face in it.

"I'd like to meet with the crewman you've chosen to make the initial survey as soon as possible and then go over communication arrangements with your bridge staff. Do you think it will be possible to maintain visual as well as audio transmissions during contact with the inhabitants, or will the watery environment present a problem in that area?"

Captain Doyle's lips twisted, and he leaned back in his chair until it squeaked.

"None of that will be necessary, Mr. Arkovic," he said, lacing

15

a set of hairy knuckles together across his stomach.

"Oh? May I ask why?"

"Why?" Doyle chuckled. "Because I have decided that you will be the one going down to meet the Marnians, Arkovic."

"Me?!"

"Yes, you. You are the only person on board with any diplomatic training."

A thread of sweat went trickling down toward Devon's collar, but he didn't like to brush it away while Doyle was watching him so closely. He cleared his throat and tried for a calm, rational tone.

"Captain, I think there's been some kind of misunderstanding. The lead negotiator always stays in the command center during First Contact. My job is to monitor the front man's progress during his preliminary survey and to provide any instructions during the initial contact. Then, based on what we learn from that encounter, I formulate a plan for the actual negotiations."

"We don't have time for all that, Arkovic. We need you to go make contact with the inhabitants and then proceed with negotiations for the search straight away."

"But I have no experience with deep sea diving! I'm supposed to run the operation from here on the ship. That's the standard protocol."

"Standard protocol be damned. We need you down there dealing with the natives directly. But don't worry, lad, no special skills are required to make the dive. You can use a regular pressure suit on the mission. I assume you have used a p-suit

16

before?"

"Well, yes, but I can't be distracted with that kind of thing during the initial stages of contact. My place is here on the ship where I can keep a clear head and use my expertise to feed instructions to the front man as he goes along."

"Well, that would be ever so nice, but as you mentioned, there are certain, er, limitations on our communications capabilities because of the amount of water involved here."

Devon's stomach went into free fall.

"You want to send me down there alone? Without even a radio link to the ship?"

His hands trembled as Doyle grinned up at him broadly. Now all the whispers and sidelong looks throughout the ship's corridors made sense.

The rumor mill must have been working overtime while I was still in hibernation. The whole crew knew that the captain intended to ambush me with this little plan.

"But I can't go alone with no communications. What if I run into trouble?"

"Trouble? What trouble could there be? In any case, with your background and experience, I'm sure you'll be able to handle any delicate situation that might arise. As I understand it, your first diplomatic mission on Parn IV involved a solo operation, did it not?"

"Well, yes, but—"

"Ventured alone into disputed territory, didn't you? Very heroic, I'm sure. Then negotiated a ceasefire among the hostiles all by yourself. Wasn't that the story?"

"Yes, but that was—"

"Got them to stop fighting and agree to commence peace talks all on your own. Most impressive. Surely you can see that no ordinary crewman could be expected to pull off a job like that?"

"I do see that, but what about sending some crewmen along to protect me? They don't need any diplomatic training for that."

"You mean a security detachment? Why, Mr. Arkovic, you don't want to scare those poor fish folk by showing up in their territory with a gaggle of armed men, do you?"

"But I'll be out of contact." Devon hated the wobble that had crept into his voice that he could not seem to control. "Alone with thirty thousand ali—that is, thirty thousand inhabitants."

"What difference does it make how many there are?" the captain growled, with a frown. "All you have to do is get down there and let them know we're coming. The hero of Parn IV ought to be able to handle that."

"It's not that simple, captain." The sweat was pouring down his neck now. "You can't just meet a complete stranger and then jump right into making demands. It takes time to gain a person's trust before you—"

"Now, now, who said anything about demands?" Doyle interrupted mildly. "All we need is permission to operate in their waters for a little while. We're not asking them to *do* anything. They just need to know to steer clear of the area while we work. Surely a clever fellow like you can handle communicating something as simple as that?"

"I'm sure I can, but—"

"Splendid. Splendid. Glad to hear it," the captain said, lounging back in his chair with a complacent smile. "Now then, the crew needs another day to prep the surface platform and the submersible for the dive, so there you go, you can spend some time getting acquainted with Marnians and gaining their trust before you bring up the subject of our little search operation."

His eyes bulged.

"One day? Captain, I can't guarantee that—"

Doyle slammed upright in the chair, fixing him with an angry glare.

"We don't have all the time in the world to coddle these people, Arkovic," the captain snapped. "You'll just have to do your best before we're forced to go ahead with the search for the Glaeon without their permission. Understand?"

He nodded numbly.

"Remember, we all agree that it is in the Marnians' best interests to have that cargo removed from their planet as soon as possible."

"Well, yes, that's true, captain. But one day isn't—"

"That's all the time I can give you. After that, we begin searching without their permission. And Mr. Arkovic," Doyle added, raising one bushy eyebrow for emphasis, "the search team *will* have an armed security detachment, so I suggest you get an agreement and get it quick."

He gulped down another fistful of objections.

"I'll try, captain."

"Very well, then. I'm glad we understand one another. Now, you will find Deck Chief Simmons hard at work in the hangar prepping your shuttle, so I suggest you get moving."

"Right now?"

"Yes, Mr. Arkovic, right now." Doyle's eyes twinkled, but there was no warmth in his smile. "I assume you have no other pressing engagements?"

Chapter 3: Un-Suitable

Well, I'm paying for all my high-minded loyalty to Dip Corp First Contact procedures now.

Devon's suit continued to practice judo on him as he sank lower, and he let out a string of profanities.

He reviled the lousy suit, this stupid planet, and his foolish attachment to protocol. But, most of all, he cursed his old friend Alistair Donahue.

Damn that silver-tongued devil. He knew exactly how to tap into every one of my weaknesses. How I'd be dying to help these poor Marnians. Itching to take my big chance to live up to my true potential and do some good in this bad old galaxy. Plus, who doesn't want to end up rich and famous with a new girlfriend and a better assignment?

Glimpses of bubbles and seaweed drifted past his faceplate while the regrets rolled on.

This is so stupid. I've ruined my entire career for nothing. Here I am alone, on an impossible mission, and Dip Corps will never take me back unless I succeed brilliantly. Who thought I'd ever miss being posted on Marvet VII? The worst gig in the Corps.

A breath caught in his throat as another twinge between his legs coincided with a compression in the upper portion of his suit.

If this really is my golden opportunity for fame and fabulous wealth, is it too much to ask that basic equipment function normally instead of being such a literal pain in the butt?

It just wasn't possible to appreciate the glorious future that awaited him while a couple of very mundane realities were wriggling around inside his orifices.

Okay, so Alistair played me for a total chump. But it was my own stupid fault that I fell for all his blarney. Now, the only way I'm going to get anything out of this is to stop feeling sorry for myself and start acting like the top-notch diplomat I was hired to be.

Clamping one hand on the top of his head to hold the evil headpiece still, he kept a sharp lookout for the underwater city.

Although he'd never admit it to Alistair or Captain Doyle, he actually had zero experience when it came to First Contact. Everything he knew came from books. As a boy, he'd gobbled down histories and biographies on every famous Encounter Specialist like candy. Later, his studies at the Diplomatic Corp Officers' Academy included every First Contact class in the course catalog.

Now, despite all his discomforts, he was tingling with impatience for a glimpse of one of the strange inhabitants of this world.

I'm going to be the first man in centuries to meet a real live Marnian.

All details about the LEAP Corporation's Glaeon production operation had been kept a closely guarded trade secret, including the full extent of the body modifications on the Marian workforce. Over time, legends grew up that referred to the people of Marna as sea people, fish folk, or mermaids. Even Alistair's information about Marna had given no hints about what the workers looked like.

Devon swelled with pride as he prepared to represent the entire greater galaxy to the people of this unique and isolated culture.

Ready or not, it's show time.

Orbital scans had pinpointed the largest building in the city, and he knew it ought to be directly below him.

His heart thumped painfully as he waited for it to appear. The water had a darker blueish tint now, but it was still remarkably clear overall. Shafts of sunlight lit the undersea world lending it an ethereal aura.

Why can't I see it yet? Don't tell me they've gone as far as dropping me in the wrong location?

And then there it was.

A set of tall towers appeared from beyond the camouflage of the slanted pillars of sunlight. Then, Devon marveled to see the towers, connected by long tunnels to a honeycomb of what he assumed might be individual living quarters. All the walls of the building undulated gently as it floated there below him, but the structure maintained a constant position overall, with no visible means of support.

He noticed a large open area near the center of the complex, so he nudged his trajectory that way.

Several people in the open courtyard or market square looked up and pointed as he floated down toward them. He could see their mouths opening, but no sound penetrated the enclosed little world of his suit.

Glancing down at the control panel on his arm, he saw that the indicator for his com channel was dark. He worked the stud with his fat gloved fingers.

At once, his ears filled with the sound of people wailing and crying as they fled before him.

Chapter 4: Annika

The babble of many voices crying out in confusion, wonder, and fear echoed down the corridor.

Annika Sharone stopped speaking in mid-sentence and cocked her head toward the sound with a puzzled frown.

There had never been a noise like this during all the time since she had returned from exile and been offered sanctuary in the Temple.

Why would people be making such a racket in a place dedicated to quiet communion with the Gods?

Annika shot a glance at the gray-haired woman across the table from her.

Her old nanny, Magda, was holding the other side of a garment that they had stretched across a table between them. The older Glae woman still held a strand of weave suspended above the place where she had been making a small repair, yet now Magda, too, stopped to listen to the unusual disturbance.

"I will find out what is happening, mistress," Magda said, dropping the strand of weave and disappearing out the door with a flick of her leg fins before Annika could object.

Although Annika was dying to know what was going on as the hubbub continued, she remained in her room like a proper

Shar lady, waiting for her Glae to return and report. True Shar never did things for themselves that a Glae could do for them.

Then Annika heard the voices of the temple choir soaring above the commotion, calling for quiet. In the ensuing hush, the voice of the elder Abang began addressing the crowd, but she couldn't make out the words.

This was more than she could bear. Abandoning decorum, Annika shot out of her chamber and raced down the corridor, hoping to catch the rest of the elder's words.

After two hands of days in the temple she still found it hard to abide by all their rules and maintain the appropriate peaceful and subdued attitude inside the holy precincts. For instance, it was against the rules for people to use leg fins to swim full speed down the corridors. Temple hallways had thick ropes of woven algae strung along the walls to assist people in propelling themselves around in the approved manner. Residents were taught to use a short pull on the rope, followed by a sedate glide with only tiny twitches of their arm fins to maintain upright orientation when traversing the corridors. Slow journeys down long temple corridors provided ideal opportunities to practice solemn meditation.

Careless of the rules, Annika pushed the upgraded muscles in her leg fins to the max. Rushing toward the light at the end of the hall where a balcony hung out over the courtyard, she hoped to get a good view of what was happening as well as hear the Abang's words. As she shot out of the gloomy corridor, she struck the netting around the edge of the balcony so hard it surprised her that the strands didn't break.

Good thing my muscle upgrades let me crash into things without doing damage to my internal organs. But I can't let anyone catch me busting up the place. The temple administrators might reconsider having allowed me sanctuary here.

Once she recovered her balance, if not her dignity, Annika flicked back to the edge of the balcony and pressed her face between the meshes of the net that kept people from diving willy-nilly off the edge. The elder Abang concluded his remarks before she reached this vantage point and the sound of the crowd resumed, in a muted murmuring of many excited voices. At the far end of the courtyard, she easily picked out the distinctive figure of the elder Abang.

Long streamers trailed from the old man's wrists and collar, fluttering behind him. Those wastefully long streamers combined with his billowing orange robe created a natural clearing in the elder's vicinity. People always refrained from touching the Abang's impressive garments.

She caught a brief glimpse of an impossibly tall, silvery figure floating next to the revered elder as he exited the courtyard, before gawkers in the crowd blocked her view.

As she straightened up, still wondering what was going on, Magda rushed to her side from a spot further along the balcony.

"Mistress." her old nanny cried, gills blurring in excitement. "You will never guess what has happened. The Abang said that strange thing is a visitor from above the upper boundary. He said the silvery covering on the visitor is a special kind of suit because—" Magda paused, eyes wide, and dropped her voice. "The visitor is an airbreather."

"An airbreather?" Annika repeated, with a skeptical quirk of the eyebrows.

"The Abang said the visitor claims he is not a God, or even a messenger from some new Holy Ones above. The visitor says that he is just a man, and that his suit is required to provide him with the air he needs in order to breathe. Do you think that is even possible, Little One?"

"Breathing air?" Annika shrugged. "I don't know. We'll have to ask Suni to research it."

The filmy mass of decorative fringe along the edge of Annika's upper fin swirled about her arm as she pointed toward the doorway where the elder and the stranger had disappeared. "But why are they leaving? Where is the Abang taking the visitor?"

"To the Ruling Assembly Building, mistress," Magda replied, having recovered herself enough to give a proper formal answer, along with the usual small bob of respect. "The visitor told everyone he met that it is urgent that he speak to the leader of all Marnians. So, the Abang is taking him to see SharScylla."

Questions raced each other to be the first past Annika's lips. "But what does the stranger want? Why is he here? Where—"

She forced down the wave of urgency as Magda cringed away.

"I am sorry mistress, but the Abang did not say," Magda shook her head, wringing her hands. "The elder just made a brief announcement to calm the crowd and then they left."

"Are you sure that was all?"

Magda gave another little bob and dipped her head. "Yes,

mistress."

Now Annika regretted not coming out earlier to see and hear for herself what had taken place in the courtyard. With a frown, she scrubbed at a spot above one eyebrow with the side of her finger, considering what to do.

Magda is far more upgraded than other Glae, but it's still possible the Abang dropped a hint that she failed to understand.

As her frown deepened, and the finger rubbed harder, she failed to notice how Magda's upper fins were squeezing together, clenching up toward her arms as her old nanny's distress grew. Soon, they had folded together so tightly that it was hard to tell that Magda even had upper fins. When Annika finally noticed how Magda was bobbing in place using leg fins alone, she snatched the finger away from her brow with a guilty start.

Oh no, I've done it again. I ought to know better than to let myself show dissatisfaction while receiving service from a Glae. I guess that the old Marnian saying still rings true. 'It is always hard on a Glae when they find themselves unable to fulfill a command from a Shar.'

She blew off a cloud of bubbles in frustration.

So much for all my grand hopes of improving life for the common people of Marna. Nothing has changed at all.

For Magda's sake, though, she crushed down any further signs of dissatisfaction with her own achievements. Or lack thereof. She knew that seeing a Shar betraying such bitterness would only reinforce Magda's belief that it was an unsatisfactory service that was making her mistress unhappy. With a glance at her poor old nanny, who had now taken to twisting her fingers together, she set out to make amends.

Quickly plucking at her upper coverings, Annika straightened up the garments that had become disheveled during her rush to the balcony. Magda's arm fins expanded and began to function again as the clothing settled back into place. Annika smiled.

A well-dressed Shar is a well-served Shar.

Careful not to let her gills flutter with impatience, she then went on to tame the wild disorder of her hair as well.

After all, there's no need to rush this and turn Magda into a nervous wreck. The visitor will have to go all the way to the Ruling Assembly Building to see Scylla, so there is plenty of time to learn all she knows about him before anything else happens.

With a calmer hand, she smoothed the long, red tangles away from her face and twisted them into a roll behind her head where they would be out of view. Then, schooling her expression into a pleasant smile, she tried again using that extra-patient tone that every Shar employs when addressing an overwrought Glae.

"Now Magda, just tell me exactly what you heard the Abang say, alright?"

As Annika listened to the word-for-word recitation, another terrible thought struck her.

Oh no. This airbreather is on his way to meet with Scylla. That madman is so quick to anger, he might kill the stranger just for daring to come here. Then I'll never find out what this visitor came to tell us.

Chapter 5: Scylla

The Leader of all Marna surged through the door of his private chamber in the Ruling Assembly Building like a great green wave. Four men from his personal pod of attendants followed him inside the chamber and lined up next to the wall mat nearest the door. Scylla thrashed his way across the room to fetch up with a bang against the window that overlooked the square in front of the Assembly Building. Stiffening spines on all four fins bristled outward, and the Leader's gills moved faster than the eye could follow.

He watched in fury as a portly man wearing the ornate robes of a council member scuttled across the square, heading for a conveyance that waited for him on the other side.

"So, he thinks he can get away with insulting me?" Scylla growled as he swung around to face his attendants, but the four men only bobbed in place without answering. Every one of them kept his gaze fixed firmly upon his leg fins.

"That is the third father in the last hand of days that I have had to listen to, mouthing the same lies and excuses," he snarled, singling out the senior man of his pod as the focus of his anger.

The senior man, Bran, floated at one end of the line of uncomfortable men by the door. Above Bran's standard gladiator fighting jacket, Scylla could see the man's face flushing darker under the undeserved criticism.

Scylla blew out a sneering stream of bubbles as he compared Bran's heightened coloring with his own.

Bran may be the darkest among my pod, but anyone would call the whole lot of them pale when compared with me.

His own skin was such a deep shade of green that it appeared almost black where the color became concentrated on his fingers, toes and the edges of his fins. Unfortunately, any shade of green only worked against him when dealing with Shar councilmen.

With a flick of his leg fins, he moved to hang over his attendants with both arm fins flexed out and upward to their full extent. The smell of his own anger was so thick in the water now that the stench of it compounded his irritation.

"You assured me that councilman SharOhare's daughter was unpromised!" he snarled at Bran.

"I apologize, SharScylla." Bran gave a submissive bob, still avoiding his eye. "Sometimes these family arrangements between cousins are not formally announced until just before the wedding."

"Isn't that because Shar women want to remain available to accept better offers until the last possible moment? Am I not a better offer?" he roared.

All his men leaned away from him until their gills brushed the wall mat behind them.

"Of course, you are, g-great S-Shar," Bran stammered. "It is j-just that these councilmen are all cowards. Too afraid to break with tradition in this matter."

"But have I not changed that law? Are Shar maidens not now at liberty to wed those who were not born Shar?" he hissed.

"Certainly, you have." Bran bobbed up and down in the stinking water like a dithering Glae.

The fourth of Scylla's attendants piped up, distracting him from Bran. "Everyone on Marna knows about all the enlightened reforms you have enacted, great Shar."

Scylla shot a sour glance at the one seeking to ingratiate himself. The fourth-of-his-pod was brave and strong, as were all his attendants, but the fellow had been too inexperienced to have earned a fighting name before being plucked from the arena to serve as one of his personal guards.

"And yet," he snapped, glaring at the young fool, "there is no Shar House that cares to claim the honor of being the first to take advantage of that new law in order to marry one of their daughters to the Leader himself."

"The Shar have always been slow to accept change," his second man, Lothic, observed. "We have seen this many times since you ascended to power. They grant you the title of Shar but in their hearts a man who *earns* that status is never the same as one born to it. As with other issues patience may produce the result you desire in time."

Scylla grunted a grudging agreement with that point. Lothic was always the most thoughtful among his companions, a man who took time to study his opponent before executing a plan of attack. He had learned to heed Lothic's words any time the second-of-his-pod chose to offer advice, but it was not always easy.

"Or perhaps it is a good thing that none of these fickle women choose to align themselves with your House," his third man, Ompire, said, with incautious enthusiasm.

He merely scorched the idiot with an angry glance.

Ompire dropped his eyes, muttering feebly in his own defense. "Such a wife would not be worthy to co-create the offspring of a great leader such as yourself, SharScylla."

"Unfortunately, Shar women from the Great Houses are the only choice I have if I am to increase my status along with that of my offspring."

He frowned, rippling his arm fins restlessly as the odor of his anger faded.

"But you are the Leader of all Marna now," Bran said. "A great and honored Shar. There is no higher status."

"And if I am so respected, then why can I find no wife?" he snapped, baring his teeth.

His only answer was more bobbing and toe-gazing, so he returned to his place by the window to nurse his rage. He would never have admitted this humiliation and disappointment to anyone else, but these four were also former Gladiators. Every Glad knew what it was like to be disrespected by an arrogant Shar.

He fretted and huffed by the window for a time, twisting his fins about and blowing off clouds of bubbles.

Even though I have raised myself up to heights that no Glad has ever attained before, those who are born Shar still snub me.

Only his pod understood. They knew what his life had been like before he lifted himself out of the bloodshed and bondage of the arena. All of them were veterans of the fighting pits, where men bit and clawed and stooped to any means just to survive. He smiled bitterly as he pictured the members of the council seated in the Chamber of the Ruling Assembly. Men who had once flocked to the arena to look down on him and judge his worth in wagers were now forced to look up, listening and nodding while he addressed the Ruling Council.

I am Leader now, and I am Shar. I must not tolerate disrespect.

Drawing himself up, he turned to face his pod and point a huge green finger at the pale and nameless fourth man.

"Summon councilman SharJimenez to meet with me tomorrow," he ordered. "Tell him I have a proposal that I wish to discuss with him."

Turning back to the window after the man left, he cast another look out over the main square and then further to take in the entire city.

His brooding eye spied a cloud of people swimming along above the main avenue. It was unusual to see people swimming along a street above the lowest level of the buildings. Apart from the fact that it was rude to pass by on level with the windows of the Great Houses that lined that street, most people found that the milder currents in the sheltered spaces lower down provided less resistance to movement.

As the cloud of excited swimmers drew closer, he heard the roaring of many voices. It sounded as if there was a festival approaching down the street. The sound grew louder as the cloud of swimmers drew nearer and they began spilling into the main square right below his window. Then he noticed the distinctive figure of the elder Abang near the head of the throng.

Gods Below! Has the Abang gone off his head and come to lead another uprising against the Assembly Building just as Annika Sharone once did?

Suddenly a commotion at the door of his suite distracted him from that astounding idea and he turned to find a messenger, red-faced with gills blurring, suspended by the arms between two of his pod.

"SharScylla," the man cried without waiting for permission to speak. "I am sent to tell you that a stranger has arrived in the city! The visitor first appeared in the Temple, and the Abang has brought him to meet you."

"What do you mean, a stranger?" Scylla growled.

"He is a creature all silver, like a phish, but he claims to be a man. A man from beyond the upper boundary."

"What nonsense is this?" Bran demanded, shaking the messenger. "Nothing lives above the upper boundary."

"I only repeat what the Abang has said," the man whimpered.

Scylla frowned furiously at the messenger.

Gods sink this nonsense! Why must some weird stranger appear now? Those cowardly councilmen will leap on his visit as an excuse to delay any marriage negotiations. Now I will have to suspend any more meetings until I can get rid of this stranger.

"Release him," Scylla barked at his men.

His Glads let the messenger go and retreated toward the door.

"Now tell me," he said softly, leaning over to pin the

squirming messenger with his most forbidding look, "why has this stranger come here?"

Chapter 6: A Visitor on Parade

It was like leading an old-fashioned parade. The noise and activity of the crowd, as well as all the strange sights and sounds of the city, overwhelmed Devon as he led the way to the Ruling Assembly Building.

It turned out that the authority figure in the fancy outfit he met at his original landing site was not the Leader of the Marnians. The old man, who was called 'the Abang,' had listened to his words, then took time to calm the crowd before conducting him on this trek through the city to meet the actual leader.

Scores of people joined the Abang on this errand, most of them trailing out behind in a long procession. However, there were quite a few bolder citizens who darted about in front of the general mass of people, trying to get a better look at him. He had no further opportunity for conversation with the Abang once they set out, because of his thrusters. Once he arrived, he quickly discovered that turbulence from those thrusters kept all the Marnians at a distance. No one seemed able to remain near enough to speak with him if they were running, so he had turned the thrusters off and perched on some structures while talking to the Abang. Now that he was chugging along on this tour through Port Bree, though, he was left literally alone in the crowd.

At least I've got an unobstructed view of the city.

Devon wasn't sure what he had been expecting from a water-dwelling society, but it was not this. The large, rambling building he had seen at his first landing site had been impressive enough. Now he realized it was only one of many fine structures in this city.

As the Abang guided him along a wide avenue, he admired the well-maintained two-story dwellings that lined both sides of the street.

The houses floated in tidy rows but seemed to have no visible means of support. So far, every structure he had seen on Marna appeared to be constructed using the same technique. Marnians employed some sort of flexible matting stretched over a frame to make their buildings.

Although he itched to know what those frames were made of, there was no way to ask anything while everyone was still on the move.

Wall mats billowed and bowed on every building all down the street as pressure from the mass of people swimming by put strain on them. Every door frame and lower window had a flap of wall mat laced in place to block entry, but the upper windows of the dwellings remained open to the street, each one filled with curious faces, all watching him as he lumbered past in his ridiculous suit.

Most of the crowd behind him swam along fluttering all four fins and appeared to have no trouble maintaining the leisurely pace set by the Abang. He caught a few distant glimpses of large vehicles, each holding several people, but these scooted away down the side streets, clearing out the main avenue before his arrival.

Although he longed to get closer and see how the vehicles worked, he never got near enough to any of them to determine their means of propulsion. However, a few people in the crowd escorting him also enjoyed the benefit of another form of transport other than their own fins.

Devon clutched his headpiece to hold it still while he peered at several Marnians straddling what seemed to be small greenish-brown logs.

Of course, they can't be logs, since Marna has no land for trees to grow on.

These 'log-riders' moved about using a short paddle, or by 'rowing' with their arm fins. Log-riding appeared to give a Marnian greater bursts of speed, at least while traveling straight ahead. However, efficient as they might be, logs could never compare with the nimble acrobatics of a free-swimming Marnian.

He strained to catch the details of how they moved with such breath-taking grace.

As far as he could tell, Marnian fins were composed of pale sheets of membrane stretched between a series of thin ribs or fingers. Fins ran down the outside edge of each Marnian limb on both arms and legs. He noted fins could fan out or collapse flat against the limb at will. The leg fins looked stronger and sturdier than the more delicate arm fins above, but the upper fins were far more flexible and maneuverable.

Arm fins remind me of fish fins, but the leg fins look more like the wings of a bird or bat.

All these observations came to him as fleeting impressions, or half-seen mirages, because of the limitations of his faceplate, as well as the fact that Marnians rarely kept still for long. Swimmers accelerated and changed direction with astounding agility and there was a constant stream of them zooming in to hover in place in front of him for a moment to get a better look. People would dart in, stare, and then race off with a flick of their fins a mere instant before the disturbing currents of his thrusters reached them.

Back at his first landing site, he had noticed that Marnians tended to be smaller-than-average people, which meant they were practically pygmies when compared with his own towering frame. As more and more curious citizens flitted back and forth around him, chattering and pointing, he became aware that he was already thinking of them as less like any species of fish, and more like a type of bird. Marnians seemed to almost fly through the water. They moved with the precision and speed of hummingbirds, flicking about in all directions at dizzying speeds. Yet they were people. They had faces and hair. Their arms and legs were only slightly longer than they would have been on a standard human and included hands and feet topped with ten fingers and ten toes. Everyone wore clothes, and at first the frilly set of gills around each neck could be mistaken for a scarf or some kind of decorative collar.

There were a few unusual things about Marnian clothes,

though. Although most of the crowd wore only a limited range of colors, the Abang stood out as the only person in this gathering wearing orange. At the building where he had first landed, many people had been wearing that shade of orange, so Devon had paid no attention. Now, besides having the fanciest garments of anyone in the crowd, the Abang was conspicuous as the only one wearing that particular color.

Could orange denote some elite status or be a color that's reserved for a certain caste within this society? Could it have a religious or military meaning?

The other odd thing he was noticing was that the clothing on most people in this crowd looked quite similar in construction and design. A standard Marnian outfit was a simple, unadorned, sleeveless jacket, overlapped in the front and secured with a sash. Some of the women's jackets were long enough to cover the short shorts worn underneath, while menswear jackets were shorter. Other than that, they were all alike. Certain individuals, especially those who hung watching him from the windows of the buildings along his route, wore much more ornate garments in a variety of intricate styles and patterns. He yearned to examine those garments more closely.

I wonder if the plainer clothing indicates mere conformity to current fashion or could the plain outfits be some type of uniforms?

It was tempting to classify the more elaborately dressed individuals as 'wealthier' and the more plainly dressed citizens as 'poor.' However, leaping to any conclusions could be a very dangerous practice this early in a First Contact.

Remember your training! Observe and curb the tendency to assign meaning to what you see based on your own cultural norms.

Suddenly, a gasp swept through the crowd and everyone around him reversed fins and floundered to a stop.

He scrabbled at his arm, seeking the thruster control button to halt his progress and switch to a hover, then squinted about, trying to see what was wrong. Following the anxious looks from the crowd, he spied a group of Marnians swooping down the street toward the crowd at great speed.

These newcomers appeared much smaller than most Marnians he had seen thus far, and as the pint-sized intruders drew closer, he could see that none of them were swimming in the usual fashion. Each one of the approaching group sat astride some kind of compact frame equipped with handlebars, plus a pair of smooth bulges that jutted out below their feet. The crowd remained frozen in place behind him as the group bore down on them. Once the riders drew closer, he saw that either these small Marnians were finless or every one of them kept their fins folded flat against their limbs.

He tensed, ready to shoot up to the surface if this was some kind of attack.

Could they be a subspecies of the original Marnians? But if this is an attack, why is no one getting out of the way?

Gripping his headpiece so as not to miss anything, he watched carefully. A moment later, the newcomers raced right up to the edge of the crowd before banking sharply. They split into two groups and then the entire troop began careening recklessly about between the houses in a series of breathtaking formation maneuvers.

It finally dawned on him that what he was seeing might be a group of rowdy children showing off their skill at riding some kind of powered vehicles akin to motorcycles. The crowd gasped as the riders skimmed so close to the houses that the occupants had to duck back inside their windows. Then several of the group peeled off to perform solo exhibitions of complicated twirls, spins and barrel rolls and the crowd began to cheer.

Devon too was lost in awe at the small riders' skills, but the performance provoked only angry yells from the people in the houses being threatened by the show. Soon, lines of darkly dressed men appeared on the rooftops of the homes on both sides of the street. Some of the dark clothed 'guardians' remained in place ready to defend the structures while the rest of them dove into the street to give chase to the little daredevils.

In moments, the riders had scattered and disappeared. Once the pursuing guardians had resumed their former positions on the rooftops, the Abang signaled for the procession to get under way again.

Devon noticed more and more of the darkly clothed men appearing on the rooftops as the noise of the crowd escorting him increased. The 'guardians' shooed spectators away if they tried to perch on the buildings to get a better look at him. They also made menacing gestures at anyone who strayed too close to the doors or windows of the homes under their charge.

Is this simple territorial behavior? Or would a building actually sink if it were to be subjected to the weight of too many onlookers?

Fresh additions to the crowd kept pouring in at every intersection as Devon passed, and the noise of the crowd increased. Soon, the route wound its way through a section of town that featured lower buildings. At that point, hordes of Marnians began flying right up over the rooftops to join the growing throng. The lower-style buildings appeared to be shops rather than dwellings, but it was hard for him to be sure as most of the window and door openings on the structures were laced closed. However, people dressed in plain-looking outfits featuring shades of blue or purple were the only ones patrolling these rooftops. These blue and purple clad people seemed to lack the intimidating authority of the dark clothed 'guardians' who patrolled the taller rooftops in the residential section. Blue and purple jackets rushed back and forth on the rooftops. The shop owners, or whatever they were, looked almost terrified as they waved off any people from the vast throng of citizens behind him who came too near. As he watched them flailing about, flapping their fins at the streams of people flying over their establishments, trying to discourage them from landing, a small seed of worry sprang up.

I wonder if we could speed this caravan up before things get out of hand. I'd feel terrible if any buildings were damaged or if any of my crowd of escorts decided to try looting these places.

He glanced sideways at the Abang who swam sedately several arm lengths away.

It was impossible to tell if this was a comfortable speed for the old man or not. The Marnian's gills moved in a blur, but there was no way to know if that was a sign of stress or just normal gill motion.

With relief, he spied a large open space coming into view a

few blocks ahead.

I'll wait and see if that's our destination. If it isn't, then I'll try to signal the Abang and ask about any danger to people or property my presence might be causing, and how best to minimize that problem.

As they continued down the street, he noticed more and more Marnians braving the uneven currents above the rooftops as he approached the open square. The waters seemed to be more turbulent above the buildings and only strong, bold swimmers were able to remain there for long. He couldn't tell if those people overhead were also making threatening gestures at him with their arm fins as they thrashed their limbs vigorously, or if they were only resisting the tricky currents they were encountering as they jostled each other for a better look at him.

The noise intensified as the procession arrived at the open square and began pouring out of the confined space of the street to occupy the wider space all around him. The Abang held up a hand to halt the crowd, but no one paid any attention.

Devon slowed his thrusters, aiming them downwards to keep from sinking, and then waited while the Abang edged closer.

"I have sent a messenger into the Assembly Building to announce your arrival to our leader, Devon Arkovic," the old man told him.

"So, I should wait here until he can see us?"

"I will not come with you to meet SharScylla," the Abang replied. "You must have important business to discuss, and I feel sure that our leader will not want my presence at such a time."

"I see. Well, in that case, I thank you for all your help, and I hope we will meet again one day."

"Indeed, I would look forward to another opportunity to speak with such a strange visitor." The old man gestured at the crowd swirling all around. "In truth, I am just as curious as everyone else to know more about you."

He smiled at the Abang, wondering if some gesture or phrase was required when saying goodbye to a Marnian. For the hundredth time in the last hour, he chafed at the lack of basic information he had about these people.

The Abang bobbed up and down looking uncomfortable for a moment.

"I hope you will not take offense if I offer you some instruction, Devon Arkovic?" the old man said. "As an Abang, my primary drives are to offer prayers to the Gods and instruction to the people. You are not one of my people, but there is something I feel you should know."

"I would not be offended at all. Any teaching you would like to offer would be most welcome."

"In that case, I would recommend that when you enter the Ruling Assembly Building, you turn off your propelling devices and swim in the usual fashion." The Abang gestured at two thruster devices attached to the waist of his suit. "The turbulence your devices cause may damage parts of the structure that are nearing rot-replacement age."

"Really? My goodness, I had no idea. I will certainly turn them off then. I have no wish to damage anything or create offense."

The Abang looked relieved but still hesitated to go. Devon waited while the old man avoided his eye.

47

"Is there something else that you think I should know?" he asked. "Some other way I might cause offense, perhaps?"

"There is one other thing about your propelling devices," the Abang said. "Perhaps inside your suit you do not realize ..."

Devon waited, unsure of what to say, while the old man's cheeks turned a delicate pink as the Marnian bobbed in place.

"There is a certain smell ..." the Abang said at last.

"A smell? You mean from me?"

"Only when your propelling devices are functioning," the Abang hastened to assure him. "I first noticed it when we set out from the temple."

"Temple? You mean the building where we first met?"

"Yes, that is the temple we built to honor the Gods Below."

Oh great. So, my first act on Marna was to stink up their temple. Wonderful.

"I deeply apologize for creating a bad smell in your sacred building. I wish I had known about the issue with my thrusters. As soon as I can, I will ask our techs if any other fuel can power the devices. For now, I can only beg forgiveness for creating any offense to you or your gods."

The Abang nodded. "I can see it was not an intentional act of disrespect, Devon Arkovic."

"I appreciate your understanding."

"Yes, well. It is a most unusual odor. Not one I have ever encountered before. It does not last once the propelling devices are off, but when they are in operation, the turbulence of your impellers spreads the smell quite rapidly all around you. I thought you should know before you meet SharScylla."

"I am most grateful to you for bringing this issue to my attention. Thank you. Be assured, I will be most careful not to use my thrusters and subject your leader to any foul odor."

"Yes, I think that would be best. Well, goodbye, Devon Arkovic. A hallowed day to you and may the Gods Below smile on your journey and see you home safe."

With a graceful gesture that might have been a blessing, the Abang left him.

Okay, so I guess I've got to get this done without my smelly thrusters now.

Chapter 7: Less Than Satisfactory

The shafts of sunlight hung in the water at a different angle by the time Devon thrashed his way back out the entrance of the Assembly Building. As he emerged into the Square where he had last seen the Abang, Devon reflected ruefully that it was now clear to him why the old man had bowed out of attending any meeting with his Leader.

Great galaxies. That guy, SharScylla, is like a bear with a sore head. Or maybe a sore fin? What a volatile, intimidating character.

The Marnian Leader reminded Devon of some of the warlords or clan chieftains he had dealt with during his time in the diplomatic service. Men who earned their positions through battle and assassination. Leaders who preferred to be feared rather than loved by the people they ruled over.

Although there were a thousand things Devon wanted to see in the city, SharScylla had declared that he must remove himself from Portbree and have no further contact with anyone until their next meeting. A grim-faced pair of guards were tasked with making sure he obeyed.

After he cleared the building structure, where it was safe to start up his thrusters, he sighed with relief as they purred into action. Aching muscles in his arms and legs relaxed at last as he was carried upward, away from the city.

A small crowd of onlookers fell behind, along with his black-clothed guardians, as he rose higher. Everything was quiet and beautiful and, for once, Devon could see clearly as the upward motion kept his headpiece in place. He hung limp, savoring a moment alone.

I suppose I'm lucky I even got SharScylla to agree to a second meeting tomorrow. Not that I'm looking forward to another session with that big green bomb.

The physical strain of swimming on his own during that entire visit to the Marnian Leader had been almost as great as the drain on his mental and emotional reserves. This respite was welcome, but short. Too soon his p-suit resumed its contortions in response to the pressure changes of the ascent. However, being treated like a balloon animal by his suit was way down the list of problems on his mind.

Since he'd been banished from the city, there was no way to avoid rising to the surface. Once there, he couldn't put off making a report to Captain Doyle. He knew the captain would be far from happy with his progress.

I wonder if I can call for a pickup and wait till I'm back on Osprey to give Doyle the bad news?

Once he rose to a level where the water turned pale green, he activated the com control on the arm panel of his suit.

"Come in, *Osprey*, this is Devon Arkovic. Over."

"*Osprey* here. We read you Devon. Over."

He smiled as he recognized Mary Chenoquen on the circuit. Mary was head of the communications department and the wife of *Osprey's* first officer. She was also one of the few people on the ship who had been kind to him during the first days of their journey, so it was a joy to hear her friendly voice after his long, stressful day.

"Hi there, Mary, I am almost at the surface and requesting a pickup. Over."

The captain's voice drowned out Mary before she could reply.

"Don't be coy, Arkovic. Did you meet with their leader? Do we have a deal?"

By this time, he had reached the surface proper and was delighted to find it much calmer now, so he was only being buffeted about in a light chop.

Still, I don't relish the idea of being left down here to toss around on the surface in a rubber raft all night. I need to make this sound good.

"Sorry, Captain Doyle, no deal yet, but the good news is I do have another meeting set for tomorrow. The Marnian leader demanded that I stay out of the city until then. So, could you send the shuttle down to get me? I can give you all the details once I'm on board, but I'm bobbing around like a cork down here, so it's a little hard to talk," he lied.

"Alright, permission granted."

Mary took over again as the captain dropped off the line.

"It will take a few minutes to finish prepping the shuttle, Devon. Maybe you should descend into calmer waters while you wait. If you barf in your helmet, chief Simmons will make you clean it up yourself, trust me. I'll let the shuttle crew home in on your locator beacon and then you can wait to resurface until they're set up to retrieve you. Over."

"Sounds good, Mary. I'll do that, thanks. Over."

"See you soon, Devon. *Osprey* out."

***

"Thanks for the lift, Chief Simmons," Devon said, sighing with relief as the old spacer pulled away the sling and unfastened the headpiece on his suit for him in the cargo hold of the shuttle. He'd never imagined being so happy to see Simmons's ugly mug again.

The chief ignored him, only pointing out a set of earphones strapped to the wall as he moved away to take his seat in the forward cabin. "Take her up, Ted," Simmons called to the pilot.

Moments later, Ted Hollander goosed the shuttle's engines and thundered aloft in fine fighter pilot style. Forgetting the earphones, Devon sprawled on the deck clinging to a support under one the seats. The shuttle leveled off as they cleared the atmosphere, and he hauled himself up to sit in a seat and put on a set of headphones. He could hear Ted making docking chat with the *Osprey* as he buckled in, but no one asked about his welfare.

He dreaded having to brief Captain Doyle on his progress once he arrived, and he also figured it wasn't likely to be a private conversation. *Osprey's* rumor mill was as efficient as a cold fusion rocket. Now that everyone on board had so much at stake, it was a sure bet that crewmen wouldn't hesitate to eavesdrop on even the captain's conversations.

The whole ship is going to be against me once word gets around that

I haven't gotten an agreement today. I'd better find a way to put a positive spin on this.

"So, you failed," Captain Doyle greeted him sourly as he lumbered down out of the shuttle.

A half dozen more pairs of eyes silently accused him from workstations around the landing bay.

"No, I wouldn't say that," Devon replied as calmly as he could. "I would characterize an invitation for a second meeting as a strong sign of goodwill and cooperation."

"And what about kicking you out of the city till then? Was that a sign of goodwill as well?" the captain sneered.

Devon shrugged as casually as he could. "A small gesture asserting control of territory. One that it costs us nothing to oblige."

"Well, I don't like these delaying tactics, Arkovic. I tell you; that pirate ship got a good look at our vector before we went to hyper."

One thing the crew had shared with Devon when he woke from hyper sleep was how a ship with no transponder had been spotted nearby as they departed the Alpha 896 system. Now, Captain Doyle glared at him as if he were personally to blame for the habits of vicious pirates.

"There's not but a few systems along this route," Doyle said, "and it won't take them pirates long before they search each one and then locate us."

Devon heard soft growls of agreement all around the bay. Exhausted as he was, he knew he might have only seconds to keep Doyle and his crew from turning against him completely.

"Listen to me!" he said, looking past the captain's shoulder and pitching his voice so everyone could hear. "The Marnian leader down there appears to be a very aggressive guy. He's used to ordering people around and getting his way. I think he wants to say yes, but if he compromises with us too fast, it could make him look weak. That means this is a tricky negotiation."

The captain just folded his arms across his chest and stared.

"If you could just give me another day, sir, maybe I could make this work, with no bloodshed."

"And how many days do you think those pirates will be giving this fishyfied chieftain?"

"I know. None. We have to cut these Marnians some slack, though. This is a lot for them to take in all at once. I've told their Leader about the cargo and about the Company. But he wants verification. I've told him that keeping the cargo could be dangerous, but you have to understand, this guy SharScylla doesn't scare easy."

"Well, then, I'd venture to guess that you're not explaining it to him properly, Arkovic. You do understand that if we're not gone before those pirates show up, then there's no hope for any of us coming out of this in one piece? Never mind your precious fish folk. Those pirates won't be doing any negotiating when they come a-calling. They'll wipe out every aquatic on the planet and then go down and raise that cargo without all this bother."

"I realize that, sir."

"Do you, now? Well, that's a comfort since we're all going to end up as little clouds of atoms if we're still here when those pirates arrive."

He didn't reply to that. Sometimes it was best to let a man vent his load of frustration and anger.

"So, you listen to me now, lad," Doyle went on, waving a finger under his nose. "It's time you stopped worrying about sparing the finer feelings of everyone below and concentrated on preserving the skins of us here above! D'ya hear?"

"Yes, Captain Doyle."

"All right then. Now, thanks to you, it's too late today to begin any operations before it gets dark. You better plan to deliver your backside onto this deck bright and early tomorrow. That will be your last chance to finish the job you were hired for, understand?"

"Yes, Sir."

***

The young, hotshot pilot Ted Hollander was loitering around in the hallway when Devon finally slunk out of the suit-up room to go hunt up something to eat that wasn't paste from a tube.

He rolled his eyes at the thought of a sparring match with Hollander on top of having delivered unwelcome news to the captain.

"Sounds like you're really earning your keep around here, Arkovic," Hollander sniggered, falling in behind him as he headed for the mess hall. "They must have been real sorry to lose you from Dip Corp."

"Go kiss a thruster fan, Hollander."

"What, and ruin my shot at becoming the richest shuttle jockey this side of Betelgeuse? No way, you gum flapper," Ted snarled, moving close enough that his next comment landed a smattering of spittle on Devon's neck. "Just remember, Dip boy, you screw this up for the rest of us and you can plan on taking a long vacation right here with your fishy friends."

He swung around to face Hollander. "Is that a threat, Hollander?" he asked the red-faced pilot.

"Just reading the writing on the wall, you *aquatic lover*."

"Oh, yeah? And what do you think the captain and First Officer Chenoquen would have to say about your interpretation of the situation?"

"I think they have as much to lose as anyone else."

Ted hunched his angry face down into his shoulders, as if preparing for a football tackle.

Time to get this bully in line.

"Maybe, Ted. I bet one thing they don't want to lose, though, is control of this crew. I might be slow to get the job done, but at least I don't cheat to make it happen."

Hollander remained stiffly defiant. "Now, what the hell do you mean by that?"

"Just that I noticed you fleecing your crewmates at cards down in the mess hall on our first couple of nights out of port. Those poor drunk idiots didn't catch it, but I did. Tell me Hollander, since when are there two Jack of Clubs cards in the same deck?"

The pilot sagged back with a quick glance over his shoulder, and Devon grinned.

"Didn't I hear that the First officer gave orders that no one could use their share of the treasure as a stake in bets or card games? So then, why is it I've heard rumors that you own four full shares now?"

Ted's face was a delicate shade of chalk now.

"That's an exaggeration!" the pilot hissed, stepping closer and lowering his voice even further. "The rule was that no one could stake *all* of their share in a game. Those guys only lost half shares."

"Oh, well, I guess everything's fine then. I'm sure the captain and Mr. Chenoquen will be relieved that it was only half shares when I tell them. I may even get another tongue lashing from the captain for even bringing it up."

"All right, all right," Hollander muttered, palms up as he backed away. "Sorry to have bothered you, Mr. Arkovic. But you know I didn't really mean any of that stuff I said before, right? I was just blowing off steam. We're all kinda tense up here. What with those pirates and so much at stake—"

"Yeah, yeah, I'm sure you cry yourself to sleep every night."

"On my honor, Mr. Arkovic, I'm very sorry. So, if there's anything you need, or anything I can do to help while you're on board, well, you just let me know and I'm on it. Extra shower time, or some of Cookie's fresh biscuit, or, or anything else you want. Just let me know and I can get it."

A long day in the suit was catching up to Devon now, so he barely had the energy to raise a hand to stem this eager tide of generosity.

"Actually, there is one thing you can do for me, Hollander."

"Anything Mr. Arkovic, sir. You just name it."

"The next time you fly me in the shuttle …"

"Uh huh," Ted leaned forward, forehead glistening with sweat.

"Could you wait for me to get buckled in before you start pulling Yeager loops at five gees, please?"

Chapter 8: Rebel's Dilemma

By midday, Annika was desperate for any new information. She made the long, slow journey down to the temple dining hall in order to loiter around, listening in on other people's chatter.

It still worried her that Scylla might have killed the airbreather or sent him away without finding out what urgent matter the visitor came to discuss.

She sat in the dining hall chewing through another bland meal but learned nothing new for her trouble. People were still exclaiming over the stranger's arrival and swapping theories about what it could mean, but no one knew anything for sure. The Abang had returned to the Temple, but all she could gather was that the revered elder had delivered the stranger to the Ruling Assembly Building as requested.

"That old jelly-head has all the curiosity of a wall mat," she complained to Magda after they returned to her quarters. "I could never have spent that much time in the company of a man from above the upper boundary without asking at least some questions. What a wasted opportunity. How could the Abang not want to know what that world up there is like? Everyone else is dying to hear about why the airbreather came to visit. Why would the old fool not ask?"

She flicked back and forth in the tiny room while Magda laced the door shut, probably hoping to keep any people passing in the corridor from overhearing her mistress's disrespectful comments.

"And I can't understand why none of our rebel friends have come to tell me what happened at the meeting with Scylla," Annika went on. "There should have been some kind of announcement by now. I hope that float-head Scylla isn't trying to hide the fact that he botched the meeting with the visitor. Perhaps we should go down to the marketplace and see if we can hear anything new?"

Magda stared back at her wide eyed. "Oh, no, mistress. You must not do that. If any of SharScylla's Goons catch you outside the temple, they will execute you."

"I know, I know. I'm still an exile as far as Scylla is concerned. But how else are we going to find out what's going on?"

"I am sure one of our rebel friends would have come to tell you if there was any real news. Why not wait until evening meal and see if people here in the temple have heard anything new?"

Annika sighed out a stream of bubbles. "You're too polite to say it, Magda, but I suppose I am being impatient. Very well, I'll wait till evening meal, but no longer."

***

Magda watched while her mistress continued to pace back and forth like a trapped jink.

I must find some way to keep her from leaving the temple. If she goes out into the streets, she will be killed for sure.

As a MAGDALENA she was driven to instruct the young and protect them from their own unwise actions.

Perhaps Annika is not too old for a little distraction.

"Mistress? How long do you suppose the airbreathers have been up there?"

Annika paused by the window of the chamber to look up toward the surface far overhead.

"That's a good question, Magda. They could have been up there watching Portbree for storms and storms without us ever knowing about it."

Magda watched with a smile as Annika's hand crept upward and her Little One absently rubbed the spot above her brow with the side of her finger, just as the girl had been doing ever since she was a child.

"Maybe the stranger was just waiting for the right time to descend. Or perhaps this arrival today was an accident. Could he have fallen into the ocean by mistake?"

Her mistress went on talking in a dreamy sort of voice as the finger sawed back and forth and Magda relaxed as her distraction put Annika's mind into full gear, darting here and there, sorting ideas and assessing their probabilities. Magda knew Annika's upgraded intellect was capable of generating entire detailed scenarios based on a single variable, then collapsing them to move on a moment later. It was all too much for a simple Glae to follow, but she smiled fondly at her mistress.

My Little One was already brilliant even when she was only a first-season adult.

"I wonder, Magda, do you think this visitor has studied politics and ethics? Maybe he's even traveled to places where one of the great political treatises was written. Historic documents like the Magna Carta, or the Foundations of Civilization, or the Bill of Sentient Rights!"

This mass of ideas toppled Magda's orientation. It was almost impossible for her to picture such far-flung notions. Instead, she clasped her hands together and imagined this first-child-of-her-heart meeting a mysterious stranger from beyond the sky. A man who might share all the lofty dreams her Little One held dear.

But that happy vision soon burst like a rotting float as she looked around this tiny room. All at once fear clawed at her heart.

This quiet, cloistered life in the temple is not something a girl like Annika will endure for long.

Big events were happening, and Magda knew how much her mistress would want a part in them.

But I am just one old Glae woman. How can I prevent a Shar like her from doing anything she pleases? How will I stop my dear Little One from risking her life, again?

***

The temple dining hall was a madhouse when Magda followed her mistress down for the evening meal.

It shocked her to see people rushing from table to table instead of sitting quietly, counting as they chewed their food. Magda trembled as she floated behind Annika in the doorway,

63

all thoughts of eating forgotten as she watched the chaos.

Rumors were flying about attacks from hordes of airbreathers or their new Gods Above. Some said the stranger had left the city, but others claimed Scylla had told him to return tomorrow. Everyone speculated about how the Gods Below might deal with this visitor.

"That's it, Magda," Annika said after watching for a few spans. "It's time we got some reliable information. I think we should go out and look up some of our old rebel comrades and see what they know."

She tugged on the girl's arm in alarm. "But mistress, it is too dangerous to go now. Even people here in the temple are hysterical. Imagine what it must be like outside."

"I know, Magda, but I've got to find out what's happening even if I have to go down to the Ruling Assembly Building and ask Scylla myself."

Magda felt her gills speeding up.

Serve or Protect? Serve or Protect?

"But Little One, if you leave the temple, you will be recognized and reported to Scylla's Goons as soon as people spot your fins."

Annika's eyes danced. "Not if they don't see them."

Before Magda could raise any more objections, the girl grabbed her hand and began towing her down the hall. Once they reached Annika's quarters, her mistress darted over to the closet and rummaged there until she located a large orange shawl.

"I thought you swore you would never wear that?" Magda

exclaimed.

Annika laughed, twirling in place to settle the shawl over her head and shoulders and check the fit.

"I might as well get some use out of it."

Magda winced as she saw how the shawl was indeed large enough to cover both Annika's hair and those distinctive upper fins.

The stubborn girl will never be talked out of trying her dangerous scheme now.

There was nothing left to do but follow along as her mistress headed for the main gate of the temple.

Chapter 9: Censored!

An over-sized conveyance pulled up in front of the Third Librarian SharCom's door just as Suni was making his way across the front courtyard to collect his next customer from the waiting room.

It shocked Suni to see any vehicle in the front courtyard, much less such a massive one propelled by no less than six double sized Mabel engine pods. Estate security Goons rushed out to turn the new arrival away before backwash from the over-powered impellors did damage to any of the delicate neural cells growing next to the courtyard.

The next moment, his eyes widened to see the Goons backing away as a hulking figure leaped from the vehicle to face them.

The Leader's hair was drawn back in the traditional fighter's queue, just like the four other former Gladiators who piled out of the convey behind him.

Suni's stomach did back-flips and any thought of serving customers or protecting the data array drained from his mind.

Scylla was even larger and greener than he remembered. The stiffening spines of the former Glad's upper fins bristled out past the black edged margins of his fin membranes to end in wicked looking points.

"Where is the Librarian?" Scylla roared at the Goon captain, who was now cowering next to the front entrance of the Estate with his men.

The Goon captain took one look at the band of green tinged muscle and whirled around to issue orders.

"Go find the master at once!" the captain said to a pair of his men. "And you, Steve," he shouted, flicking a fin at the Estate houseboy, who hovered just inside the front door with his mouth hanging open. "Have Marisol bring a drink bulb to the waiting room for our Leader."

Suni saw the Goon captain glancing his way after Steve disappeared, but it wobbled his orientation when the captain pointed at him next.

"You there, Suni. Go and clear all the customers out of the waiting room so that our Leader may use it."

Suni froze for a second, trying to process the Goon captain's demand for a service that was not one of his usual tasks. In all the seasons he had served on this Estate, the Goon captain had never tried to order him around before.

Bobbing a little bow of respect in the Leader's direction, he forced himself to obey.

"No!" Scylla's voice boomed out, freezing everyone in place. "I want SharCom brought to me here," the great green terror rumbled, stabbing a finger toward his feet. "Immediately!"

While the search for SharCom proceeded, other Estate staff members trickled out into the courtyard to see what was going on. Each Glae then found themselves trapped, unable to depart once they had beheld the Leader waiting there impatiently.

No Glae likes to witness an ugly scene between two Shar, but all the staff were terrified to leave the area without permission. They remained clustered together in quivering little groups against the barriers of the yard, waiting anxiously for SharCom to arrive. None dared disturb the great SharScylla by asking authorization to depart. Suni huddled with two other Glae while the wait went on and the stink of fear in the water became sickeningly strong.

The other Glae whispered about the deliberate insult of summoning a Librarian to a conference in his own courtyard. However, it appeared to Suni that insulting the master of the Estate was exactly what Scylla had in mind.

A double handful of disappointed customers trailed out of the waiting room and swam off past the angry former Glad as the Leader waited. The Shar customers all shot dirty looks in Scylla's direction while skirting his massive vehicle on their way to begin the long swim back toward the Grand Eddy, where they might catch rides to their homes in the city.

The Leader's pod of attendants arranged themselves around him, muttering and scowling and aiming threatening looks at any Shar who stared at Scylla for too long.

Suni secretly admired both the impressive physiques of the former Glads, and their effective intimidation of the customers. Of course, he knew that only the largest and best trained Gladiators had the good fortune to be chosen to serve in the Leader's personal guard. Still, it was awe-inspiring to see them up close.

Every one of Scylla's men seemed to be big and tough and

utterly loyal to the man who had scooped them out of the pits and given them status as one of his pod. Their green, algae-infused skin was no longer a stain that prevented these men from ever leaving the pits. No more were they pitiful men who lived and died for the entertainment of others. These were the green-tinged guardians of the Leader himself. The Glads who feared no one. But their discipline was excellent, and the four refrained from attacking anyone without a signal from their leader.

Scylla himself simply ignored the customer's angry glances as he hung there waiting for the Librarian to arrive, with arms crossed over his chest and gills flicking.

When SharCom appeared at last, Suni noted his master had taken the time to assemble a full cadre of Goons to accompany him. However, to Suni's eye, the Estate security men seemed a scrawny bunch when compared with the Leader's personal guard. SharCom seemed oblivious to that fact though, as he glided out into the courtyard at the head of his band of Goons.

Suni smelled the usual whiff of arrogant sourness that always tinged the water around the Librarian. He cringed as his master immediately called out to Scylla without waiting for the Leader to speak first.

"What madness is this?" SharCom addressed Scylla in a high and scolding tone, omitting any greeting, courteous or otherwise. "What do you mean by approaching my array with a vehicle? Perhaps you do not know that this is forbidden, but your Conner could have told you!"

As the Librarian huffed out a disdainful cloud of bubbles, he aimed a poisonous look at the Glae chauffeur, who sat at the controls of the Leader's convey.

Suni wondered if this was a deliberate attempt to redirect all the ill feeling in this meeting onto that unlucky Glae's shoulders.

The Conner appeared not to hear, however. The man sat absolutely still at his controls, staring straight ahead out over the vast fields of neural cells as if blind and deaf to all that was happening around him. Standard Glae posture while awaiting a Shar's next command.

"There was no time to observe your stupid protocols today, Librarian," Scylla snapped. "I have had a visitor today. A stranger who says that he comes from beyond the upper boundary. The man wears a suit of unknown material that covers his whole body because he also claims to be an airbreather. The stranger told me he was sent from the regions above to bargain with us. He says that his airbreather people left something here on Marna long ago. Some equipment with a precious cargo. Now this stranger wishes to bring others of his kind into our ocean and dive into the Deep to retrieve this cargo."

SharCom shrugged. "And what has this to do with me?"

Scylla frowned. "I have come for information, obviously. I need to know if there is any data in the ancient files of your hoard that confirms these claims. Is it true what this stranger tells me? Did airbreathers bring our people to this world from some other place long ago? Is it true that the Gods Below did not create us? Does the stranger speak the truth when he says that some powerful House of airbreathers called 'The Corporation' own this cargo that he seeks? Or is he trying to trick me into allowing these airbreathers to invade our ocean so they can steal from the Gods Below?"

Suni could tell from the set of his master's jaw how angry SharCom was. As one of only ten Librarians, SharCom expected fawning deference from others, not bullying and humiliation.

And when has any Librarian ever liked to give away information?

As he watched SharCom's face twist into a scowl, Suni recalled the many times he had heard his master refer to Scylla as just a jumped-up Gladiator who fancied himself to be a real Shar now that he'd stolen the Leadership from Annika Sharone. So, it was no surprise when the Librarian unwisely adopted a haughty lecturing tone as he replied to this demand for free services.

"Your information is correct," SharCom said with a dismissive flick of the gills. "The most ancient files in my hoard do indeed tell that Marnians are an aquatic subspecies of airbreather humans, created elsewhere, long ago. The original Marnians were altered from the standard airbreather body format, then placed in this ocean to work for a wealthy Family of airbreathers known as the LEAP Corporation."

Scylla's forehead swelled visibly and Suni gagged as an acrid gush of fury pervaded the entire courtyard. He and the other Glae along the fences shifted in place and looked sick, but none dared draw attention to themselves by trying to leave.

"What?" Scylla bellowed. "How dare you conceal such important information from me?"

71

Behind Scylla, Suni saw the pod of Glads tense and grip their jagged-tipped struts and strangle cords, alert for any order to attack.

Suni's gills whipped up and down, marking double time as he trembled in his place. However, his master, the Librarian, still appeared unconcerned.

"Important?" SharCom scoffed. "No airbreather has been seen on Marna for generations. Their entire House was believed to have fallen. How could it be important for you to know about a defeated House of airbreathers that no one thought we would ever hear from again?"

"Yet now I am faced with negotiating with this airbreather and his House. All without ever having heard of their existence. As head of the Ruling Council, these are facts you should have told me about!" Scylla roared.

SharCom let loose a large and disrespectful bubble. "No Leader has ever needed to know these things before."

"And this is the reason you have concealed such vital information from me?"

"What Librarian could expect a fee for such a useless bit of data?" SharCom demanded peevishly. "Even Leaders cannot expect to have free access to all the information in a hoard. A Librarian is entitled to his secrets."

It sounded perfectly reasonable to Suni, but Scylla appeared incensed by SharCom's attitude. The big green man's face contorted, and his fins moved in a blur as he lunged forward to seize the Librarian by the neck.

"You traitor!" Scylla screamed.

SharCom only had time for a startled squeak before the Leader's massive hands closed around his gills.

Suni felt his own gills falter in sympathy as the former Gladiator bared his teeth, glaring down into his victim's eyes as he squeezed. Like all the other staff Suni could only watch helplessly, keeping as quiet as possible while his master flailed in the Leader's grip. Even the Estate Goons remained fixed in place as the horror went on and on.

When the Librarian finally hung limp in Scylla's grasp, a foul odor of loosened bowels wafted across the courtyard. A small sigh escaped all the former Glads behind Scylla once SharCom's struggles ceased, but the Leader's howl of triumph sent shivers down Suni's spine. Each of the watching lieutenants placed one hand atop the other in front of their chests, fins and gills extended as their Leader raised the dead Librarian overhead. Scylla shook the limp form of his opponent twice, asserting victory, then tossed the broken body aside.

After the corpse spiraled down into the dark, Suni watched from the corner of his eye as Scylla prowled along the edges of the courtyard. The Leader glared at each of the Estate staff in turn, where they cowered next to the barriers, almost fainting with fear. When Scylla reached the group where Suni huddled with two others, the former Glad leaned forward to stare a little longer at him.

As the Leader's voice boomed out right above his head, he gulped so hard he almost swallowed his own tongue.

"You," Scylla growled, reaching out to hook a dark tipped finger under Suni's chin. "I know you."

Quick currents brushed Suni's gills as the two other staffers darted away from him while Scylla leaned closer.

"Are you not the SUNI who once came to the arena with that little MAGDA to bargain with me for a data cable? Back in the days before the revolution."

He quaked under the Leader's burning gaze. "Yes, Shar."

"Then you must also be that clever Suni who helped Shar-Annika stage her Glae uprising."

"Yes, Shar."

A surprised mummer swept through some of the staff in the courtyard, but it died away immediately under another glare from the Leader's pod.

"Is there no other SUNI here at this array?"

"No, Shar. I am the only one."

Scylla cocked his head on one side, boring into him with bloodshot eyes. "Then your master SharCom did not know what a dangerous rebel he had working for him?"

There was no way to pull off a convincing lie under that searing gaze, but it curled Suni's gills to answer that particular question.

He kept his eyes fixed on his clasped hands as the Leader's finger dug deeper under his chin. "No, Shar."

It was impossible not to wobble as he waited for the final blow to fall, so it almost collapsed his buoyancy sac when Scylla burst out laughing instead and then released him.

"So, a rebel Glae in the Librarian's own staff. But one clever enough to have an instinct for survival," Scylla remarked to the members of his pod with a grin. "I suppose he will have to do."

The Glads smiled and nodded in return, and Suni saw them eying him more curiously now that he had gained their Leader's approval.

"And what do you know of these strangers from beyond the upper boundary and this cargo they seek?" Scylla asked, turning back to face him.

"Nothing, Shar."

"Nothing at all?"

As the Leader's brows drew down in anger again, Suni felt his arm fins shrink down into quivering little stubs. He wrung his hands together, bowing again as he explained to the angry former Glad.

"I am sorry, great Shar, but Mistress Annika never required the knowledge to which you refer. Also, I was never assigned to help a customer access the master's oldest data files, which he said were the ones that told of such things."

"Then you will go seek out the data that I require now!"

"Yes, Shar. Immediately, Shar. Whatever files you need. If you will come inside and wait a few spans, I will locate the files and prepare them for you to download at once."

A heady wave of relief filled his nostrils as all the staff all around him awaited new orders with joyful anticipation. Serving a customer who desired data was something everyone on the Estate felt confident of doing well. Plus, if they were called upon to perform their professional duties, they would all soon have an excuse to leave the Leader's presence.

"I have no time for data bursts today," Scylla said gruffly, turning away to stare out over the vast fields of neural cells with a frown.

Suni was struck dumb.

No one ever refuses the offer of a data upgrade.

As a confused mummer from the staff rose and then fell away, even Scylla's attendants looked surprised. The Leader seemed to swell with anger as the expressions of wonder around him registered.

Every fin on the vast body of the Leader bristled outward. As a vein in the great green forehead throbbed, Suni felt himself trembling again.

"As of now you are in charge of this facility," Scylla roared at him. "I want you to search every file in this hoard if necessary. I need every fleck of information that concerns these airbreathers and their Corporation. Do you understand?"

"Yes, Shar."

"Check all the oldest files in the array first. Nothing is off limits."

"Yes, Shar. Thank you Shar. B-but may I ask, who will receive the fees from the customers from now on?" he quavered.

"Sink all of you, and your sludge-slicked fees," Scylla swore. "There will be no customers, and there will be no fees. Do you understand? You will spend your time doing research for me. Find as much data on these subjects as you can and download it yourself. You have my permission. Tomorrow morning, you will come to my chambers in the Assembly Building and report to me all that you have learned."

"Yes, Shar." Suni bowed again. "I will have answers for you by first light."

"See that you do."

At last Scylla turned away and swept a hand at his men, shooing the members of his pod aboard the convey ahead of him. Once the Leader had taken his own seat in the vehicle, the Conner started up the Mabel engine pods and aimed the magnificent conveyance back toward the city.

Suni hung as limp as a wall mat while he watched Scylla depart. A wide vee of turbulence spread out across the fields of the array, setting all the clusters of globular cells filled with precious data dancing about in his new master's wake.

Chapter 10: The One Who Whispers With Gods

Some temple residents they met in the hallways still recognized Annika despite the shawl. They stopped to bow and murmur polite greetings to "The One Who Whispers with Gods" as her mistress hurried by.

Annika's gills stiffened every time someone used that name, but Magda could console herself that her mistress's displeasure was not because of one of her failures, this time.

Good thing I cannot be expected to protect her from hearing that name.

Magda hid a smile behind her hand, remembering Annika's reaction the first time someone used that reverent moniker to her face.

***

Three days after Annika took up residence in the temple, a young acolyte scratched politely at the chamber door.

Bored and restless, her mistress rushed over to see who it was, easily beating Magda to the door.

"First Light Blessings, oh One Who Whispers with Gods," the young man said as Annika appeared in the doorway.

A sudden stiffness appeared in her mistress's fins, and there was a quick uptick in the motion of Annika's gills as the girl took in this pious new title.

Magda cringed but checked an impulse to intervene. Her mistress was the one Shar who preferred not to be fussed over by her servants.

"What is your purpose here?" Annika asked in a brusque, very Shar-like tone.

The acolyte bobbed and beamed as happily as if she had blessed him in return, proffering a neatly folded shawl.

"I bring a gift from the temple council of elders."

This time, Magda quivered in place as her mistress made no move to accept the gift.

"There must be some mistake," Annika said. "I cannot wear Aban-orange since I am not one of those dedicated to the service of the Gods."

"There is no mistake. The elders wish you to know that they are happy to have you here with us and they hope that their gift will keep you warm when you attend temple services in the evenings."

As the stiffness spread to include Annika's spine and jaw, Magda gave in to her urgent compulsion to protect her Shar.

I must prevent Annika from offending the temple elders.

"Well, how generous of the elders," she spoke up before the girl could say anything else. "Was that not a thoughtful gesture, Mistress? It certainly is quite chilly in the main courtyard during the evening service." She prattled on, sidling between the other two to take charge of the gift. "Here, let me take that and hang it

79

up in the closet for my mistress."

Snatching the shawl from the acolyte, she continued. "We thank you, young man, for bringing this gift from the council all the way out here to the guest quarters. It was very good of you to go to all that trouble. May the Gods Below bless you for your flawless service. A hallowed day to you and may your faith never rot. Goodbye now."

Once the acolyte was gone, she faced the irritable young woman floating in the center of the room.

"Do people have to keep cultivating this ridiculous idea that it was some whispering from the Gods that inspired my actions during the rebellion?" Annika said.

Magda thrust the offending shawl far out of sight beneath a pile of other clothing in the closet before risking a reply.

"Now, now, Little One." Magda chuckled as she looked at her mistress with wide-eyed innocence. "Is it not better to allow people to think that the revolution happened because a little Shar girl once heard the Gods whispering in her ear?"

Her only answer was a deeper frown on Annika's face.

"Think mistress, would you not prefer people to see you as a faithful servant of the Gods, rather than having them think of you as a traitor? A Shar who *chose* to raise ignorant Glae up to be equals with her own kind?"

For a moment, Annika looked as if she was about to explode, but then the girl she had raised to be a Shar lady in one of the Great Houses of Marna brought herself under control.

"Fine," Annika said. "Let people call me whatever name they like. But I will not encourage this nonsense by dressing up as an

Aban and going to evening services."

"Will you not, mistress? I have heard that attendance at evening services has increased fivefold since you arrived at the temple. Many people come only because they hope to see you, but donations to the temple have still increased greatly. The council of elders must be very glad they offered you sanctuary here when you returned from exile."

"Oh, I'm sure that they are. Alright, Magda, you've made your point. I'll go to services so people can see me. But I am not wearing that shawl."

"Yes, Mistress."

It did not happen often that she won an argument with Annika. But how could any Glae take pleasure in a victory that made one's Shar unhappy?

***

Although it was not yet dark, crowds of anxious people filled the streets outside the temple's main gate. The water was thick with odors of uncertainty and speculation. Everywhere clumps of citizens huddled together, discussing the visitor.

Magda trembled as they headed down the street toward the marketplace. Although she longed to make Annika happy by helping with this errand, the uneasy crowds made her wish she was safely at home with her husband and daughter tonight.

She was still not used to having her mistress back in the city and spending every day away from her own Little One at home. Serving a Shar was an honor, of course, but it was far more exhausting than she remembered to always be worried about serving her mistress well. Annika was sad so often now that Magda struggled with a constant, nagging sense of failure.

There were pairs of Goons patrolling the perimeters on all the Great Houses down the avenue. She skirted their vicinity nervously.

The guards seemed tense, alert for any trouble from the long line of restless people that snaked down the street from the entrance to the temple. Hands upon hands of the faithful still waited their turn to make offerings to the Gods Below and beg for their protection.

Their weeping and wailing sent shivers down Magda's spine.

It seemed that the lack of response from the Gods Below had only increased the hysteria among the residents of Portbree. Many Glae and Shar people alike had expected their Gods to ascend in fury and strike down the invader. Now impatience turned to fear as length after length passed and there was no sign that the Gods Below intended to do anything to rid the world of this marvelous menace.

Now Magda was very glad she had not chosen to leave Annika alone to gather information.

A Glae's place is at her mistress's side. My own paltry concerns can wait. Perhaps this time I can make up for all the times I have failed her in times past.

"Let's go to the shot house in the marketplace," she heard Annika whisper. "That's the most likely place to find some former rebels we can trust."

They hurried on their way until they reached the marketplace. There she paused beside Annika to listen to a shopkeeper perched on his rooftop addressing a small crowd in front of his store.

Magda was intrigued by how well The GLEN spoke, captivating his listeners like an Aban telling stories. But his dire warnings about the airbreather visitor echoed the same rumors they had heard in the temple dining hall. His odd behavior gave her chills.

"First, this one stranger comes," The GLEN cried, waving one finger over his head, "but mark me neighbors, it will not be long before there are many more invaders polluting our ocean. These airbreathers have no ocean of their own in the over-realm, so they probably have no proper homes of their own either. Soon, there may be squads of them coming down here to take over our whole city!"

"I heard that some new Gods Above sent the visitor," one man in the crowd yelled out.

"Maybe his Gods did send him here," the GLEN said. "But who comes just to talk? And what will happen if we refuse to give these strangers what they want? We all know how it ends when the Shar disagree. First, they talk in Assembly to settle the issue. Then when they cannot agree, there is a raid where Goons and servant Glae get killed."

"Yeah!" another man from the crowd screamed. "First, they talk, but when Shar want something they cannot get, there is always a raid!"

"I tell you, neighbors," the GLEN warned, "soon there will be airbreathers everywhere trying to take what is ours and killing those that oppose them."

"But will the Gods Below not protect us if there is an airbreather raid?" a third voice from the crowd quavered.

"The airbreather has been here all day and the Gods have done nothing!" the GLEN said. "My brother-offspring is an acolyte in the temple, and he says the arrival of the airbreather means that the Gods Below are punishing us for neglect."

"My Shar says that the Gods Below do not exist, and that the appearance of an airbreather proves it," a MARISOL in the crowd yelled, bobbing up and down.

"Proves it how?" the GLEN sneered. "We have all seen proof that the Gods Below exist, neighbors. There are quakes and smoker mountains that disturb our waters to remind us that powerful beings live way down in the Deeps."

"I am only telling you what my Shar said," the MARISOL grumbled, subsiding.

"Your Shar is only trying to frighten you." A woman next to the MARISOL put an arm around her.

"Your Shar is a very cruel man," another woman added.

"It is as the Aban have always taught us," the GLEN cried, recapturing everyone's attention. "The Gods Below made us. Therefore, we owe the Gods Below our lives. And if some foreign airbreathers have come here to pollute the ocean which the Gods have given us for our home, then we should fight back!"

The crowd roared approval, flourishing fists and flaring out their leg spines.

Magda cast a worried look at Annika. "Mistress, why is this GLEN deliberately sowing fear and violence among these people?" she whispered.

"I'm not sure. A GLEN usually has only two drives: serve his customers and maintain a healthy business. This man seems strangely driven to share all his ideas with others."

"He speaks like one who received our rebel upload files."

"I agree. Our upgrade included an urge to share ideas and information with others. But this GLEN seems to want more than that. He is trying to incite the crowd to fight the airbreathers."

"Could this man's rebel upgrade have failed to integrate properly, mistress?"

Annika narrowed her eyes as she watched the GLEN whip his audience into a frenzy.

"Perhaps that would explain it. Our basic rebel upgrade files never included anything about persuading other people to violent action, though. Directing the actions of others is a leadership trait."

The idea of this angry GLEN possessing leadership traits made Magda tremble.

The only Glae who learned how to influence others was Scylla, and it earned him leadership of the Ruling Council.

"Could this GLEN have been influenced by the religious ideas he hears from his sibling in the temple?" she asked Annika.

"Maybe. Although, I have never a heard a GLEN or a rebel speak like this. He seems to care less about the welfare of others and more about influencing them to share his hatred of the airbreathers."

"So, what can we do? How can we stop him? Since we no

longer have access to the rebel upgrade files, how can we correct this man?"

Annika shook her head sadly as she beckoned Magda away from the screaming crowd.

"We can't do anything about it, Magda. Every person has the right to use the data we gave them in any way they choose. Even if we don't approve of their intentions."

"Of course, you are right, mistress." Magda's gills drooped as she followed her mistress away across the marketplace. "But I tell you, this GLEN worries me."

***

On the other side of the market square, Annika stopped outside a shot house where, in earlier times, rebels had passed messages back and forth to help plan the revolution.

The place was louder than Magda remembered, and there were several patrons rendering a very explicit love song for the entertainment of the others.

It shriveled her gills to think of entering such a rowdy place alone.

But it would be far too suspicious for Annika to go inside with me while wearing the orange shawl. No Aban would ever go into a shot house.

She hung back, fanning her arm fins, caught between her distaste for navigating a drunken crowd and the desire to please her mistress. It did not seem to her that this raucous establishment was a likely place for gathering any coherent information. But a nudge between her shoulder blades urged her

86

forward.

"Go on, Magda, at least no one in there is spewing hateful sludge to the crowd about resisting airbreather invaders," Annika said.

Gliding toward the doorway, Magda made sure that the light streaming from the entrance would allow the STEVE on duty at the door to see her gray hair and plain gray uniform. She did not want him to mistake her for a LISA seeking a customer for the night.

"Greetings neighbor," she said. "Is there room for one more inside?"

"If you wish," the STEVE replied. "But watch yourself in there MAGDALENA."

Although it was comforting to know that Annika was just outside, waiting in the shadows if she ran into any trouble however, it was vital to avoid needing any rescue from her mistress.

It is my job to protect her, not the other way around.

She could just picture the reactions of the shot house patrons if an Aban in an orange shawl, or worse, the famous Old Leader Shar-Annika herself, were to appear, ready to do battle, with fins swirling and hair flying.

Edging through the door past the STEVE, she tried not to jostle any of the other patrons as she worked her way toward the bar. A few angry eyes turned in her direction but then lost interest once they saw it was just an old woman in a MAGDALENA uniform wiggling by. The man behind the bar was not the former rebel that she had been hoping to find, so she ordered an unfermented drink that she could finish quickly and then leave.

"Let me buy you a proper drink," a blue-clad JOHN squeezed in next to her at the bar said. He had to yell in order to be heard over the sound of the finned-out trio, who were harmonizing loudly just off to their right.

"No thank you, neighbor," she said, with a brief smile and a little bob.

"You cannot come to a shot house and not have a shot," the JOHN persisted. The man stank of intoxicants and lust as leaned closer.

"I prefer Lana juice," she said, not looking at the fellow this time.

The JOHN blew out a stream of bubbles. "Lana juice is for spawn," he bawled.

"The correct term is offspring," she said, twitching her MAGDALENA uniform at him and emphasizing the word to underline her disapproval.

"You only think that coz your upgrade tells you to." The JOHN lurched from side to side as he over-corrected his orientation. "But here we are off duty. No Shar to answer to. No punishment for speaking your mind."

He sounds like another Glae who once uploaded the rebel training files. Too bad he is so drunk he cannot answer any questions discreetly.

The bar tender arrived with her Lana juice, and she tossed him two squares of yellow algae while he floated the bulb in her direction. Scooping up her drink, she turned to face her unwelcome admirer. "Well, since you care about my freedoms, neighbor, perhaps you will be good enough to get out of my way and let me go enjoy my Lana juice in peace."

The JOHN shrugged and turned away. "Huh. There is no cure for being stupid," he said.

She edged away, trying to put more distance between her ears and the harmonizers at the end of the bar. One fellow sang while his companions did the backups, making boom sounds and zither noises, both of which were out of rhythm with the lyrics.

Checking over the crowd as she drank her juice, she looked for any faces she recognized from the days of the rebellion. No one looked familiar though, so once her bulb was empty, she dropped it and gave up.

Yet another disappointment for my mistress. That seems to be all I do for her these days.

Gills drooping, she wormed her way through the crowd and on out the door to rejoin Annika.

"I am sorry, mistress. The former rebel STEVE that we called Tillius was not behind the bar this evening, and I did not see Tal, Undina or Rocio either."

Annika drew her further into the shadows between two shuttered shops.

"I've had no luck out here either. No one that I've spoken to has heard anything but rumors. Everyone says there were no public announcements from the Ruling Assembly Building after Scylla met with the stranger today. I did overhear two councilmen talking, and they were praising Scylla for having his Goons send the stranger off to the upper boundary right after their meeting, so itis probably true that he is gone until tomorrow."

"Then why not go back to the temple and wait in safety until there is new information?"

Magda clasped her hands in hope.

Perhaps once Annika is safe, I can return home in time to see my little Umiko before she goes to bed.

Annika only tapped a finger on her chin in thought, ignoring the suggestion.

"Is it possible that no one here knows anything because they are all Glae? Those councilmen had the best information I've heard so far. I wonder if some of the other high level Shar might know more than our old rebel friends?"

"But mistress, there is no one among the Shar who will speak with you. Not anymore."

"There is one who might. I can pay a call on Trent."

"The artist Trent? But his workshop is all the way out at the west end of the city. We cannot go so far this late at night. Desperate, hungry people roam the streets during the full dark. Some of them even kill people after they steal from them. You may be eager to make use of your combat files, but I am too old for such adventures."

"I know, Magda, and don't worry, I wasn't thinking of going tonight. The stranger's next meeting is not until tomorrow, so there is no rush to go see Trent."

"It will still be dangerous to go so far from the temple, even in daylight. What if someone recognizes you?"

"Well then, I'll have to keep using my shawl so that I'm not recognized, won't I? Why don't you go home to your family now, and we'll argue about whether to go in the morning?"

"As you wish, mistress."

Magda gave a little dip and bowed her head.

By the time she looked up, Annika was already halfway down the avenue that led away from the temple and out toward the west end.

Chapter 11: An Artist and a Gentleman

Once she was certain she'd left Magda behind, Annika proceeded toward the western side of town at a pace that would not draw attention. She knew she couldn't wait until morning to visit Trent, since Magda would insist on accompanying her, and that would be far too dangerous for her dear old nanny.

As she hurried along the deserted streets, homes and shops soon gave way to the warehouses and factories of the west end business district. The west end of the city extended above the slopes of Mount Charlize because many industries required proximity to the fierce heat blasting from the summit of the underwater volcano.

Businesses that produced everything from fermented shots to ordinary wall mats could tap into streams of water with temperatures high enough to be useful for their manufacturing processes. Although it was already full dark, some factories here were still running. Since the volcano ran day and night, many factories did too.

Once Annika reached this commercial sector, she slowed down, moving stealthily to avoid run-ins with any nighttime predators. Around the businesses that were still in operation, patchworks of light and shadow made ideal spots for an ambush. Annika flitted across each lit section, pausing in the shadows to check for any sign she was being followed. Although she had integrated quite a few martial arts upgrades prior to the rebellion, Annika knew that if she had to defend herself, it would mean dropping her shawl to free up her hands. Much as she hated the shawl, losing her disguise would be a disaster, so she took her time and remained alert for danger.

Working her way northwest through the district, she headed to where the artist Trent had his facility near the Grand Eddy.

The Grand Eddy was the other reason that the west end, near Mount Charlize, was the preferred business location in Portbree. The Eddy was a fast current of cold water that wrapped three quarters of the way around the city. It functioned like a highway, facilitating the movement of people and goods all over Portbree. Businesses that manufactured their wares in the west end could then easily ship the finished products to customers all over Portbree using the Grand Eddy.

The sub-surface topology of the volcanoes surrounding the inhabited region of the planet created the strange, hooked shape of the Grand Eddy. The four volcanoes stood in an elongated diamond shape, with Charlize occupying the western point of the formation. Portbree spread out above Charlize's eastern flanks toward the center of the diamond. The Eddy began as a fast-moving ocean current that approached the inhabited area from the west side of Mount Charlize. When this current struck the western slopes of the mountain and encountered the scalding column of heat issuing from the top of Charlize, it was deflected north. There, heat from Mount Dornan at the northern point of the diamond and from Mount Ishvan on the east side continued to bend the path of flowing water to form the curving stream of the Grand Eddy. The Eddy encircled most of the perimeter of the city before it lost cohesion and dwindled away across the fields of crops toward Mount Onclat, far, far to the south.

Annika had heard that Trent's patron and business partner, SharAsherman, had purchased a large building in a prime spot close to the Eddy for the artist's use. Here, Trent created all his sought-after sculptures, and supervised production of the innovative structural columns he had invented.

She was very young when Trent first became famous, still a little girl growing up in her father's House. The artist had originally begun playing around with growing algae in the shape of hollow tubes in order to support one of his larger sculptures. Since then, Trent-tubes had exploded in popularity. Multiple forms of rigid, hollow columns and smaller solid struts had revolutionized everything from buildings to conveyances on Marna. In fact, new uses for all sizes of these innovative products were still being identified almost ten storms after Trent first introduced them.

Even so, the size of the artist's operation astonished Annika when she peeked in through the door. She gasped to see rows and rows of tables lined with Glae workers attending to the various steps in producing short, hollow tubes of algae.

The true genius of Trent's invention had been the realization that even though rolled mats of algae would only grow in short lengths, he could stack several short sections together to make longer, extremely useful columns.

It was not just the enormous size of the Trent-tube factory that impressed Annika. Although the workers seemed to toil long hours here, they all wore rot-free uniforms of an unfamiliar color. Their workspace was well lit by whole families of bioluminescent glow globes held together in nettings on the ceiling. There were even some glows in small enclosures on the tabletops. The tables themselves were supported with Mabel-under-the-table units rather than being suspended in the usual way with bunches of floats. This minimized shadows on the work surfaces to facilitate meticulous tasks.

Annika sidled up to one of the Glae working at a table near the door. "Is the artist here this evening?" she asked.

The man bobbed in place as he looked sidelong at her orange shawl. "The artist is in his studio, Honored One," he said, pointing to a large open doorway at the end of the room.

Nodding her thanks, Annika squeezed along behind the ranks of busy Glae toward the doorway, keeping a tight hold on her disguise to hide her fins.

At the threshold of Trent's personal studio, she paused to take in a view of his latest piece. The sculpture was huge. All of Trent's pieces tended to be oversized now that he had perfected the framework to support them. She saw several decaying models made of algae paste on a table to the left of the door, but the pose of the work in progress did not match any of them. The paste models showed figures in several static positions, sitting or standing. The piece looming over her portrayed its subject in a more aggressive posture, with both arms outstretched and legs flexed. But it was the face of the figure that made her breath catch in her throat. The expression on that face had captured Scylla down to the last detail, and its fearsome grimace left no doubt in her mind how the Leader felt about the imaginary enemy he faced.

A scolding voice from somewhere on her left startled her, snatching her attention away from the sculpture.

"No previews!" the voice cried. "No previews allowed!"

A middle-aged Glae wearing the blue uniform of a JOHN scooted toward her from behind the sculpture, making shooing motions.

"I'm not here to view the piece," she said. "I came to see the artist. Is Trent here?"

"Of course, I'm here," another voice said from behind the sculpture. "I'm always here."

Trent's head appeared over his creation's shoulder, giving the eerie impression of a small extra head perching on Scylla's shoulder.

"It's alright John," he called down to his assistant. "Take a meal break now. This is just an old friend come to visit me."

Trent waved a fin to dismiss the man and Annika waited as the JOHN scuttled off and Trent floated down from the sculpture's shoulder.

"At least I'm pretty sure I recognize that voice." Trent chuckled, peering at her more closely until she dropped the shawl away, letting it dangle from one hand, revealing her arm fins in all their glory. "And so, I was right. Tell me, dear lady, what brings Annika Sharone to my humble workshop this evening?"

"First, I dispute that there is anything humble about this place," she said. "And second, I have a question for you. Why in the waters is an artist of your caliber making that?"

She blew out a large, derisive bubble as she gestured at the unfinished piece with a frown.

"Wonderful, isn't it?" he said with a father's pride in his eye. "So much energy and malice."

Trent had always been impervious to criticism.

"An exceptional likeness."

"Ah yes, I believe I've exceeded expectations with this one. Those other attempts were stultifying." He wrinkled his nose as he waved at the figurines on the table. "I think this piece captures the essence of the subject."

"I'm sure he'll love it."

"Actually, he may not." Trent shrugged. "Scylla wanted something dignified and flattering. He preferred that second one of the two seated poses."

"In that case, are you sure it's wise to make something so radically different?"

"I can't compromise my artistic aesthetic to accommodate the wishes of a patron who doesn't possess even a fleck of taste, now can I?"

"Apparently not."

"So, to what do I owe the pleasure of a visit from the hero of the revolution? Don't tell me you have a new scheme in the works that you want my help with?" he laughed. "No wait. Please tell me you *are* planning another coup that will remove

SharScylla from power. I'd be happy to forgo my fee on this commission in that case."

"Sorry to disappoint you Trent, but haven't you heard? I'm not in the rebellion business anymore."

"Oh yes, I forgot. It's Annika the saint now, isn't it?"

She flicked her gills at him in annoyance. "Not by my choice."

"And yet here you are, orange robe and all."

"It's not a robe, it's a shawl, and I'm only using it as a disguise."

She flung the shawl onto the table next to the paste models.

"Ah yes, to hide those most exquisite fins. Whatever happened to that delightfully eccentric fighting jacket you used to wear when you visited me before?"

"It rotted. Did you think it was made from some everlasting weave?"

"Such a shame," he murmured, "you looked positively magnificent in it."

"Well, why don't get your new pal Scylla to send me another one? Then I can hide my fins in that when I pay you a visit, instead of using the shawl."

Trent clapped his hands, making a quick twirl in the water. "You promise? Oh, imagine the fee for a sculpture of the famous Old Leader all decked out in her fighting gear?"

She laughed and then sobered. "Speaking of strange gear, Trent. Have you heard about this visitor coming down from beyond the upper boundary?"

"Naturally, my dear. My patron SharAsherman tells me

everything. Not that I listen to most of it. But that item was of some interest."

Her gills drooped. "So, you haven't seen the visitor for yourself?"

"No. Why? Should I have?"

"I was curious to know if you had examined this suit he wears. I hear it's made of some strange material that doesn't shed. People say the suit holds a pocket of air around the stranger because he cannot breathe water."

"Indeed? I must have missed that detail. How intriguing."

"I would be most interested in your impressions of the substance. And the man. Do you think you could procure an invitation to the Assembly Building to see the suit for yourself?"

"But, my dear, I am always at the Assembly Building. SharAsherman, refers to this manufacturing space as the Assembly Building you know? For assembling our columns, you see?"

"Yes, I see. Very amusing. But wouldn't you be curious to see a new material that doesn't rot? Think what you could create with such a substance. Artwork that would last for generations. What a treasure that would be."

"I see you are back to appealing to my lust for everlasting fame," he said, eying her with suspicion. "So, what is it you want from me this time?"

"I only want to understand more about this stranger. Don't you find it odd how there's been no public announcement about why the visitor is here? It made me wonder if perhaps this airbreather's suit makes communication with him difficult. You and I might work together to solve that issue. Remember how we had such a successful collaboration last time?"

"You don't fool me, Annika Sharone. You're not interested in working to solve some communication problems. All you want is direct access to this stranger."

"And what if I do? We've been contacted by a representative from a world beyond the sky, Trent. Everyone knows Scylla is no statesman." She nodded toward the sculpture that seemed to threaten them with mouth gaping wide and fins akimbo. "Don't you think it would be better if this visitor encountered someone who would bring intelligence and rationality to the meeting, rather than just a Gladiator's fin-flick attack reflexes?"

"Hmm, I see your point. So, you think that if I became involved in facilitating communications with this airbreather visitor that I could then suggest including a certain former Leader in the negotiations?"

"My only concern is for the welfare of the Marnian people."

"Of course." Trent idly trailed a finger along one arm of his sculpture. "However, as much as I would love to help you, dear lady, I regret that I do not have the kind of influence with our great green Leader that would score me an invitation to his next meeting with this visitor."

She arched an eyebrow at him. "Really, Master Trent? I can't believe that your curiosity about the stranger's remarkable garment would let you rest without at least inquiring if such a thing were possible. Why, the benefits to your own work would be immeasurable."

Trent chuckled as he turned to face her. "Still the charmer, eh?

Well, this time, your flattery will not work."

"How can you call it flattery when I kept every one of my promises to you after the revolution?"

She offered Trent her most charming smile.

"Oh yes, you preserved images and memories of my work just as you said you would. But there is no guarantee SharCom won't destroy every one of those files if he finds them in his hoard."

"Nonsense! Suni Jorah has given your files innocuous names and buried them in a stack of mundane data where the Librarian will never review them. Images of your work are going to be protected and remain preserved in SharCom's hoard for all time."

Trent blew out a thoughtful stream of bubbles. "Humph. I suppose any chance for my work to be preserved is better than nothing, especially since all those sculptures have already rotted to sludge. Only the records in the array remain now. But what good is a buried file? An artist wants his work seen and appreciated by as many people as possible."

Annika gave a little bob of apology.

"I understand, but that's all the more reason you should want to help me ease back into a position of power. Think how famous you would be if I were to regain my place at the head of the Assembly, and could grant people access to any data file from the Libraries they want?"

"Ah ha! I knew it. I knew you must be working on a way to worm your way back into the Leadership."

"Only for the benefit of all Marnians. Just think, if I were

Leader, we could create an entire database with images and memories depicting great works of art, including yours. Free access to information is not only about extra professional upgrades for Glae workers, you know."

"Yes, yes. No need to quote your revolutionary slogans to me, my dear." He flapped an impatient fin at her. "I agree, it is not only art that suffers under our current system. Why, without my patron to pay the exorbitant fees charged by the Librarians, I could never afford to create files to preserve the instructions for producing my columns and struts."

"And what a loss that would be. Your struts and columns have changed our world over just a few storms. Wouldn't you like to see how other things would change once we break the Shar chokehold on access to data? Imagine images of your work from the library files still being admired by people long after you're dead. I think that would be a splendid thing."

Trent snorted. "Well, when you put it like that ... I can hardly disagree, can I?"

He smiled as she began darting from side to side as her enthusiasm overflowed.

"My dream is to give people the opportunity to see things in their lives differently. Through art, through knowledge, and even through sharing their personal histories. People shouldn't have to be limited to seeing themselves as just one more pampered, greedy Shar, or another insignificant JOHN or MARISOL. My Glae rebels learned to see themselves as unique individuals who *deserved* a better life." She speared him with an earnest look, as the delicate scent of hope swirled across the water between them. "Can you picture an entire world where every person thinks of themself as unique? A person worthy of knowledge and opportunity? It would be amazing. So, yes, of course I want another chance at seeing that dream come true. Wouldn't you like to see a world like that, too?"

Trent shook his head, fins drooping. "You weave a lovely image, my dear lady, and as an artist, I admit it would thrill me to see that world. However, my wishes do not change the fact that this time you are asking too much."

Her gills went stiff, but she held herself in check, unwilling to damage her relationship with the one remaining Shar in Portbree who would still speak to her.

"I was not being modest when I told you before that you've over-estimated my influence with SharScylla. The fact is, that these days I am barely tolerated by our new Leader and never venture near his Assembly Building at all."

She forced down her disappointment, twisting her own lips to mirror his regretful smile. "I see."

"No, an invitation for you to meet with this stranger is not something I can provide. Your beautiful visions of a better world will have to wait a little longer and find some other way to come true. This time I cannot help you."

"In that case I should let you return to your work, master Trent," she said, with a graceful dip that sent her fin fringes coiling out in all directions.

"Good night, dear lady."

"Good night."

Swiftly wrapping the hated shawl over her head and

shoulders, she turned and skimmed away out of the workshop.

Chapter 12: Crowd Control

Scylla whirled away from the window of his Audience Chamber and threw himself into a chair suspended from the ceiling.

"Bring me a shot bulb," he ordered one of his Glads.

Outside his window down in the Square, a clamoring group of citizens protested the imminent arrival of the airbreather for his second meeting.

Their noise made Scylla want to cover his ears like a child. Instead, he broke the seal on the drink bulb his Glad handed him and flung it at the little SUNI from SharCom's Library, who floated next to the window, head bowed. Scylla eyed the fellow with a scowl. The man's entire report only confirmed every infuriating detail about the airbreathers that the foul-smelling Librarian had told him yesterday.

So, now I cannot just kill this Gods-cursed airbreather to get rid of him. I need a way to deal with the stranger's unholy requests.

His Glads were lined up next to the doorway as usual, and Scylla gestured for the SUNI to go join them.

He may be useful once this airbreather arrives.

The shot tasted bad, but he slurped most of it anyway, as the people in the Square began synchronizing their voices into chants, hoping to make their messages heard.

"KEEP OUR OCEAN PURE. KEEP OUR OCEAN PURE."

"LEAVE OUR GODS IN PEACE. LEAVE OUR GODS IN PEACE."

"SINK THE STRANGER. SINK THE STRANGER."

Scylla rolled his eyes.

Those idiots will never understand why I cannot just sink this stranger or tell him to go away.

Scylla wished he could make the noise stop so he could think clearly. Being angry made him itch to break someone in half.

If only I could sink a few of those irritating float-heads out in the Square. What satisfaction that would be.

The happy image lasted only until he pictured the Ruling Assembly's response if he were to kill a group of innocent citizens. His old reflexes were of no use for winning political contests. The last thing he needed was more trouble with the councilmen while he was trying to negotiate for a bride.

Scylla crushed his empty drink bulb, reflecting that life as the Leader of all Marna had not turned out at all the way he expected.

I ought to be surrounded by Shar groveling for favors. Instead, I have councilmen rejecting me as a husband for their daughters, and insolent citizens screaming outside my window.

The noise from the crowd reminded him unpleasantly of spectators at the arena.

His fins tensed, and he ground a fist into his forehead, trying to stave off those memories.

How dare these impudent fools question my actions? I deserve respect.

Aiming another poisonous look at the window, he signaled the men of his pod to approach.

"I cannot have a meeting with the airbreather while all that noise is going on. The stranger will lose respect for me if he sees my people behaving so rudely."

Bran dipped in place before speaking. "Shall I take some Goons and go disperse this crowd, Shar?"

Scylla almost smiled, until he looked at his second man, Lothic. Lothic wore that expression that said he had a different solution to this matter. With a surly flick of a fin, he gestured for the Glad to speak.

"We could chase these rude people away before the airbreather arrives," Lothic said, with a flick of his own fin. "But we cannot control a crowd of citizens the way you control an opponent in battle. They will only return and resume their disturbance later."

"What is it you suggest?" Scylla snapped.

"I believe there is an old Gladiator saying that applies here. 'Never start a fight which you cannot win. It hands your enemy the advantage.' Therefore, if using force will only bring defeat, consider avoiding this conflict. You can simply ignore these people. Treat them as if their behavior does not matter."

Scylla's nose wrinkled as he considered this advice. It did not sit well to let these people go on flaunting their disrespect. However, the other alternative appealed to him even less. He squirmed inside to think of losing a contest in front of the airbreather if he could not end the crowd's disrespect.

I could go out there and crush every one of them, but now is not the time to give in to foolish impulses. I won the Leadership by being smart as well as strong.

As usual, Lothic is correct. I am not under attack, so there is no need for a show of force. Let this crowd scream like spoiled spawn. Let them scream until they sink from lack of gases. The important thing is that the airbreather must not see me as weak for failing to control a few noisy protesters.

Chapter 13: Second Meeting

Apart from having to spend more time in the same room with Scylla, Suni was glad to stay for the second meeting with the visitor. Accumulating new information was one of the principal joys of his life, and today was his first chance to see a real live airbreather up close. People outside the Assembly Building did not share his enthusiasm, though. The noise from the crowd of protesters in the Square had been growing louder ever since the airbreather arrived.

The mob kept howling up at Scylla's window, objecting to a stranger with no gills being entertained by their Leader. Of course, there was not much entertaining going on since the airbreather's suit isolated him completely from the Marnian environment.

The visitor's clunky garment intrigued Suni. It was so heavy that it often threatened to sink the airbreather. At the moment, the one who called himself Devon Arkovic was using a tether tied to a ceiling support to keep from dropping right out through the bottom of the building.

It was funny to watch the man writhing and kicking on the end of that line from time to time. Suni's face gave no hint of how much he enjoyed the visitor's antics, though. He had long years of practice at keeping his face impassive, no matter what was going on around him.

The only good thing about the stranger's ungainly suit seemed to be that it provided Devon Arkovic with air to breathe. Since the stranger had no gills, without the suit, he would die. That an air breathing man had overcome this obstacle was an amazing feat in Suni's opinion, no matter how inelegant the solution was.

Suni took care to hide his interest in the details of the visitor's suit because Scylla was angry. Again. The entire room stank of it.

"Come and see what you have caused!" Scylla snarled at his guest, gesturing toward the window.

Suni doubted that the airbreather's suit would provide any defense if the Leader became angry enough to attack the man, but he hoped he would not have to find out.

Perhaps the airbreather will jet away using his impellors if attacked.

One of Scylla's Glads untied the stranger's tendril so the airbreather could swim clumsily toward the window. Apparently, Devon Arkovic had already learned not to use the small impellers attached to his suit to help maintain his position or move from place to place while indoors. Suni was relieved, as he had seen and smelled the impellors in action when the visitor arrived in the Square.

SharArkovic could probably burst right out through the wall and escape if he wanted to.

However, without the help of his impellors, the visitor could only thrash his finless arms and legs to make his way to Scylla's side at the window.

110

Suni hung back while the Leader and the visitor looked out over the Square in front of the Ruling Assembly Building. A roar went up from the people when the stranger appeared. The bulky, silvery suit made Devon Arkovic recognizable, even at a distance. Suni could hear various groups out in the square attempting to synchronize several voices to make their slogans heard again. He even thought there was one chant that sounded like, 'Kill the Airbreather.'

Scylla shot an accusing glare at his unpopular guest. "Even the Aban have warned me that any journey into the Deeps could disturb the Gods Below."

"We only want to retrieve our equipment," Devon Arkovic repeated patiently.

"And why is this equipment so important that you must disturb the realm of the Gods?" Scylla demanded.

The Leader returned to his chair, leaving the visitor to follow him and have his tendril fastened back on the ceiling beam by one of the Glads.

"As I tried to explain yesterday," the stranger said, "the equipment holds an important cargo, and we are here to fetch it."

Suni suppressed an awestruck wriggle.

Here to fetch it from very far away according to what I learned from the files yesterday.

It had been a dream come true for him to have free run of his former master's great data array. Suni had always wanted to see those most ancient records in the vast trove of information. However, SharCom had kept those files carefully sequestered from the rest of the data in his hoard, so Suni had never had an opportunity to satisfy his curiosity before. Now that he had seen the files, he completely understood SharCom's precautions.

Much of the information he had downloaded during the last full dark was nothing less than fantastic. He had been awake till first light, downloading hands upon hands of files made during the founding of the original colony on Marna. The files told him all about why the LEAP Corporation came to Marna. He even saw records made right up to the time the company abandoned its colonists here to fend for themselves.

Although he knew he might have missed some details of that saga, Suni had seen enough to know that Devon Arkovic wasn't telling the whole story. So far, the stranger's words had focused only on the sunken equipment he sought.

Why is he hiding things from Scylla?

Curious as he was, self-preservation was very high on Suni's personal agenda today. After witnessing the slaughter of SharCom, he'd decided the wisest course of action would be to play the dumb Glae during this meeting. It was always acceptable for a Glae to answer only the questions asked and offer no additional information.

Then I will not risk rousing the Leader's anger for saying anything he does not want to hear.

Suni had a strong sense that Devon Arkovic was also afraid of Scylla, but the stranger's body language was hard to read since most of that body remained hidden inside what the visitor referred to as his 'spacesuit.'

Space.

That was another incredible concept Suni had learned about last full dark. Many of the ancient records casually referred to a vast 'galaxy' beyond the world of Marna. One file, which seemed designed to educate young offspring, showed a picture of a galaxy and defined it as a collection of thousands of worlds in orbit around bright stars. The file also explained that a great emptiness which stretched enormous distances between those stars was called 'space.' Other more technical files talked about how space contained mostly 'vacuum.' Vacuum was a sort of waterless, airless nothing. A great, cold blackness where nothing could live. The very idea made Suni feel faint.

"And why do you airbreathers deserve to have this cargo instead of leaving it with the Gods Below?" Scylla demanded.

Suni leaned forward to catch the reply. It was this idea that airbreathers intended to steal from the Gods, that was making the people out in the Square so angry.

He had heard from others at the array that some Aban from the temple had started this rumor that the airbreathing strangers were going to steal from the Gods Below.

"Didn't your Librarian confirm my information about the LEAP Corporation and the equipment they brought here?" Devon Arkovic asked.

The Leader's frown deepened at the mention of the dead Librarian. Turning away from the window, he returned to the center of the room with a flick of his black edged fins.

"Yes, the Librarian confirmed your story," Scylla rumbled.

"Well, maybe he could join us and explain to you about this cargo as well," the stranger said. "This Glaeon we came to find is of no use to you, but it is valuable to me. Your Librarian ought to be able to confirm that too."

Suni quivered in place as Scylla shot a warning glance his way before pointing him out to the stranger.

"This SUNI is now in charge of that data hoard," Scylla told the visitor shortly, omitting any mention of the SharCom's fate. "He will be the one to confirm or deny your information today."

As both men turned to look at him, Suni bobbed twice, locking his fingers together to keep them still and chose his next words with care.

"The visitor is correct, SharScylla," he said. "The cargo SharArkovic seeks is only of value to airbreathers. According to the ancient files, Glaeon is worthless to Marnians."

He gave another little dip to show that he had finished rendering a service, and then fell silent with his head bowed.

"You see?" the airbreather said. "Everything I told you is the truth."

From the corner of his eye, Suni saw Scylla's expression turned predatory for a second. The odor of malice that accompanied the look almost shriveled his gills.

How does this stranger not flinch in the face of such obvious danger?

"All of that may be true," Scylla said. "But if this cargo is valuable to you, and you want my help in recovering it, what do you offer me in exchange?" Scylla's eyes glittered as he waved a fin toward the window where the roar of the crowd filled the Square. "As you can tell, it will not please my people if they think I am helping you steal from the Gods Below."

"I am sorry if they object, SharScylla, but I'm afraid there is something more that I haven't told you yet."

The airbreather spoke hesitantly and even though he sensed danger, Suni's eyes went round at the prospect of acquiring even more new data today.

"My group—that is me and my companions onboard the *Osprey*—we are not the only ones who seek this cargo. There are other ships carrying other airbreathers who are also searching for this load of Glaeon. We expect that one or more of those ships will arrive here very soon."

"*Ships*?" Scylla frowned, turning away from the visitor and glancing at Suni for a translation.

"Conveyances, Shar," Suni explained. "Ships are the vehicles which airbreathers use to travel great distances."

"I see." Scylla leaned back in his chair and flicked a fin at the stranger. "So, you have rivals. Continue."

"Please understand, these other ships do not come from the LEAP Corporation as I do. They carry dangerous men called pirates. Pirates are killers and thieves. They live by searching for items of great value to steal." The stranger spoke slowly, and Suni could see him eying Scylla to see if the Leader followed this explanation. "These pirates are on their way here to Marna right now. Once they arrive, they will not ask permission to retrieve the cargo or pay anything for what they find. Pirates take what they want and kill any who oppose them."

Scylla gave Devon Arkovic an appraising glance. "And these pirates who steal, they are like you? Airbreathers in clumsy suits?" He blew off a contemptuous cloud of bubbles. "My warriors will defeat them."

"They are airbreathers, yes. But pirates have powerful weapons. Weapons that they will use from far above the surface."

Scylla turned to Suni again to explain this mystery, but he could only fan his fins in bewilderment. Nothing he had seen in the ancient files mentioned weapons of this kind.

"What are these 'weapons' you speak of?" Scylla asked.

"It may be hard to understand," the stranger said. "These weapons can kill people—many people—from a great distance. You will have no opportunity to fight men in suits." Devon Arkovic gestured at his own bloated outfit. "The pirates will stay on their ships and launch many of these weapons until everyone on Marna is dead. After there is no one left alive, they will come down in their suits to take the cargo. Do you understand?"

The furious expression on Scylla's face left no doubt he understood. "And you and your airbreather companions will not do the same?"

The skin on Suni's back crawled as the stink of hostility permeated the room. Scylla spoke in the same fierce tone he had used when he called SharCom a traitor. Right before he went berserk and killed the Librarian. The reek of anger made Suni want to wriggle away and hide, but the airbreather still did not back down.

This stranger cannot smell his danger, not while locked away inside his suit.

"The crew of the *Osprey* does not wish to hurt anyone."

Suni marveled at how the visitor looked Scylla straight in the eye without flinching.

"We want the cargo, and we will pay you for it, as I told you yesterday. But we must remove it before the pirates arrive. We believe this is the best way to ensure the safety of your people and mine."

Scylla folded his arms across his chest, gills flicking. "And how will it ensure *our* safety that *you* possess this cargo?"

The stranger gripped his headpiece with one hand as he faced the Leader.

"Once the Glaeon is gone from your world, there will be nothing of value here for the pirates to steal. When they see the cargo is gone, we believe the pirates will depart without killing anyone."

"And how will these others know that the cargo is gone, eh? What if they also wish to dive into the Deep and see for themselves? Will these dangerous men not use their weapons and kill us all so they may conduct their search in peace?"

"We have a plan to prevent that from happening, SharScylla. When we find the harvester that contains the Glaeon, we intend to preserve the equipment intact. We will raise the machine to the surface and leave it there empty for the pirates to find. Once they see that the cargo is gone, we believe they will leave Marna to seek elsewhere for some other treasure to steal."

"Will they not use their weapons to kill us in anger because their prize is gone?"

"We do not think so. Each weapon is so expensive that a pirate will not use one unless there is a treasure to be gained. My captain does not think pirates will waste any weapons when there can be no profit."

Scylla nodded. "I can see the reason in that. But how long must we leave this airbreather equipment cluttering up our skies?"

"That is another issue I wanted to discuss with you today, SharScylla. We would like you to leave the equipment there permanently, because it is the LEAP Corporation's wish to resume shipping cargoes of Glaeon from Marna, just as they did before."

"So, you wish to turn Marna into some kind of farm to produce a product only airbreathers can use? Do you take me for a LAGE?"

The airbreather looked confused. With a small dip of apology to Scylla, Suni supplied a translation.

"A LAGE, SharArkovic, is a Marnian trained to grow foodstuffs and then transport them here to the markets in Portbree."

The stranger held up a hand. "No, SharScylla, I can see you are no LAGE. You are a wise and great Leader. When the Marnian people produce new cargoes of Glaeon, then I foresee that you, as the Leader of Marna, will be in charge of a great volume of trade. You do have trade here, don't you?"

"Of course, we have trade," Scylla snapped. "What is it you offer?"

"If Marnians learn to operate the equipment and produce new cargoes of Glaeon, then we airbreathers can trade with you for many things wonderful things."

"What do you offer," Scylla repeated.

"You can see that my suit is made from materials you do not have here on Marna. Airbreathers have many such things. We have new materials to create houses with stronger walls. Clothing and conveyances that do not rot—"

"That is impossible," Scylla interrupted. "Everything rots. Do you take me for an idiot spawn?"

The visitor once again turned toward Suni, silently appealing to him to confirm these outrageous claims.

Ruffling his gills, Suni bobbed from side to side. He had seen many wonders in the records, including stories about people traveling enormous distances through the vacuum of space in airbreather ships.

But how will Scylla take a direct contradiction?

Suni bit his lip as he noted the stream of bubbles obscuring one side of Scylla's surly expression.

Airbreathers could not travel great distances if their conveyances succumbed to rot as quickly as ours do. Even if there was air for them to breathe between the stars, no one would plan to travel so far if they knew their conveyances would rot and breakdown.

He composed his features into a blank mask as he bowed his head before the impatient Leader.

"The records confirm airbreather ships often travel great distances, SharScylla. It is not clear that the materials used to make them *never* rot. However, from what I have seen in the files, airbreather conveyances do last much longer than ours." The stranger shot him a curious glance, no doubt picking up on the evasiveness of his reply, so he broke his own rule about not offering extra information before Scylla noticed the airbreather's expression and became suspicious. "I viewed one record that spoke of an airbreather ship which lasted longer than a man lives, SharScylla."

After concluding with the customary small dip, he and the stranger remained silent while Scylla took time to digest this incredible concept. After a small interval, Devon Arkovic broke the silence again.

"Do you remember what I said yesterday about how my captain will pay you for this first load of Glaeon? Just wait till you see some of the wonderful things we have to offer. We have many materials and tools you will find useful. Once you see them, I think you'll understand how you can benefit from trading with us."

"And what of the warriors with the terrible killing weapons?" Scylla asked with a sly look. "Will you also offer weapons we can use to defeat them?"

Devon Arkovic shook his head carefully.

"I cannot promise that. I know that once we deliver this first load of Glaeon, the LEAP Corporation will send soldiers—that is, warriors—to defend you from any pirates who might try to come here and harm you in the future. The LEAP Corporation wants to provide everything you need to restart production of Glaeon here on Marna. They plan to send men here to teach you how to use the harvester equipment and lots of warriors to make sure you stay safe. Then, when you have Glaeon to offer, LEAP will establish regular trade with you for the cargoes you produce. Do you think those pirates who are on their way here now have any interest in developing future trade? Not a chance.

They only want to steal the Glaeon you have now and give nothing in return."

Scylla shrugged. "The strong take what they will. But I shall not be their victim. I will offer my help so that you and your corporation can recover this lost cargo. But remember, if you break your end of this agreement, then I will order that any airbreather who appears from beyond the upper boundary shall be killed on sight."

"Agreed," said Devon immediately, holding out his hand to Scylla. "You will see. If we find this cargo of Glaeon, the LEAP Corporation will return and make the Marnians prosper."

Scylla's look was menacing as he touched the stranger's hand. The expression gave Suni the same chill he had felt earlier, when he thought Scylla might be about to attack the airbreather. It was no accident that this vicious man had taken over the leadership. The same dangerous cunning that had kept Scylla alive in the Gladiator pits while other competitors fell still lurked just below the surface of those deep green features.

That look means bad news for someone. What can he be planning now?

Scylla dropped the visitor's hand and then wiped his own fingers on the top spine of his leg fin. "First, we must calm the fears of my people regarding you disturbing our Gods Below with your journey."

"I'm open to ideas."

"I believe it would reassure my people for a Marnian to be present during this dive Below."

"But the pressures at that depth are extreme. No Marnian

121

could survive there, SharScylla."

Suni could see the Leader's gills stiffening as the airbreather's reaction only encouraged his suspicions.

A stubborn look twisted Scylla's features. "A Marnian representative must be on hand to advise you on this journey. Or to beseech the Gods on our behalf should you disturb them. Understand me airbreather, I will not allow this journey to proceed unless a Marnian accompanies you."

"I see."

Suni watched the stranger's brow furrow.

At last, the man is worried about something.

"Perhaps I have not been quite clear, SharScylla." the airbreather said, carefully. "You see, our submarine—that is the special conveyance that makes it possible for us to survive the pressure of such great depths—is a very small vehicle."

"Do not worry, SharArkovic," Scylla chuckled, "the one I will send to watch over you is not large."

Suni froze, his gills pausing in mid-beat, while he waited to hear his name pass the Leader's lips.

"I still don't think you understand, sir," the airbreather cut in, holding up a hand to silence Scylla. "I will not be going on this mission. My job is only to conduct negotiations and learn about your world and your people to facilitate our future trade arrangements. I do not have the correct training to operate a submarine, so it will be one of our best pilots who will control the craft during the retrieval of the cargo."

Now it was Scylla who waved the other into silence.

"I think it is you who do not understand, airbreather," the

Leader sneered. "I do not care which stranger makes the journey. Only that a Marnian goes with you on the search for your cargo."

"But Marnians cannot travel in a submarine, SharScylla!"

Suni noticed that the stranger now seemed almost as agitated as he was. The man poked at his headpiece and twisted his features this way and that before calming himself and trying to explain.

"With respect, SharScylla, a submarine is an airbreather vehicle which is not designed to carry aquatic passengers."

This time Scylla waved his massive palm toward the open window.

"Do you hear that noise out there, airbreather? Those people are on the verge of rioting. They believe you will anger the Gods Below with this journey. I cannot grant permission for you to go meddling around in the Deeps unless a Marnian is there to intercede for us in case your activities should disturb the Gods. I tell you, one of the Aban must go along on this journey."

Suni flicked both fins to stabilize his orientation.

Bless my gills, I am saved. It is an Aban he plans to send on this terrible journey, not me.

As the heady aroma of relief spread around him, Suni almost missed what Scylla said next.

"This is the only way to reassure my people, so I will not give permission for this journey unless an Aban goes along."

The stranger began twisting his hands together in anxiety, almost like a Glae.

"But SharScylla, what about the pirates?"

"I have only your word that such a danger exists. Perhaps we should just wait and see if any pirates arrive?"

"That would not be wise ..."

"I will not have some flailing jink spawn telling me what is wise," Scylla interrupted. "My job," he said, imitating SharArkovic's patient-yet-patronizing tone, "is to protect the interests of my people, not to do favors for strangers in badly fitted garments who show up uninvited spinning bedtime tales of cargoes and pirates."

"I'm sorry, SharScylla. Believe me, I would like to respect your wishes in this matter. I just can't think of a way for an airbreather and an aquatic to share the same vehicle. I'm only trying to help, but without your cooperation, we cannot remove this cargo that presents a great danger to your people."

Suni trembled in place. This talk of pirates was terrifying. He wished he could support the stranger's argument but to do so would be suicide when Scylla was in a mood like this.

"This discussion is over," Scylla told the visitor. "If you wish, you are welcome to convince that crowd out there to listen to your stories about pirates with magic weapons coming to kill everyone in the city. Just be sure you are ready to jet up to the surface with those cursed smelly thrusters of yours, because I do not think my people are in a very receptive mood. They might decide they would rather send you down to meet the Gods Below right now. Without your marvelous diving vehicle."

With that, Scylla turned away, gesturing at his pod to remove the stranger.

Chapter 14: Diving Solution

As SharScylla turned away, Devon's hopes sank to his boots and puddled there.

What am I going to tell the captain this time?

He pictured Doyle sending down the surface platform and posting armed crewmen around its perimeter with orders to shoot any Marnians who interfered with operations.

But why should these people believe any of my stories about pirates with torpedoes and deadly energy weapons that can be launched from orbit?

He racked his brains for another argument that might be more convincing, but his mind only spun in panicky circles as Scylla's security detail moved in to surround him. Just when he thought the four green musclemen were about to lay hold of him and eject him from the Audience Chamber, Devon noticed the small Glae retainer who had been answering questions during the meeting bobbing up and down in excitement.

"Excuse me, SharScylla," the little fellow said. "Perhaps SharArkovic could lend our citizen one of his special suits to use during the journey."

The security men around him paused their approach, waiting to see how Scylla would react to this suggestion. As the big

Leader glared down at the little retainer, the man humbly dropped his gaze to his clasped hands. However, Devon could see the little fellow watching from the corner of one eye, also waiting to see what the Leader would answer. SharScylla's burning gaze shifted away from the nervous servant and aimed directly at him instead.

"Well?" Scylla demanded.

"Oh, er, yes," Devon floundered, trying to think of how to explain why the idea would never work. "Unfortunately, our suits only provide a person with air, not water. And the submarine is also filled with air," he added, quickly.

He thought that would settle the matter, but then the little Glae began bobbing again. This time the fellow shot a timid glance at the Leader, silently asking permission before posing his question, and receiving a grudging nod in return.

"Excuse me, SharArkovic," the Glae said, turning to face him with folded hands and arm fins tucked in tight, "Could you not fill your conveyance with water instead of air? Then the airbreather could wear a suit during the journey while our representative had plenty of water to breathe."

"Yes!" Scylla exclaimed.

"No!" Devon cried, unwisely throwing out his hands to halt this idea before it went any further.

Sadly, the sudden movement sent him twisting out of control on the end of his tether again. Security men scattered, making no move to help him, so he was red-faced and huffing like an ox by the time he righted himself. Peering at the Marnian leader through a faceplate now streaked with drops of sweat, he tried again to explain.

"I'm sorry, SharScylla, but the sub is just not designed to have water inside it. Exposure to water would damage the control systems of the vehicle so that the machine would cease to function."

The Marnians all stared at him, looking completely baffled.

They probably think I'm either a liar or some kind of lunatic. Everything in their world functions in water all the time.

He tried another objection they might more readily understand. "Also, I'm afraid that even if the inside of the sub could tolerate exposure to water, our pilot could not operate the controls of the vehicle while wearing gloves like these."

This time he raised a hand more slowly, then wiggled his fingers inside one bulky glove.

"You have given me another idea, though," he said. He carefully lowered the hand to his side. "The sub is equipped with an airlock. That is a small space which is designed to hold either water or air. We use this airlock to go in and out of the vehicle when it is underwater. It might be possible to fill that airlock with water and then have your representative ride in there during the mission. However, I must emphasize that it is a tiny space."

He looked at the muscular form of the Marnian leader doubtfully.

Scylla only laughed, rising from his chair and twitching his arm fins outward in both directions. "Do not worry about the size of the space, SharArkovic. As I told you, I will not be the one making this journey. For this we will need someone who has influence with the Gods Below. And I know the perfect person for the job. I am going to send dear Shar-Annika."

"No!" the clever little Glae retainer burst out. "SharScylla, you cannot risk her safety on a dangerous journey like this. What if she is killed?"

"Silence!" the Leader snarled. "Annika Sharone is exactly the person we need for this task. People already say that she speaks with the Gods, so it will reassure everyone if she is on hand during this mission. She has always claimed that her only goal is to help the people of Marna, so I am sure the great old Leader will be delighted to be of service to them now."

Something in Scylla's tone set the hair on the back of Devon's neck prickling, so he remained silent as the big green leader hovered over the small Glae retainer, issuing orders in a manner that brooked no interference.

"You will go now and conduct our visitor to the Assembly Building dining room. After that, you will bring Shar-Annika from the temple to meet with airbreather and discuss arrangements to make the journey."

While the Leader barked orders at his servant, Devon stayed quiet, consumed with his own thoughts.

Wow, this Marnian sure moves right along, doesn't he? Using the airlock was only an idea, but now he's talking like this is the plan we've agreed on. Crap! Will this even work? I'm no tech. But the guy is so easily irritated I don't think we can argue it anymore. I can't wait to hear what captain Doyle has to say about this. He's going to kill me.

Scylla turned to face him once he was through issuing commands to the little Glae. "You may make your journey tomorrow," he said.

"Wait, what? Tomorrow?" Devon imagined trying to sell that timeline to his captain. "I'm sorry SharScylla, but it will take a day or two minimum for preparations. First, we must set up a surface support platform for the sub. Er, that is a conveyance that remains on the upper boundary while the sub dives below."

Scylla frowned. "You claimed that the er, pirates—the warriors with the great killing ways—will come soon."

"Yes, that's true, but if any alterations to the airlock are required so a Marnian can remain there during the dive mission, that may delay preparations as well."

"A Marnian must accompany you or you may not go."

"I understand, and we will work as fast as we can, believe me. We want to have that cargo safely removed before the pirates arrive, for all our sakes. But shifting heavy equipment takes time. Perhaps you could use those days to prepare your people for our arrival, so they don't interfere with our operations." He gestured at the window where the noise from out in the square continued. "You should tell them they will need to stay clear of the entire area between the last bend of the circular current and the volcano in the west. That is where we must place our surface platform in order for the sub to reach the equipment down below."

"Beyond the last bend of the Grand Eddy? Well, why did you not say so before? Your airbreathers will not be disturbed in that area. That region has only algae farms, so few city dwellers ever go there. As for the LAGEs who work the farms, my Glads can easily maintain order among them." The Leader waved a massive hand toward the window. "Those citizens who are complaining out there in the Square are never even going to see your airbreather companions or their conveyances."

"But don't you think it would be a good idea to tell them to avoid the area, anyway? Just to be on the safe side?"

"No. I see no need to inform anyone of the plans we have agreed upon today."

Devon opened his mouth, intending to offer a friendly word of advice about keeping secrets from the public, but then closed it again as the proud green Marnian turned his back to aim another stern glance down at his little Glae retainer.

"You will now arrange the meeting," Scylla snapped.

I wish I knew why the little guy thinks taking this passenger is a bad idea. But SharScylla is already so irritated that I hate to ask. It gives me a bad feeling the way he's just taking over all the planning on this. At least I got permission to do the dive. But Captain Doyle is going to hit the roof when he hears that I let them push me into agreeing to fix up the airlock to carry an aquatic.

Chapter 15: A Goon for All Seasons

4th Goon of the Leader's Guard dragged the visitor through the halls of the Ruling Assembly Building by a tendril attached to the central part of his suit. It seemed to him a very undignified way to transport an important visitor, but luckily for 4th Goon, the stranger did not seem to mind. The visitor's 'spacesuit', as the man called his garment, made the stranger quite awkward and slow in his movements. The fellow also had an alarming tendency to sink when not thrashing his way forward by beating his arms and legs in all directions.

It was 4th Goon's misfortune that he was the one assigned to stand guard outside the Audience Chamber today. This meant that once the Leader was through screaming at his guest, 4th Goon was stuck escorting the odd visitor over to the dining hall for another meeting. He felt a momentary panic following this unwelcome assignment, as he eyed the stranger floundering out of the Audience Chamber like a dying float. Fortunately, the little SUNI who trailed the visitor out of the Chamber intervened to bridge the awkward moment.

"Perhaps SharArkovic, it would be best if our escort," here the SUNI gestured at him, "were to provide a little assistance by towing you to the dining hall?"

4th Goon's eyes bulged, but he stared straight ahead, pretending he had not heard.

How can this SUNI dare say such a thing?

The SUNI was a squat little man, so it did not surprise 4th Goon that the fellow had been dedicated to work as a SUNI rather than being chosen to serve as any kind of Goon. SUNIs had no need for the size and strength required for Goon tasks. Brains were far more important in a SUNI's work.

Still, after hearing the fellow speak to a guest of the Leader in such a fashion, 4th Goon could not help but wonder if even the brains on this SUNI were lacking, given his age. The SUNI looked to be about forty storms of age. His smooth Asian-style features made it hard for 4th Goon to tell for sure.

"Oh yes, that would be very helpful," the visitor agreed.

The airbreather's voice had a weird, distant quality, as if the words were echoing down a Trent-tube, but otherwise the stranger was easy to understand. 4th Goon could see parts of the visitor's face through the small clear patch on the ugly thing that covered the man's head. The stranger's head covering differed from the rest of his phish-colored suit. None of the materials that made up the garment looked familiar. It was a spooky alien thing that gave 4th Goon an itchy feeling in the back of his brain, so he did not know whether to feel scared or curious.

"Thank you," the stranger added.

4th Goon was not sure if the visitor was thanking him or the SUNI. He also was not sure what he ought to say in reply if the stranger had been speaking to him.

Better just shut up and do as I am told. That always works in unusual situations.

Wrapping the tendril that protruded from the front of the bulging silvery suit around his hand a couple of times, he began towing the stranger down the hallways, doing his best to keep the visitor and his 'spacesuit' from ripping through any walls when they went around corners. Earlier he had heard some of the other Goons in his cohort swapping rumors about how this airbreather must have been sent by some new Gods From Above. Some of them even said that this fellow Arkovic himself was some kind of God. Yet as far as 4th Goon had seen, the Leader treated this airbreather like any other man.

SharScylla was just as rude and irritable with this stranger as he is with everyone else. Any visiting God hoping to squeeze some sign of deference out of our Leader would have to be a lot more impressive than this poor flapper.

4th Goon chuckled to himself over that idea as he swam along, dragging the airbreather like a load of vegetables. As they threaded their way through the halls of the Assembly Building, it also amused him to hear the stranger shooting one question after another over his shoulder at the SUNI. The little 'linker trailed along behind, patiently answering every childish question the visitor asked.

"What is this substance that forms the walls?"

"How do you maintain buoyancy?"

"Do you wear clothing for protection from the elements or to just preserve modesty?"

4th Goon kept all his attention on navigating around a group of people who were half blocking the next intersection while the

SUNI fielded that one.

"Tell me," the stranger said next, gesturing at a group of Glae passing by in the opposite direction, "do the single-color garments many people wear denote some particular function or status within your society?"

People who think this fellow is some kind of God from above the upper boundary ought to hear how he talks. He is worse than an idiot spawn. What kind of God would not know such basic things?

"Glae workers wear single color garments, SharArkovic," the SUNI said. "The color of the garment indicates each worker's profession."

"Do you mean that every person in a profession wears the same color?"

"Yes. This way a Shar can tell on sight what services a worker can provide before they issue any orders. That is why every Glae wears the uniform color allocated to their profession after they receive their professional upgrade."

"Professional upgrade? What is that?"

4th Goon wallowed in surprise, then recovered quickly.

How can anyone not know what an upgrade is? Perhaps this visitor needs an upgrade himself, so he can stop asking so many stupid questions.

4th Goon rolled his eyes, but the SUNI was as patient as ever.

"When a worker is first hired for service in one of the Great Shar Houses, his new master pays for the Glae to receive a neural upgrade. After the worker receives this data burst from one of our library arrays, he or she immediately possesses all the knowledge, as well as any physical skills needed to perform their new duties."

"So, you mean they get some sort of data download?"

"That is correct. The employer pays to have data files delivered to the worker via direct neural uplink. This guarantees complete competence in a Glae's new profession."

"Really? I'm surprised something as advanced as neural link technology still exists on Marna."

"Of course, you have seen very little of our world, but I assure you, SharArkovic, we are not a primitive society. Perhaps you would be interested to know that Marna has no less than ten vast data arrays that contain every fleck of information in existence."

4th Goon fought to keep his eyes forward and his pace unchanged. The SUNI's tone was so clipped that he might have been scolding some naughty spawn rather than addressing a guest of the Leader.

"Not only do we possess neural uplink capability, SharArkovic, our data arrays contain all knowledge needed to maintain life here. All ten Libraries maintain multiple copies of these critical files, among many others. Multiple backups keep our information safe from the endless ravages of rot. Every Marnian knows that any data lost from our arrays would be lost forever. That is why generations of Librarians have dedicated their lives to tending these data hoards."

"I see," the visitor said, with a trace of hesitancy in his voice.

4th Goon couldn't help releasing a small proud huff of bubbles.

Perhaps this fool has come to realize that he is overstepping the bounds of propriety with all his questions.

There was a blessed silence for a few spans after that, and they all drifted single file down the next long hallway in peace. Then 4th Goon heard the small crackling sound that occurred each time before the visitor's odd sounding voice demanded attention with another question.

"So, who is this Shar-Annika that I am going to meet?"

Although the SUNI was a scrawny little runt, the fellow answered that question in a rich rolling baritone.

"Annika Sharone was the leader of our revolution."

"Your revolution?"

The SUNI delayed answering since they had arrived at the dining hall.

"If you will please wait here, SharArkovic," the SUNI said to the visitor, "I will bring Shar-Annika for your meeting."

4th Goon almost smiled to see the SUNI finally make a polite bob in place and adopt the correct, deferential tone for a Glae to use when speaking to a Shar. Then the fellow ruined his show of good manners by making another insulting suggestion.

"If you wish, I can secure you to the beam overhead while you wait, SharArkovic," the SUNI said.

4th winced. The situation left him torn. The visitor was already sinking toward the open lattice that formed the base of the room now that they were not moving forward anymore. Although he hated the idea of dangling any kind of Shar from a ceiling beam like a bale of foodstuff, he worried his captain would hold him responsible if the visitor fell out of the building altogether.

"Oh, yes, please," the stranger replied.

4th Goon gladly turned over the tendril to the SUNI and then edged back toward the door of the dining hall to await further instructions. Doorways always felt like the right place to go in situations where there was no specified guard position.

"Er, I'm sorry," 4th Goon heard the visitor saying to the SUNI while he settled in by the doorway. "What was your name again?"

"Suni SharCom," the little 'linker said as he worked to secure the tendril around a support beam overhead. "I am the 1st uplink integrator for the 3rd data array. Or I was until yesterday. Now that my master SharCom is dead, I am not sure what my designation is anymore." The SUNI gave a last pat to the knot on the visitor's tendril. "But I do not plan to ask," the little man confided to the stranger with a wink and a wry chuckle.

4th Goon frowned.

I have never heard a Glae making jokes when speaking to a Shar. Perhaps it is performing such intimate services on the neural data ports of Shar customers that encourage such bad habits in this SUNI.

The visitor did not respond like an insulted Shar, though. In fact, since the stranger seemed unmoved by the 'linker's over-familiar manner, it left 4th Goon wondering what he ought to do. Goon priorities were to protect one's Shar and ensure that other Glae did not break the rules. His Goon captain had ordered that the visitor should be treated like a Shar until it could be determined what his true status was.

Does that mean I ought to report the SUNI's off-color remark? The visitor does not act like a Shar. So, maybe the SUNI's slip does not quite count as disrespect?

"I will return soon with Shar-Annika," he heard the SUNI say before the little man turned and skimmed past him out the door.

4th Goon gave up on figuring out whether to report the SUNI as he watched the visitor from the corner of his eye. The airbreather was examining a cluster of perfectly ordinary floats from among the many that supported tables throughout the room.

One thing is for sure—if this stranger is a Shar, then he is the dumbest one I have ever seen.

He clenched his jaw to keep from laughing as the visitor poked at the floats, muttering comments and appearing to count the number of them in the groups at each corner of the table.

Do they not have floats where the stranger comes from? If airbreathers have no floats, then why are strangers not falling out of the big emptiness above the upper boundary more often?

It all made his head hurt to think about. None of it seemed possible. People living in the over-realm. Men who breathed air.

Yet here the fellow is. A stranger in a weird suit dangling on a tendril like a bale of kelp.

He noticed that his instinctive dislike of the un-mannerly stranger along with this uncertainty about the visitor's status was making it more and more difficult to maintain a properly impassive Goon façade. That ideal non-expression which reassured any nearby Shar that a Goon cared only about his duty and was paying no attention to the conversations of his betters. He looked away from the airbreather, trying to settle the turmoil in his gut.

139

Assessing the threat level in this area is a valid guard duty I can perform.

4th Goon halted the progress of his rebellious thoughts to focus on that priority task. He scanned the entire dining hall, which was a large space packed with tables. At the moment, there were no other people in the room except a few low-level staff gathered around a table halfway down the hall. The workers were all staring at the stranger in the shapeless suit with their mouths open, their meals forgotten.

Ok, rude, but not an imminent threat to my subject.

Still, the exercise was a calming routine and 4th Goon felt better for having done his survey. Once the visitor finished looking at the floats, he wiggled his suit round to face 4th Goon.

Gods Below, please do not let him start asking me his stupid questions now.

4th Goon froze his features in place, trying to make his expression look as blank and unchatty as possible.

"And what is your name?" the visitor asked.

Cranking his posture another notch straighter, 4th Goon lifted his chin. "I am 4th Goon of the Leader's Guard here at the Assembly Building," he replied formally.

"I see. And do all those in the Leader's guard wear a black uniform?"

"Yes, Shar. All Goons wear black."

"All Goons wear black. Interesting. So, then the men wearing black that I saw on the rooftops in the city must also have been guards of some type."

4th Goon was not sure if this was a question directed at him or not. His orientation wobbled and he could smell his own growing uneasiness wafting around him. While he floundered in the stink, the visitor switched back to his previous line of questioning.

"What I meant was, what should I call you?" the stranger asked.

"Goon," he replied, staring at a point over the visitor's head and willing himself to generate an aroma of calm and confidence instead.

"Goon? But you said you were 4th Goon. What if 3rd Goon was here also? How would you know I was speaking to you instead of him?"

The question seemed pointless. 4th Goon shot a quick glance at the visitor, wondering if this was some kind of test. He decided to play it safe.

"When a Shar speaks, the nearest Glae of the appropriate designation to perform the required service shall answer," he said, reciting from the 'basic rules of service' file.

"I was asking about your own name," the stranger persisted. "Your personal name, not your professional designation. Like, for example, the man who was just here tying my safety line," the stranger pointed at the place where the SUNI had fastened the tendril to the ceiling beam. "He said his name was Suni."

"SUNI is also a professional designation."

It was terribly uncomfortable to say something that sounded like he was correcting a Shar.

"Oh? What kind of designation?"

4th Goon remained at attention, twitching his eyes around,

hoping to see someone else nearby who could come and take over. But there was no one. Even the people who had been staring at the stranger earlier had all left.

Probably gone to spread the news to their co-workers that they have just seen an airbreather with their own eyes. Well, they are all welcome to him. Him and all his silly stink-making questions.

"SUNIs work for Librarians at their data hoards," he replied as briefly as possible.

"Doing what?"

"SUNIs are Sub-occipital Uplink to Neural array Integrators."

The visitor only looked blank, so 4th Goon added a little more.

"The SUNIs are 'linkers. They assist a Librarian's customers with uplink connections when people get neural upgrades from the Librarian's data hoard."

The visitor thought this over for a few moments before asking his next question. "So, then SUNI is an uplink technician? He's not some kind of personal secretary to your Leader SharScylla?"

4th Goon shook his head, giving in to the unpleasant obligation to correct a person who might or might not be a Shar.

"The SUNI is a Glae specialist who works for a Librarian. Librarians are the Technicians. They are DATAShar. Data Accumulation Technician Advanced," he quoted in a tone of deep respect.

"So, who is in charge of the Librarian technicians, then?" the visitor asked.

4th Goon was scandalized. He lost every bit of gas in his speech sac as he gaped at the visitor, then his gills blurred into

142

action to refill the supply as he peered at the airbreather through the clear portion of the stranger's head covering.

Is this some kind of trick? Does he really not know? There seems to be no end to this fellow's ignorance.

At last, he collected sufficient gases to allow him to reply. "No one is in charge of Librarians. They are the keepers of the data hoards. Preservers of all knowledge, as the SUNI mentioned before."

"I see," the visitor said.

4th Goon doubted that he did.

"And so 'Librarian' is a Shar designation, then?"

4th Goon nodded. "Yes."

"But your designation is Glae?"

He nodded again. "Yes."

"And the Glae take orders from the Shar?"

"Of course."

"And a Shar just addresses you as Goon?"

"Yes."

"Well then, what do other Glae call you?" the visitor asked.

The stranger's expression hinted that the man thought he had just said something really clever. 4th Goon could not repress an irritated flick of gills this time.

"Goon," he repeated. "Or sometimes, Assembly Building, Leader's 4th Goon. But that is very long, so people just say Goon."

The visitor threw up his hands in despair, which set him spinning on the end of his tether like a defective impeller. Keeping his expression neutral, 4th Goon moved in to halt the visitor's spin and place the man upright next to a table again.

He cannot swim, he cannot breathe, I cannot see how he eats, and he knows nothing about the world. Maybe he will grow tired of being so stupid and helpless and go back to where he came from?

"Thanks," the stranger gasped as he clutched the table to maintain orientation. The stranger dangled in silence for a few minutes after that, and just when 4th Goon thought it was safe to relax, he heard the crackling sound again.

"The Shar have personal, or rather, er, individual names, isn't that right?" the visitor asked.

4th Goon did succeed in suppressing the flicking of his gills this time. "Yes. The Shar each have a separate first name, plus a House name."

"But the Glae only have designation names?"

4th Goon wondered how many times the stranger was going to go over this.

"Yes," he repeated with an emphatic twitch of his arm fin. Then he thought he might save some time by offering the one other thing he knew on the subject. "Although I have heard that Glae members of the reformist revolution also had individual names," he said. "I never understood why," he added, before the visitor could ask.

The stranger fell silent again and seemed satisfied at last. Then the brief crackle came again.

"Do you know this woman Annika that I am waiting here to meet?"

"Everyone knows of Shar-Annika, although people call her by many names."

"Many names? Such as?"

"Some call her Aban, or The One Who Whispers With Gods. The Shar often call her The Rebel or sometimes That Disgrace to All Shar. But everyone knows her as the Old Leader."

His brow crinkled for a moment before he asked his next question. "So, she is — an elder, then?"

4th Goon thought for a moment. "Shar-Annika had many, many knowledge upgrades before she led the revolution. She is a great and wise Shar. She is near the same age as my eldest offspring, who was born four hands of storms ago," he said, holding up both hands and extending all his fingers twice.

"Then why is she called the *old* Leader?"

"For a time following the Glae revolution, she was our Leader, which was before my master SharScylla won the contest to head the Ruling Council."

"So, there was a contest between them? Do you think he deserved to win? Is Scylla a better leader?"

4th Goon narrowed his eyes in suspicion.

What does he expect me to say? A Goon has no business having an opinion on such a matter. Is he trying to lead me into making a disloyal statement about my master SharScylla? This stranger is not only full of foolish questions, he is very dangerous to talk to.

Before he had to answer, though, 4th Goon saw the SUNI appear in the doorway of the dining hall, trailed by two women.

Chapter 16: Her Place in History

"You have to come. The airbreather is already waiting."

"So?" she said, looking away.

"Scylla ordered the stranger to meet with you before the expedition, so you have to go."

Annika frowned. "Well, if our illustrious Leader has already decided that I'm going along on this little voyage. What is there to meet about?"

Her voice was heavy with sarcasm.

"Just come to the meeting, please."

"Oh, Suni, don't be such a Glae. Just because some Shar gives you an order—"

"It is not only that," he said with a hurt look. "Magda told me you were searching everywhere for information about the airbreather yesterday. And now you want to pass up a chance to meet him? This is a visitor from another world. His arrival is a momentous event in Marna's history. You must want to be part of it."

"Of course, I do. I just hate being assigned my place in this piece of history by that tyrant Scylla. Don't you understand he's handing me humiliation, not a privilege? I should meet this airbreather as an equal, not as some powerless underling Scylla

146

chose to tag along and observe on a mission."

"But the meeting is already arranged. And wait till you see the airbreather. He has this amazing suit."

"Yes, yes, I heard about the suit. No one at the Temple could talk about anything else all day after he appeared. But since I have no choice about going along on this dive, then there's no reason for a meeting, is there? I won't be paraded in front of the visitor just to please Scylla."

Suni winced as she mentioned the Leader's name.

"It will be good enough if you just show your face at the meeting," he begged. "You do not have to stay long or even say anything."

Annika studied him as he jittered in front of her, clasping and unclasping his fingers. It wasn't like Suni to keep pressing her in this way, so there must be a reason he was so insistent.

The most obvious reason is that any person who likes to go on living always makes sure they complete any task assigned by Scylla. He's so touchy about being obeyed now that he's no longer a low-status Glad taking orders himself.

"All right, I'll come," she said. "Only for your sake, though, not because *he* wants me to."

Chapter 17: Worlds Collide

Devon was glad to see Suni returning so soon.

Oh good, maybe now I'll be able to figure out why he doesn't want their Old Leader to go on the dive mission. Talking to this Goon hasn't been much help.

Suni coasted into the dining hall accompanied by women. First came an older Glae in a plain style outfit with her graying hair pulled back in a braid. Behind her was a striking young woman with long red hair.

This must be Shar-Annika.

He could feel his heart thumping as he watched the famous Marnian approach. Shar-Annika had the most beautiful and elaborate upper fins that he had yet seen in this world. They reminded him of the long, decorative fins on certain varieties of koi or betta fish. The trailing fringes swirled about her arms and shoulders as she swam, cloaking her in a semi-translucent mist. Her ruddy hair reminded him of sunset clouds as it billowed out to frame her pale face when she came to a halt in front of him. The expression on her delicate features was calm, but the look in her green eyes seemed to pierce straight down into his lonely soul.

She's so beautiful, yet there's a hint of sadness here, too.

That suggestion of tragedy made him yearn to lift those burdens from her heart. He was almost stunned by the powerful effect of her presence after only a few moments.

How thoroughly exotic and mysterious she is.

The Marnian year was slightly shorter than a Galactic Standard cycle, so he calculated that Shar-Annika must be what airbreather folk would call eighteen years standard.

Too young to be so serious.

4th Goon crowded forward to hover protectively as Suni introduced Shar-Annika, so Devon hesitated to shake the famous girl's hand, afraid that a clumsy touch from his rough-surfaced gloves might damage those extraordinary fins and create an incident.

"Please call me Devon," he said.

It gave him a wonderful glow to imagine her saying his name, but Shar-Annika only nodded and drifted away to take a seat.

The scowling Goon backed off out of earshot once the three Marnians settled into a row of chairs on the far side of a table from him and the meeting got under way. Shar-Annika remained reserved, swaying in her chair slung from the ceiling and saying very little at first.

She's like some silent hermit torn from her spiritual retreat to appease a demanding follower, and now having trouble remembering how to speak.

He studied her as the older woman whom Suni referred to as Magda, fielded another question on her mistress's behalf.

This famous 'Old Leader' was taller than the average Marnian woman. She appeared to be one hundred and seventy

2

centimeters high, in a world where even the men topped out around one hundred and fifty centimeters. She wore a simple sleeveless coat and a long skirt-like garment in a dark brownish color with no excess ornamentation. He had already observed that Marnian life required clothing that left one's fins free. Most ordinary people accomplished this by wearing nothing more than short shorts on their lower body. The length of Shar-Annika's flowing lower garment immediately set her apart from the Glae around her. The item was not quite a skirt, since it appeared modestly joined in the middle. The bottom hem of the garment ended in a tie around each ankle, but it was slit to the hip on both sides to leave her leg fins free. These changes made what at first appeared to be a long skirt into something more like a dramatic pair of slashed-seam harem pants. Yet the lack of pattern or decoration in Shar-Annika's clothes still lent her a rather ascetic air.

After the first few minutes, the older woman, Magda, leaned across the table to interrupt him before he could frame his next query.

"Perhaps you would be better off consulting Suni Jorah for the answers to these questions, rather than bothering my mistress any further?" she said, shooting him a quelling look before turning to face Suni.

Annika also raised an eyebrow at the little specialist.

"Of course," Suni said. "You can return to the temple, and I will send a message when SharArkovic's conveyance is ready to begin the journey."

Annika rose from her chair, making a graceful gesture with

her arm fin in his direction. "It has been very interesting to meet you, Sh - Devon. I hope we can speak again before you leave us."

As she moved closer, he felt his mind going a little numb at the edges. Her face filled his entire field of view, surrounded in a filmy cloud as those marvelous fins coiled and swirled around him.

"Uh, er, yes, I would enjoy that very much. I have to inform my people on the ship that we have an agreement to proceed with the dive so they can begin preparations. But after that, I am at your disposal, Shar-Annika."

"There is much I would like to discuss with you about life on other worlds," she said.

His heart pounded as her face drifted even closer and his hand itched to reach out and touch her. Only the fact that the suit would prevent any actual contact stopped him.

"Our knowledge of other people and societies is very limited," she continued. "We know only what our ancestors uploaded into the Librarians' arrays. I would be most interested to compare our data with what you know about ethics, law and government on other worlds."

Wow, a gorgeous girl who likes to talk about political science.

"By all means. I'm sure it would be most enlightening for us both."

She smiled again as she drifted away before turning and signaling Magda to follow her.

"But you can't go yet," Devon protested, wracking his brain for some way to delay her departure. "I haven't heard about how a woman dedicated to the service of the Gods ended up becoming the leader of a revolution. It sounds like a fascinating story."

Magda and Suni shot nervous glances at one another, but Annika only smiled.

"The revolution happened before I went to live at the temple," she said. "Back when I was just a daughter in one of the Great Houses of the Shar."

"Not just any House," Devon heard Magda mutter.

"What was that?" he said.

He tried to catch the older woman's eye and give her an encouraging smile, but she stubbornly avoided his gaze. Suni intervened before the situation became awkward.

"What Magda means is that Shar-Annika was once the daughter of the Leader himself," Suni explained.

"You mean …?"

"Oh no," Annika laughed, seeing his look of horror. "Not this current leader, Scylla. My father was Andronikos Sharone, a previous tyrant of the Ruling Assembly."

All three Marnians chuckled at what seemed to be an inside joke, while Devon looked from face to face in bafflement. Suni came to his rescue as usual.

"Shar-Annika is referring to the fact that life on Marna under her father's rule was little better than it is now under SharScylla."

While Suni explained, the two women drifted back to the table and re-seated themselves.

Then Magda spoke up, nodding sober agreement with Suni's

assessment. "Yes, it was the cruelty and greed of Andronikos Sharone that first inspired Suni to dream of a revolution and then think of a way to create a better leader for our people."

Devon felt his jaw hit the collar ring on his suit. It was a shock to hear that it was Suni who was responsible for planning their revolution. Prior to this, he'd thought that all Glae were simple folk who lived from day to day with no thought of the future.

"May I ask how you went about *creating* a leader?"

Although he addressed the question to Suni, it was Magda who replied.

"Suni knew it would take someone special to carry out his plan. A Leader who would be eager to re-shape our society along new lines."

She nodded at Suni, and he took up the tale.

"I knew this person would have to be a Shar, since only a Shar could rise to power within the Ruling Assembly to become Leader. You see, my original plan was to have our specially prepared Shar take over the Leadership and then enact legislation to bring about a complete social overhaul. The problem was that Shar offspring are not raised to cherish principles like fairness, equality, and respect."

He smiled at Magda, and she continued. "Suni reasoned that our candidate would require a very different upbringing. An education that would instill a yearning for the changes we hoped to achieve."

Devon gaped at the two Glae floating tranquilly before him. "And you chose the Leader's own daughter for this plan? That was quite a bold move."

Suni smiled. "Not quite, Shar Arkovic. My wife was employed as the MAGDALENA in the Sharone household at the time I first conceived this plan." He waved a fin in Magda's direction.

"Wait, wait," Devon risked holding up a hand. "You mean you and Magda are married?"

Good thing I'm recording. There's so much to keep straight I'd be bound to get something wrong trying to remember it all later.

Both Glae nodded, then Suni continued. "Since Annika was born into Magda's care, she was the most accessible Shar youngling to use for our plan."

"I see. So, you convinced your wife to alter the upbringing of a child she had access to, so you could use her in this plan?"

Suni ruffled his gills for a moment before offering a more precise interpretation. "I did not convince Magda. I upgraded her with a series of files from the Librarian's array. After she had integrated that data, Magda agreed that the idea of molding this young Shar to become a better leader was more likely to succeed than trying to change the corrupt leader we already had."

Devon glanced wide-eyed at Annika. There was a touch of ruefulness in her smile now, but overall, she seemed unconcerned by this description of her childhood.

Imagine being raised as part of a plan to destroy your own father. She seems pretty calm about having that destiny laid out for her by a pair of scheming servants.

"Then you believe it was the data that changed Magda's mind, not you," he said to Suni. "You just broadened her perspective on the issue with new information."

"Exactly." The little man bobbed up and down with a beatific expression. "Access to more information can change the entire course of a person's life. Even if they are Glae. Magda and I proved that principle on ourselves long before the revolution."

Seeing Suni bobbing up and down, looking so smug, Devon couldn't repress an admiring chuckle.

"Okay so, once you both agreed that you'd need a Shar who was tailor made for your plan, Magda subverted the current evil despot's own daughter, right under his nose. Very nice."

Magda frowned at his flippant tone. "I raised my charge to the best of my ability, as all MAGDAs do," she said with a lift of the chin. "Once Suni gave me the upgrades, I simply used that increased knowledge to further enrich the upbringing of the offspring in my care."

"Of course," Devon replied, hastily. "You must have done an excellent job too, since I understand that your plan was a success."

"Success?" Annika's voice rang out, startling him with its bitterness. "Sometimes I think we are all worse off than before," she said, blowing off a cloud of bubbles and tossing a lock of hair off her forehead.

"Mistress!" Magda scolded, "You must not say things like that."

"Why not?" the girl shot back. "Face it Magda, I failed. Everything we did was for nothing."

The two women glared for a moment, then spun away from each other, folding their arms across their chests. Suni seemed anguished as he watched this abrupt change of mood between the women, but he seemed to have no more idea than Devon what to do.

Huh. It doesn't bother her that her servants manipulated from birth. It's that she failed in her appointed task that seems to distress her most. I wonder if this is the source of that sadness I noticed in her earlier.

"Your efforts can't have been a total failure," Devon said, addressing the back of Annika's head. "You removed your father from his position, right? I know you must have accomplished that much because I've heard people calling you 'the Old Leader.'"

"That's true." Annika flicked her gills dismissively. "I took over the Leadership from my father, and then, I couldn't even hang onto power long enough to enact any significant reforms."

Magda wrung her hands, with gills hanging limp at her neck. "But the people know you tried, Little One. It was not like you had the support of the councilmen in your efforts. And no one could have predicted that Scylla would win the election against you."

"He's a Glad, Magda. Winning contests is what they do. Plus, it was we three that helped him get every upgrade he needed to learn all the dirty tricks he used to defeat me."

Devon looked at Suni while the women ran through what appeared to be a well-worn argument.

"What is a Glad?" he said quietly to Suni.

"A Glad is a Gladiator, SharArkovic. A green-skinned man who fights in the arena. SharScylla is a former Glad."

Annika pressed her lips together, then nodded at Suni. "Go ahead, Suni, tell him the rest. He ought to understand who he is dealing with."

Suni gave a little dip, then reeled off a rapid summary.

"Although most Glads are condemned to the arena for some crime, a few of them like Scylla were ordinary Glae sold into service at the arenas as children. One of Shar-Annika's first acts as Leader was to free any Glads who were not criminals and allow them to choose a life in any profession they wished. When Scylla was freed, his choice was to seek the Leadership. During our first election, he challenged Shar-Annika and won by opposing every goal of the revolution."

Magda took over the recitation of events while Suni pumped his gills to replenish gases.

"Scylla advocated continuing to restrict Glae persons to menial work and service professions. He vowed to deny them access to any extra knowledge downloads, permitting them only essential professional upgrades."

"He also promised extravagant gifts to any potential supporters on the Ruling Assembly Councilmen," Suni added. "For all these reasons, SharArkovic, Scylla's campaign was successful."

Suni dipped again, and Annika took over the explanation.

"So, although I replaced my father as Leader, and reinstated elections for the Ruling Council, what did I achieve? Nothing. All I did was to give that sludge-hearted beast Scylla an opening to snatch the leadership. Now we're all stuck under his thumb instead of my father's."

Magda shot a nervous glance at 4th Goon, where he floated like a statue near the entrance to the hall.

"I see the things we accomplished during the revolution as a good first step," Suni disagreed calmly. "We must all be patient while those first changes beget more change. Meanwhile, Scylla is the first *Glae* ever to become Leader. That alone is a radical change in our society."

Devon couldn't help but notice that even though Suni accompanied this remark with the customary polite bob, somehow the little fellow's demeanor was much less cringing with Annika than it had been when he was speaking with SharScylla.

Annika only flicked her gills again and looked away, refusing to be comforted by his logic.

"Scylla may not be a true Shar, but he sure acts like one when it comes to getting his way. Boil him!"

Magda looked like she was on the verge of a nervous breakdown, fluttering and fanning both gills and fins, trying to hush Annika. The girl went on, now attempting to keep her voice down somewhat for Magda's sake.

"Remember how he behaved during the election? That devious slime went around telling councilmen everything they wanted to hear, just to get himself elected. And remember how all the ones who didn't join his side right away ended up dead? Anyway, now that he's in charge, there won't be any more elections. He's just one more tyrant, like every Shar Leader before him, including my father."

Annika's tirade was beginning to worry Devon for a different reason than the one that concerned Magda.

Gee, I could tell Scylla wasn't the best person to have in charge here, but she makes him sound like a total monster. Is he that bad or is she just exaggerating because they are enemies?

"A new *Glae* tyrant," Suni reminded her gently. "Having him as Leader will always have that one significant benefit. He may be a violent person who prefers a repressive society, but now no one can ever deny the fact that an upgraded Glae like him is capable of more than anyone thought possible."

Annika blew off a cloud of bubbles with a disdainful snort. "Repressive? That's an understatement. All Glae are required to be servants under his regime. Even the ones with multiple upgrades. I think things are worse than before."

Suni bowed his head but did not contradict her this time.

Uh oh. Scylla sure sounds like another evil despot and even Suni doesn't disagree. There is so much going on here that I didn't understand before I opened negotiations. If only I'd had more time to get to know this culture first. What a mess I've made. Now a dangerous, calculating thug is going to have control over the galaxy's Glaeon supply. And LEAP will probably just go along with whatever Scylla wants to do. Alistair's investors are totally focused on getting rich. They won't care if an entire population of aquatics is enslaved by their own leader to boost the Glaeon harvest. And I'll be blamed for launching the whole hideous scenario. Damn.

Chapter 18: Doubling Down

Devon twirled on the end of his tether, wracking his brains for a way out of the mess he had created.

Here, I thought my job was almost over. I was going to cruise around the city seeing the sights, and then hang out on the ship relaxing while the crew wrapped up the recovery of the Glaeon before we all went home rich. Now, how can I just leave knowing what's going to happen to these poor people? They're all doomed to be betrayed by their own leaders.

He almost squirmed to picture it.

The Glae will be enslaved by evil selfish Shar on the Ruling Council, who are all in the pocket of the biggest tyrant of them all. Just great.

I can't get involved, though. Diplomatic Corp regulations forbid interfering in other cultures' laws and business affairs.

Then it hit him.

But I'm not in the Corps anymore. I resigned to run off and get rich and famous on this First Contact treasure hunt. That means I'm free to do whatever I think is best here. I may burn my bridges with Dip Corps if I go rogue; but that's better than just standing by and watching while the Marnians are forced to harvest Glaeon to make a bunch of greedy airbreathers rich.

He glanced up at Annika and her companions. Already he

thought of them less as servants and more like undercover co-conspirators.

But how can I stop this disaster from happening now? Scylla would probably kill me on the spot if he even thought I intended to help these rebels.

He shot a look at the Goon posted by the door, listening in on this treasonous conversation.

As it is, these three will be lucky not to end up in pieces at the bottom of the ocean once I'm gone. Wow, I have messed this whole thing up. Some diplomat I am.

The only good thing I've accomplished so far is making progress on preventing all the Marnians from being murdered by pirates.

Annika and the two Glae were still rehashing their memories of the revolution, so he tried to organize his thoughts into a plan.

What am I going to do?

Priority one: keep the mission going to get that Glaeon out of here before the pirates blow us all to bits.

As he tuned back into the discussion between the Marnians, Suni bobbed once with a brief nod.

"More downloads from the Libraries would be good," he said. "But because of you, every Glae has the one piece of knowledge that is most important. They know now that the Shar have lied them to their whole lives. Having a former Glae become Leader is daily proof that Glae people are capable of more than the servant professions the Shar limited them to for generations."

"It still doesn't seem like enough after all the sacrifices made during the revolution," Annika said.

Her lips trembled and her chin dropped so that her hair swayed forward, hiding her face. The sorrow and bitterness in her voice was so great that Devon looked away out of respect.

"I know it is not what you hoped for, Little One," he heard Magda whisper.

When he lifted his head, he saw the older woman move closer to slip an arm around the girl's waist, just the way he wished he could do. As Annika lifted her head to smile at her two faithful allies, she also noticed him dangling nearby at the end of his tether. An outsider intruding on this very private moment between former rebel comrades. In an instant, she transformed from a vulnerable girl whose every cherished dream was smashed to bits, into a cool, poised young woman in complete command of herself.

"I trust this has answered your questions about me and the revolution, SharArkovic?" Annika frowned, brushing her hair back from her face.

He could only admire how steady her voice was.

If only someone like Annika was in charge during the negotiation with LEAP. Then I'd be sure the interests of the Glae would be protected.

"Yes, it has," he replied. "Please know that it sounds to me as if you all made heroic efforts to attain your goals under very difficult circumstances. I am astonished at the sheer scope of what you set out to accomplish, and I think you should all be very proud of what you achieved."

There has to be a way to have this marvelous young woman be in charge of dealing with LEAP.

"Thank you for that," she said, allowing a touch of genuine warmth to creep in. "It's good to hear praise from someone who must have so much more experience with such events."

"Yes indeed. I have witnessed revolutions on several worlds, and I agree with Suni that significant change often takes time. And the cost of lasting change is not always what people expect to pay."

And if I don't fix my screw ups, they may have to pay even more.

"I suppose not," she sighed. "At the moment, though, one of those costs is that we must all obey orders from our latest tyrant SharScylla. Even sent-from-the-Gods airbreathers have to bow to his will these days. Isn't that right, SharArkovic?"

"It's Devon, please. And I hope you do not believe that foolish story about me being a messenger from some Gods Above."

"No, no, Suni has shared with me the story of the true origins of the Marnian people as revealed in the ancient files from the data hoard. He also tells me you are here to recover a lost shipment of that product, Glaeon, which your company created our ancestors to harvest."

"Exactly."

He caught himself raising a hand to his face, only to have it meet the barrier of his head covering.

If I want her in charge of negotiating with LEAP, then I have to keep her alive first. Suni is right, she shouldn't risk going on this dive. She's too important.

"I'm very glad you understand about that, but I'm so sorry you have gotten caught up in this search for the Glaeon. I hope you also understand that it was not my idea for you to take part in the recovery mission. In fact, I would strongly advise you against agreeing to go along on this dive."

"Surely, if it is safe for you to go, then it is safe for me?"

He felt himself blushing. The mere idea of diving into the great, cold blackness below sent invisible fingers curling around his heart.

"I'm afraid I am not trained to operate a submersible, so it will be one of our most experienced pilots who will take the sub down to perform the search. But in any case, the real *issue* is that the interior of a submarine must remain dry in order to function. The controls and systems of the vehicle will stop working if we flood the inside with water for an aquatic passenger to use."

Annika frowned. "I'm sure I was told that I would have to ride *inside* the airbreather vehicle in order to survive the immense pressures of the deeps." She aimed an accusing look at Suni.

This time, the little fellow's gills trembled as he replied. "Yes, mistress. SharArkovic suggested that the Marnian representative could ride inside a small part of the vehicle called the airlock. I was told they *can* fill their airlock with water. SharScylla insisted a Marnian must ride in the airlock and accompany the airbreathers, or he will not agree to let them dive and retrieve their property."

Annika turned her piercing green gaze back to him. "So, you have suggested this plan, yet you do not recommend it, SharArkovic? Is this mission so important to you that you would risk the safety of a Marnian to achieve it?"

"The mission is important, but I would never wish to endanger anyone to accomplish it."

"Then why do you advise me against your plan?"

This is it. Better get it right, boy.

"I fully expect that if you decline to go, SharScylla will choose another Aban to make the dive and the mission will proceed."

"Do you think I would allow another person to take my place on a dangerous mission?"

"Of course, I never meant to imply any such thing," he assured her. "Please know that our most skilled technicians will prepare the airlock so that any Marnian passenger will remain safe during the journey. It is only my diplomatic training that makes me suggest avoiding even the smallest risk to a very valuable member of society such as yourself. I meant no offense."

He waited a beat and then put all the persuasion he could muster into his next words.

"Please forgive me for valuing your life above another's. It's just that I believe there may be an important role for you to play as Marna reconnects with the greater galaxy. There are going to be extensive changes to your world once the LEAP Corporation returns and trade resumes. I think having someone with your compassion and vision guiding that process will be essential to safeguarding the future of the Marnian people."

All three Marnians stared at him, and there was no way for him to cross his fingers while he waited for a response. He'd noted a distinct gleam in Annika's eyes when he mentioned an important role for her in the future, and the idea of protecting the interests of her people. Now he could only hope that she would agree with his suggestion.

"Perhaps you are correct," she said. "My presence on this dive does not seem essential. Since we know now that here are no Gods Below to be disturbed, I think I may safely leave this job to one of the Aban."

"I'm so happy to hear that," he said, remembering at the last second not to nod.

Annika made another graceful gesture with one arm fin. "Very well then, Magda can inform SharScylla of my decision so he can choose another representative for the mission. You said you must report this plan to your companions, so I will return to the temple for now. Perhaps tomorrow we can meet again, and you can answer some of my questions for a change?"

"Sounds fair," he grinned.

Chapter 19: Mission Critical

After Shar-Annika departed, 4th Goon waited to escort the Leader's guest out of the Assembly Building as ordered. The stranger, of course, was back to asking questions again.

"Shar-Annika said that she was not one of the Aban, so why is she returning to the temple?" the visitor asked the SUNI.

"Shar-Annika lives in the temple since her return to the city from exile. Some people refer to her as Aban, but she is not truly one of those who has dedicated themselves to serving the Gods Below."

The SUNI had bobbed politely before giving that reply, but he still failed to ask permission before ascending to untie the visitor's tendril from the ceiling support. 4th Goon wrinkled his nose and blew out a large bubble, but he had other more serious matters to consider. Although he had removed himself to a position on guard near the door during the meeting, he still heard everything that was said. His head was buzzing with the huge number of infractions he had observed during the last length. Top of the list was the fact that the Glae woman, Magda, had used the revolutionary name Suni Jorah when she referred to this badly behaved SUNI.

The SUNI, as well as the MAGDA, are obviously rebels. And, they spoke with open disrespect for my master. I can excuse the stranger for such rudeness since he is just a giant silvery, possibly Shar idiot. But no Glae should speak that way about our Leader.

Again, he agonized over which of his duties was most important. He had orders from SharScylla himself to escort this visitor out of the building after the meeting was over. But it seemed equally important to inform his Goon captain of all the infractions made by the two Glae traitors.

While he was weighing his choices, the SUNI signaled him to approach and take hold of the tendril again. The SUNI continued answering the stranger's questions while 4th Goon began towing the visitor out of the building.

"Although some people believe Shar-Annika speaks with the Gods, she does not make that claim herself. Originally, she was just a daughter in one of the greatest of the leading Shar Houses, as we explained before. Since then, she has gained more recognition for her own accomplishments. For example, even before she led the revolution, she was the first one to invent the concept of history." The SUNI's eyes twinkled. "First Historian is her favorite title of all."

4th Goon carefully maneuvered the stranger out into the corridor while the SUNI lapsed into silence following this lengthy speech. The little man's gills blurred beside his neck as he replenished his gases, but 4th Goon felt no sympathy.

Imagine sharing such private things about our Old Leader with a complete stranger! I will certainly report every one of this terrible man's infractions as soon as the airbreather is gone.

But the visitor just looked puzzled rather than impressed to have the SUNI confiding those very personal details to him.

"How can someone invent the concept of history?"

"That is difficult to explain, SharArkovic. It is unfortunate that you cannot access one of our data arrays to understand all the things you wish to know."

Now 4th Goon's surprise over the SUNIs gases replenishment rate was nothing compared to his dismay at the mere suggestion of connecting an airbreather to a data array. 4th Goon felt himself dipping like a child, as a blast of astonished bubbles escaped him while the SUNI prattled on.

"However, your need for the spacesuit makes uplink connections impossible." The SUNI pointed to the back of his head, where uplink portals were typically situated with a rueful look.

"Well, Suni, you may not know this, but uplink is also used by norm—that is, by airbreather people too," the visitor said. "Like most of my people, I am equipped with an uplink port. I'd just have to get the ship to send down the type of helmet that has an uplink connection access patch built in. Why don't I ask *Osprey* to include one along with a fresh gas splitter after I make my report? I would be delighted to see the records in your data array for myself."

4th Goon ground his teeth as they all halted at an intersection to let a delivery float pass by. He shot a warning glance at the little SUNI, but the fellow had his head cocked on one side, rubbing his chin as he considered the airbreather's idea.

"I understand from our friend here," the stranger said, pointing in 4th Goon's direction, "that you're an uplink

169

specialist?"

The SUNI gave a nod and a little bob, and the stranger's grin widened.

"It's going to take a couple of days for my people to prep the surface platform for the dive and make the modifications to the airlock to allow a Marnian to join the mission. What do you say we try to whip up a way for me to view your records while we wait? I want to learn everything I can about your society while I'm here and uplink will make that go much faster. Also, I bet you have some fascinating records from the time when the aquatics were first brought here to Marna."

Brought here?

4th Goon felt as if he were a Glad taking blow after blow in the arena. This conversation seemed like a bad dream, but as he resumed towing the stranger toward the Entry Hall, 4th Goon couldn't help slowing down the pace so that he would not miss the next part of their discussion.

"Many people I know would love to understand more about how your people survived after—after."

"After the airbreathers abandoned us here on Marna?" the SUNI supplied calmly.

4th Goon could feel his mouth dropping open and the smell of disbelief swirling out into the surrounding water.

What does he mean, airbreathers abandoned us here?

He was so distracted by the outrageous ideas he was hearing that he failed to correct the visitor's trajectory and the stranger smacked into a support column instead of gliding out into the center of the main Entry Hall of the Assembly Building. The

SUNI deftly scuttled aside, leaving him and the visitor to sort out the resulting tangle.

Resuming his impassive Goon façade, 4th Goon worked to set the visitor upright beyond the support column while he thought about what he had just heard.

I have always believed the stories that the Aban tell us. How the Gods Below created us to live in the warm zone so they can look up and be amused by the antics of their creations.

Now he wondered if any of those stories were true.

Have the Aban lied to us about the Gods Below? After all, I have never seen one of them.

He looked at the visitor floating right in front of him, all covered in that amazing silvery suit, and then up toward where the upper boundary covered the world.

How many other strange things might exist up there beyond the sky?

4th Goon felt his head packed with so many uncomfortable thoughts that it might break off and go zooming away like a punctured float at any moment.

"Well, it wasn't exactly intentional that your ancestors were abandoned here," he heard the stranger explaining to the SUNI defensively.

Could this foolish stranger really know another explanation for why we are all living here on Marna?

The visitor was still talking, but it was hard to follow what he meant.

"You see, the LEAP company collapsed, and the location of this planet was a secret—so there was no way to send a rescue

171

ship. I assume those original colonists had to overcome some tough challenges once they realized they were cut off. The story of how they survived must be remarkable. I'd love to see if I could experience the records from those times for myself."

The SUNI ruffled his gills and bobbed in place for a moment.

"Why not?" the little man said at last. "It could be an interesting challenge to find a way for an airbreather to access data from a hoard."

This time, 4th Goon positively wallowed as he lost orientation.

Surely, it is exceeding a SUNI's authority to grant an airbreather free access to a data hoard! Even a rebel dedicated to the idea of free information for everyone should have some limits!

He almost opened his mouth to object before he remembered that doing so would mean that he himself would be guilty of over-reaching his bounds.

I would be very angry if a SUNI advised me about a security issue.

Hunching his massive shoulders with a scowl, he reconsidered the idea of challenging the SUNI's right to grant the visitor access to an array.

Why is it that there is never a Goon captain around when you need one? They are always there when your badge is on crooked, or another Goon has just told you that your ass is the size of a house and you are winding up to slug the fellow for it. But never around when you need to make a judgment call like this.

He shook his head as he towed the visitor toward the main entrance. The stranger was still babbling over his shoulder to the SUNI about connectors and cables.

But if I tell my captain every infraction I have heard today, he will be angry at me for allowing the offenders to escape. They are all extremely bad people. Even the airbreather and Shar-Annika have committed numerous offenses. But how can I tell the captain that? Can a Goon report a Shar? Even a Shar who is an exile? Or a weird airbreather visitor-Shar?

As they passed through the doors of the Assembly Building into the Square outside, he felt a flood of panic instead of the relief he imagined he would feel.

Oh, no. I chose wrong. I think I should have towed the visitor to the security office instead. Curse this stranger and all the confusion he brings. Now I must let them both go and say nothing. If I report what has happened after these offenders are gone, then I will be the one who is punished.

But it was too late to change his mind. They had already reached the outer limit of the area where he held any responsibility for security.

Now, because of the stranger, I have failed in my duty.

"You may now resume using your impellers," he informed the visitor.

4th Goon retreated a short way to watch as the airbreather stowed his tendril inside his spacesuit before activating the garment's impellers. Water all around the stranger blurred, then a horrible smell washed over 4th Goon as the impellers took hold. An instant later, the visitor surged upwards with the SUNI following behind.

I wonder if all airbreathers are as awful as this SharArkovic.

4th Goon watched as the stranger in his ugly suit disappeared

173

into the glare of the upper reaches.

I hope his greedy brain bursts from stuffing in too many data files.

Chapter 20: Magda's Errand

Magda hurried through the halls of the Assembly Building, rehearsing the message in her head. She was not looking forward to performing this service for her mistress. If she was lucky, she could leave the message with one of Scylla's attendants rather than having to speak Annika's words to the Leader himself.

"I have a message for SharScylla," she told the Goon on guard outside the Audience Chamber.

The Goon scratched at the Audience Chamber door and one of Scylla's personal attendants answered.

"This Glae has a message for SharScylla," the Goon told the Glad, who answered the door.

The Glad flicked a suspicious glance over her as if suspecting her of carrying poisoned weapons.

"Very well," he said, lifting the flap higher to let her in.

Scylla sat reclined in a sling chair behind a long table suspended with clusters of multicolored floats at each corner. He had a shot bulb in one hand, and the remains of a meal floated about the kelp leaf food containers stuck to the table before him.

"What is it?" he asked, without bothering to look at her.

"I bring a message from Shar-Annika," she said.

She took care to keep her eyes humbly fixed on her leg fins.

"Proceed," Scylla said, sounding bored.

"My mistress says she declines to accompany the airbreathers on their dive into the Deep. She suggests you choose a real Aban for this mission."

Scylla sprang out of his chair, tossing his drink bulb aside. His eyes blazed as he hung over her.

"She suggests! How dare she presume to advise me? I am not interested in her opinions or her preferences. And her participation in this journey is not optional."

Magda could feel herself sinking lower as her arm fins clamped down in terror.

"As you wish, great Shar," she managed to say. "I will return to my mistress at once and convey your message."

She began backing away, but suddenly Scylla swooped in and hooked one massive hand under her chin. Slowly, he forced her head up, glaring down into her eyes.

"I know you," he rumbled. "You are the MAGDA who came to bargain with me at the arena on behalf of your mistress. Back before the revolution."

Magda quivered in his grasp.

"Yes, Shar."

"You were not so timid in those days."

He chuckled, but it was not a cheerful sound.

"I had less to lose back then, great Shar."

"Ah. So, you do not live only to serve your mistress anymore?"

"I still serve my mistress faithfully."

"Then tell her this. When I visited SharCom's array, I saw that SUNI who came with you to the arena there. And now, I know that you serve Shar-Annika at the temple. Let her know that if she does not go on this dive with the airbreathers that I will kill both you and the SUNI from the Librarian's array."

"No, Shar, please! We have a young offspring. Our Umiko will be all alone in the world without us."

This time, Scylla's answering chuckle chilled her to the bone.

"Do not worry about your daughter. I will see that your Umiko is brought here to me once the two of you are gone."

She just gaped at him, unable to reply.

Chapter 21: Surfacing

It took Suni some time to identify what he was feeling. It was such a rare thing for him to have an unscheduled afternoon at his disposal that he could barely recognize the sensation of freedom. Since the Third Librarian's business was shut down, he had no line of customers waiting to be served at the array. There were not even any orders to fulfill for his new master, SharScylla. His time was truly his own for once, so he tagged along after Devon Arkovic without the usual guilt that worried him when he pursued a project of his own.

He still had mixed feelings for quite a different reason as they made their way toward the upper boundary. As intriguing as it was to think of experimenting with connecting an airbreather to a data array, he wished it didn't require visiting these upper reaches. This trip would take him higher than he had ever been before. The idea of rising to the very edge of the world made him tremble. Slitting his eyes against the increasing glare as they went higher and higher, he noticed his gills pumping a little faster and a wave of dizziness passing over him.

Does the water have less oxygen here? Or is it just the horrible sight of the boundary tossing around over my head, making me nervous?

He looked away from the sight and concentrated on trying to

catch a glimpse of the city far below. The visitor explained that he needed to be as close as possible to the surface in order to speak with the others of his kind and call down the shuttle.

This chance to see a shuttle will make all my discomfort worthwhile.

Ever since he had studied the ancient records last full dark, he had hungered for the chance to see a spaceship with his own eyes. So, he endured the heat and searing brightness as well as he could, huddling in the airbreather's shadow as much as possible.

Devon Arkovic began speaking, but Suni could not hear anyone reply. It made the airbreather seem like one of those sad people who had lost their mind and floated around talking to themselves all day.

Suni felt like he might end up that way himself soon. The smell from the stranger's impellors had grown very concentrated now that they had stopped moving. That foul odor turned his stomach, and even worse, the way the surface swelled and heaved above him had him teetering on the verge of panic. It terrified him to think that he might be about to experience the touch of the awful, waterless expanse above.

I am being foolish and weak. Nothing bad is going to happen to me. And having this opportunity to spend time with a real live person from another world is an extraordinary gift.

He glanced at the bloated silvery form of the visitor, swallowing down another wave of nausea.

It is just that I never expected that people from another world would be so radically different.

Learning that the descendants of the people who wrote the

179

words which had changed his life were these weird, finless beings who breathed air instead of water was tremendously unsettling. The visitor was strange in so many ways that being around SharArkovic was far more unnerving than oh-so-rational Suni liked to admit. Even the simple fact that no one knew for sure whether this airbreather was just an ordinary person or a high-status Shar contributed to that anxiety.

Is it right for me to follow this stranger around, trying to be of service? Or should I be treating him the same as I would treat one of my neighbors? Someone that I can help if I have time or ignore if I am busy.

There was no answer to such questions. But Suni comforted himself with the thought that at least he was not shirking any real duties to be here serving the visitor.

It is probably fine to play it safe and continue to render service to the best of my ability.

He resigned himself to remaining as still as possible and waiting without complaint for span after span while Shar-Devon continued to speak to his invisible friends.

"Yes, Captain Doyle, we have an agreement, so you can begin surface preparations right away," he heard the visitor saying enthusiastically. "That's right. Yes. Thank you, Captain Doyle. No sir, I would like to stay here in Portbree in the meantime and continue my work researching the Marnian society. Yes sir. Of course, sir. Well, there are some things I could really use if the shuttle could drop off a care package on the way to the operations site for the dive. Yes, sir. Perhaps I could go over the list with one of the com techs. Yes, sir."

Suni shifted sideways to squeeze another finger width or two of his leg fins into the shade. Devon Arkovic gestured as he spoke, and the motions meant that the airbreather's shadow was a moving target. He firmly avoided looking at the heaving boundary only a few meters above him as visitor chattered on and on with his invisible friends, like a madman. At last, Devon Arkovic turned to face him with a big grin.

"We'll have to wait here for a few minutes for them to drop my package," he said, sounding strangely apologetic again.

Suni did not know what to expect, but after a few more spans, there was an odd trembling in the water. The sensation reminded him of times in seasons past when the vents and smokers on the slopes of Mount Rozan in the east had belched forth clouds of debris. His gills quivered along with the water, and he could not make them still. Then a roaring sound grew louder and louder. Just as he was about to dive for the safety of the normal levels below, he saw Devon Arkovic pointing to something overhead. He desperately wanted to see 'a shuttle' but he could not help cowering behind the airbreather's bulk like a child.

Peeking out from that meager refuge, he watched in awe as a tiny object appeared far away in the dreadful air overhead. The bizarre object expanded rapidly until it was almost the size of a mansion. His heart was shaking, and his gills could barely flutter as the conveyance thundered down to hover overhead, whipping the water at the surface into a storm. He was terrified that this massive vehicle would keep falling from the sky and crush him, but Devon Arkovic never moved as the shuttle howled above their heads. Suddenly, the storm on the surface shot a short distance away. A dark square appeared in the bottom of conveyance while he watched, and then the visitor gave a loud cheer as a smaller object fell from the shuttle and hit the water with an enormous bang.

White plumes ascended from the spot where the object landed, and Suni felt a pressure wave shoving both him and the airbreather man away from the site. He worked all four fins hard to remain in place so as not to miss a thing. His heart pounded with fear and excitement, but now that he had seen this much, he had to stay and see the rest. The shuttle rose upwards and then departed with another blast of noise, quickly growing smaller. Devon Arkovic remained where he was for a few more spans, watching while his 'package' bounced and floundered on the surface. A thousand questions bubbled through Suni's mind, but he dared not disturb the airbreather who seemed to be concentrating intently on this thing that the shuttle dropped.

What is he waiting for?

All at once, the object on the surface began expanding at a stupendous rate. Devon Arkovic jetted toward it as it grew, and he followed cautiously in the airbreather's wake.

Once the visitor reached the now circular object, he was aghast to see Devon Arkovic clamber right out of the water to sit on top of the small structure. The sight of a man thrashing his way out of the water caused a fresh wave of dizziness. Suni fixed his gaze on the bottom of the object until the feeling passed.

This must be another airbreather conveyance or maybe a small residence. It seems designed to stay on the surface without sinking and to hold the occupant up into the air. Of course, an airbreather would like that.

Once he felt better, Suni drew closer and inspected the strange craft for some means of support or locomotion. It was composed of other unfamiliar materials and the bottom side seemed utterly smooth, with no sign of an engine pod or flotation system. Moving further away so he could observe Devon Arkovic atop his airbreather device, he peered up through the distortion of the uttermost limits of the ocean. He watched the airbreather retrieve a pair of well-wrapped packages from the floor of this odd craft. The visitor set one package aside and then leaned over the side of the structure to put his head back in the water and beckon Suni closer.

"The navigation and communications officers told me these items can tolerate exposure to water," the airbreather explained, proffering some sort of pouch. "Why don't you wait in the raft's shadow and open this up to have a look while I take on some lunch? Ok?"

Suni obediently retreated to the shade under the 'raft' and inspected the package of gifts from above.

The next time he ventured out to ask his companion a question, Suni got a chill down his spine. Devon Arkovic sat bare headed atop his conveyance with his pale face raised toward the sunshine. The airbreather's strange head covering was gone, and the visitor was busy gobbling down some kind of oddly colored food that his fellow airbreathers must have sent down for him. The raft bobbed gently on the waves as SharArkovic enjoyed his meal, sitting up there smiling and laughing instead of choking and dying from being exposed to that great dry expanse. It took a tremendous effort for Suni to remind himself that the visitor was meant to do these things.

He is well and happy and back in his natural state. Breathing air.

Tearing his eyes away from the ghastly sight, Suni returned his attention to the items in the pouch. The crew on the *Osprey* had gone all out to supply him with anything he might need for his little project. There was a double hand worth of all different connectors, plus several lengths of various cables.

Seems like I am not the only one who is curious to see if it is possible to link an airbreather visitor to a Marnian data hoard. I wonder if I will ever meet the men who sent these things from that ship flying so far above my head. Will I ever be able to share my success with them if I do accomplish this task?

Devon Arkovic spent a few more minutes finishing his food and enjoying being able to scratch the back of his neck, while Suni pondered over the connectors in the pouch.

Perhaps airbreathers are not so different from Marnians after all. Those men on the ship share my curiosity about the data transfer. Even Devon Arkovic mentioned how he would enjoy discussing politics and government on other worlds with Shar-Annika. I wonder if he shares other goals with us.

With that thought, another wonderful idea sprouted in Suni's mind.

SharArkovic said he understood how Magda came to think as I did after her upgrades. Could I perhaps modify him in the same way? Since he is asking to be connected to the array, this might be my best chance to help him along.

His fingers tingled as he pictured how easy it would be to slip a few extra files into the stranger's download and make him an ally.

This man can call down a shuttle and an unsinking surface conveyance on command. And here are two hands' worth of neural connectors. He says he is not a god, but he must be a very wealthy and powerful person. He told Shar-Annika that he admired our efforts during the revolution. What if he adopted more of our revolutionary goals? What a great asset to our cause he would be.

Suni tapped a finger on his chin. He knew that many of the people he had modified had not appreciated having expanded knowledge after their upgrade. Quite a few had been very unhappy to fully understand the injustice of their lives and then be condemned to live on, yearning for a better world.

Will Devon Arkovic also be unhappy if I modify him to support our cause when our prospects of victory are so small?

All his musing scattered to the tides when SharArkovic returned to the ocean. With a loud tearing noise, the airbreather smashed his way through the upper boundary. Suni barely had time to be shocked before both he and the small conveyance were shoved aside with great force. Once he fluffed out his gills and righted himself again, he saw a great mass of bubbles before him. When he looked upward, he noted with awe that the boundary overhead was once again whole and undamaged. The airbreather's violent arrival had not left a gaping hole behind that would allow the horrible air above to touch him.

Once he made sure of that important matter, he saw the bubbles had cleared revealing SharArkovic floating serenely before him with a brand-new head covering attached to the top of his suit. The new covering resembled a single enormous bubble that surrounded the airbreather's whole head. It seemed strange at first that he could see all of the visitor's head. The airbreather's pale yellow hair remained unnaturally still inside this new protective bubble, but apart from that weird detail, SharArkovic's face appeared mostly normal now that Suni could get a better look at it. The eyes were a clear shade of blue, like the sky. Which made sense. There were even a few Shar families who possessed that rare color of eyes. But unlike most Shar, the visitor's face wore a very pleasant smile.

I am sure many women would call Devon Arkovic an attractive man. That is, if they could ignore the missing gills.

The new head covering was quite rigid, unlike the previous one, and Suni thought he could see two spots in the middle of a dark area behind Devon's head that might be the promised access ports for data cables.

Ah, now I see how he plans to give me access for connection to the array.

The sight sent another tingle through his fingers, and he gripped the pouch of connector cables tighter.

I must not miss this chance to recruit such a valuable person to our cause. Who knows if I will ever have a chance to upgrade an airbreather again?

"Ok, Suni, I'm ready when you are," the visitor said, still with the echoing quality in his voice. "Let's go see if we can hook me into your data library."

What a pleasure it will be to speak with him without having to stop and explain things to him as if he were a fourth storm offspring. He is not stupid, only ignorant, and I can fix that easily. Yes, yes, with a few upgrades I think SharArkovic will make a very fine ally indeed.

Chapter 22: Red Two Deep

Devin floated just under the surface, next to the raft, facing Suni. He was all ready to go with a full stomach and the new uplink-equipped helmet, but the little Marnian seemed reluctant to lead the way. The 'linker kept bobbing up and down, keeping his eyes fixed on the ends of his toes.

"Is something wrong, Suni?" he asked.

"I regret I have something I ought to attend to before I can take you to the array, SharArkovic."

Devon glanced involuntarily at the gauge on his arm panel. But of course, the replacement gas splitter that *Osprey* had sent him along with the other supplies still had a full charge.

"Well, I'm in no rush, so it's no trouble for me if you have an errand to do before we head out to the Library. I haven't had a chance to see much of the city yet, so wherever you have to go will be just as interesting as visiting the data array for me."

Devon paused as a sudden worry crossed his mind. Scylla had banned him from the city before and it wasn't clear whether he would approve of Suni showing him around Portbree. He hated the idea of getting Suni into any trouble if he was caught playing tour guide against Scylla's wishes.

"As long as you're certain it will be okay to bring me along?"

188

he asked Suni.

"My home is in a Glae section of the city, SharArkovic. I am sure no one there will complain about your presence."

"So, we are going to your home? How wonderful! I'd love to see where you live and meet some of your neighbors."

Suni gave another of his apologetic little bobs.

"I am afraid that most of my neighbors are away from home working at this time of day, so this will not be an ideal opportunity to meet them. But my errand will not take long, I promise you, and then we can move on to visiting the array with no further delay."

"Please don't worry, Suni. You take all the time you need. I'm sure I will find it a fascinating experience to visit a Glae neighborhood."

Suni bobbed again, looking doubtful.

"Very well, SharArkovic," the little Glae replied. "If you will please follow me?"

They descended to the city, then turned into one of the major thoroughfares that led away from the Ruling Assembly Building. People on the street turned to stare, then shied away from him, darting into shops and homes all along their route. Devon was constantly aware now that his thrusters were causing a problem for other people, despite their curiosity. He soon found himself hoping that this side trip of Suni's was not going to take too long.

After a few blocks, Suni paused at the entrance to what looked like a deep shaft.

"This is where we go down, SharArkovic," Suni said, giving

one of those deferential little bobs that Devon was coming to see as a substantial part of any Glae person's day.

"How far down does it go?" he asked, eying the gaping hole dubiously.

"There are eight levels below this one, SharArkovic. We use the first five as residential districts for the Glae population, as well as commercial zones. Everything below that is considered the chill zone."

"Chill zone? What is that used that for?"

"Certain products require lower light and temperature conditions for storage or manufacturing."

"I see."

"Mostly it is where waste accumulates before the daily tides carry it away. The delay allows bottom feeders time to pick through the discarded items and recover anything edible or otherwise useful to them."

"I didn't realize there were any scavenger species on Marna. Are bottom feeders some kind of fish or more like a crustacean?"

"It does not suit phish to live in the chill zone. They require lots of light to maintain their body heat, which is why we use them in ceiling slats. And I regret I am not familiar with the term crustacean."

"Crustaceans are small soft creatures which have a hard outer shell around their bodies."

"Bottom feeders are not crustaceans. They are people with nowhere else to live."

"People?"

"Most are Glae who have lost employment and housing through some misfortune. Occasionally, a Shar family sinks so low, but Shar rarely last long in the chill zone."

"I see." He gazed down into the inky depths with a shudder.

"If you turn off your thrusters, SharArkovic, I will guide your descent through the transit chute."

"But how will I know when it's time to turn them back on? I don't think I'm ready to take a tour of your chill zone just yet."

"Do not worry, SharArkovic. I would never let you sink so far. We are only going two levels down, so the drop will not be long. When we are approaching the intersection, I can signal you to re-start your thrusters by squeezing on your ankle if you will permit me."

"Okay, let's try it."

Being dragged down a deep, dark hole was everything he imagined it would be. Light levels dimmed significantly as he sank down the shaft and water churned all around him as Suni released a mass of bubbles in order to decrease his buoyancy enough for his weight to sink them both. Devon wobbled along in Suni's wake, feeling like a balloon on a string in a brisk wind. By the time he felt the squeeze on his ankle, he was disoriented, and even a bit nauseous.

"That was not so bad was it, SharArkovic?" Suni asked, once they were both stabilized in the transit chute once more.

"It was fine," he lied.

Suni had anchored them both in place by grasping the tendrils of a large moldy looking float held in place by what looked like a netting full of garbage.

The little man smiled, rocking the float back and forth, causing the two strands of red algae attached to the top of the balloon-like object to flutter about.

"Welcome to Red Two Deep," Suni said.

The little Glae gestured for him to head left down the street away from the transit chute.

Glae homes seemed to differ from the buildings he had seen on the upper level in a couple of obvious ways. All the buildings here were much smaller, and they all showed far more advanced signs of rot. Ramshackle dwellings hemmed him in on both sides as he went along, and he worried that even a gentle pulse from his thrusters might cause damage here. Support posts were blotched with multi-colored patches of mold. Wall mats stretched across between these mottled posts were all fuzzy with decay. He could see the mats shedding clouds of slimy bits every time they moved, and buildings all up and down Red Two Deep had a somewhat ghostly appearance because of the pervasive haze of suspended filth.

As Suni had predicted, the neighborhood was mostly deserted at this hour. Devon could see a few older people moving up and down the street carrying bundles, but it was the children of Red Two Deep who captured his attention. Dozens of cute chubby little cherubs swooped and darted here and there among the houses, shrieking and laughing, just as groups of children do all over the galaxy. Given their diminutive size and astonishing dexterity, however, Marnian children were particularly irresistible.

You just want to scoop them up by the handful and take a bunch

192

home.

Of course, the children all rushed away screaming at first. Then, once Suni was recognized escorting the big silver monster down their street, the children's curiosity overcame their fear and Devon was surrounded. First came the chorus of high-pitched voices complaining of the smell in his vicinity, but soon tiny fins and fingers almost covered his helmet as they came close enough to peer in at him. He could feel other tiny unseen hands grabbing at his suit as little ones on either side of him tested the currents produced by his thrusters. He became concerned, however, when the children moved on to investigating the control panel on his arm. Worried that they might shut off the thrusters and allow him to go plummeting down into the chill zone, he tried to cover the controls with his other hand.

"Er, Suni? A little help, please."

"Back! Back all of you," Suni cried, flapping his arm fins at the little devils. "Be still and stop behaving like a pack of Five Deep spawn in front of the visitor."

" — But who is he, Suni? — "

" — What is he? — "

" — Does he talk? — "

" — Does he bite? — "

" — What is he wearing? — "

" — Where are his gills? — "

"Quiet, all of you," Suni called out in a surprisingly deep and carrying tone.

There was immediate silence.

"Now, I would like to introduce Shar Devon Arkovic. He is a visitor from above the upper boundary. He has come to Portbree on business. Shar business. But today he is visiting Red Two Deep. You are all very lucky to see a man from beyond the upper boundary, so show some manners and stay back to say hello like well brought up children."

A dozen pairs of wide, solemn eyes stared up at him as they obediently formed a half circle in front of him. At a gesture from Suni, they all bobbed once in unison.

"Greetings, Shar," they all called out. "How may I be of service today?"

"Greetings, children," he replied, performing the standard Dip Corps folded hand gesture in front of his chest. He dared not attempt a bow in return lest he end up in an ignominious tailspin. "I thank you for your welcome."

" — he does talk — "

" — he sounds funny — "

" — can he do any other tricks, Suni? — "

" — can I touch his garment again, Suni? It feels weird — "

" — let me try — "

" — me first! I never had a turn yet — "

"Back! Back all of you!" Suni scolded. "You must not crowd the visitor."

" — but we want to talk to him, Suni. Can you make him say something again? Please! — "

Suni looked at him over one shoulder, seeking permission. He smiled and remembered not to nod.

"Alright, the visitor has consented to talk with you," Suni

said, sounding like he was doing the little imps a great favor. "But only if you stay very still and remain three fin lengths away."

Suni stretched out his own arm fin to emphasize the distance requirement. Every tiny little body immediately darted back to their original semi-circle and went into hover mode using the smallest fin motions possible. None of them moved a centimeter, but every mouth started moving at once.

" — why is he dressed like a phish, Suni? — "

" — how does he eat with that thing on his head — "

" — what does he eat? — "

" — where does he sleep, Suni? — "

" — why does he wear smelly Mabel pods on his belt? — "

" — do all visitors smell bad? — "

" — why is he visiting Red Two Deep? — "

Suni waved his arms for quiet.

"When I said that the visitor would talk with you, I meant he would talk and that you would listen," Suni said to the children in a severe tone, "not that you would all shout questions at him."

The children blushed and hung their heads. Suni gestured for him to begin addressing them, but Devon had not prepared any remarks for this type of encounter. He fell back on some standard phrases from Dip Corps First Contact Procedures.

"I am very pleased to be here. It is good to see so many of you interested in meeting a visitor from another world. I hope that today will be the beginning of a long and productive friendship between us."

The children stared back and forth between him and Suni, possibly wondering if that was all he was going to say. He regretted that his canned lines had not addressed even one of their questions.

Maybe it will be enough that they saw me and heard me speak.

"All right now, go and play all of you and let the Shar get on with his tour of the district," Suni said, shooing the children away with both arm fins and blowing bubbles into their wake as they flicked off in all directions.

"I apologize SharArkovic," Suni said, not looking at all upset by the incident now that the children were out of earshot. "Children can be most curious and insistent when they encounter something new."

Devon could not help but chuckle. "I guess that's one thing we have in common then," he smiled at Suni. "Children are the same all over the galaxy."

"I am pleased you were not offended by the little ones."

"Not at all. And I can see now where you get all your patience with me. It seems you get a lot of practice answering questions from these neighborhood children."

"I do indeed," Suni nodded. "With them and with my own little Umiko at home."

"Umiko? Is that a daughter?"

"Yes. We were going to have a Tommy too, but after Shar-Annika went into exile, our income was so reduced we could not afford another offspring."

Any further explanation was interrupted as a small, dark-haired girl erupted out of a house near the end of the street. The child zeroed in on Suni like a torpedo, zooming toward him at full speed, whooping and giggling.

"Father!" she cried, flinging herself into his arms.

Suni caught his little girl and went into a full spin with her while the child shrieked in delight.

"You are so late, Father. Is mother coming too?"

"No, Little One. I only came to say that I have more work to do, and to ask Marisol to give you dinner."

The girl pulled away with a frown, crossing her tiny arms across her chest as she scowled at her parent.

"But, Father," she began, working herself up toward a full whining fit.

"Umiko," Suni cut in with a stern look, "if you were paying attention, you would see that I have a guest with me."

She stared, popping one chubby finger into her mouth as she gazed up at him.

"This is SharArkovic," Suni told her. "He is a visitor from far, far away."

"A visitor?" the little girl repeated.

"Yes. A very important visitor who will only be here with us for a short time, so I must accompany him out to the array before he has to leave on a great journey."

"A journey?"

"Never mind. I will tell you all about it tomorrow. But right now, I must arrange for your dinner and then go back to the array. Will you be a good girl and eat dinner with Marisol and her family?"

"Yes, Father."

With a quick bob in his direction, which Devon took to mean that he should wait here in the street, Suni took his daughter by the hand and flicked away to poke his head in at the window of a house nearby. He saw Suni reach into his sash for something and hand it through the window as he and the person inside concluded their brief conversation. A woman's head appeared in the window to stare at him as Suni waved goodbye to his little girl and swam back to join him in the middle of the street. Suni's neighbor was not the only curious one. The children he had met earlier had spread the word of his arrival and by the time Suni returned to his side, a small crowd of adults and children alike had gathered around, staring at him.

"Greetings, neighbors," Suni addressed them all as rejoined Devon. "This man is SharArkovic. He is a visitor from beyond the upper boundary. I am sorry there is no time for you to meet him now. The visitor has urgent business to attend to. But I promise I will tell you all about him when I see you tomorrow."

That promise seemed to satisfy Suni's neighbors, and the crowd parted to let them through.

I suppose Glae are used to giving way to the needs of a Shar. Even one as strange as I am.

People backed away, covering their noses as he increased power to his thrusters to follow Suni back down the street toward the transit chute.

"I thank you for waiting, SharArkovic," Suni said. "Now I am ready to take you out to the array and begin our experiment."

There was a disturbance in the water at the entrance to the transit chute as they drew nearer. A gush of debris poured out of the opening, followed by a shadow, signaling the arrival of some person at the intersection. Flecks of filth clouded his view, but Devon could still make out a small figure in a gray uniform exiting the chute while he and Suni remained floating off to one side, awaiting their turn.

"Magda!" Suni called out, darting forward to brush fins with his wife. "What are you doing here?"

"Oh Suni, thank the Gods Below!"

Magda barely paused before seizing Suni's hand to begin dragging him back down the street.

"Where is Umiko?" Magda asked as they hurried along. "Is she safe? Have you seen her?"

"Of course, she is safe," Suni replied. "I left her with Marisol at number six."

Suni tugged at her hand, swinging her around to face him.

"Now wait a minute, my dear. You had better tell me what is going on. Why would our Umiko not be safe?"

"Because of that horrible SharScylla," Magda cried, wringing her hands and trembling in every fin and gill. "He said if Annika will not go with the airbreathers on their dive mission, then he will sink both you and me and then take Umiko to live with him in the Assembly Building."

"What?" Suni wobbled so hard Devon almost reached out a hand to keep the little man from tipping over.

Magda didn't wait for him to recover though, she immediately resumed dragging Suni toward the house where Marisol was caring for their daughter.

"We have to get Umiko out of here, Suni. We have to take her away and hide somewhere before Scylla sends his Glads to take her prisoner."

"But, what about Annika?" Suni said. "Will she not be in danger if we all go missing?"

"The temple is the safest place for her if she is determined not to do as Scylla wishes. She has been granted sanctuary there, but we have not. We have to get Umiko away now and find somewhere for all of us to hide."

"But where can we go that he will not find us?" Suni said.

The sheer terror in Magda's voice sent shivers up Devon's spine, but he was also disturbed by Suni's stunned reactions. So far, these two Marnians had struck him as particularly thoughtful and steady people, so to see them both on the verge of panic was very unnerving.

"Is there any way I can help?" he asked.

"Have you not done enough SharArkovic?" Magda replied tartly. "You said that it might be dangerous for Shar-Annika to travel in your airbreather conveyance and that she ought to refuse to go. Now she has angered the Leader by following your advice."

"But I thought SharScylla would just assign someone else to make the dive. I had no idea he would threaten your family in order to coerce her to go."

Suni seemed to be recovering his wits to some degree. The little man ruffled his gills and made a small bob in place as usual before speaking. "To Scylla, her refusal must seem like a challenge to his authority. Now he will not give up this fight until he wins. That means Annika will end up going on the mission just to prevent any harm to us."

"But she cannot do that," Magda wailed. "She should not risk her life just to save us."

"And how will you stop her?" Suni asked.

Magda's gills wilted. "But ... maybe. What if we had already gone into hiding? What if she knew we were already safe?"

"You know that would never work, my dear," Suni told her gently. "Annika knows that just as the former Gladiator will never give up his fight with her, he will also never stop hunting for us. Scylla does not tolerate disobedience from anyone."

Chapter 23: Research

Devon gazed at the two Glae in an agony of guilt and pity. Despite his best intentions, he had once again caused disaster for someone else.

Will the cost of protecting Annika from my mistake be the lives of these two and their daughter? No, Annika will never allow that. Suni is right. She'll risk herself in the submarine before letting them pay for her disobedience.

He had never felt okay about the prospect of any Marnian being sealed in the airlock of the submersible, committed to the tender care of Ted Hollander. Ted would be preoccupied with piloting the craft and recovery of the Glaeon. Devon could easily envision what would occur if some difficulty arose with the jury-rigged airlock while Ted was distracted with other matters. That issue had been nagging at the back of his mind ever since he suggested this plan. Now, he even questioned whether Ted would lift a finger to assist a Marnian in difficulty, whether he was busy piloting the sub or not. Somehow, Devon had known what he would have to do ever since he met Annika. But it was seeing Suni and Magda sharing a hopeless look that gave him the courage to take the last step.

"I think I may know how I can help."

As the two Marnians turned their desperate looks his way, a strange feeling of weightlessness swept over him. The idea of descending into those crushing depths still terrified him. But, from that very first moment, he had yearned to help Annika Sharone.

This is my chance to do something for her that even these two most faithful friends cannot.

"Since it seems inevitable that Annika will go on this dive," he said, nodding toward Suni as if to concede that point, "Then I am going to go with her."

"Really, SharArkovic?" Suni said, springing forward to take his hand and stroke it with a fin. "You would do that for her? And for us?"

"My presence may not eliminate all risks to Annika, but at least if I am there watching out for her, I think it will give her a better chance of surviving the journey."

***

Once Suni and Magda said their goodbyes, the little uplink specialist led the way back up the transit chute to the main level of Portbree. Devon followed Suni through several posh looking neighborhoods out into a sunny open area surrounded on three sides by commercial buildings, with a stream of traffic passing by on the fourth side. It appeared to be a busy docking area where conveyances were landing and launching, loading and unloading.

Devon could see a stream of vehicles of all sizes sailing briskly downstream beyond the calm waters in this sheltered space that seemed set aside for embarking and debarking. Several large vehicles floated nearby, well out of the main current, tied to docking frames. With a thrill, Devon realized he was at last going to get a closeup view of the Marnian transportation devices.

"If you permit, we will take a taxi from this point, SharArkovic," Suni said.

Suni went to make arrangements, while Devon gave in to his curiosity and glided toward the nearest large conveyance. Men in purple uniforms were unloading bales of some product from a similar vehicle nearby, so he assumed that this wide, flat platform was a transport vehicle. Both the purple clad men and then others all down the docking area stopped to stare at him as usual as he approached to examine the craft.

"What causes this vehicle to remain afloat and to move?" he asked when Suni reappeared at his side.

His personal encyclopedia launched into an explanation. "Conveys are both supported and moved forward or back by one or more Mabel pods."

"Mabel pods?"

Suni pointed underneath the vehicle at eight large, bulging structures. As he leaned closer to see how they worked, Devon was startled when a button near the front of the pod swiveled to inspect him in return, and then blinked.

"It's alive," he exclaimed, flailing to maintain orientation after having flinched away from the thing.

"Of course," Suni said, looking puzzled. "Mabels function by generating and storing large amounts of gas which they expel through a rear orifice, creating forward motion. They work in much the same way as your impellors, except they do not smell so much."

"So, your vehicles are literally jet propelled? How clever."

"Only so long as the beast lives and can consume food and produce gas."

"Is the same system used to support homes and other buildings?"

"It is, but those Mabels never produce forward thrust. Their body shape has been modified to aim the force of the expelled gas in a downward direction only."

"I see. So, there are subspecies of the animal for different purposes?"

"Yes. Some Mabels are by nature inclined to work in tandem with others, producing forward or back motion or simply maintaining station keeping."

"What happens when you need to replace some but not others? How do you train new members to work with old ones?"

Suni held up a hand. "I am a SUNI, SharArkovic, I am not a CONNER. It is not part of my professional knowledge to understand all the details of how a Mabel works. I just know that they do."

The little man turned pink as the purple clad Glae drew back in shock at his disrespectful tone.

Damn it, I'm doing it again and Suni can't scold me like a kid from his neighborhood when I get demanding.

"Of course, I apologize, Suni. I get carried away with

investigating new things sometimes and forget that not everyone knows everything about how the world they live in works."

***

Devon hovered in place, using his suit thrusters to maintain buoyancy, once again waiting for Suni to lead the way. They were floating next to the Grand Eddy, where the taxi had dropped them off at what was supposed to be a point nearest the former Librarian's Estate, but there was no building or indeed anything in sight.

"Where is this array of yours, Suni?" he asked, looking around the deserted area.

He tried to keep his tone polite, reminding himself not to badger Suni like a child.

"The array is that way," Suni said, pointing in a direction away from the Grand Eddy. "I will carry the equipment sent down from the ship SharArkovic. But you must now swim over to the Estate on your own." Suni's tone was apologetic, but the little man's expression was firm. "I am not strong enough to assist you as 4th Goon did in the Assembly Building, and from this point you must remove the impeller units from your suit."

"Remove my thrusters! Why?"

Suni appeared uncomfortable again, bobbing up and down and keeping his eyes on his toes. "Everyone who visits an array is required to approach the Estate either by swimming or using only a standard conveyance once they leave the Grand Eddy."

"What's a standard conveyance?"

"An unpowered roll."

"A what?"

"An algae roll with a paddle," Suni said. "A standard convey does not produce a wake in the way that vehicles which use impellers do. No vehicles that produce a wake are allowed in the vicinity of any data array. The information contained within the neural cells of a hoard is irreplaceable. All arrays are deliberately situated in calm areas like this, beyond the natural current. That way, we do not risk unnecessary damage to the cells from currents or from careless driving. The penalties for using any kind of powered transport near an array are quite severe."

"So can I have a standard conveyance then?" he asked plaintively.

"A standard conveyance has only enough buoyancy to hold up its own weight. A Marnian does not require more. So, I regret that a paddle roll will not prevent you from sinking, SharArkovic. Also, the balance required to use one, uh, takes practice. I do not recommend it for a—a beginner."

Suni looked away from him, seeming uncomfortable again.

"I'll take your word for it."

"I promise I will keep your impellers safe and return them to you when you leave the vicinity of the array, SharArkovic," the Marnian said, extending a hand for the devices.

Devon hesitated, remembering the strain of floundering around without thrusters that whole afternoon when he first met with SharScylla.

I guess this is my chance to be the polite guest for a change instead of just a pestering nuisance.

"Ok, I guess if I want to visit an array, I need to conform to

207

local rules."

"I appreciate your understanding, SharArkovic."

"You know, Suni, you don't have to keep calling me SharArkovic. My name is Devon."

Suni bobbed up and down, rubbing his jaw in thought, as Devon worked to unfasten the thrusters from his belt.

"I will address you as you wish, of course," Suni said at last, "but I do not like to seem disrespectful."

"And 'Shar' is an honorific placed before a person's name to show respect, right?"

"Not just for any person. We only use the term Shar when addressing a high caste person. One who belongs to a Great or a Minor House of Marna."

"And so, what exactly does 'Glae' mean, then?"

"Ordinary people like me are referred to as Glae," Suni replied calmly. "According to records in the array, Glae was originally a derogatory term created from the letters spelling algae, minus one. As in, dumber than a clump of slime with some missing."

Devon was shocked silent for a moment before he could collect himself.

"On my world, Suni, it is not a sign of disrespect to call a person by their first name when invited to do so," he said, eyeing the other man carefully. "However, if it will make you more comfortable, you may continue to address me as SharArkovic when there are other people present."

As Suni nodded and smiled in relief, Devon enjoyed the warm feeling of having done the right thing for once.

Surrendering his thrusters was a much harder feat. His teeth clenched as Suni secured them inside multiple folds of his sash, wondering if he would regret this attempt at courtesy.

"Very well then, Devon. If you will follow me. I will go slowly so that I do not leave you behind."

***

Regret did not take long to arrive. It was impossible for Devon not to think about the kilometer deep drop below him as he swam along behind the little uplink specialist. Without his thrusters, he knew that if his arms and legs weren't up to this trip, the bottom of the ocean was exactly where the *Osprey's* submarine would find him.

"I'll never complain about EVA again," he muttered to himself.

Water was so much more resistant than vacuum that his muscles grew tired in the bulky p-suit. The suit engineer on the *Osprey* had emphasized that it would be important to conserve energy and avoid exhaustion when moving in water. The engineer had also said that Devon should learn to get the most out of each pull of his arms when swimming, and to synchronize his kicks so that they propelled him forward rather than in circles. Easier said than done. It all sounded so obvious and straightforward when he was up there on the ship. But now Devon could feel the muscle fatigue creeping in all over his body.

Forcing himself to breathe steadily, he tried to use the rhythm of his lungs to time his strokes, keeping his movements as smooth as possible. First, he would exert and then glide forward on momentum for a moment while relaxing the contraction of his muscles in order to stretch them briefly and prevent a fatal cramp. Suni swam below him so that he could follow without lifting his head. Watching Suni gave him something to focus on other than the gloomy depths below. However, it was an impossible mental discipline to resist the urge to crane his neck up periodically and check to see if the Estate was in sight yet.

The effort went on and on. Small muscles he never knew he had were threatening to cramp all over his body. If that happened, he would end up plummeting into the blackness below. He imagined his family getting the news that he had drowned on a mission to Marna. His friends in Dip Corps putting up his picture in the base dining hall, then shrugging and going about their day. After a while, a fall into the blackness began to seem more like a blessed relief instead of a terrifying ending. Exhaustion sent him teetering on the brink of hallucination and he pictured floating downward like an airy speck of dust. Drifting and sinking lower until at last he'd be extinguished like a candle flame in one quick puff.

Far, far away, beyond those visions, he heard a knocking sound and woke from that dreamy vision of death to see Suni peering in through his helmet. The little man was pointing out the grand sight of the enormous fields of neural cells as they approached the Estate. But with his helmet fogged and running with drops of sweat, Devon was far past caring about sightseeing. He only roused his screaming muscles into a final effort to reach the dark bulk ahead that might be the Estate

Building. A last spark of the desire to live carried him to the threshold and then just inside to reach Suni's uplink room.

After that, he dangled limply, rotating at the end of his tether, utterly spent after his harrowing crossing.

When at last he recovered enough to grab onto the tether and pull himself upright once more, he looked around Suni's 'office' curiously. The room measured only a few meters square with the standard wall mats, open lattice floor and overlapping phish arranged into slats covering the ceiling. The slats were angled open, so the room was filled with light, but the water in this enclosed space was rather on the cloudy side.

Although he could tell that the environment on this Estate was far superior to the squalid conditions he'd seen in Red Two Deep, he still noticed that fragments of algae were constantly shedding off the mat-like fabric of the walls of the chamber. Seeing such a high level of pollution, even in an upscale location, made Devon glad for once that his suit isolated him from direct contact with the Marnian ocean.

Everything on this planet seems to exist in a constant state of decay. I sure don't envy Suni those gills right now. Yuck.

Although the Marnian didn't have to worry about his oxygen supply, at the moment Suni was subject to inhaling all sorts of filth. While the living collar of gills around his neck flared and clenched in a steady rhythm most of the time, Devon could see those layers spasming now and then as they ejected some overly large bit of debris from between their ruffled layers. Suni's face tended to be so impassive that Devon was unsure whether that retching process was actually uncomfortable, but the sight disgusted him.

He was envious of the way Marnians seemed to effortlessly maintain their position, however. While he was forced to either dangle on his tether like a lump or go to the effort of holding himself upright on the line, it took only the tiniest of ripples along the edges of Suni's pale grayish fin membranes to keep him upright and stationary.

At least that's true while we're here indoors and not speaking. Maintaining orientation in any kind of current or while carrying on a conversation seems to require a Marnian to make more significant fin effort.

The waves of exhaustion were passing now, and Devon's curiosity returned, along with his strength. He noticed the room was sparsely furnished, with a narrow armless couch in the center, and a small table near one wall. Suni floated next to the table, examining the connectors and cables that had been sent from the ship, so it was an ideal opportunity to study a Marnian up close. He had already speculated that their aquatic modifications must include some kind of internal float, or swim bladder, that kept people from sinking downward. Beyond that, staying in position under ideal conditions seemed to be only a question of delicate balancing. It had puzzled him at first to see the Marnians' gills pumping madly after expending gases to speak. Now, as he thought it through, he realized that even rapid gill action could not produce enough gases on demand to keep vocal cords functioning properly. Therefore, Marnian anatomy must include some special reservoir of gases dedicated solely for speech purposes. He had noticed that Marnians did not carry on long conversations without pausing for some period of contemplation.

Those pauses must allow time to refill that speech reservoir. Either that or they have a very polite and sedate culture when it comes to communication.

Looking back over his time on Marna, he wondered how people from such a society might perceive him.

I must come across as a run amok babbler the way I go on talking with no breaks.

Watching Suni going about his work so quietly also made Devon wonder if he'd also been unintentionally rude to the specialist in that way on numerous occasions.

And now, here is Suni going to all this effort to help a stranger access the data archives and what do I ask to see? Records about when airbreathers abandoned his ancestors.

Wouldn't it be more tactful to ask about the current Marnian civilization first and then work backwards? Or perhaps I should ask about their revolution? It couldn't hurt to know more about that incident since the beautiful Annika was so involved.

There was only one way to find out.

"So, tell me, Suni, why do you think your Leader wants Shar-Annika to be the one to make the dive below?"

Suni turned gracefully in place, holding a piece of gelatinous looking cable in his hand.

"I do not know for sure Sh-, er, Devon. But I assume it is as he explained to you. Shar-Annika is both well known to the people, and many of them believe she is Aban."

"Believe she is Aban?"

213

"Ever since the revolution, it is a common belief that the Gods Below persuaded her to carry out the removal of her father from power. Because people believe she serves the Gods, they will trust any report that Shar-Annika makes about the journey. They will also have faith that she can calm the Gods if this airbreather intrusion disturbs them."

Devon thought that idea over while Suni pumped his gills at high speed.

"I doubt we are going to run into any Gods, so she won't have much to do on that score."

"Perhaps not, but Scylla knows that there are many foolish people in the city who still think that you yourself might be some new kind of God."

"I told everyone when I first arrived that I have nothing to do with any Gods," Devon said, restraining an impulse to rake the hair off his forehead as he often did when upset. "I said right off that I am a man. A physical being like all of you."

"And yet your suit does not shed," Suni pointed out. "It is not made of living things like plants or phish. No one can touch you to be sure you are flesh." He gave an apologetic dip. "These things confuse people. So SharScylla must send a trusted person to accompany you. He has made a bargain with you for the cargo inside the equipment, but that does not mean the people do not still fear that raising this cargo from the deeps means you are stealing it from the Gods Below."

"You know that we're not stealing it. You said that you saw in the records that it belongs to the company."

"Yes, I know this from viewing the records in this data

hoard," Suni agreed, gesturing at the surrounding complex. "But others do not understand about the corporation that brought the equipment here long ago."

"Ok, I can see how people have come to believe that there are Gods down below. But why don't they understand about the company? Don't you have stories about how you came to be living on this planet? About the LEAP Corporation who brought your ancestors here?"

"No. None of that is considered useful knowledge for either Shar or Glae."

"Well then, how did Scylla know what I was talking about when I first arrived, and I started talking about the company and the equipment they left here?"

"He did not know. No one knew," Suni shrugged. "SharScylla came out here to the array and asked my former master, SharCom, about the company right after you had your first meeting."

"Then how is it you know about these things from the past then?"

"I only know because SharScylla ordered me to search the records to confirm several aspects of your story. That was after he killed the Librarian."

"What? He killed the Librarian? Why?"

"SharScylla claimed that the Librarian was a traitor to have withheld vital information about the airbreathers and the Company from him. He then became enraged, killed SharCom and ordered me to take charge of the facility."

"But how could the Librarian withhold that knowledge?

Doesn't everyone know how you all came to be here?"

Suni shook his head. "Such information is not in demand therefore, no one knows it. I also think that my former master, SharCom, made it undesirable to know these things by charging very large fees to access his most ancient records."

"But that's outrageous. That is all part of your history! Isn't that kind of thing public knowledge here?"

"There is no such thing as public knowledge. All data comes at a price. Most people know only what they can afford to know."

"How awful. I didn't realize, Suni. There is so much about your world that I don't know."

Suni bobbed and nodded.

"When Shar-Annika was young, she came to believe, as you do, that it is a crime to deprive people of their history. The primary goal of our revolution was to increase access to information of all kinds, for all people. Not just the wealthy."

"Yes, I remember how you explained that, but now it makes more sense. I don't think I understood before how restricted access to information is here."

"Annika also believed that personal history, in particular, is very valuable. She helped Glae people in our rebel movement to differentiate themselves by sharing and preserving their personal stories. She also gave them unique names rather than just designations to honor each person's great deeds. That is why we former rebels call her the First Historian. When she taught us the value of history, we learned who we were."

Suni lapsed into silence again with his gills blurring beside his neck. But there was little time to mull these new ideas over as the little 'linker approached, with the neural connector cable in hand and a strange expression on his face. For the first time Devon felt a splash of worry over letting this stranger from such a foreign culture handle uploads into his brain. He kept talking to stave off the moment when he had to submit himself to Suni's care.

"Imagine teaching a world of undifferentiated people to see themselves as individuals. I think Annika is the most extraordinary person I've ever met."

It hurt his heart again to think of Annika blaming herself for a failure when she had, in fact, accomplished something so profound.

I wonder how much else there is to know about her that would amaze me?

Suddenly, he found himself truly more interested in the present than in the distant past.

"You know what, Suni? I'm glad that I'll be going with her on this dive. I really think she is vital to securing the future of your planet once the Glaeon starts flowing again. In fact, I've changed my mind about the records I want to see. The best way to prepare for this dive mission would be to understand as much as possible about her. So, how about you show me everything you've got on this revolution of yours? Especially anything that pertains to Annika's involvement. She is a key player here, and I want to be sure I know everything there is to know about her."

Chapter 24: Party of the Gods

"Good evening neighbors."

Glen stood on a worktable and waved both arm fins to get the crowd's attention. Once they were quiet, he began his pitch.

"Now I think everyone here has heard about this airbreather who came down from beyond the upper boundary. Am I right?"

The handful of glow globes that lit the crowd in Trent's manufacturing building sent shadows flashing around the walls as men nodded.

"Then you must also have heard how this stranger entered our temple uninvited and how he pollutes our ocean with his stinking impellors."

Now the crowd made hissing sounds and angry gestures with their fins.

"I suppose you have even heard the rumors that this airbreather intends to dive into the Deeps and steal from the Gods Below."

Glen smiled to himself as the noises from the crowd grew louder.

"My neighbors, I am here on behalf of a group called the True Believers. We True Believers are loyal to the Gods Below.

Therefore, we see it as our sacred duty to stop this blasphemous journey. The True Believers want to defend our Gods from these airbreather invaders. We say it is time to put a stop to any desecration of the holy realms of the Gods Below!"

The crowd roared agreement, setting the water quivering. He saw gills blurring on every neck as the workers yelled their defiance, filling the water with the stink of outrage and impatience.

Finally, he held up a hand for silence. It was all going much better than the meetings he had tried to run in the marketplace outside his shop. In this more private location, men seemed to feel freer to let loose their secret resentments. At first, the idea of using a factory belonging to a Shar worried him. Now Glen was glad that he had taken the time to chat with the customer who often came into his shop after a shift in this factory. The man had begged Glen to hold a rally here for his fellow workers, and the fellow was right. These men were ready for action.

"My neighbors, I think you know it is not only the airbreathers who disrespect our Gods Below."

Glen shook his head sadly as surly mutters and hisses rippled through the crowd.

"Yes, there are now Marnians among us who intend to help these strangers with their desecration. First, SharScylla ignored our protests and invited the airbreather right into the Ruling Assembly Building. Since then, we have heard tales that the Leader will send his Goons and Gladiators to help the strangers to steal from our Gods."

Snarls and hisses came from all sides until he waved them

down again.

"And SharScylla is not the only stranger-lover. Oh no. There are many others in this city saying we should give the airbreathers what they want. People who say we should let the airbreathers steal from the Gods so they will go away and not harm us. Do you know what the True Believers call people who say those things?"

"Cowards!"

"Traitors!"

"Defilers of the Gods!"

"Kill them all!"

As the crowd roared, Glen flared out all four fins and raised his fists above his head, letting them scream until they were all dipping from loss of gases.

"Oh yes, neighbors," he said once they were quiet once more, "it is time some of these people learned that there is a price for disloyalty to the Gods Below. Look, here is my own brother who is an acolyte in the temple." Glen gestured for his brother to join him on the table. "My brother tells me that there are Aban in the temple who agree with us True Believers. These Aban say we need to demonstrate our faith in the Gods by punishing those would disturb them."

His brother's fins trembled, but the acolyte raised his voice high enough for most of the audience to hear.

"It is true. Many of the Aban are saying we must show the Gods Below our devotion."

"Show our devotion?"

Heads turned as a familiar voice spoke up from the back of

the crowd near the door. Glen cursed his luck as factory workers automatically parted to make way as the artist Trent glided between them up toward the table where he and his brother stood.

"I see my workers have all stayed very late tonight, John," Trent remarked to the Glae who swam at his heels.

The JOHN dipped acknowledgement without replying, shifting his eyes about as if counting the number of angry men surrounding him and his master. Glen frowned as he looked the servant over. His customer at the shop had often complained about how this JOHN's upgrades earned him the easier job of assisting the artist in his studio. That privileged status made the JOHN very unpopular among the other workers at the factory.

"I don't recall anyone asking me if my workshop could be used for a meeting," Trent said.

The Shar's tone was mild, but he spoke loud enough so that even those in the back could hear. Heads throughout the crowd dropped as men took time to inspect their lower fins. Glen ground his teeth as the artist darted up onto the front of the table, forcing him and his brother to step back.

"And do you think this is a temple where you can debate what Gods may or may not desire?" Trent mocked the crowd.

Although the Shar deliberately blocked the crowd's view of him and his brother, Glen could see over the artist's shoulder, that a few resentful faces were glaring at Trent after that last remark.

"I think you should all go home before I have my JOHN make a list of your addresses and have you all discharged from work here in my factory," Trent said.

The JOHN's gills quivered as grim faces turned his way now.

"Do you hear me?" Trent snapped. "I said go home and forget all this nonsense."

"Nonsense?"

Glen felt like cheering when he saw how stiffly his brother's gills stood out on either side of his neck as the acolyte flicked forward to confront SharTrent.

"How dare you call the words of the Aban nonsense? Do you also lack respect for the Gods Below?"

Now every head in the crowd was up, and every eye rested on SharTrent waiting for his answer.

"What I believe is of no importance," Trent said turning away from the acolyte to face his workers. "What matters is that you should all believe that you will be without work if you don't do as you're told and leave here right now. You Glae ought to know better than to meddle in affairs you don't understand. Go home and leave dealing with the airbreathers to educated Shar who know what they're doing. Get out and take these two fools with you." Trent waved a fin at the GLEN and his brother. "The Gods don't need your help. They can take care of themselves."

"Blasphemer," shrieked the acolyte, pointing back at Trent. His fins began flailing as he lost control, but he kept on screaming. "Faithless, greedy, selfish Shar. Traitors like you should be dragged to the temple to answer for your disloyalty to the council of elders. And may they cast your body into the boiling heart of the mountain. Evil men like you do not deserve to take the Big Dive and be gathered into the arms of the Gods

Below."

Glen wriggled with glee as Trent paled and backed away while his brother's rant went on and on.

"Time for one who disrespects the Gods to pay the price, right neighbors?" he said, beckoning some men in the front ranks of the audience forward.

Eager hands reached out to pluck the artist off the table. A small red cloud formed around Trent as a circle of men ripped at his clothes and fins. Other Glae who could not get close enough to lay a hand on the Shar rushed to his studio and hauled the artist's latest sculpture out into the factory workspace.

"Ah, yes," Glen called out to his followers. "Let the Shar see the last piece he will ever make. And bring his servant forward also."

The JOHN was hustled forward, and Glen saw him share an anguished look with Trent.

"Now tell me," Glen said, bending to look the JOHN in the eye. "What is an artist's most important tool?"

The terrified man only shook his head, gills wilted and limp by his neck.

"Alright now neighbors," Glen called out, beginning to enjoy himself, "I think we should let the artist know what we think of his work."

He mimed out an action for his followers, then scooted aside for a better view.

The artist's JOHN gasped as one by one his master's fingers were snapped apart like fresh kelp buds. Once both hands were mutilated Glen waved the rest of the crowd forward to take a turn with the blasphemers.

Later, after two clouds of red fluid soured the water in Trent's factory, from wall to wall, he addressed his followers again.

"And now neighbors, just as my brother said, let us make sure that the final journey for these two traitors ends in the hot belly of the mountain, rather than in the arms of our beloved Gods Below."

Soon a mob of brand-new True Believers had gathered up the broken bodies of the artist and his servant and set off to launch them into the searing caldera at the top of Mount Charlize.

Chapter 25: Suni's Remorse

Suni hung huddled below the upper boundary, watching the airbreathers from beneath the shade of a small raft. It was the same kind of conveyance that Shar-Devon had used before to snatch a hasty meal and exchange his old headgear for the clear, hard bubble kind. In Suni's opinion, however, this puny craft was useless for quelling any of the terror involved in remaining so close to the upper edge of the world.

Everything about these trips to the upper reaches was hateful to him. The light was painfully bright, this high up, and the heat made his whole body feel heavy and sluggish. He had heard tales of adventurous souls who ventured to the upper boundary at dawn in order to experience that strange form of water called dew. There were even reckless thrill seekers who boasted about rising this high when storms raged in the over-realm. Fools who ascended here, seeking a taste of rain. However, he had never been the kind to aspire to wild adventures. His greatest joy was pottering about in the vast data hoard of the Librarian, discovering little gems of unique and valuable information.

Squinting upward into the searing light, he watched several men moving about on a large platform nearby. The airbreathers had caused this great flat thing to come down and rest upon the

225

upper boundary without sinking. The strangers seemed to possess an unlimited supply of astonishing items, all made with materials he had never seen before. Just as Shar-Devon had promised during the meeting with SharScylla back at the Ruling Assembly Building. Yet, everything the airbreathers made looked impossibly heavy and strangely hard to Suni. Despite his curiosity, he remained where he was under the raft, afraid to go any closer to the dangerous-looking things.

Several airbreathers were walking about with Shar-Devon on the platform, doing mysterious things to a large object that rested there. The thing was as round and white as a wiggler's egg, yet almost as big as a house. Shar-Devon had explained that this was the special conveyance for journeying down into the Deeps that airbreathers called a 'sub.'

Suni sighed as he gazed up at the vehicle.

Now poor Annika will have to go inside that terrible hard thing and travel into the black unknown with the strangers, to search for this lost Glaeon.

He was not sure how much of what he'd heard about that amazing substance he believed. If Glaeon could indeed grant a man long life and a youthful body, then it made sense why the airbreathers were so eager to possess it. It would also explain why other violent, greedy pirates might come and kill everyone in the city in order to claim that prize. But Shar-Devon's tale of pirates hunting this treasure still seemed like bedtime stories for offspring. Foolish nonsense from the same far-away dream world where people could consume a magic food and then live on and on forever like mountains.

Can the data I have seen about Glaeon possibly be real? How could some extract of bree make a man live so long? And why would it only work on airbreathers? It has to be a trick of some kind. Yet Shar-Devon is here risking his life to seek the cargo of Glaeon, and he is no fool.

Suni shook his head to clear it. He was sure of only one thing right now. Shar-Devon had tried to dissuade Annika from going along on this mission. Therefore, once again, his dear girl must be squarely in the path of danger.

And this new danger is all my fault too. Not only is she forced to make this risky journey today to protect me and my family. I was the one who set her onto the path that led to this moment all those storms ago. What a fool I was back then. So blinded by the glorious future that my modified Shar would one day bring forth.

It didn't help Suni to remember that at the time he conceived his plan to change the world, he had been counting on a much safer method. He dropped his head into his hands and ground the heels of his hands into his eyes.

Yet, even when it came to mounting a rebellion, I convinced myself that a certain amount of risk and sacrifice was acceptable in order to achieve our noble goals. Too bad most of those sacrifices were not mine.

Guilt claimed a few more slivers of his soul as he reviewed the sum of his failings.

In raising the poor girl to become the one to lead us into that shining future, not only did I isolate her and put her in constant danger, I also stole Annika's chance to be happy with any lesser destiny.

His body shook with sobs and he drifted lower as his limp gills failed to replenish the gases he was losing.

Magda tried to tell me there would be trouble for our Little One. But

I would not listen. I took every sign of her being different as a step toward success.

Although he still believed in the revolutionary goals and principles that he helped Magda instill in Annika throughout her childhood, these days he was not so sure about having guided an innocent girl onto a path that had so often led her into sacrificing her own safety for the good of others.

As he drifted down into the full sun, Suni hugged his arms across his body despite the heat.

It is too late now. We are all trapped by those choices I made so long ago. Me, Magda, Annika and now even Shar-Devon.

Suni could tell that Devon was no happier about making this voyage than Annika. Yet the stranger had opted to go for her sake. He returned to watching the weirdly distorted airbreathers up on the platform.

At least I am sure that Shar-Devon is making this dive of his own free will. I did not even have to modify him. He chose this path on his own.

As Suni examined the group of airbreathers working to raise the sub off the platform, he noted how these men differed from Devon Arkovic. Their coverings looked well worn, and they spoke in harsh voices, shouting terse instructions at each other as they winched the vehicle up from the deck and swung it outwards over the water. During pauses in their work, he could hear them laughing loudly as they traded insults and meaningless gestures, or simply lounged against their equipment, awaiting their next task. They must be Glae, since they were the ones performing the heavy work of moving the sub. However, their manners were unlike those of any Glae that he had ever seen.

Suni glanced at another group of men standing in a group off to one side of the sub. They were dressed in tidy outfits decorated with shiny circles down the front and stood watching the progress of the work while discussing something with Shar-Devon. Clearly, this second group of airbreathers were Shar, but even they seemed different from Shar-Devon.

Shar-Devon is a born explorer. One who lives and breathes to ask questions.

Many of those questions had been very difficult for Suni to answer, so connecting Devon to the data array had taken an immense burden off his shoulders. Throughout most of the previous day, his new airbreather friend had remained at the array, integrating an astonishing quantity of data about the revolution and Shar-Annika's personal history, along with some records from ancient times.

Suni bobbed in place with a smile for a moment as he imagined Shar-Devon carrying Annika's story far across space to people on distant planets. The visitor had solemnly promised to see that done when he opened his eyes after reviewing her personal history files from the time of the revolution.

And I never even had to add to his downloads to encourage him. He just naturally wants to help us. Wants to help her. So now Annika will be famous throughout the galaxy.

Imagine all those people hearing what she accomplished. That is more glory than our dear Little One ever dreamed of.

It was a genuine thrill for him to think of Annika's story

spreading across the galaxy. A fitting tribute for Marna's First Historian. But Suni couldn't help blowing out a sad slow bubble as he peered through the surface distortion at the airbreather sub.

At least she knows her story will be told on countless worlds beyond the upper realm. Even if she does not survive this next heroic sacrifice.

He shied away from dwelling any further on the idea that this might be the last day of Annika's life. It was improper to taint his observations with that unlucky thought when he had been granted the honor to be the designated historian for this event. Charged to bear witness to this joint venture, and then record a file for storage in the array in case Annika herself failed to return and give a first-hand account. To that end, he watched every detail carefully as Shar-Devon and another man climbed down through a doorway on top of the sub.

The Glae airbreathers on the platform caused the sub to swing out over the side, then lowered the swaying vehicle down to break through the upper boundary.

Suni sighed with relief as he dropped away from the inadequate shelter of the raft to follow the sub's descent. The outer door to the airlock was open, and Suni shivered to see the small dark space yawning ominously below him.

Poor Annika! Imagine being crammed into one tiny place to make this descent. And what can she do if there really are Gods Below and the airbreathers disturb them? She will be trapped in that terrible little room while the strangers do whatever they intend to do. Will they even hear her if she does make any objection?

Heat and light quickly decreased to a bearable level as he

moved lower. Suni pushed his arm and leg fins harder to dodge aside as a sudden stream of shiny bubbles gushed up from the sub. He also adjusted the gas in his buoyancy sac to allow his body to sink faster and continued on down, staying level with the big, curved side of the sub now.

His eyes relaxed as the light level returned to normal. Once his vision cleared, he could see a small group of Marnians gathered on one side of the path that the sub was following in its descent. Annika's distinctive haze of red hair, mixed with long trailing upper fins, caught his eye first. Then he spied what must be his own dear Magda floating behind her mistress's right shoulder, as usual. The rest of the group appeared to be a few Goons, and several Aban from the Temple, attended by a few acolytes.

So few witnesses to Annika's latest act of selfless courage.

Suni gave the sub a wide berth as he scooted over to join the group waiting with Annika. He saw her eyes flick toward him as he passed, but she gave no other sign of noticing his presence as all the Aban began reciting a prayer to bless her journey. Her hair and fins floated around her, as usual, but she wore only short shorts and a sturdy, almost utilitarian upper garment today. While the ceremony continued, Suni could see Annika studying the airbreather's conveyance with no sign of fear. His own gills fluttered, and his lips trembled at the memory of that horrible, dark little room in the center of the sub. Yet now that he was facing the front of the conveyance, Suni could see Devon Arkovic and another airbreather inside. They were visible through one of those clear hard spaces, just like the one Devon had on the front of the first type of head covering he had worn with his silvery suit. Devon looked quite different without the bulky garment. Frail and vulnerable.

For the first time, it struck Suni that Devon too was at risk here today.

If he does not return, it will not matter that an airbreather has downloaded the story of Annika's great deeds straight from the array. Her story will never reach the stars without Devon Arkovic.

As the chant from the Aban went on, Suni found himself sending out a plea for the safety of both Annika and Devon.

If you Gods Below do exist, then please watch over these two precious people. Send them back to us unharmed today.

When the ceremony ended, Suni opened his eyes and saw Devon waving and smiling at Annika, then pointing toward the top of the sub where the airlock waited to receive her. Devon had assured him that the cramped space of the lock would maintain a watery environment at a constant pressure and oxygen content for Annika. Still, the very name *airlock* made his skin crawl.

Annika gave Magda a quick nod, then detached herself from the group of Marnians and glided toward the sub. Only his obligation as historian for this event drew Suni forward to follow that lonely figure up the curve of the sub toward the entrance to the airlock. As he came to a stop at her side, he could hear Devon's voice emanating from a speaker next to the lock, providing instructions for operating the door.

So, it is true. The airbreathers will be able to communicate with her during the descent.

232

He bobbed in place with his gills flaring as Annika gently glided inside the lock. Carefully tucking her hair and fins inside. Suni could see her gills moving with slow deliberate beats while his own speeded up into an absolute blur. A giant lump filled his throat as the terrible door clanged shut.

She is in Shar-Devon's care now.

A round thing on the outside of the door turned a few times as he watched, and then his heart leaped to see Annika's face looking out at him from a small, empty space set into the collar that stuck up around the doorway. He felt a flood of relief as Annika gave a little smile and waved to him.

If she can see me, then at least she is not utterly in the dark in that small space.

He raised an arm to wave back, but then a voice suddenly boomed out in all directions. He flinched aside, clapping his hands over his ears before he forced himself to stop and try to process what the airbreather voice was saying.

"ALL SPECTATORS PLEASE MOVE BACK. EVERYONE IN THE AREA MUST MOVE TO A SAFE DISTANCE DURING SUB DESCENT. REPEAT, MOVE TO A SAFE DISTANCE NOW. SUB DESCENT IN TEN SECONDS."

Suni backed away, but he could not bear to leave. His gills still blurred away at top speed, and he dug his fingers into the fabric of his upper covering to keep them from tearing at his fins. He wanted to hang his head in shame, but he could not take his eyes off the pale face peering out at him from the sub. His heart swelled as he locked eyes with her. Then his fingers dug deeper into the fabric under his hands, and he wished with all his might for her safe return as the airbreather's voice counted down. "THREE ... TWO ... ONE. COMMENCING DESCENT."

Chapter 26: The Dive

Devon wondered if it was only his imagination that an icy breath of air kept whispering past his cheek from the curved wall to his left. Now that they had left the light from the surface behind, there was nothing to see out the window except an endless blackness. The cold and dark pushed all his fears about this dive to the forefront of his mind, shoving aside all other thoughts.

Casting a glance to his right, he silently envied Ted Hollander the distraction of checking dials and readouts on the controls. He had nothing to do as they descended except wait and think about the millions of tons of water outside, eagerly waiting to crush the small craft at the first sign of weakness.

So far, the front window looked strong and intact, but according to the *Osprey's* submersible engineer, that didn't mean a thing. Everything he'd learned from that cheerful fellow while the sub was being prepped for launch reeled through his head, in fast forward.

"Don't worry, Mr. Arkovic, they designed this sub to easily withstand the pressure at the depth you'll be working in today. So as long as Ted doesn't go crashing into the harvester in the dark, you'll be fine."

"And if he does bump into the harvester?"

"Jarring the vehicle can cause uneven distribution of stress on critical areas."

"Critical areas?"

"Certain parts of the sub are more likely to fail first if exposed to uneven pressures. Window seals, seams between bulkhead plates, the door on the airlock."

"What would be a sign that they might fail?"

The man clapped him on the shoulder with a chuckle. "Don't worry about it, sir. If you see a crack in the window or a seeping wall seam, it's already too late."

"Terrific."

"Seriously, you have nothing to worry about," the engineer said again, "The sub has plenty of exterior lights and Ted knows what he's doing. Betcha this ride is gonna be smooth as silk."

"Just like Hollander's shuttle runs, eh?"

Devon closed his eyes to shut out the sight of all the blackness outside. He lifted a hand to his mouth pretending to cover a small fake cough as an excuse to wipe away the film of sweat collecting on his upper lip.

"Hello?" said a small voice in his headphones. "Is anyone there?"

He realized he'd left his comm channel to the airlock open, and that Annika had taken his throat clearing noises as a prelude to conversation.

"Yes, yes. We're here," he answered quickly. He glanced over at Hollander again, but the pilot ignored him. Either Ted was not listening in, or he just couldn't be bothered to chat with passengers. "That is, I'm here. It's Devon Arkovic. The pilot is busy right now."

"Oh?"

"Yes, but everything's fine. Uh, I mean, we're descending normally. Umm, how are you?"

"Well, it's cold, and it's dark, and I can't see anything out this little window."

"Gee, I'm sorry. I don't know if that airlock even has a light, but I'll check, okay?"

He fumbled with the switch to put the channel on standby so that he could talk to Ted without Annika hearing him.

"Hey Hollander, is there a light in the airlock that we can turn on for Annika?"

"No, there isn't," Ted snapped. "Now shut up."

As if to underline that comment, a loud groan punctuated with sharp popping sounds emanated from the walls of the sub. Devon gripped the bar protruding from the front of his control panel just as a loud clang reverberated up through the floor and he felt himself being tossed sideways.

"Holy hells! What was that?"

"Hang on," Ted ordered tersely, gripping the steering yoke a little tighter as he squinted at the controls.

Devon felt his seat tilting forward till he was literally hanging over the control board. His breath made panicked little patches of fog on the armored glassteel of the front view port as he waited to see what would happen next. The engines revved higher and there was another jolt accompanied by a softer bang and then the motion of the sub smoothed out again. Ted slowed the vehicle and leveled its attitude.

"There we go," Ted said, sagging back into his own chair. "We're okay now."

"What happened?"

"Thermocline," Ted shrugged. "Layers of water at different temperatures. Gave us a little resistance the first time, so I had to take a run at it to get through."

"I see. Well, thanks for the heads up on that Hollander."

He wondered if Ted had even considered the consequences of 'uneven pressures on critical areas' before he muscled the sub through that obstruction.

"Sorry, sorry. I didn't expect it to be such a problem. But I'll let you know the next time one is coming up."

"Next time?" Devon's heart did a little flip-flop. "How many of these things are there?"

"Depends," Ted shrugged. "Sometimes only a couple, sometimes more."

"Terrific."

"Aren't you going to answer?" Ted asked, pointing at a light on the control panel that was flashing. "Looks like Little Miss Fish tails wants an update."

"Oh geez, is that the com signal light?"

Hollander just laughed while he fumbled around, trying to reopen the circuit.

"Annika? Annika, are you okay in there?"

"A little bruised, maybe. That was quite a bump."

"Yeah, sorry about that. The pilot says we had a little trouble getting through the thermocline. He'll try to warn us next time if it's going to get bumpy."

"That would be nice."

"I'm sure we'll both appreciate it."

He smiled as he detected a trace of a chuckle from her end of the line. Just as he had hoped, rather than compounding her own misery, hinting at his own discomfort had indeed cheered her up.

"So, did I hear somewhere that you have greater than normal strength along with an upgraded intellect?" he asked her, switching topics.

"Yeah, so?"

"I was just thinking that's a feature that might come in handy on a carnival ride like this."

"Carnival ride? What's that?"

"Well, you Marnian girls sure don't get out much, do you?"

"What?"

"No carnivals, and probably no bootleg off-world vids either. So what do you do on a first date around here?"

"Well, on my first date, we went to the arena and watched some gladiators pound each other to death."

"Really? And where did he take you on the second date?"

"We never had a second date."

"Glad to hear it. How did you end up dating such a loser in the first place?"

"Oh, he was one of the three men that my father picked out as contenders to be my husband."

"I see. So you had a very limited pool of options for this first date. Seems like your dad had great taste in men."

"Well, let's just say his priorities were a little different than mine."

"I guess so, since you did lead the revolution that removed him from power."

"Yeah, well, what are you gonna do? Some families have all the tyrants."

"Rough patch coming up," Ted interrupted.

"Hang on back there," Devon called to Annika, reaching for his own grab bar.

This time, the turbulence was minor.

"Hey what happened to this carnival stuff you promised me?" Annika said.

"Sorry, ma'am, we'll try to do better next time."

"Would you two cut the chatter?" Ted growled. "We're almost to the ocean floor."

"What's wrong now?" Annika asked.

"The pilot says we're close to the ocean floor now, so hang on for some maneuvering while we search for the harvester."

Headlamps illuminated a space in front of the sub, but there was still nothing to see. Devon closed his eyes and clung to his grab bar, bracing for the crash that would end it all. Ted muttered and fussed over his instruments, relaying what he saw on the scans to some techs on *Osprey* far overhead. Don't worry. Don't worry, he heard the submersible tech repeating over and over inside his head.

The sub began edging to the left and Devon risked cracking open an eye to get a glimpse of any sign of the harvester through the window.

"Hold position *Dive One*," he heard the voice of the captain order. "Now angle left two degrees."

"Roger, *Osprey*."

Devon switched on the channel to the airlock while Ted continued to maneuver the sub for more scans.

"I think we might have found what we were looking for," he told Annika.

"And I assume that there are no signs of any angry Gods to dispute your claim," she replied, again with that trace of a chuckle.

"Not so far. But I'm keeping my fingers crossed."

"Oh really? Is that what you do to scare an angry God?"

"No, but I would've tried it for that bumpy ride through the thermocline. If I hadn't been busy hanging on with both hands to keep from falling out of my seat."

"At least you have a seat," she shot back.

Devon did not reply, as he felt his eyes go wide. He sucked in a shaky breath as a murky shape loomed into view, lit by the beams of the headlights.

"Is that it?" he cried, pointing.

The shape outside the window crept closer as Ted inched the sub toward one end of the ancient machine.

"*Osprey*, this is *Dive One*," Ted said. "I can see the harvester."

***

Ted ignored the excited diplomat next to him but kept the channel to the ship open as he maneuvered the sub closer.

"Standby *Osprey*, I'm going closer to check out the cargo hold," he muttered into his headset.

A camera set into the waldo on the sub's articulated arm showed a view of a small portion of the harvester. The camera view was displayed in the top corner of the sub's front window. As Ted delicately maneuvered the sub closer, the waldo reached out and activated an algae-encrusted panel on the side of the machine.

Suddenly, the faint sound of cheering tumbled from the speaker on the control panel.

"Readings show an eighty-two percent load!" a voice from the speaker blurted out, omitting all the formal com protocols.

A manic laugh burst from Ted's lips and he shot a quick look at his companion.

"Hot damn, Dip boy, we're gonna be rich," he cackled.

Arkovic only stared at the ancient harvester in silence. After releasing the waldo, Ted leaned back from his console and closed his eyes for a moment, taking advantage of this quick break from the intense concentration of piloting the sub while waiting for orders from the ship.

"So, what's next?" he heard Devon ask.

He didn't bother to open his eyes or look over, but he did grant the nervous Dipper a brief rundown. "Well, the Captain will look over the rest of the data from our scan of the harvester before deciding how to raise it. He could decide to deploy the other sub. But that'll take time."

Ted massaged the back of his neck. He was just picturing everything he intended to buy with his share of this treasure when the yammering from across the cabin started again.

"Is it possible for this sub to lift that gigantic machine by itself?"

"No, no, we'll use airbags to raise her. It's gonna be a three-legged bitch to get them in position, though, with her belly down on a soft bottom like that," Ted groaned. "We were hoping for some rock that would leave gaps to place the bags in."

Arkovic had just opened his mouth to ask something else when there was a squawk from the com panel.

"*Dive One*, this is *Osprey*. Begin deploying airbags. We have shuttle two with *Dive Two* on board in case you can't do it on your own, but you're the best we've got at handling the sub so, the captain wants you to give it a shot. Over."

"Roger that, *Osprey*. Deploying airbags. Will advise when ready to lift. *Dive One* out."

He got to work punching in commands to bring the waldo back to pick up the first airbag but his companion just couldn't seem to take the hint when someone was busy.

"So, how long is this going to take?" Arkovic asked.

Ted shot him an irritated glance. The Dipper looked sweaty and antsy, and Ted hoped he wouldn't end up having to trank the guy. "I don't know. Two or three hours, maybe."

Arkovic's jaw dropped, then he gulped and turned pale. For once, Ted had the satisfaction of seeing Dipper Devon with nothing to say.

Chapter 27: Bathys-Fear

Devon tried to remain patient as Ted worked, but the excitement of finding the treasure soon waned. It was replaced by an oppressive awareness of the sheer amount of cold, pitiless water pressing down on the tiny sub.

It had been an hour since he had taken to pulling out hairs on his forearms to keep his mind off the thought of imminent death here in the cold black depths. Each time his throat started closing down so that he couldn't breathe, Devon would slowly extract one of those hairs so that the pain forced him to gasp up another breath.

I hope I won't have to resort to pulling hairs further down before this is over. That could get embarrassing.

While he was busy with his defoliation project, Ted Hollander had been working to place several small servos connected to pancake-like airbag mechanisms in specific spots around the harvester. Each servo was controlled by a technician up on *Osprey*. Hollander used *Dive One's* stronger com channel to boost signals from the ship so that a group of technicians up in orbit could take control of the servos remotely and coordinate efforts to dig the bags under the harvester, then inflate the airbags simultaneously. Unfortunately for Devon, it was a very tricky operation, as they needed to make sure that the harvester remained level as it ascended. Balancing the lift on multiple airbags through hundreds of feet of pressure changes would be no small feat.

After everything was set up, Ted would move *Dive One* into position above the harvester and, using the sub's articulated arm, attach towing cables to various points on the ancient machine. The sub would only provide a small amount of lift while they raised the harvester to the surface, but it was essential for guiding the ascent.

Devon chatted on and off with Annika, trying to distract himself while Ted worked. He wished the designers had thought to include a window in the hatch that led to the airlock, but the chamber was only a solid faceless tube in the center of the sub. Although he knew how lucky he was to be here in a warm cabin, with lights and anyone at all sitting next to him for company, Ted was becoming more and more surly as his efforts to deploy the airbags ran into one snag after another.

"So, you said it might take an hour or two to position the airbags," he said to Ted.

Ted slapped some switches and squinted at the read out before he answered.

"Better not be longer because we don't have much more air than that."

"What? You mean we might have to leave the harvester here if you can't get these lift bags to work?"

"Maybe," Ted heaved a sigh. "But I'd rather not give up too soon. It will slow things down if the other sub has to take over.

That Adorian pilot, Cruglal, isn't nearly as good with the subs as I am, and I know my way around down here already, so it would be better if I stay and finish this."

Devon frowned but refrained from commenting. For all he knew, Ted was right about Cruglal. Everyone seemed to agree that Hollander was a particularly gifted pilot. He switched ground.

"But what about our air supply?"

Ted spared him a quick look.

"It might get a little tight, but we'll manage."

"And how about Annika? Does the airlock have enough O2 to keep her breathing that long?"

Ted shrugged in exasperation. "I don't know. Probably. But if you would let me get back to work, we will certainly all be better off."

Devon gritted his teeth as another section of that submersible engineer's little pre-launch pep talk ran through his head.

"There are readouts on the control panel to show oxygen status in the cabin. Don't worry if the readings get low, that only means your supply is running out. You will only experience hypoxia once the reading dips into the red range on the monitor. At that point, you won't be getting enough, but all the way until then, you'll be fine."

"How will I know if the airlock has adequate supply?" he asked the engineer. "Is there a separate readout for that?"

"No. The airlock isn't normally supplied with oxygen when it's filled with water, so we've had to rig up a conduit to bubble oxygen through that area, but there is no way to determine saturation level."

"Then how will we know if Anni–I mean the Marnian–is getting enough?"

The engineer shrugged. "Who knows? It was their idea to have one of their people ride along. This was the best we could do on short notice."

Devon took a firm grip on his temper.

"Listen, this Marnian is a very important person. Isn't there something more we can do to ensure she'll be able to breathe down there?"

"I don't know what," the engineer shrugged again. "But if they are anything like us, I would be more worried about a buildup of CO_2 in the lock. There was nothing we could do to set a up a wet filter for CO_2 in the time we had."

The idea of using concern for Annika's welfare as a way to make Ted give up and let the other sub pilot take over flitted through his mind and kept right on going.

Ted will never give up his fight for this pile of riches for her sake.

It was a harder decision whether to tell Annika about the danger. In the end, he just bit his tongue and kept quiet. He had enough problems of his own dealing with these delays without adding any distress from her into the mix. In fact, after talking with Ted, he found that he was no longer able to look out the sub's viewport without breaking into a sweat.

"Are you ok, Devon?" a warm, concerned voice in his headphones asked a few minutes later.

He wondered if she was asking because she'd noticed how the sound of his breathing had turned heavy and labored.

"Well, I'd trade all this waiting for any kind of carnival ride right about now," he replied weakly.

"Me too," she said. "If I never spend half a day in a cold, dark airlock again, I think that will be just fine with me."

"So, tell me more about these storms of yours."

"Oh, uh sure. Well, when the storm comes, it brings us the purple algae. It's a rich source of nourishment that is quite rare during all other seasons. That is why parents and their Moddrs always time the decanting of our offspring with the beginning of the storm. That way, there is plenty of food for the new little ones and their parents during their early days. While the storm lasts, gathering supplies of the purple is as easy as laying out containers and letting them fill themselves."

"So, food just falls from the sky, does it?"

"From the sky? No, but the entire warm zone from Mount Dornan in the north to Onclat at the South point is filled with the stuff. The entire city turns purple and there is no point in wearing any other color, since it will become stained in no time."

"That must be quite a sight."

"Yes, purple is the color of celebration. The storm is a time of plenty. A brief respite from concern about food. Some call it a shower of grace to welcome the new offspring."

"So, all babies on Marna are born during one brief span of days each year?"

"Is that uncommon?" she asked.

"Well, many species have what is called a breeding cycle that is timed so that abundant food is available soon after the young arrive. But it is one feature of standard humans that we are not limited to procreating at a single season during the year. Airbreather humans can conceive and bear children during any season."

"Well, your Moddrs must appreciate that arrangement," Annika laughed. "I know ours find the pre-storm demand for their services very tiring."

"Actually, Annika, standard human couples do not require any kind of assistance from anyone in order to procreate."

"Really? Do you grow your own, er, connectors for the process? And how do you check the zygotes for coding errors? And what about upgrades for the embryos? Surely, you're not all able to do your own upgrades for your offspring?"

"Uh, Annika, I think we've strayed into an area that is beyond my ability to explain."

"Oh? Well, I suppose it is complicated. Perhaps when we have access to download files with diagrams, you could show me what you mean."

"Yes, I think that might be best," Devon muttered.

The uncomfortable warmth that had spread over his face wasn't helping the queasy feeling in his gut at all.

"Let me check in with Ted and see how much longer it's going to be before we start back up to the surface."

"Oh yes, that would be wonderful. I've been bracing my feet against the wall to keep my fins from bumping, but now I think the pattern of the bolts behind me is going to be permanently imprinted on my back."

"So, Ted, how goes it?" he asked the pilot.

"Not good," Ted growled. "Servos three and ten can't get their airbags to respond, so I may have to go and trigger them manually and hope that doesn't tip the harvester over before we even start the ascent."

"Oh, uh, so do you have an idea how long that will be?"

"No Arkovic, I don't," Ted snapped. "Now, will you shut up and let me concentrate here?"

Devon squeezed his hands between his knees and tried not to check the time display on the console again. He could swear that the cold from the window was seeping into the bare skin of his neck between the collar of his ship suit and the bottom of his hair. Worming its way down into his bones. Freezing his blood so that his heart stuttered to a stop and …

He sank down under the console to escape the draft from the window. Then he went back to pumping Annika for interesting tidbits about Marna to keep his mind off his multiplying fears while he waited.

"So, Annika! What's the deal with these gladiators? How come they all have green skin when no one else does?" he said.

"They get an infusion of symbiotic algae when they are first dedicated to the pits. It's supposed to help them with stamina during their bouts because the gill covers they wear while fighting limit their ability to process oxygen. The longer they survive in the arena, the more algae they grow, so they may gain a greater advantage over time."

"While becoming ever more weird looking."

"Yeah, they do look kind of hideous. Maybe it helps them intimidate their opponents. But it also means that they can never leave the pits and do any other kind of work. They are marked for life as Glads."

"And how do you know so much about all this?"

"Remember, my first date? That guy knew a hoard's worth of information about Glads."

Devon found that he could no longer hide the fact that he was shivering uncontrollably as he slid lower to lie curled in a ball under the console.

"P-p-perhaps we c-could talk about something e-else for a while?"

"Are you okay, Devon? Devon? Hello?"

His teeth were chattering too much for him to respond.

And I came along thinking I'd be taking care of her.

Despite Annika's efforts, he could feel the edges of his mind beginning to unravel under the constant pressure of claustrophobia. He thought about asking her if she knew any jokes, except that he worried that if he started laughing, he might not stop.

Blast and damn Alistair. How did I ever let him talk me into this? I'm going to die down here and it's all his fault.

"Hey Arkovic," he heard Ted's voice saying from far away. "What's going on? Talk to me, man."

As his hands came up to cover his face, the terror he'd been holding at bay finally rolled over him. The last thing he felt was a quick sting on the side of his neck before his mind slipped away to lose itself on a dark plain of memories.

Chapter 28: A LEAP Too Far

All concerns drifted away as the drug hit Devon's system. Nothing bothered him anymore and he felt light and almost giddy. He'd just been thinking about Alistair when Ted snuck up and dosed him with something, so his mind drifted happily back to the memory of where this all began. Back to that meeting with Alistair on Marvet VII.

It was quite a surprise when the base com tech delivered a message pad telling Devon that he had a visitor arriving today. These days, most people communicated by subspace com rather than making tedious journeys through space to speak in person. The message said Alistair had urgent business to discuss.

What business could be so important that anyone would travel all the way out to Marvet VII on a freighter?

Devon spotted his old pal immediately as he sauntered into the recreation area after the day shift. Red-haired, laughing, and with a beer in each hand, Alistair Donahue hadn't changed a bit.

"Over here!" Alistair roared out, waving a beer in case Devon was too blind to spot him.

"Good to see you, Alistair."

"Come and have a drink," Alistair said, as he slid into a booth cradling his precious cargo. "Not one of these, though. They're mine."

"I'll be right back then," Devon nodded, changing direction to head for the bar.

He edged his way through a jolly group of off-duty personnel who were all toasting Commander Norfolk as the hero of the beer run. The commander had returned from the sector supply depot today on the same freighter that delivered Alistair. Norfolk had made the run personally to take charge of a few classified communiques from HQ, plus a large quantity of mission critical beer. He was the man of the hour, and Devon had to throw a few sharp elbows to get near enough to place his own order at the bar.

"Ok, Alistair," he said a few minutes later, sliding into the booth with a glass of his own, "so what's so important that you had to come all the way out here to talk to me instead of just sending me a COM?"

Alistair cast a glance at the rowdy celebration going on all around them.

"Can we take this somewhere more private, Devon? How about your quarters?"

"Actually, I've been having a few problems with the AI in my quarters, so if this really is important, maybe somewhere else might be better."

"You can't even trust your personal AI? What kind of dump is this?"

"Yeah, it's a long story. How about outside by the shuttle pad? No one is going to be out there now that we have beer on the base again."

***

They took a case of beer and a couple of oderet zappers to make their departure for the privacy of the shuttle pad less conspicuous.

Oderets were the local scavenger species on Marvet VII and on a personal level, Devon felt that they were tailor-made to arouse every anti-reptilian, anti-insectoid, anti-rat phobia that existed in the human psyche. They looked like a snake, a tarantula, and a dock-rat had a baby together and then flattened it with a shuttle.

Over the years, these disgusting pests had broken the nerve of more than one Dip Corps officer assigned to Marvet VII. Finding one grinning up at you when you had just dropped your pants in the Personal Sanitation Chamber was enough to make even the steadiest Dipper want to run screaming to find a hermetically sealed medico capsule to mail themselves home in.

In addition to their nightmarish looks, oderets had voracious appetites and chewed everything they touched to bits, even if they didn't eat it. Apart from the dust, the tedium and the general hopelessness of the mission, oderets were one of the worst aspects of a posting on Marvet VII.

Fortunately Dip Corps HQ shared the general opinion on the subject of oderets. So much so that every employee on the base was charged with the responsibility of making sure none of the little horrors ever made it into a shuttle or cargo container to escape the planet. Dip Corps was determined not to be held responsible for aiding the revolting things to colonize the rest of the galaxy.

Faithful to those orders, Devon had spent many long hours honing his skills with a zapper, so he anticipated scoring a big win off Alistair in tonight's competition.

"Alright, let me get this straight, Alistair. You want me to go lead the team that makes First Contact with this isolated society, abandoned over three centuries ago on the fabled planet of Marna?"

"That's about the size of it."

"Well, that sounds great, Al. Just one question, though. What makes you think that you even know how to find this planet? It's supposed to be lost, remember? Co-ordinates shrouded in the deepest security. So how do you, of all people, know where it is?"

Alastair leaned forward, eyes gleaming. "Ah, but I do know!"

"On your right, Al," he interrupted, pointing with the muzzle of the zapper in his right hand while trying not to spill the beer in his left.

Alistair splashed him with a liberal dose of beer while drawing a bead with his own zapper on a small form scuttling through the brush toward the shuttle.

"Damn. Missed him," Alistair swore, frowning at the blaster in his hand then consoling himself with a large slug from the container in his other fist.

They had positioned themselves with their backs against a large rock close to where the freighter's shuttle stood cooling in the night breeze. Devon knew that heat given off by any vehicle that had just made atmospheric entry would attract hordes of oderets. Given how fast they scuttled around on their eight scaly legs, it was always a tricky task to draw a bead on one with a zapper. Between the distraction of consuming several rations of beer and explaining the reason for his visit, Alistair was having very little luck in their game.

"Don't worry, Al, you'll get one, eventually. Now, you were saying you know the location of the planet. How, exactly?"

"Ah yes, Marna. Chance of a lifetime. Are you in?"

"Like I was just saying, all the bedtime stories about Marna say that its location was a secret. So, how did you come to know where the LEAP Corporation's supply of Glaeon came from?"

"I know, because my grandfather used to be on the board of directors at LEAP."

"Oh, stuff it out an airlock, Alastair. Hey. Three on the right."

This time Devon took out the lead oderet so the other two would pause to investigate the barbecued remains, allowing Alistair an easier shot.

"Got him. Got one of those beasties at last," Alistair crowed. "Great Galaxies. What is that smell?"

"Yeah, that happens sometimes when you hit one near the hind end. But let's get back to this yarn of yours. You were trying to convince me that your grandfather—"

"Oh yes, grandad was on the board of LEAP. Ready for another?"

Alistair fished in the case of beer, searching for an unopened container, and held one out toward Devon, looking as innocent as a child.

"Now stop trying to take me for a fool, Alistair." He accepted the container with a nod of thanks and broke the seal. "I know very well that when you and I were in school together, we were both poor scholarship boys. I also know you always shipped out to spend every holiday in Brock City on Vallos. Not exactly the stomping grounds of the rich and famous there, buddy."

"And don't I know it?" Alistair grimaced. "But do you know what I used to *do* during all those school vacations, Devon?"

"No, but I feel sure you're about to tell me."

"I'd spend the entire time listening to my grandad telling me all about how he used to be a big shot at LEAP. The old coot would ramble on for hours about his glory days when the company first got started. Bragging about how rich he used to be before the invention of synthetic Glaeon ruined the company."

"Is that right?"

"Yes, that's right. Look there. On the left."

Alistair blasted another target and hoisted his beer in a joyous toast.

"I'm not kidding, Devon. My grandad was really *old*. He had Glaeon anti-aging treatments from the very beginning. My mom too. Of course, grandad got a bit daffy near the end. Not from Synthetic Glaeon Psychosis, you understand. His treatments were completed long before that crappy stuff came on the market. No, it was just normal old age stuff you'd see in anyone over the age of two hundred. But he used to show me holos of the atmospheric racing shrike he used to have, and the big estate where he and Mom lived. Even pointed out the little moon he'd once thought about buying on the system maps. Everyone from our dumpy neighborhood in Brock City thought he was just a crazy old man making up wild stories. But he always insisted that he was in on LEAP from when it first started. Then after he died, I found the coordinates for Marna in his valuables vault. Willed it to me, he did. There was even a note saying how grandad wanted to be sure that I would be the one to carry on the family secret."

"Uh, huh."

"You don't believe me? Well, how do you think I made it into Thurston Haus then? Private schools like that are for spoiled brats from the families of high-level politicos and the cronies of royalty."

"Hey, what? Who are you calling a spoiled rich kid?"

"Not you, Devon. You were the only decent sod in the whole place. But the rest of that lot all bleed platinum when you punch their little noses."

"Yeah, it was certainly no picnic being a scholarship boy at Thurston. Aim left."

They shot and drank again, finishing their containers.

"Yeah, I guess we both hated it there," Devon sighed. "But my parents were so proud that I qualified to get in that I just stuck with it."

"To parents and their cherished dreams," Alistair chuckled, passing Devon a fresh beer without spilling any of it.

They touched containers, and Devon sucked in a generous amount as they both took a moment to remember their youth.

"But at least you earned your scholarship," Alistair said, pounding on his chest to hammer loose an enormous belch.

"What do you mean?"

"This is what I'm telling you, Devon. I didn't qualify for Thurston Haus. My mother was a LEAP Corporation heiress who got a pity scholarship for me out of some of those vultures at Sorenson Brothers who picked LEAP to pieces after the bottom fell out of the Glaeon market."

"Uh, huh? So, if your mother was an heiress, then it was your family who stranded the colonists on Marna after the company collapsed?"

"Well, it wasn't like they had a choice. Ma said liquidation arbiters appointed by the courts swooped in to break up LEAP after the Sorensons' announcement about their invention of synthetic Glaeon. It was the liquidators who wrote off the Marnian operation. Once all the company debts were paid, they claimed there were not enough assets left to finance a voyage to retrieve the colonists, never mind reverse their body mods once they got home."

"I see."

"Honest. All the top brass over at Sorenson Brothers came out of that deal with fat little fortunes. The liquidators awarded them a big chunk of LEAP assets because they held senior bonds from the early financing of LEAP. After they took their share, there was nothing left in the kitty to rescue the colonists."

"Well, that stinks. How could they just abandon those people? I thought Sorenson Brothers was such a reputable company."

"Not in those days. Competition was cutthroat and the big boys over at So&So were no saints. But my old ma heard about a few other shady things the Bros pulled over the years. She held

259

onto that info too. Used it to wring a few favors out of the assholes from time to time."

"You're making all this up. Your mother was no LEAP Company heiress."

"Four on the right."

They shot, scored, and drank again.

"Sure, she was. Way before I was born, my mom was married to Plantario Oomatzi."

"Who?"

"Oomatzi. He was the third largest shareholder in LEAP. The silent partner in the venture, so you never heard very much about him. But it was Oomatzi who got grandad onto the board of directors at LEAP to help manage our family's share of the stock."

"Oh, give it a rest, Alastair. Shoot left."

"Damn, missed again."

They drank anyway.

"You expect me to believe that you are related to one of the original partners in LEAP?"

Devon accidentally wiped his mouth with the hand holding his zapper.

"Upon my honor! My mother was an Oomatzi before she married a Travers. And then a Wershott. And then a Donahue."

Gulping down the last of his drink, Devon stared at the empty container in one hand and then the zapper in the other.

"That's a very inspirational story, chum, but—"

"Yes, once they go Irish, they never go back! Dad was a real keeper."

"I'm sure."

"No, I'm serious. Dad was a goalkeeper for the New Belfast Ballers. Continental champions six years running. Would've made it to the All Planet Finals if their star forward hadn't snapped a tentacle."

"Alastair?"

"Yeah?"

"Shut up a minute, so I can think."

Alastair pouted quietly while Devon worked out what was wrong.

"You know, we might be a little too drunk to be using zappers."

"You think?"

"You almost shot your nose off trying to scratch your ear just now, and I can't figure out which hand to lift to get a sip. Yes, I'm sure."

"Damn, just when my aim was improving. Well, power them down then and we'll put 'em in here with the empties," Alistair grumbled, holding open the empty beer case. "Don't know how you stand it here with the beer rationing and creepy crawlies and the damn dust everywhere. Why aren't you jumping at a chance to leave?"

"Listen, Al, you know I would love to get off this rock and go help with whatever slagbrained scheme to restart the family business you've got going on. But can you imagine me waltzing into Commander Norfolk's office to tell him I'd like to take a few months off to go chase down the Legendary Lost Colony of Marna?"

"Well, why don't you tell him something else, then?"

"Are you suggesting that I lie to my commanding officer?"

"Oh, for the love of fairy farts, why not?"

"It may be news to you, buddy, but lying is frowned upon in most of the rest of the galaxy, not occupied by Alistair Donahue. Besides, I'd feel bad about abandoning my post after I just signed up for another three-year hitch here."

"Why in all the blazing novas would you do a stupid thing like that?"

Devon felt his cheeks warming. "There was this girl."

"Ah, of course there was."

"No, I mean a really special girl."

"Well then, why don't you ask this feminine wonder to come along? What's her area of expertise, anyway? Apart from tickling your fancy."

"She's an exobiologist."

"How perfect. I'd love to have her join the expedition to Marna."

"Then you can just head over to Galva III and invite her. She transferred there to study some new ruins they discovered two months ago."

Alistair roared with laughter, sending dozens of oderets scuttling away through the underbrush.

"Right after you signed up for three more years in this hellhole? Oh, that's rich. So, there's nothing holding you back from going to Marna then?"

Devon drained the last of his beer and slammed the container back into the case of empties.

"Of course, there's something holding me back, Al. I can't go because I have my career to think of. Also, I still believe there's a chance Dip Corps could end up doing some good here on Marvet VII by providing a neutral party to arbitrate this destructive conflict."

"What a bunch of 'cycler sludge." Alistair sniffed, rolling his head back and forth on the rock they were leaned against. "The negotiations here on Marvel number nine—"

"Marvet VII."

Alistair waved a hand in time with his head. "Whatever. The point is, talks here have been stalled for years. The newsies don't even report on this fiasco anymore. From what I can see, no one will even miss you."

"Gee, thanks."

"What I mean is, the idiots on this dust ball have been arguing for decades. What makes you think they are suddenly going to come to their senses and start behaving rationally at any point during your lifetime?"

"I can't just up and leave my post because Alastair Donahue thinks the situation is hopeless."

"But Dip Corps doesn't need you like I do," Alistair whined. "I've got to have a friend I can trust to run this negotiation with any descendants of those colonists on Marna for me. Come on Devon, I'm offering you the chance to make First Contact with a society that has been living isolated from the greater galaxy for generations. How can you pass that up?"

"Yes, Alistair, of course. It would be great to be involved in some important work like that. But I can't just put my career on

263

hold, to run off and do a job for you. Be reasonable."

"But isn't this kind of thing right up your alley? As a career diplomat, I mean. Just think, you'd be helping those vulnerable people make the transition to a better life. Don't you Dippers always yammer on about how it's your job to make a real difference or some such thing? How are you going to do that if you're just rotting out here on this dust ball with your thumb up your butt?"

"Well, it's true this is not the best assignment I've ever had since I joined the Corps."

"Not the best? I'd call it an absolute disgrace to have a man your talents wasting away out here. Weren't you the savior of the whole mission on Parn IV? The one who risked his life to negotiate a ceasefire? Why it still brings a tear to my eye that it was my best friend who prevented the loss of thousands of lives that day. Millions even. Do you know how many times people have bought me free beers when I've trotted out that thrilling tale?"

Alistair stared at him pointedly until he grunted a grudging agreement to allow his guest to claim the last unopened container of beer.

"It's nothing less than criminal for someone of your caliber to be wasting away out here, Devon, and you know it."

"Alright, Alistair. I admit it would be nice to have something a bit more challenging to sink my teeth into."

"Of course it would. Haven't you always talked about the day when you'd be in charge of your very own mission? Well then, here's your chance! Your day has come. You, Devon, could be famous for making First Contact with those people out there on Marna. As well as a share of the profits."

"I'm sorry, Al, I really am. But I'd be risking my entire career."

"So what? Why can't you risk your career if you want to? You've got no wife or kids to support. Not even a girlfriend to consider now."

"Thanks for reminding me. I do have parents and a sister back on Calandria, you know."

"Ok, so you have family. Don't you want to become famous and make your parents proud of their wonderful son?"

"Of course, I do. But I doubt they will be proud of me for abandoning my duties to wander off chasing fame and riches."

"Whatever you wish to believe," Alastair murmured, inspecting a fingernail. "But I'm sure they'll be delighted when you come back and show them your share of the profits from this little jaunt."

"Yes, profits. Naturally, that would be great. I've always wanted to do more for my parents financially."

"Of course you have. I know if I still had a father, I'd jump at the chance to break away and go on a real adventure that would set me up for life, so that I could provide for him and my old ma. Just think, after this mission, your parents will never want for anything ever again. And you'll be rich enough to retire yourself."

"But I don't want to retire, Alistair. Apart from this assignment, I really love my job."

"Ah, but after this trip to Marna, think how famous you'll be.

I bet Dip Corps will be falling all over themselves to hire you back. They'll offer you your pick of assignments once you're known as the man who made First Contact with the people of Marna."

"Well, you could be right about that."

"Of course, I'm right. This mission could improve things for you in so many ways. You know it's the chance of a lifetime I'm offering you here, Devon. So come on now, what do you say, buddy?"

"Honestly, I really would like to go, Alistair. For a lot of reasons. It's just that I can't see any way to get an extended leave of absence. Commander Norfolk is way too smart to give anyone time off from this assignment. He knows that once people get away, he'll never see them again."

"In that case, perhaps this is our lucky day, my lad," Alistair chuckled, pointing with his chin through the recreation area window. "From what I can see, you could get halfway to Marna and back before your Commander Norfolk has even raised an eyelid after tonight's bender."

Following the direction of Alistair's gaze, he saw the very proper Commander Norfolk sitting tilted over in a booth, head bobbing as he giggled over a story that another officer appeared to be slurring in his direction.

"Just you leave that fellow to me," Alistair said, rubbing his hands together with a smile. "I promise, inside of ten minutes, I'll have him *ordering* you to ship out tomorrow morning or he'll fire you from the service himself."

"Wait what? What are you planning to say to him?"

"Trust me, it will be another tale to bring a tear to your eye," Alistair said, patting him on the shoulder. "But go ahead and rub some dust in yours first before we go in, will you?"

"What for?"

"We might as well make this look good, even if your commander can never recall a thing about it afterwards. Now drink up and let's get on with this before the fellow passes out."

He took one more drink for courage, then passed the container to Alistair.

"Are you sure this is necessary?" he asked after reluctantly scrubbing dust-covered knuckles into both his eyes.

"Well, you want to go on this mission, right?"

Alistair offered him a hand to help him to his feet, peering intently into his eyes.

"Yes. I have to admit I do."

"Fine. Then let me handle this part now, so you'll have a chance to do your part later."

The ground heaved and wobbled as Devon followed, half-blinded by dust, while Alistair led the way back toward the entrance to the dome. Oderets scurried and rustled about in the dark beyond the patch of light cast by their safety lights, heading for the warm shuttle. The idea of boarding that craft and permanently escaping this world made him almost giddy.

"Am I doing the right thing, Al?" he asked one more time as he poked around on the panel, trying to hit the correct button to open the door to the recreation area.

"Trust me, Devon, going on this mission is something you will never regret."

267

Fiona Kolodzy

Chapter 29: Ascent and Dissent

Devon almost gave into a fit of giggles as the memory of Alistair's words shredded and he returned to reality. The cold deck pressed into his cheek and the skin on his arms was burning where he'd sacrificed the hairs.

Sure, I'll never regret it, Al. Because very soon I'm going to be the galaxy's flattest diplomat. Its squishiest treasure hunter. I won't have to worry about how to spend my share of the profits 'cause I'll never see them. I'll never see anything else except black water and metal walls ... and ...

He dug his fingers into his leg with a painful grip to stop the rambling when his ears caught the distant sound of some chatter from the ship.

"... slow and steady, *Dive One*. Last thermocline coming up. After that, it's smooth sailing."

The movement had been so gradual that he hadn't noticed it while locked away in the vivid drug-assisted memory of that evening on a dry, dusty planet far, far away.

He raised his head from the deck trailing drool, then risked crawling back into his seat to strain through the front viewport for a glimpse of light or hope beyond. So far, there was nothing, but the voices from *Osprey* continued to talk about the ascent, so he pinned his hopes on that.

"Ah, you're awake," Ted said. "Good timing. Better strap in."

He fumbled with the buckles just in time for the appalling bump and screech as the sub shouldered its way into the next layer of ocean on its way to the surface.

The surface.

Devon could hardly wait. The fog was clearing from his brain, but it still felt like ants were scurrying over his skin. He was just selecting another hair to part with when he remembered Annika in the dark airlock.

How long has she been alone in there while I was drugged out on the floor?

His finger was just reaching for the com button when he realized how tight his throat was.

I don't want to scare her with some squeaky voice. Not after that big bump we just had.

He set about trying to clear his throat, so he'd sound normal, but every time he glimpsed the blackness outside the window, he felt another wave of dizziness overtake him.

Come on, Devon, pull it together. You're supposed to be here to help her, so help.

He punched the button without another thought.

"Uh, er, ahem. Uh, Annika? How are you doing?"

"Devon? Ish tha you?" Annika's voice drifted through his earphones. Her words sounded blurry somehow. He forced his eyes open a little further to check whether his vision was also fading along with his hearing. The ribbed walls of the sub still seem pretty clear, however, so he reached up a hand to settle the earphones back into place.

"'S awfully dark in here," Annika slurred. "When did ya say wur goin' home again?"

"Annika? Annika, what's wrong?"

"I dunno. M' gills feel funny. Like I can' lift 'em."

In a split second, all concern for himself sluiced away in a wave of fear for her safety.

"Ted! Ted, I think something's wrong with Annika. Can you tell what's going on in there?"

Ted shot him an irritated look, but he slapped a few switches and screwed up his face to peer at some readouts. Devon shut off the com link so that Annika wouldn't hear any bad news that Ted might decide to share.

"Looks like the O2 level has gotten pretty low in the lock."

"What? Why?"

"The tank they hooked up to recirculate the water and replenish the oxygen is almost empty. They didn't know the dive would go on this long, so the tank is running out now."

"Well, what are we going to do, then? Can't you hook up another tank for her?"

"No. Because there are no other tanks. We didn't bring any extras. Like I said, the geniuses who set up the airlock for her to ride in didn't know the mission would be this long, so they figured the tank they were using was already going to be more than enough."

Devon could feel his blood slowing and thickening in his veins as Ted's words washed over him. He pictured Annika suffocating alone in that upright coffin.

No way. Not while assholes like Ted get to live and breathe in comfort.

"But there has to be something we can do," he said to Ted. "We can't just sit here and let her die."

"Hey, it's not my fault. I didn't set up that system," Ted said.

"No one is talking about whose fault it is, Ted. I'm saying we have to try something—anything—before it's too late."

"What is it you want me to do? I'm a pilot, not an engineer."

"Well, engineer or not, you are the only one here with any technical expertise. Please Ted, I'm begging you, try to think of a way to get some oxygen into that system. She may not have much time left."

"So? Why am I suddenly responsible for saving her? It wasn't my choice to have her come along."

He backed off at Ted's belligerent tone. Riling the man up would not gain him Ted's co-operation.

Perhaps an appeal to his self-interest will do the trick.

"You know, Ted, those Marnians up there practically worship this woman. By the time we get back, there will probably be a bunch of them on hand, waiting to hear her report. If they don't see her swim out of that airlock alive and well, there could be a riot. Do you really think they are going to care which one of us screwed up and let her die?"

Precious seconds ticked by as he tried to imitate a rational man who had all the time in the world to debate these interesting issues.

"They could kill us both along with any other airbreather they can get their hands on, Ted. And if the Marnians go berserk, then our crew won't be able to finish getting the cargo off the harvester. Think about all that wealth floating right below the surface, just out of reach. If the Marnians decide to interfere with the recovery of the harvester, we could end up having to leave all that Glaeon behind when the pirates show up. Is that what you want?"

Ted scowled as he considered that scenario. "Well, there is one thing that might work," he said after a sullen pause. "We each have a small air tank attached to our personal dive gear."

"We have dive gear on board?"

"There are low depth dive suits with air tanks in that locker." Ted pointed. "In case we have to swim for it if we can't grapple the sub onto the surface vessel for some reason."

"So, we can hook one of those tanks up to the circulation system for the airlock?"

"Well, you can hook up your tank, but I'm not giving up my air for any fish-girl. I don't care what kind of prophet her people think she is. And that goes for you too, by the way. If you give up your air to her, don't expect me to be sharing my emergency tanks with you if we run into any problems later."

"Okay, okay, I get it. Just hurry up and do it, will you?"

He reopened the com channel to the airlock while Ted got busy digging out the emergency dive gear.

"Annika? Annika, can you hear me?"

There was no answer. He kept talking anyway, telling her what was going on. Hoping she could hear him and that it would help her hang on until oxygen started flowing again. He shot an anguished look at Ted when the pilot returned to his seat after hooking up the tank.

"Hey man, I've done all I can." Ted shrugged. "I hooked up the tank, and the gauge says the oxygen is flowing. She's either okay or already dead, but there's nothing else I can do for her.

Chapter 30: On Their Own

Devon sucked in a deeper breath as water outside the viewport went from black to deep blue and then green. The invisible bands locked around his chest loosened, but the longer he waited for a response from Annika, the hollower he felt inside. The airlock loomed behind him in the center of the room like a round upright metal coffin. It sickened him to think of Annika banging around in there, limp and helpless. Or even dead.

Ted seemed utterly indifferent to her fate, though. Hollander busied himself checking readings and then hailed *Osprey* to report their status as they ascended.

For the first time, there was no immediate response from the ship. The light outside was growing brighter though, so Ted sent out a pulse to home in on the surface platform's locator beacon.

"That's funny," Hollander said a moment later. "My scan shows no beacon within range. The current must have pushed us much further west than I realized."

Devon bit his lip, torn between calling out to Annika again and not annoying Ted while he was concentrating on this important task. He squirmed on the edge of his seat while Hollander slapped a control, muttering about increasing the range of the locator pulse. Just as the pulse went out for the third time, there was a crackling from the com circuit.

"*Dive One,* this is *Osprey.* Do you read? Over."

Ted's face lit up. "We read you, *Osprey.* Go ahead. Over."

"Be advised there is a large group of Marnians headed your way. They surrounded the surface platform a few minutes ago and threatened to scuttle her, so we've had to lift the vessel with our shuttles to prevent damage."

Ted shot a glare at Devon as if this mob he had predicted was his fault.

"Unless we can get the Marnians to stand down, the captain will have to order the shuttles to bring the platform all the way back into orbit," the com tech on *Osprey* said. "They can't hover with that much weight forever. Until it's safe to operate on the surface again, we can't risk setting the platform down to recover the sub or the cargo. Over."

"Copy that, *Osprey,*" Ted replied. "Hey, there they are. I see the Marnians approaching on scan. There sure are a lot of them. Over."

"Assume they are hostile, *Dive One,*" they heard the voice of Captain Doyle cut in on the com circuit. "Take the harvester back down to a depth where they can't follow and wait. Over."

"Wait for what?" Devon wondered aloud.

His forehead wrinkled as he puzzled over why Scylla and his men were not keeping these people away from this area, as agreed.

Scylla seemed so confident that people wouldn't even notice our operations the last time we spoke. Something is way out of whack here, unless it's Scylla's men who attacked the platform.

He wished Ted had mentioned their loss of contact with Annika to the captain. If she was unconscious, someone would need to help her out of the airlock from the outside. Dropping the sub below the habitable level would mean the Marnians could no longer assist her.

And if we stay down too long, she might die. Who knows how long it will be before the captain thinks it's safe to head to the surface again?

On top of his concern for Annika, the last thing Devon wanted was to descend into the black depths again. Jabbing at his com console, he added his voice to the link with the ship.

"Hey, hello, this is Devon Arkovic. Can somebody tell me what's going on? Why are the Marnians threatening us? Has anyone even talked to them?"

"Is that you, Arkovic?" the captain demanded.

"Yes, yes, I'm here! What happened with the Marnians?"

"All I know is that they attacked two of my divers in the water and then started trying to puncture one pontoon on the platform. The Chief got our divers back on board and called the shuttles for an emergency lift. Over."

"But did the divers say why were they attacked? Did something happen that upset the Marnians?"

Ted leaned across to growl at him. "You're supposed to say 'Over,' stupid, so they know it's their turn to talk."

But the captain didn't wait for protocol. "As far as I know, our guys were just doing their work under the platform when a bunch of Marnians showed up screaming insults and attacked them. No major damage, just cuts and bruises, but the two of them were pretty shaken up. Over."

Devon gritted his teeth as the view outside the window darkened again.

"But we have a deal with the Marnian Leader for safe passage to recover this cargo, so there's no reason they should be attacking us. Are you sure the divers didn't provoke them? Over."

"Captain Doyle," Ted interrupted. "Scan shows a couple of hundred of them out there and they've moved to surround us. If I keep descending, I can't avoid hitting some of them. Request instructions. Over."

"Ok, *Dive One*, hold position. We don't want to antagonize them. They might try to grab onto the load and destabilize it. Then we'll lose the harvester. Over."

"That's true, captain but we can't just hang around down here. We'll run out of air. What's the plan? Over."

"Just hold position there, *Dive One*. Shuttle Two has some explosives on board and Chief Simmons thinks he can improvise some kind of depth charge to scare them off. Over."

Devon's hair stood on end. And from the look on Ted's face, they were in total agreement regarding that idea.

"But sir," Ted said. "What if the explosion ruptures the sub? Or even just destabilizes the load? Isn't there something else we can try? Over."

Every instinct was telling Devon he should take charge before things got out of hand. He poked at the studs on the com panel to rejoin the conversation.

"Captain Doyle, sir?" Devon said, "I recommend we talk to

the Marnians before we start dropping bombs on them. I made a deal with their Leader. Perhaps if I can find out what's gone wrong, I can fix it. Let me try to talk to them before you try scaring them away."

"Stand by, *Dive One*," a voice from the ship replied.

He and Ted shared a worried look as they waited for the captain's decision. Meanwhile, they could see the mob shifting closer to the sub every moment.

"They'd better not start grabbing onto the cable. If they destabilize our load, the harvester might pull us down along with it," Ted said, keeping an anxious eye on the scan.

"Can't you just detach the cable and let the harvester fall? Then maybe the other sub could go down after it once this situation with the Marnians is resolved."

"You don't know what you're talking about, Arkovic," Ted snarled. "If we drop the harvester, the cargo hold might break loose on impact, and get damaged. If it does, the entire cargo might get ruined."

"But won't the airbags slow the fall of the harvester and cushion the impact?"

"Maybe, but if the hold comes loose but doesn't fully separate from the harvester, we can't cut it free with a torch in the pressure at those depths. And we might not be able to pull the harvester up again if the hold is hanging off one side. It would make the load too unbalanced for us to handle. Plus, the hold could tear off and fall if the ascent got bumpy. And all of that supposes that we're allowed to go back down and get it another day and that the pirates haven't already shown up to blow us all to hell first and—"

"Ok, ok, I get it Ted."

There was another long silence as he and Ted watched more and more dots appear around the icon on the screen representing *Dive One*. All at once, shadowy figures appeared in the water along the edge of the pool of light cast by the sub's arc lamps. He looked at Ted for direction, but Hollander just shook his cocked his head and shrugged. Only static hissed from the com channel as the seconds ticked past and more Marnians appeared. At last, the captain's voice boomed out from the speaker again.

"Alright, *Dive One*, it seems like there's nothing to lose now. They're too close to the sub and cargo to try a depth charge. You try talking to them, Arkovic. *Osprey* out."

Devon resettled his headphones and took a deep breath. "Ok, Ted, which one is the control for the external speaker?"

Ted leaned over and punched a stud for him.

"Attention, citizens. This is Devon Arkovic speaking to you from inside the vehicle. Is SharScylla there with you? I would like to speak with him."

There was a long pause while clouds of silt and fragments of algae blew past the view port. Then the outlines of three people appeared, moving into the circle of light around the sub. Devon felt a wave of relief as he recognized the compact form of Suni between two larger Marnians.

At least I know Suni will care about helping us get Annika out of the airlock.

"Hello, Suni," he said, giving the 'linker a little wave. "It's good to see you again. Can you tell me what's going on here?"

The two larger ones shoved Suni closer to the view port and then fell back a short way.

"Greetings, SharArkovic," Suni called out formally without returning the wave. "SharScylla is not here. I am sent to convey the words of the leader of the True Believers to you. He does not wish to be contaminated by contact with foreign machines that have defiled the realm of the Gods Below."

"I see. But Suni, do these True Believer people know we got permission from SharScylla and the blessing of the elder Abang before making our journey? Are they aware that the Marnian representative Annika also accompanied us, to ensure that we caused no offense to the Gods on our mission? I assure you, we have adhered to all our promises, and not disturbed any Gods."

Suni glanced left and right, then clasped his hands together, moving a little closer to the sub.

"I believe you, SharArkovic, but this group is concerned that the—item—you obtained," he inclined his head at the harvester dangling below the sub, "is, er, the rightful property of the Gods. They claim they and not the Aban are the only true and faithful servants of the Gods Below, so they must defend the divine property and—"

The two larger Marnians moved forward to snatch hold of Suni at that point. Ted stared wild-eyed as Suni was dragged away, so Devon touched the studs to close the external com and open the channel to the airlock instead.

"Annika? Are you there? We have a problem."

281

Chapter 31: Negotiate or Die

When Annika awoke, it was less dark than it had been before, but the water in the airlock tasted stale. Her head ached and her gills still felt curiously numb. Twitching her arm fins aside, she inched her way upward to where the short stem on top of the sub, which held the door to the airlock, had a small window. The water outside was dark blue, but there was no way to know what amount of pressure was present out there. After so long trapped in this dark, cramped space, she felt an overwhelming urge to just open the door and take her chances. Then she remembered the two airbreather men in the other part of the sub.

If I passed out, then something might have happened to them, too. I can't just leave without making sure Devon is ok.

"Devon? Devon are you there?" she called out.

His response was immediate.

"Annika? Great galaxies, it's good to hear your voice. Are you okay?"

His question, along with the relief she could hear in his voice, brought it all back to her. The terrible suffocating sensation creeping over her, then the smell of fear swirling around her before she blacked out.

"I'm better now," she said. "I can see some light from the window, but we aren't moving. What's going on?"

"Ah, yes. Well, we are closer to the surface. But there is a large group of Marnians blocking our way."

"Blocking us?" she said. "Why would they do that? Aren't they Scylla's men?"

"No, I just spoke to Suni. The leaders of this mob sent him forward to speak for them. He says this group calls themselves the True Believers, and he hinted they are a new faction not under the control of Scylla or the elders of the Temple."

"Hmm, well, I've never heard of them, so Suni must be right. Did he say what they want?"

She craned her neck for a glimpse of any people out the tiny window, but there were none in view.

"Suni tells me this group believes we stole the harvester from the Gods Below. I think they might want us to give it back."

Annika's brain went into overdrive, assessing the possibilities of this new situation.

"Devon? I think I should go talk to them," she said. "Many people see me as Aban. Since this is a religious group, I think there's a strong chance that I can gain influence over them. Then I can tell them to let you two go, even if they still demand that you return the harvester."

If I get control of these fanatics now, then after Devon is gone, maybe I can use them to build up a base of support for a new movement to oppose Scylla.

Her eyes gleamed at the prospect of toppling another tyrant.

"You just wait here, Devon. I'm going to get you out of this, I promise."

"Annika, wait. You can't go out there. These people might be dangerous."

Ignoring him, she returned to the top of the lock and flipped up the cover on the controls for the hatch.

"Annika, stop. This isn't a good idea. There's more I need to tell you."

She could hear Devon pleading with her, but the idea of freedom just outside that door drowned him out. Besides, it made no sense that any Marnian other than Scylla might wish her harm. Within moments, the wheel on the door spun and a gush of clean water flooded in around her. Shoving the hatch of her prison wider, she sprang out at last, into the open ocean beyond.

***

Devon sat on the cold metal deck of the sub, yanking on the lower half of a wetsuit while the airlock pumped down. Ted stood beside him, arms folded, looking doubtful.

"I can't let her face that mob alone, Ted. The captain said they've already attacked people today, but I didn't have time to tell her about that. Who knows what kind of mood they're in? They might kill her before she even gets a chance to speak to them."

"I don't know, Arkovic. What is it you think you can do that she can't?"

"She may be a leader, Ted, but it is literally my job to negotiate with hostile people. *Osprey* can't do anything to help us and there's no sign of Scylla's men, so we're on our own. We've got to do something before the sub runs out of air. I'm thinking if I approach them in her company, at least some of them will hesitate to attack us, which will give me time to talk to them."

Ted still looking unconvinced while Devon wriggled into the top half of his suit.

"Look, Hollander, these people believe in the Gods Below, right? I have an idea of how to use their religious superstitions to save our cargo."

"Sounds good, but what am I supposed to do once you get yourself killed out there, playing hero?"

"I don't know, Ted. I'll do my best to get a deal for you and the cargo, but if things go bad, you're the pilot. Maybe if you dump the harvester and then blow the ballast for an emergency ascent, you might have a few minutes for the shuttle to pick you up before they find you." He held up a hand to silence Ted before Hollander could tell him everything that was wrong with that idiotic plan. "Look, I don't have time for this. Are you going to help me suit up or what?"

"And I suppose you want my air tank so you can go out and try this crazy stunt?" Ted grumbled. "First, I was gonna be filthy rich, and now I'll end up lynched by a bunch of mermaids."

Devon couldn't picture anyone being lynched underwater, but he set aside that distraction.

"Just get me out there and let me do my job, Ted. It's your best shot at getting out of this in one piece."

"Oh, swell. Now give me the good news."

Fiona Kolodzy

Chapter 32: Captured

"How much time will I have using this thing? Devon asked as Ted connected the air tank to his suit.

The form fitting wetsuit was a vast improvement over the awkward pressure suit they had forced him to use before, except that it was old tech and therefore incompatible with the fancy gas splitter he'd grown used to.

"These little tanks have about two hours of air max," Ted replied. "But your helmet has the same kind of set-up as the p-suit, to detect and eliminate carbon dioxide so just breathe normally and let the system handle your gases for you."

While Ted struggled with the final closure, to seal the full-view helmet onto the locking collar of the suit, Devon watched the view from the sub's exterior camera. It was projected on the front window of the sub and showed Annika heading away from the sub, swimming slowly toward the mob of Marnians. Suddenly, dozens of Marnians armed with short struts and lengths of netting converged on her position.

Devon could only watch in horror as the scene faded from view, lost in the darkness beyond the arc lights. He wanted to scream with frustration at the delay while he waited for the light on the airlock to turn green. It seemed to take forever while he shifted from foot to foot with a hand at the ready on the wheel, but at last the light changed. After he'd scrambled inside, Ted handed him a set of webbed large foot fins.

"Here, take these; they'll help you swim faster. But wait till you're outside to put them on," Ted advised. "And good luck."

Then the door thumped shut, and he was alone in the appalling little closet where Annika had recently spent so many hours. It seemed impossible that she had managed it. Had it been him trapped in this cramped, dark space, he was sure he would have gone insane in minutes.

And she was locked in here all that time, telling me stories and trying to keep me from losing it during the dive. I never would have made it through without her. Now it's my turn to help her.

Once he was outside the sub, Devon activated his thrusters and put himself into a steady hover, then began forcing the first foot fin over his boot. By the time he had yanked the first one into place, Ted hailed him on the com channel inside his helmet.

"Devon? Can you hear me out there?"

If he hadn't known better, he would've sworn Ted's voice held a hint of anxiety.

"Yeah, I'm here," he said, straining to work his second boot into its foot fin.

"I think I can see our girl on scan," Ted reported. "I see one person surrounded by a ring of others about thirty meters to your left. She must be holding them off from attacking. They are moving away from the sub toward the larger group surrounding us, though. That group is holding position about fifty meters out on all sides."

"How many are in the group around Annika?"

"Maybe a few dozen."

"Hmm, could be some kind of polite escort for a revered public figure. How many are around the sub?"

"Might be more than the couple of hundred we saw at first. There are some dense clumps where it's hard to—Devon, look out!"

Since there was nothing in front of him, he swung around to locate the threat. A Marnian with a net in one hand was approaching from below around the curve of the sub. He considered staying where he was and using the sub to protect his back. However, he doubted he could drive the Marnian off before some others joined this first attacker.

Besides, finding Annika is more important.

He pushed off from the side of the sub, and with a big kick of his foot fins, shot off into the darkness to look for her. Although he was nowhere near as agile as a Marnian in the water, the wetsuit was orders of magnitude better than the clunky p-suit he had used before. Experimenting quickly, he made a few minor changes of attitude and vector as he swam off into the gloom in what he thought was the right direction.

I hope that Marnian will just keep following me without trying to trap me in his net.

"Ted? I'm going after Annika. Let me know if I pick up any more company on my tail."

"Roger that," Ted replied.

A few more vigorous kicks brought him to the scene of the standoff where a globe of assailants surrounded Annika. She was trapped, but the Believers hung back at a respectful distance without trying to lay hands on her. It seemed obvious to Devon that if they all rushed her at once that they would prevail. Even with her upgraded strength and speed, she was no match for that many bodies. But her attackers seemed very wary of her.

"I don't think they've hurt her," he told Ted. "Maybe she does still have some influence if they are so reluctant to just grab her."

Ted only grunted in reply.

Devon noted that his own sheepdog also seemed content to hang back out of reach now that he had moved away from the sub. So he stayed where he was and watched to see what Annika would do. Three of the Believers on one side of the globe finally got up the courage to rush in together and try to overwhelm her. However, because all three came in on the same vector, Annika simply twirled aside and let them pass her by. The three continued forward to crash into their fellow attackers on the far side of the globe. Devon couldn't understand why other members of the group hadn't moved to surprise her from behind when the group of three rushed her from the front. Even Annika didn't have eyes on the back of her head. Then he remembered the limitations imposed on the average Glae person. He knew that a Glae generally received only a single download from a data hoard during their lifetime.

That download must focus only on things they need to know in order to do their job. Skills for figuring out how to handle any new situation must not be included.

As he watched Annika's attackers floundering about making

foolish choices, he realized these must be just a bunch of houseboys and farmers trying to work out battle tactics on the fly. Unfortunately, the novices were facing a woman with a vastly upgraded intellect and extensive expertise in martial arts. Annika's would-be captors were about as effective as a pack of domesticated puppies trying to subdue a full-grown wolf.

Just as he began to worry about how this stalemate would end, he heard Ted yell another warning.

"Devon, behind you!"

Before he could dodge, he felt the strands of a net dragging down his arms and tangling around his legs. Watching Annika had so distracted him, he'd forgotten about the man lurking behind him. Apparently, even an inexperienced fighter would pounce if his prey stayed still long enough.

"Damn!" he swore, struggling to free himself from the meshes of the net before his adversary could get a grip on him.

His movements must have distracted Annika though, because he saw her lift her head and look his way. As soon as she realized he was in trouble, she charged the crowd, trying to force her way through to help him. This was a grave error, since it was all the open space around her that had been protecting her. Reluctant as her attackers might have been to cross the clearing in the middle of the globe to reach her, once she left the hollow center, it collapsed behind her. The people in front of her were slow to retreat as she rushed them, and as she checked her speed to avoid hurting them, it gave those behind her time to close the distance. The last thing he saw was her disappearing under a tide of struggling bodies.

291

Meanwhile, Devon's own attacker had secured a firm hold on him, making it impossible to free himself from the net. Then he felt hands fumbling along his belt and tugging at his thrusters.

"Hey, stop that. Don't. Wait, I need those!"

But the Marnian ignored his protests. In seconds, his captor had torn the thrusters off and tossed them away into the dark. Now Devon had to fight down a wave of panic, as the only thing holding him up were the hands of his attacker. He refrained from struggling, fearful that the Marnian might lose his grip. Fortunately, it took little original thought for the fellow to realize he needed help to hold up a much larger airbreather. Two other Believers soon moved in to lend a hand. As the guards clustered around him, Devon strained for a sight of Annika amid the flailing blob of her attackers.

He prayed that fins were not like fingers, that once gone, they were gone forever. Fin lore wasn't something he had studied during his time at the Librarian's array. All he could do was watch and worry for Annika's safety in the melee, while also dreading that she might damage some of her attackers. If any Believers were injured, it could ruin his chances of a successful negotiation.

I've got to get her to surrender before anyone gets hurt.

He wriggled to bring his arms together in front of his chest before the net got any tighter.

There was now a coordinated swaying of the crowd around Annika, and it appeared as if she was attempting to shake loose her heap of attackers. He watched in awe as the great mass of people rocked back and forth, building speed. At any moment now, he expected their combined motion was going to cause some of them to lose their grip, like in a giant game of crack the whip.

Crawling the fingers of his right hand up over his left, Devon strained to reach the control panel on his forearm. Another few wiggles and he found the button he was aiming for.

"Annika," he called out as the button activated the external speaker on his suit. "Stop, Annika! Don't hurt them!"

There was no reply, so he tried again. "Annika, it's alright. Don't fight them. Trust me, I have an idea."

Slowly, the ball of people heaved to a stop and broke up. He gnawed his lip until Annika reappeared in the center of the crowd.

"Are you ok?" he asked over the com.

"I'm fine," she called back. She was frowning like a thundercloud, but all her limbs and fins seemed to be intact. The mob still hovered only centimeters away, ready to seize her if she tried to escape. He could see gills and fins twitching among the crowd as they eyed her, looking determined not to lose their prisoner.

"So, what's this big idea of yours?" she yelled over her shoulder. She was keeping herself in motion, turning in place and constantly changing her orientation to discourage the crowd from taking hold of her again. "Whatever it is, you better do it quick."

He had to chuckle to himself.

She isn't going to like this plan.

"Diplomatic playbook page one," he called back. "Let them

corner you, then say 'Take me to your leader.'"

Chapter 33: Gods Above

Trussed up as he was, Devon could not very well swim for himself. His guards towed him along while Annika and her escorts followed behind.

He'd never been a prisoner during a negotiation before, and the idea of bargaining from such a position of weakness was daunting.

What can I offer these people for the sub and harvester? And why should they back down now that they have two hostages? Three if you count Ted inside the sub.

Too late again, he questioned his decision to leave the safety of the sub and attempt this negotiation.

No, as bad as this situation is, I know I made the right choice. Negotiating at a distance through Suni would never work. That would give my opponents too much power to cut off talks on a whim. And if I hadn't come, Annika would be out here alone.

Squaring his shoulders as best he could inside the confines of the net, he prepared for the coming encounter.

His captors dragged him toward a small group floating apart from the others. He could see the tiny figure of Suni floating on the fringes of this group, still flanked by two much larger guardians. Seeing the little 'linker there cheered him somewhat.

Suni's calm, rational manner would be an asset in this situation, and he knew he could count on his friend to help smooth over any cultural blunders.

As he arrived near the smaller group, Devon tried to orient his body so he would have a view of both Suni and what he hoped were the leaders of the True Believer group.

Suni gave him a quick welcoming smile, but most of the little 'linker's attention was on Annika. The group guarding her had stopped at some distance away. Although Devon assumed that was a safety measure, so she could not pose a threat to these important men, he almost chuckled. Based on what he'd seen in the records made during the revolution, Annika's upgraded speed and strength meant that she could easily harm any of these people if she chose.

I bet they're counting on the fact that Shar-Annika, Rebel Leader and Friend of the Glae, would never do anything dishonorable or hurtful to others.

But the way she had risked injuring others when they captured him made him wonder about that.

Does she care more for my safety than that of her own people?

A little thrill ran over him at the idea. It was humbling to think that she would see him worthy of that much regard.

She's so isolated among her own people. As lonely as I am on the Osprey. I wonder when Annika last sat and talked with someone for hours the way we did during the dive?

Listening to her stories had been more than a pleasant distraction from his claustrophobia. The tales of her own adventures had left him lost in admiration. Thinking back on the courage and humor she maintained throughout all the difficulties during the dive brought a lump to this throat.

She's wise and strong and … And thoroughly distracting me. I've got to buckle down and focus on saving all of us. This may be the last chance I ever get to do something to help her.

"Uh, Devon?" Ted's voice interrupted from the com link.

"I'm here Ted."

"Any progress out there?"

"Not yet, Ted, hang tight."

"Yeah, about that. I think we have another problem."

"Oh great, what now?"

"Well, after all these delays, I'm running low on O2 here in the cabin already."

"How much do you have left?"

"Half an hour maybe, then I'll have to get in my wetsuit and use the tank, which will buy me about another fifteen minutes. After that, I'll have to head for the surface."

"Fifteen minutes?"

"Yeah, we used up most of this tank keeping Annika alive during the ascent. Now there's almost none left for me. So, work fast out there, will ya?"

A cold knot clenched inside Devon's stomach. Much as he didn't care for Ted, the thought of Hollander suffocating to death was even less appealing. Plus, Ted was still needed to pilot the sub and harvester to the surface if there was any hope remaining to retrieve this cargo they'd gone to so much trouble to secure.

"Ok. Understood. Hang in there, Ted. I'm working as fast as I

297

can."

Tearing his gaze away from Annika, he studied the man in the center of the group of True Believers. Their leader was a long, lean fellow with a dour tilt to his gills. Although the other Believers appeared to defer to him, the man wore only plain purple work clothing, so Devon assumed he must be a Glae. As the leader's icy gray eyes skimmed over him, Devon felt himself being weighed, measured and found wanting.

To him, I'm just some nasty foreigner, fouling up his ocean. About as welcome as a hyena at a garden party.

Though it was hard to project a strong, calm image while bundled up in a net, Devon tried to catch the leader's eye with a confident smile. The head True Believer pointedly ignored him and instead went off to inspect Annika inside her circle of captors. Devon's hopes sank and a bead of sweat trickled down between his shoulders when he saw a hungry expression cross the True Believer's face as the man looked Annika over.

If he's already decided what's going to happen to her, then my job just got much harder.

"Greetings," he called out over his suit speaker. "Do I have the honor of addressing the leader of this group?"

Devon's escorts jabbed him in the ribs for speaking without being spoken to, but his suit protected him from any actual harm. He could see Suni nodding encouragement in his direction, so he tried again.

"I was hoping to speak with you about a matter of mutual concern."

The leader glanced in his direction this time, then turned

away again to speak to his advisory group.

One of Devon's guards leaned closer to hiss at his helmet. "Quiet, airbreather. The GLEN is too busy to flap gums with the likes of you."

He ignored the Marnian, and raising the volume of his voice, he tried once more. "Excuse me Glen, but I think I can offer a solution to our problem."

One of his guards yanked on his net, spinning him around to face away from the leader.

"I told you to shut it airbreather!" The man shoved his face right up next to the helmet with a menacing growl. "Now I mean it, you hold still and keep quiet, or I will send you back down to meet the Gods again. And this time you will not be using your infernal conveyance."

Devon tried to duck his head inside the helmet to show submission as he spoke. "If I can't talk to your leader directly, perhaps you could take a message to him for me? You see, what I have to tell him is important and we haven't much time."

He spoke as loudly as he dared on that last part. Before the guards could punish him further, the one they called Glen drifted closer with one eyebrow raised.

"And why do we not have much time?" the GLEN asked.

Suni was nodding again, more eagerly now, and miming a bow, so Devon tried to nod his thanks to the True Believer from within the confines of his net. "Thank you for speaking with me, great leader."

"Never mind your flattery, airbreather," the Marnian said with a flick of the gills. "Just answer the question. Why do we not have much time?"

"Because here in the water, we airbreathers must carry our gases with us. Just as you will die in the over realm without water to breathe, we die here in the ocean once we consume our gases."

"And why is it any concern of mine whether some blasphemer who has offended the Gods runs out of gases?" the leader asked in a sneering tone.

"Because there is another man in the sub—that is our round, white conveyance—if that man dies, it will be impossible to resolve this problem between us."

The leader shrugged, preparing to turn away again. "Another airbreathing sinner whose fate is also of no consequence."

He could see Suni trying to come to his aid and being restrained by his own pair of guards.

"Will it be of consequence when the Gods Above seek vengeance for their dead messenger?" he called out loudly.

Suni's eyes widened, and the GLEN spun back to face him, gills whirring. But before Devon could say anything, one member of the advisory group darted forward. The advisor was a lean man of about the same age as the leader, wearing Aban orange.

"You told the elder Abang that you were not a messenger from any Gods Above," the one in orange cried.

Ah ha, I have their attention now.

"Yes, but I think we both know that only Gods could live unseen in the over realm."

With an internal wince, he imagined what the Diplomatic

Council would have to say about one of their officers using this sort of tactic during a negotiation.

Well, I'm not in the Corps now and we are in big trouble here. Ted sure won't care if I have to throw away the rule book to save our butts, and neither should I.

Besides, this mob doesn't strike me as the type to respond to traditional diplomacy. There will be time enough for rational negotiations when this is all over. Some other Dipper backed up by a phalanx of security men can take all the time he needs to make superstitious Marnians listen to reason.

Today it's down to me and any dirty tricks I can think of.

He cast a pious look up to the sky then spoke to the Marnians using the tone and cadence of a cleric preaching a sermon.

"You should know that our Gods Above look down, seeing all that passes here. Just as your Gods Below look up and observe the world of mortals," he told them.

The orange-clad Believer's pale eyes gleamed feverishly. "Yes, yes, the Gods Below see all. They have seen your theft just as we have. Soon, you will be punished for it."

Devon spared the man a tolerant smile. "Ah yes, Gods are such jealous creatures, aren't they? It is the same with our Gods Above. They watch and they will be angry if their costly diving conveyance is lost. Yes, very angry. But I tell you, you cannot imagine the depth of their rage if one of their airbreather servants dies. And how do you think they will they show that fury, other than by sinking some of your group?"

The GLEN ducked involuntarily with a quick glance toward the sky, but the orange-clad one cried out fiercely. "Your Gods would not dare harm any of the True Believers! Our Gods Below would never allow their most faithful servants to be harmed for the sake of one airbreather."

"Then there will be war!" Devon declared in ringing tones. "And when the Gods go to war, it is you who will suffer the most. They will catch you Marnians right in the middle of their terrible battle."

The leader's chin trembled as he considered this idea, but his voice was steady. "We cannot abandon our task. We are sworn to protect the property of our Gods Below."

"And so you should," Devon assured the Marnians earnestly. "Airbreathers must not take away things that belong to your Gods Below. I believe that our Gods Above are only entitled to the cargo they lost here long ago. After we have removed the property of our Gods Above from that Marnian machine, we can return it to bottom of the ocean if you wish."

The orange-clad man pushed forward with a frown once more. "Everything on Marna belongs to the Gods Below!" he shrilled, bobbing up and down and pointing a trembling finger at the deeps.

"Ah, but there is something you do not know about this ancient machine." Devon jerked his head in the general direction of the sub and the harvester. "You should know that long ago, before it sank into the depths, that device took on a load containing the food of our Gods Above."

"I do not believe you!" the Marnian screamed. "It is a trick to let you steal from our most holy—"

Devon's escorts tightened their grip on him as the orange-clad man raged on, and even the crowd around Annika began an ugly muttering.

"It's not a trick, and I can prove it."

"How?" the GLEN demanded, waving the orange-clad man down.

The crowd grew silent, and Devon took a slow breath to calm his beating heart.

If I blow this chance, I won't get another.

"That machine carries a cargo of special food belonging to the Gods Above. It is not normal Marnian food. You can taste the substance for yourself to see if I speak the truth. Once the machine reaches the surface, we must open the container before we carry the food it contains up into the over realm. Before we return this foreign cargo to our Gods Above, you may first sample it and see for yourself. There will be plenty of time for this. You can ask that SUNI there. He watched the whole process when we arrived. The platform you saw earlier must set down on the surface of the ocean and remain there for some time in order to unload the food of the Gods. This will give you ample opportunity to sample the contents and stop us from carrying the cargo away if you find my words are not true."

Actually, he had no idea how this tasting would be accomplished, but at this point, he was ready to say almost anything that would get him and Ted up onto the platform in the open air.

"As you know, our conveyance is vulnerable while on the surface, so we must have your agreement to retrieve this food for our Gods. But after we have recovered what belongs to them, we can leave your machine on the surface where both the Gods Below and all the Marnian people can see we did not steal it from you."

The leader looked thoughtful, so Devon dared to add one more thing.

"I think that if we work together, we can placate all the Gods. Then there will be no war and no Marnians need to get caught in the middle and be killed."

The GLEN waved a hand to stop Devon's words, then bobbed in place, rubbing his chin for a moment as the orange-clad one whispered in his ear.

"And how will I know what food for your Gods from Above tastes like, airbreather?" the leader asked.

Devon managed to nod his head slightly, conceding the point. "You are a wise leader," he said. "Although you may not know what food meant for our Gods Above tastes like, I am sure you will recognize whether it is any kind of food you are familiar with."

"And if this cargo be strange, as you say?"

"Then let us take the un-Marnian food away so that we may avoid a war between the Gods."

The GLEN floated before him, brow furrowed in concentration. Marnians all around were looking at their leader with a hopeful gleam in their eyes. Devon held his breath, wondering if his reminder about avoiding a war would do the trick. His guards had eased their hold on him while he made that appeal, and even the group around Annika was looking sheepish.

Then, before the leader could agree, the orange-clad one flung up his head, eyes flashing.

"No!" he cried loudly. "Even if this cargo is food for the Gods Above, that does not mean it belongs to them anymore." He turned to face the GLEN, wringing his hands as he poured out his reasoning. "When the Shar do battle with other Shar, the winner often takes goods and food from the House of the loser. Your Gods Above have lost this food, therefore it now belongs to our Gods Below." As the GLEN nodded agreement, the one in orange turned to face Devon with a triumphant sneer. "And we will see that everything that belongs to our Gods is returned to them!"

A roar went up from the crowd in response to this rallying cry and Devon's escorts crowded closer, tightening their painful grip on him.

Damn, now we're going to lose all that Glaeon, after everything we went through to get it.

Chapter 34: Sacrifice

Devon's heart sank as the GLEN nodded his approval of the orange-clad Believer's sentiments. Any hope of saving the cargo dimmed as the cheering went on and on.

So much for appealing to their desire to avoid a war between the Gods.

His eyes squeezed shut as he racked his brain for anything else he could say that might change the Believers' minds. Losing the harvester was a bitter pill to swallow after everything he'd been through today, and he was sure Ted felt the same. He didn't have the heart to call Hollander on the com and tell him how the gambit had failed.

The most important thing now is to get busy convincing these True Believers to let Ted go before they sink the harvester. Ted said that if the harvester goes down while the cable is still attached, it could take the sub along with it. I've got to get them to allow him to leave before they do anything rash.

In the back of his mind, he still figured that Annika could fight her way free and probably get him to safety as well. But that would leave Ted trying to swim for the surface alone.

And what will he do when he gets there? No, we need the Marnians' cooperation to give the shuttle time to come and pull me and Ted out of the ocean.

The orange-clad Believer still floated nearby with a gloating look on his face, while their leader hung behind him, appearing less pleased, yet resolved.

No hope there. If only I had something to offer that would convince them to let us go.

All at once, it struck him that what these Believers wanted was to punish someone.

If I give them a chance to prove their loyalty, maybe the idea of avoiding a war between the Gods will seem more appealing.

He licked his lips as he faced the two Believers, choosing his moment to make this final offer.

"You may be right," he called out, nodding to the orange-clad one. "Your Gods deserve some form of atonement after this attempt to steal their property."

The rest of the Marnians froze, waiting to see how their leader would respond to his words, so Devon forged on while he had their attention.

"But I still think there is a way for us to appease both the Gods Above and those Below. I am the one who led the expedition to retrieve the cargo of food for my Gods. Therefore, I should suffer the consequences of that crime. You can send me back down to meet your Gods Below, but why not let the man inside our vehicle go free? That way, both the Gods Above and the Gods Below will have reason to be pleased and you may yet avoid a terrible war."

He waited, watching the GLEN's face anxiously.

At last, the leader drew himself up and glanced around to

make sure he had everyone's attention. "All three of you blasphemers took part in stealing from the Gods Below. So, it is only right that all of you pay the price for desecrating the sacred realm of the Gods."

This time, the leader's words were met with dead silence from the crowd.

Before Devon could say anything else, the GLEN nodded to a man nearby who held a length of netting in his hands.

"No! No!" Annika screamed, before the surrounding Believers moved in to restrain her once more.

The crowd began cheering as the man with the net moved forward and secured one end of the mesh to the bindings wrapped around Devon's body. Devon only realized what they intended when, at a gesture from the GLEN, other men from the crowd came forward to toss their weapons into the new net.

"Wait, wait," he said. "My friends on the ship can offer you and your Gods many rewards if you let me go."

"Hey Arkovic, what's going on?" Ted called over the COM.

Devon didn't take the time to answer. He wriggled inside his bonds as the Believers secured the loose end, then released the load to dangle freely below him. The bindings of the new net cut sharply into his legs as the weight took hold. The guards holding his arms ignored his struggles, but Devon could feel their leg fins creating stronger currents as they churned to keep him afloat.

He expected some last words once preparations were complete, but they would have been lost in the noise of the crowd, so the leader of the True Believers merely waved a hand once all was ready. At this signal, Devon's guards released their hold on his arms and darted aside. The weight of the full net immediately dragged at his ankles, and he quickly sank below the level of the crowd, lost in a cloud of bubbles. He could hear Annika shouting, cursing the True Believers, calling them savages and fools as he descended in the net's wake. Then he was alone, falling into blackness and death.

Chapter 35: Attack

Suni's heart sank as Shar-Devon disappeared from view. He was a 'linker, not a fighter, and now flanked by two big guards, with their meaty fingers digging into his arms, Suni felt more helpless than ever.

Annika had her hands full dealing with the mob of Believers trying to keep hold of her. She was angrier than he had ever seen her before, and the sight of her in full battle-mode shocked him. The way she darted about inside the cloud of her attackers, landing blows, then using disabled ones as missiles against the rest, chilled him. The GLEN's words left no doubt the Believers intended to truss her up and send her to the bottom of the ocean next. But Suni realized she was not only fighting to get free, but she was also frantic to dive down after their airbreather friend.

All this chaos was so different from the grand historical events Suni had expected to be recording today, that it took every bit of self-control he had to not close his eyes and block out the awful things he was witnessing.

Then suddenly, he heard a new sound over the shouts of the crowd assaulting Annika.

***

4th Goon swam in Scylla's wake carrying the great green Leader's spare weapons. At least he assumed his master was still green under the elaborate upper covering Scylla was wearing while on campaign. The garment looked quite impractical as a fighting outfit, but very impressive. 4th Goon pondered the cost of the outfit, wondering how long it took to make, and if keeping it clean was the reason they were swimming so high above the fields of bree.

He had never been to the agricultural areas before, and his first view of the vast fields of crops spread out in all directions astounded him. There was no time for sightseeing, though. Loaded down as he was with weapons, it was an increasing strain to keep pace as Scylla led his force of Glads and Goons speeding along above the crops.

They were charging toward what sounded like a battle up ahead. It occurred to 4th Goon that since Scylla was making no attempt to surprise the people they were approaching, his master must not expect to encounter any military presence there.

But the Goon Captain told us that citizens were not allowed in this area today. How odd that so many people would ignore that order. Although it explains why the Leader is so angry. Again.

Although 4th Goon did not enjoy knocking heads among the citizens, he was philosophical about the need for punishment when it was deserved.

At least it will give us Goons a taste of action for once.

He pushed his leg fins faster, enjoying the thrill of charging into battle among a company of true fighting men. The load of weapons he carried gave him pause, however, and 4th Goon glanced down at them with a frown.

It is supposed to be an honor to be assigned a task by the Leader himself. But how can I fight while carrying all this stuff?

With a sigh, he resigned himself to remaining at his master's side and perhaps missing out on the battle this time.

As they whipped past the edge of the last field of bree, the site of the disturbance came into view. 4th Goon's lip lifted in a sneer as he took in a mob of Glae all bunched up in a ball, flailing and yelling.

"Amateurs." he snorted under his breath.

SharScylla waited a moment for the last of his troops to arrive and form ranks before signaling the attack.

Knots of struggling Glae froze in place when they heard the battle cries of real warriors bearing down on them. It was rather comical to watch how the fools dropped their weapons and darted off, shrieking in fear. One even dove straight down from the center of the pack, seeking escape.

There was only a single small group who kept their wits and their weapons to face the oncoming tide of professional fighters. As far as 4th Goon could tell, this band was protecting the retreat of a few men behind them. The holdouts kept casting glances over their shoulders as they waited for the Goons and Glads to overwhelm them. It seemed they were mostly concerned with whether the ones they were protecting were being pursued.

When SharScylla beckoned him forward, 4th Goon hastened to move up, offering the Leader's weapons. Scylla waved the weapons away and instead pointed to the group of men 4th Goon had been watching.

312

"Tell the reserve group commander to chase down those men and bring them to me," he ordered, pointing to the ones who were fleeing for their lives.

4th Goon was stunned silent for a moment. He had never passed on orders to a superior officer before. However, it would not do to delay.

"At once SharScylla," he said.

His armload of weapons prevented him from adding any gesture of respect. He simply sped off as fast as he could go, taking the weapons with him rather than questioning his master on whether to leave them.

Once the reserve troops had departed on their mission, 4th Goon had time to observe the mop-up phase of the engagement while he returned to SharScylla's side.

The water was dark with blood now, and the smell of fear and death hung everywhere. Pathetic injured men paddled their fins weakly, leaking fluids and crying for help. Scraps of clothing and bits of fins drifted among the dead and dying.

SharScylla was interrogating a trio of battered prisoners when he returned. The terrified Glae cowered before the Leader as he hung over them.

"—so, then you took the airbreather and Shar-Annika prisoner?" Scylla was asking as 4th Goon slid into position behind him.

"Yes Shar."

"Why would you do that?" Scylla thundered.

The prisoner wobbled but remained upright.

"We are the True Believers, pledged to defend the Gods

313

Below, great Leader. It is our duty to stop the blasphemers who stole from our Gods."

"And where are the two of them now?"

One captive gestured downward with a flat palm. "We already sent the airbreather down to meet the Gods Below, great Shar. He took the Big Dive just before you arrived."

Scylla glanced down and then back at the prisoners. 4th Goon could see a vein above Scylla's ear bulging and throbbing.

"You dared to sink an airbreather?"

"He was an outsider, great Shar. A stranger. A pollution in our ocean. And he stole from the Gods Be–"

The man quavered to a stop as Scylla's glance withered him til he was dipping.

"And what of Shar-Annika?" Scylla asked, turning to one of the other captives.

"I do not know, great Shar. We had her penned in, but when your men arrived, I threw down my strut and tried to escape. I did not see where she went."

"Cowards and fools, all of you."

Scylla's arm fins flared outward and points on his fin struts gleamed malevolently.

"We only wished to defend our Gods, great Shar. We are the faithful servants of the Gods Below and—"

"Faithful you say? You are all fools and traitors," Scylla screamed, shaking with rage.

The smell of hostility almost choked 4th Goon. He closed his eyes, hoping to miss seeing Scylla strike the entire group dead. When no sounds of death and agony came, he cracked one eye open to find the Leader turned away from the quivering captives, to hang frowning out over the battleground.

Contemplating the results of the action beside his master, 4th Goon shuddered.

So many dead!

He was now glad he had taken no part in this slaughter.

Even if these people were defying Scylla's orders by being here, how can it be right to kill Marnian citizens for opposing the airbreathers?

Then he recalled how that little SUNI and the airbreather visitor had talked about airbreather ships bringing people to Marna long ago.

If airbreathers brought us here, then we were never created by any Gods Below. Are these True Believers right to be here defying SharScylla for the sake of Gods who might not exist?

He looked down at the heap of unused weapons in his arms.

I am just the Leader's 4th Goon. Should I even have opinions, or simply do my duty and not question?

Once again, his head ached with that overfull feeling of too many thoughts.

Ever since I met that airbreather, I have not felt sure of anything. Perhaps it is the best thing that has happened today, that he is sunk and gone at last.

Chapter 36: Doom

This was the thing Devon had been dreading ever since he got his first glimpse of Marna out the viewport of the shuttle three days ago. Sinking. Drowning. Being crushed to death in the black depths.

He struggled madly, but his bindings held firm. Within seconds, his ears popped, and his eyesight darkened. Fleeting figments of landmark events in his life flashed before his eyes, to be replaced by a single vision of Annika.

It was cold comfort to know he had offered to sacrifice himself for her. The thought of Annika suffering this same fate broke his heart ...

I failed her. Why couldn't I find a way to save her? Even if there was nothing I could do for Ted?

As the world went black around him, Devon thought that the roaring in his ears was the final sound of his helmet failing under pressure. Then, all at once, a dim figure swooped in beside him, thrashing up a mass of bubbles. Then Annika wrapped her arms around his body, and he felt the speed of his fall slow. He could hear her calling out to Suni, but most of his faceplate had fogged over, and he couldn't see the little man anywhere. He felt some tugging at the ropes around his legs, but the drag on his ankles didn't change. Annika was kicking hard and working her lower fins, but he couldn't tell if that effort was moving them any higher. All he knew was that the water was still pitch dark and his legs were still trapped.

As strong as she is, I am so much bigger and weighed down with this heavy net.

Annika said something else that sounded like an order to Suni and at once he saw a shape streak past his faceplate, heading upwards.

Time stretched and contracted as they hung there together in the blackness. From the corner of his eye, he could see Annika's gills blurring as they worked away at top speed. Her fingers kept slipping, then grabbing back onto him, and he wondered how long it would be before she'd have to let him go.

How much deeper can she go without damage? Should I tell her to forget about me and save herself?

Then he hesitated as he recalled that moment in the sub when he was pleading with Ted to find a way to add some more oxygen to the airlock.

I could never have lived with myself if I hadn't done everything possible to save her.

He kept silent while his heart swelled with tenderness and the arms around him trembled with fatigue.

*****

As the horde of Goons and Glads raced toward the True Believers, Suni felt his guards release his arms and dart away in opposite directions. Shar-Devon was already out of sight, so he searched for any glimpse of Annika among the bubbles and fleeing bodies surrounding him. Then a bright shape streaked straight downward from the center of the crowd. With no hesitation, he followed.

The noise of the battle overhead dimmed, and it grew darker and darker. Annika was calling out for Devon as she rocketed into the deeps, so Suni followed the sound of her voice. The terrible cold and pressure of these depths worried him. He had only ever descended into the chill zone once. Many times since then, memories of that trip to the murky underworld of the city had kept him awake at night.

But if there is any chance of saving Shar-Devon, then Annika will need my help.

Just when he thought he couldn't stand to go any deeper, Suni heard Annika's voice change.

She did it. She actually found him. Now if only he is still alive.

Shar-Devon was a pitiful sight as he came near. The airbreather was trapped in lengths of netting, and the clear helmet he wore was almost completely clouded over.

"Oh, Suni," Annika gasped when she saw him approaching. "Quick, see if you can get off the tendrils holding the net below him."

Suni darted downward, pleased to see that Annika had slowed the rate of Shar-Devon's fall. The tendrils of the netting were invisible in the gloom, but he felt along the airbreather's legs, clawing at the knots and checking the fibers for any areas of rot. It was all hopeless, though. His fingers were clumsy with cold, and the tendrils were fresh and strong. The odor of his own despair sickened him.

"It is no use, mistress," he called out to her, between chattering teeth. "I cannot free his legs."

"Then go for help. Quickly. Offer them anything you can think of, but get some of those men up there to come and help me."

He didn't stop to reply as he shot past her toward the upper reaches. Pushing his fins and gills till he thought they would fly off him, Suni surged upwards like a runaway Mabel.

Even before he arrived at the scene of the battle, the rain of debris and mangled bodies told the grim tale of how the True Believers had fared in the fight.

And how are the victors going to receive my pleas for help on behalf of an airbreather?

Setting aside that worry, he blasted on upwards to reach the location of the recent battle.

The first thing he noticed was that most of those who remained upright were black-clad Goons.

No help there. A Goon would never take orders from me. I must find the commander of these troops. Annika is counting on me.

As Suni glanced in the direction of Portbree, he saw a group of green tinged men floating together. Among them, he spied the unmistakable figure of Scylla himself. Hope flared large in his heart as raced toward the Leader.

Suni never even saw the two Goons rushing to tackle him from both sides. They struck him almost simultaneously, and all three spun off on a different vector together.

"So, where do you think you are going, little man?" Suni

319

heard a voice growl in his ear.

The Goon on his left looked angry and disheveled, but the man maintained a firm grip on him.

"I must speak to the Leader at once. It is urgent," he managed to say, gills blurring to replace his gasses.

The Goon flapped a hand toward Scylla, who was turned away, ignoring the incident. "Go to the Assembly Building and make an appointment," the Goon on his left shrugged, while the other Goon snickered. "Our Leader may make time to see you after a double hand of storms or so."

Both Goons laughed out loud, then the one on Suni's left let go of his arm to re-adjust his upper garment. It was the chance he had been waiting for. The second Goon had a looser grip in deference to his arm fins, so Suni wriggled sideways, then shot straight up, flourishing the stiffening spines of his leg fins in both Goons' faces. The Goons fell back, losing orientation while Suni darted forward to end up just short of Scylla's face.

"SharScylla!" he cried out. "The airbreather Devon Arkovic is sinking and Shar-Annika needs help to save him."

Scylla brushed out a hand to wave him off, but Suni avoided the gesture and remained at eye level, pushing his case.

"You must not let SharArkovic die, great Leader! It might sink your deal with the airbreathers along with him."

There was no time for him to say anything else as two Gladiators from Scylla's group seized him along with the Goons he had escaped from. This time rough hands spared no thought for his fins.

"Wait," Scylla's voice rang out.

Everyone froze, using only the tiniest movements of their fins to maintain position.

"Release him," Scylla said. "You three." Scylla beckoned to some of his Goons. "Follow this SUNI down and see if you can recover the airbreather unharmed."

Scylla's men took a split second too long to gawk at their Leader.

"Go! Now!"

Swimming down into the dark again was hard, even after emptying his buoyancy sac. Suni's dread of the cold and dark, combined with the fear of not being able to find the missing pair, slowed him down. The Goons followed him as ordered but did not spread out and increase the odds of locating the sinking man. After what seemed like an achingly long time, Suni thought he heard a faint call below him and off to the right. He looked around at the Goons to see if any of them were hearing it, too. They stared back at him through the gloom with the incurious eyes of a pack of phish. He ground his teeth.

"SharScylla will punish all of us if we return without the airbreather," he reminded them.

Galvanized by that warning, the Goon swimming on the right flank turned his head in the direction of the sound Suni thought he had heard. Before it was too late for any hope of success, Suni led his reluctant rescue party that way. Then the voice called again, from right below him. He immediately dropped lower, straining his eyes in the dark. His heart pounded, then felt like it might shatter his ribs to pieces when he spotted his dear Little One peering up at him.

The Goons streamed past him to seize hold of the limp form of the airbreather, ignoring Annika since she was not included in their instructions. Suni hovered next to her, worried she might not have the strength to ascend by herself after all her exertions. She cast him a weary smile, letting her fins rest as her buoyancy sac took over to lift her slowly upwards.

"I knew you would find me," she said, reaching out to squeeze his hand.

When Suni turned back to check on Shar-Devon, he saw the airbreather make a quick bounce upwards as the weight came off his legs. Then the three Goons set about dragging their prize back to the upper reaches and their master.

Chapter 37: Ally

Annika disappeared as the circle of strangers surrounded Devon. The newcomers checked his fall, then he felt them ripping away the tendrils around his legs.

At first, he couldn't believe that help had arrived. His rescuers were just ghostly blobs seen through a fogged faceplate. Disoriented in the black emptiness, Devon had a moment of terror, wondering how these strangers would know which way to go once he was free of the net.

How stupid I am. A Marnian's buoyancy sac will always take them upward. It must be the dark and the cold getting to me.

As the deadly weight finally dropped away from below him, the reality of his rescue hit home.

I'm saved. I'm still alive and still breathing. It's going to be alright.

Leaning his forehead against the faceplate of the helmet, he let grateful tears flow down his cheeks to drip off his chin.

Devon's head was still spinning once his rescuers hauled him back up into the brighter reaches. As it grew light enough to see, it surprised him to see that the ones who had saved him were a squad of black-clad Goons. He checked the gauge for his air tank and was relieved to see it registering a sixty percent supply remaining. Raising his head to look around, he saw many more

Goons gathered near the edge of a floating mass of crops.

"Bring him here," a familiar voice growled somewhere to his left. "And get the rest of those nets off him."

As the fog cleared from his faceplate, he saw Scylla floating before him, with two green Glads and a great many Goons at his back. Once the netting no longer hindered him, Devon was delighted to find that he could maintain position with easy kicks of his large foot fins. The lost thrusters had been useful for adding speed, but they weren't essential while he was just hanging around in one position.

"Are all those disrespectful zealots gone?" Scylla asked as another of his Glads appeared at his side.

"We believe they are, SharScylla," The Glad said. "We have chased the trouble-maker citizens back beyond the algae fields. Some may have hidden in the village, but most seem to have fled all the way back to the city."

"You believe?" Scylla snorted. "If you cannot be sure, I suppose we must deploy the men in a guard perimeter while the airbreathers complete their work."

The Glad nodded to acknowledge the order and began issuing instructions to other Glads. At once the water filled with shouts and froth, as squads of Goons fell into formation.

"I believe this satisfies my agreement to protect your airbreather friends while they recover your cargo," Scylla said. "Do you not agree, SharArkovic?"

Devon gathered his scrambled wits as the impatient Leader glared at him.

"I do, indeed. Thank you, SharScylla. I am so glad you arrived when you did."

The fact of Scylla's presence, and now this unexpected gift, almost made Devon giddy.

I'm going home!

With Scylla's help, the moment when Devon could rip off his helmet and breathe clear air again was so close, he could almost taste it. It was funny how the confines of the *Osprey* seemed so much more appealing now. After days stuck in a suit, a harrowing dive, and nearly being sunk, returning to the stinky old freighter sounded like a trip to paradise.

As Devon enjoyed his moment of anticipation, the com circuit in his helmet activated with a burst of static, followed by Ted's voice.

"Devon. Devon, are you there, buddy? Over."

It threw him a little to think of Ted Hollander as his 'buddy.' At the moment, though, he was so glad to hear Ted was alive that he was willing to let that fact alone be the basis of a new solidarity between them.

"Yes, I'm here, Ted. Only by the skin of my teeth, but I'm okay now. Good to hear your voice. Are you alright? Where are you?"

"I'm almost out of air, but the sub is near the surface. You sure took your sweet time getting those Marnians off the harvester. I was starting to think you weren't going to pull it off. Whatever you did, though, it worked just in time."

Some of his relief that Hollander was safe melted away under that faint praise. However, it would take more than a few barbs from Ted to ruin the blush of happiness that they had both survived this ordeal.

"So, you didn't have to drop the harvester?"

"Nah, I've still got it. I'm just about to disengage the towing cable and let the techs on *Osprey* finish raising it the rest of the way on the airbags. Seems like you saved both us and the cargo. Didn't think either of us were going to make it there for a while. I guess I owe you one, Dip boy."

"Well then, I'll be sure to collect. See you soon, Ted."

"Roger that. But hey, don't take too long saying goodbye to your fish friends. I've had enough of this place. I vote we blast on out of here as soon as possible. *Dive One* out."

Scylla's Goons were all organized in tidy ranks by the time Devon finished speaking to Ted. He watched in awe as each Glad lieutenant peeled off smartly, leading a squad to take up guard stations, around the sub and harvester.

Perhaps I misjudged this SharScylla. He seems to be a man of his word, after all. I didn't even have to ask him to arrange all this. Now if only I could be sure that Annika and Suni are alright too.

It concerned him that he had not yet seen them anywhere, but before he could ask, there was another burst of static in his earphones and he heard Mary Chenoquen calling his name.

"Devon? This is *Osprey*. Do you read? Come in, please. Over."

"Devon here. Read you loud and clear, Mary. Over."

"Well, that's a relief. We've been worried sick up here. Where have you been all this time? Over."

He had to grin. It was stretching the truth that anyone other than Mary had been worried sick, but he still appreciated the sentiment.

"I've been gathering some reinforcements so we can collect our loot and scram," he laughed. "Happy to report the area around the sub is now secure. Over."

"Say again, Arkovic," the captain cut in, overriding Mary as usual. "Did you say you have the area secure? Over."

"Yes sir, Captain Doyle. All Marnians in the vicinity now are troops under the command of the Marnian Leader. They are friendlies, here for our protection, so we can lift the cargo without interference from the group who attacked us before. Over."

"Good work, Mr. Arkovic. We'll send down the platform as soon as possible. Can you hold out where you are while the shuttles set her down? Over."

"I'm safe now, sir. Over."

"Acknowledged, Devon," Mary's voice resumed. Apparently, the captain had other business. "Please move away from the vicinity of the sub so the shuttles can begin platform deployment. Estimate ten minutes. Over."

"Roger that, *Osprey*. Over and out."

Just as he completed the call with *Osprey*, Devon spied Suni pushing his way to the front of Scylla's remaining troops. The little fellow was almost lost among that crowd of hulking warriors, but Devon could see him waving and bobbing up and down in delight.

And then, with a gush of pure joy, he saw Annika appear. She was floating a short distance from Suni, sandwiched between a pair of pale green Glads. Her face and posture appeared somewhat tired, but otherwise, she seemed fine. He looked her guards over with a critical eye as they chivied her forward. Even in a state of exhaustion, he had to wonder if a mere two Glads could prevent Shar-Annika from leaving if she chose to make a break for it.

Would those two really fight and maybe die if she tries it?

He shook his head as he caught the grim look in the Glads' eyes. Their absolute dedication to duty astonished him—especially given who they worked for.

Dip Corps would never ask one of their own to make such a sacrifice.

The Corp's methods were slow and strategic rather than brash. They demanded patience from their officers. Discipline and adherence to the rules so that the Corps was always above reproach in its behavior. Dip Corps would sit waiting for literally years in order to broker a settlement, but they would never order an officer into danger for the sake of the mission. All that was required of a Dipper was to man his post and wait.

And wait. And wait. And die by inches instead of in a blaze of glory.

At last, here in the Marnian ocean, watching not-quite-human Gladiators do their duty, Devon finally saw how Dip Corps had stolen decades of his life. Condemned him to a career of waiting for something to happen. Waiting and waiting, while all the people in his world moved on. His parents, his sister and her family. School friends like Alastair. And finally, even the girlfriend who once said she loved him.

Yvette jumped at that opportunity to transfer to another

assignment. She just up and left me there on Marvet VII, counting the grains of sand blowing past the window. Now, she's working with the real pioneers, living in dicey regions on the fringe of the galaxy. Meanwhile, the Corps keeps claiming my psych profile makes me unfit for such adventures.

He snorted.

Unfit for hazardous duty. Despite my damn stupid heroics on Parn IV. I wonder what Yvette would think if she could see me now. Down here, risking my neck. Breaking all the rules, so a pack of fortune hunters can claim their prize. Not exactly Dip Corps SOP.

With a last chuckle, he pictured the look of amazement on his former lover's face before the image dissolved and then dropped into the abyss.

His eyes sought Annika as thoughts of Yvette fell away. During his career, he had met many extraordinary people on many worlds, yet she still stood out in that elite company.

She's both philosopher and visionary. With a concern for less fortunate people that is quite rare among those raised in upper-class families. She's also the most beautiful woman I have ever seen.

His heart beat faster, then slowed as he recalled how he must leave her today.

Will she miss me when I'm gone?

Learning details about Marnian culture and Annika's own life during the dive gave him a sense of how lonely her life must be.

Concepts like freedom and individual rights are so foreign here she is almost as much an outsider as I am on Osprey.

It made him cringe to think of leaving her behind here in this brutish culture.

If only I could go over there and at least make sure she's okay after all her efforts to rescue me.

But he knew there were other priorities. He should not delay informing Scylla about the arrival of the platform. Also, Suni seemed to be urgently trying to attract his attention. Since Scylla was busy talking to one of his men, Devon edged closer to the little 'linker first.

"Is something wrong, Suni?"

"Not wrong exactly, SharArkovic. But I am hoping you will ask our Leader for a favor before you go?" The little Marnian barely waited for Devon to nod. "I think it would be wise for Shar-Annika to have an escort to see her back to the temple."

"An escort?"

"These Glads tell me that some True Believers might still be hidden in the local village. If there are more than a few, Annika may not be safe from them until she is back inside the temple."

"Of course. I'd forgotten about those bloodthirsty lunatics."

"SharScylla is not a friend to Annika." Suni continued, bobbing and casting a nervous glance over his shoulder at the great green Leader. "Once you are gone, there will be no way for anyone else to compel him to see to her safety."

Hearing Suni refer to his departure jammed that reality right in Devon's face.

I'm leaving. And there's no guarantee that I'll ever be able to return to Marna. This may be the last time I see her.

Yesterday, he'd nursed dreams that he might help Annika regain some position of power before he left Marna. A role in the negotiations for restarting Glaeon production that would give her a chance to protect her people in the years to come. Instead, because she had taken part in his treasure hunt, her status seemed worse than before.

What kind of life does she have to look forward to now? I've got to do at least this much for her.

"I understand, Suni. Let me see what I can do."

Now that the last of Scylla's men had been dispatched to guard the sub, Devon took his opportunity to approach and make requests.

"Excuse me, SharScylla? My ship has informed me that our surface vessel will be here in a few minutes. Uh, that is, a short space of time. I recommend everyone move to a safe distance from the sub as the arrival of the new vehicle will create violent motion in the water at the surface and for some depth below. After the platform is on the surface, you may approach and examine any of our vehicles more closely without risk of harm."

"I see," Scylla rumbled thoughtfully.

"I ask this not for my benefit great Leader, I only wish to ensure the safety of all your people."

"So, I am 'great Leader' again, am I? Yet you still think I need you to tell me how to care for my people."

"I meant no disrespect."

"These men are warriors. They do not expect safety."

"Of course. I apologize. But I would consider it a great favor to me if you and your men remain undamaged while we reclaim our cargo."

"We will withdraw as far as the center of that field of bree," Scylla said, indicating the crops behind him with a jerk of the head. "The guards on the perimeter will maintain position in case the True Believer mob attacks again."

There was no way to argue with that decision, so Devon just smiled and bowed. Inside, he winced to think of asking anything more from the irritable Leader, even for Annika's sake.

I hope I haven't used up his entire supply of goodwill already.

As they retreated above the field of bree, Devon glanced over at Annika to bolster his nerve. She swam a short distance away, still flanked by her two Glads. A heart-breakingly beautiful sight, as she moved gracefully, trailed by the filmy haze created by those spectacular upper fin fringes. It brought a lump to his throat, and once again, he longed to rush over and take her in his arms.

She looks like an angel wrapped in wings of glory. I've just got to pull off this one small thing for her before I go. I owe it to her for saving my life.

The entire company stopped at Scylla's signal, and they all cast their eyes upward, waiting for the surface platform to appear. Firming his jaw, Devon turned away from the sight of Annika's loveliness to concentrate on the deep green features of the Marnian Leader.

"Er, pardon me again, SharScylla. I wonder if I might speak with you while we wait?"

Scylla eyed him with a frown. "Have you come to ask still more favors of me, Devon Arkovic?"

A chill stole over him at the Leader's silky tone.

"There *is* one more thing I could use your help with, SharScylla. You have already been so generous, and I apologize that I have nothing to offer you in return for this service."

Scylla's face split in a sly smile that brought a cold lump to Devon's stomach. "Oh, I think you have already brought me that which I desire most, airbreather."

As the big man chuckled, some of the Glad lieutenants nearby joined in the laughter. Devon had the sinking feeling he wasn't going to like whatever Scylla was hinting at.

"Well, I am glad you are pleased, SharScylla. May I know how I have accomplished this?"

"No, no, you tell me first," Scylla insisted. "What is it you want now, airbreather?"

Devon forced a smile while his skin crawled at the look on Scylla's face.

"I was hoping you could assign some of your men to escort Shar-Annika back to the temple. Just in case any of those True Believer fanatics are still around, waiting to make trouble."

As Scylla's horrible grin grew wider, the icy lump inside him dragged Devon's stomach down another notch.

"Shar-Annika *will* have an escort," Scylla said. "However, she will not be going to the temple. Since you have so kindly delivered my enemy right into my hands, she can serve as payment for all the favors I have granted you this day."

Devon bit his lip as he caught a look of anguish crossing Suni's face.

"I have waited a long time to find a way to capture Shar-Annika," Scylla went on. "Once we are through here, I will have my guards escort her to my residence, where she will take her place as my prisoner."

Chapter 38: For Lack of a Jink

Suni thought he might just take the Big Dive himself from shock. His fins trembled and he detected a whiff of panic in the water around himself.

There is no doubt Scylla means what he says.

His mind raced, but nothing useful occurred to the little Marnian. All he could think was that his temporary assignment as designated historian was going to become a very permanent role if Scylla had his way.

Devon Arkovic looks just as worried as I am but what can one clumsy airbreather do to save my Little One from Scylla and all his Glads?

While his mind continued to spin like a punctured float, Suni heard Shar-Devon's com channel crackle and the tiny voice of another airbreather seep out of the suit into the surrounding water.

"Devon? Come in, Devon, this is Ted. Over."

"I hear you, Ted."

"The platform is about to arrive. Chief Simmons says he wants you and me to take the second shuttle back to *Osprey* so we're out of his way during the recovery operation. Over."

"Yeah, about that. I've run into another situation here so I'm going to need a bit more time, Ted. Over."

"More time? How long? Over."

"I'm not sure. I need to speak to the captain first."

"Ok, but what's the problem? Why are you still messing around down there? Over."

"Annika is in danger, Ted. I can't leave until I know she'll be safe. Over."

"I knew it had to be some problem with that damn fish girl. She is a magnet for trouble, that one."

"Well, this time *I've* got an idea how to save her, Ted, but I need some time to pitch it to the Marnians. Just stand by, ok?"

"Alright, Arkovic, I'll try to cover for you with the chief. Hollander out."

A small spark of hope leaped to life in Suni's heart as he listened to the exchange. He didn't know what Shar-Devon had in mind but given what he knew about his airbreather friend it probably had nothing to do with fighting to get his way.

Shar-Devon is a man who uses his wits to win.

He paid close attention as Shar-Devon turned to face Scylla once more.

"So, do I understand that you intend to hold your main rival prisoner, SharScylla?" Devon said.

The airbreather gestured at Annika who floated between her two guards nearby.

Scylla shrugged. "She is one of my citizens and I will do what I like with her. Not that it is any concern of yours, airbreather, since she has nothing to do with our bargain."

"No, of course not," Devon raised a hand. "It's just that I

understand she is still revered by some of your people. Don't you worry that they will object if she is not returned to the temple?"

"What I choose to do with her is none of their business either," Scylla snarled. "I am Leader. I answer to no one."

"Certainly not," Devon agreed, casting a warning glance at Annika that seemed to say 'keep quiet and let me handle this'.

Suni clasped his hands tightly and hoped that the airbreather knew what he was doing.

"A Leader must project strength," Shar-Devon nodded to Scylla. "You should not be subject to the opinions of others."

Suni tried to suppress the instinct to bob up and down in agitation. This was starting to sound like Shar-Devon supported Scylla's decision.

"Believe me, airbreather, even the Shar on the Ruling Council will not dispute my right to take this woman as my mate."

Suni's blood froze in his veins, and he gaped in horror at this new development.

"In fact, I expect that the members of the Council will be delighted that I have found a co-parent for my dynasty who is not one of their daughters."

Casting an anguished glance at Annika, Suni noted how a double handful of Scylla's Goons had moved to surround her in a globe of bodies just as the True Believers had done earlier. There was no way she could fight her way free now against two former Glads plus this cadre of fully trained Goons.

"Hmm," Shar-Devon said, appearing to consider Scylla's plan. "I wonder, though, why do you choose to bestow such an honor on your greatest enemy? Will your children command the respect they deserve if their mother is such an unpopular person?"

For the first time, Scylla showed a trace of doubt and Suni applauded inside as Devon pressed his advantage.

"It occurs to me," Shar-Devon held up a finger, "that a more fitting option would be to remove this rival from your society altogether."

Now Suni was so appalled and surprised that he had to hold himself back from springing at the airbreather's throat. Even Scylla hunched his shoulders and twisted his fins to and fro.

"Well, I can always execute her after the procreation process is complete," Scylla frowned. "Or even before that, if she proves too troublesome to hold on to."

"True," Shar-Devon said.

His calm agreement made Suni want to spin in circles and howl.

What is this airbreather doing?

"But execution will only make Shar-Annika a martyr in the eyes of those who adore her," Shar-Devon said. "Trust me, I've seen it happen after a popular figure dies, and it always causes trouble. No, I had another solution in mind for your situation."

Scylla's expression was suspicious, but his gills twitched upward. "Another solution?"

"What If I told you I could remove Shar-Annika from your planet entirely? Take her away with us in our ship, but keep her alive? Then your rival would be gone, but no one could resent you for executing her."

Scylla looked almost as surprised as Suni felt.

Can he really take her away? Save my Little One from this terrible fate?

He dared not look at Annika or even wiggle a gill while Shar-Devon went on.

"Wouldn't it be better to have your enemy leave this world entirely, rather than remain here where either she, or her memory, might become the focus of a new uprising one day?"

"Well, that would be better," Scylla rumbled. "But then who will be co-parent to my offspring?"

"Surely these councilmen you mentioned cannot be allowed to get away with defying your will. Are they not marrying their daughters to men less worthy than you? I think any of them should be honored to join their families with yours."

Scylla's chest puffed up, and he nodded thoughtfully as Devon pressed on.

"A man like you should not be forced to settle for a woman who is your enemy. There must be better options than that for a great Leader such as yourself."

"It is true that Shar-Annika lacks status. She is no longer even the daughter of a Great House since the rebellion. There are plenty of other high-born Shar women I would prefer to have as my co-parent."

"Then why not let me take this problem off your hands? Call it an act of gratitude for saving me from being sunk by those True Believers."

"And you will take her away in your ship?"

"Absolutely."

Suni's hopes rose so high he had to blow off some bubbles to keep from rising to the upper boundary.

Imagine my own dear girl being the first Marnian to travel in a spaceship. To visit other worlds and see sights that no other Marnian will ever see.

"My people can provide Annika with everything she needs to live a life away from Marna, so you will never be blamed for her death."

At those words, Suni's heart clenched once more as the beautiful dream dissolved. Shar-Devon was smiling as he continued to explain but as soon as Suni glanced over at Annika, he could tell that she had realized the problem with the airbreather's plan too.

If only she could be safe and truly have everything she needs to survive.

Suni couldn't bear the idea of watching Annika remaining here as Scylla's prisoner and forced to become co-parent to his odious offspring. But neither could he stand to think of her dying a lonely death far from home.

Scylla will never tell Shar-Devon why his plan won't work. He would let poor Annika leave and condemn her to a lingering death. But how can I interrupt two Shar? Scylla might kill me for it. I must do something though. While there is still time to stop this.

Annika was surrounded by her mass of Goons so there was no way to ask her advice on the matter. Which meant he must make the choice himself. Suni gritted his teeth as he moved closer and waved a fin discreetly, trying to gain Shar-Devon's attention a second time.

When the airbreather glanced over, he made terrible faces and beckoned his friend nearer.

"What is it now, Suni?"

Shar-Devon sounded impatient and annoyed. That irritable tone rattled Suni so badly, he had to dig his fingers into the fabric of his upper garment to keep from cowering away from the disapproval.

"SharArkovic, I know you mean well and hope to help Annika, but there is something you do not know."

"Tell me quickly."

"Your plan will not work."

"What? Why not?"

"You said you can take Shar-Annika away. I have known her since she was a small child. As dedicated as she is to her people, I am sure she would choose to go with you rather than suffer what Scylla has in mind for her. But you also said that you can provide her with all she needs."

"And I will. She will have a water environment and our technology can synthesize any foods she needs to meet her nutritional requirements. I am certain of it. She will be safe and well cared for I assure you."

"But SharArkovic, Annika is no ordinary Marnian. She has many upgrades and body mods."

"I'm aware of that. Why is that a problem?"

"Her upgrades will require a Moddr's jink to tend to them."

"A Moddr's jink?"

"Yes, SharArkovic, without a supply of jinks, Shar-Annika will die."

Chapter 39: Jinksed

Annika's hopes rose and dipped so many times while Devon and Scylla talked that she felt dizzy.

Devon was so clever the way he pandered to Scylla's pride while leading him along to agree with this radical idea. Too bad it won't work.

For a brief moment she considered leaving with Devon just for the chance to visit other worlds. But the idea of dying somewhere along that journey boiled off her enthusiasm for the plan.

No, I'll have to stay here and try to fight my way free the first chance I get. No child of mine is going to be raised to become Marna's next tyrant.

She saw Suni draw Devon aside and caught the look on his face as Suni broke the news to him.

The main thing now is to appear calm and confident. I can't let Devon see how hopeless I feel, or he may do something that will provoke Scylla into killing him. Devon needs to go back to his ship and move on with his airbreather life. There's nothing else for him to do here.

***

Devon was stumped. Suni was talking and obviously the little man believed what he was saying, but Devon couldn't make any sense of it.

"Suni, I have no idea what any of that means," Devon whispered back. "Talk plainly. What does Annika need to survive off-world?"

"I do not know about 'off world' but on Marna, in order to remain healthy, a Shar with many physical and mental upgrades must have regular maintenance. That involves tasks performed by small creatures called jinks. Jinks which perform body maintenance tasks are bred by our Moddrs."

Devon just shook his head, still confused, so Suni tried again.

"Moddrs are those who attend to the care and maintenance of our bodies and oversee the procreation process."

"You mean a doctor?"

"No. A *Moddr*. That is a modifier and a doctor."

This time, Devon threw up his hands in frustration and almost went into a spin. Suni looked ready to explode by the time he was upright again.

"Ok, Suni, let's try this again. So, what do Moddrs do?"

"A Moddr is one who can repair a body and alter the genetic makeup of individuals and ..."

Devon held up a hand before they got bogged down in a long explanation. "Wait. Wait. Never mind, we don't have time for this. Let me ask you this. What is the problem with my plan?"

"The problem is that Shar-Annika must take at least two jinks with her if she leaves with you, or she will soon die."

"Die? Are you sure?"

"Very sure. You must think of some way to convince

SharScylla to obtain some jinks for her, or your plan will fail."

Devon took a fast peek at his air supply which was still in the green.

"Okay, I'll believe you, Suni. But where can we get these jinks, she needs?"

"The Moddr in the local village should have a breeding pair."

"I see. But isn't that where some of those True Believers might be hiding out?"

"So the Glads say. I can go there and fetch some jinks for her, but I think an escort would be wise. If I have a few Goons with me it will help persuade the Moddr to part with some jinks."

Devon would have traded a tall stack of credit chips to be able to wipe the sweat from his face. It seemed to be one of those times when nothing could go smoothly. Plus, he still had to call Captain Doyle and convince him to go along with this hare-brained idea. With so many points of potential failure in his plan, it felt like he was riding a rickety roller coaster along a path strewn with disasters.

But Annika has no other options. I have to make this work.

"Alright," he said to Suni. "Let me see what I can do."

Just as he turned away to go talk to Scylla, he paused and then drifted back to Suni for a moment.

"Please, tell me there are no other reasons my plan won't work?"

"I believe we have discovered all the flaws, SharArkovic."

"And you're very sure Annika will wish to go with me?"

"Quite sure. Once she learned of the existence of other worlds the idea of visiting them captivated her. Now since she can no

344

longer serve her people if she remains here, I am confident she will feel free to indulge that desire."

"Very well, you stay here while I try to convince my big green buddy to do me a few more favors."

Scylla was frowning as usual when Devon returned to resume their conversation after Suni's interruption. He cringed to think what penalty Suni might pay for that faux pas but there were some battles he had to pass up.

"Please excuse the interruption SharScylla, Suni has been kind enough to point out an issue of which I was not aware. It seems there is one thing we airbreathers cannot provide for Shar-Annika. I am told she will require some jinks."

Scylla's gills twitched in irritation. "Ah yes, jinks."

"We could send Suni to get some in the village nearby, but it might be wise to have him escorted by some of your Goons–"

"*Wise* to have him escorted?"

Devon's heart sank at Scylla's sharp tone.

Uh oh, I've offended him again by using that word.

"What I mean is–"

"You mean that you know better than me how to organize a simple mission."

"No, that's—"

"A mission and another favor that are not part of our deal."

"I understand SharScylla, but–"

"But you will continue to ask favors until the storms bring the purple algae."

"I didn't mean—"

345

"Enough," Scylla bellowed, setting the water trembling. "There will be no more free favors."

It took all Devon's courage to speak again after that utterly final pronouncement.

"What if I can pay for this favor?"

He waited while Scylla's wounded pride warred with his greed.

"What do you offer?"

"I have something of value, but I must ask you to bear with me while I explain."

Scylla crossed his arms and nodded.

"When production of Glaeon resumes, you will receive a share of those profits. Is that not correct?" Sylla nodded again. "There are certain other people who have also been promised a share in those profits as well. I happen to be one of those people."

Scylla's eyes gleamed as he waited now.

"My offer is that I will give up my share of the future Glaeon production to you, in exchange for your help with obtaining these jinks."

"So, you have nothing to offer me now." Scylla made the deal sound contemptible.

"I assure you, there is an enormous demand for Glaeon among the airbreathers of the galaxy, so my share of the future profits will be extremely valuable."

He risked a glance at Annika while he waited for Scylla's reply. Her eyes were so full of hope, Devon prayed he was not about to see that light extinguished.

"I see," Scylla said, at last.

The Marnian mimicked Devon's own way of speaking those words exactly. There was a glint in the Leader's eye, however. A look that said Scylla was just toying with them now. With a stern reminder to keep his temper in check, Devon lifted his chin as he held the Leader's gaze.

"So, do we have a deal or not, SharScylla?"

Once Suni was on his way to the village trailed by a Glad leading a small squad of Goons, Devon braced himself for his next uncomfortable conversation with Captain Doyle. SharScylla had chosen to take his opportunity to inspect the surface platform and harvester, so they were all on the move, heading back to the landing zone. Devon swam slowly, ending up at the tail end of the group while he put in his call to the ship.

"This is Devon Arkovic calling *Osprey*. Come in, please. Over."

"This is *Osprey*. We read you Devon. Over."

"Hi, Mary. Listen, I need to speak with the captain, and I'd like a little privacy. Can you patch me through to his cabin or something? Over."

"Can do, Devon, standby while I set that up. Over."

Captain Doyle was his usual charming self when he came on the circuit.

"Arkovic, this the captain, do you read? Over."

"Right here, captain. I mean, I read you fine, sir. Over."

"Ok Mary, I've got it. You just let me know if there are any messages from the surface vessel."

"Yes, sir. Mary out."

"Alright now Arkovic, what's the big mystery? I'm a little busy here, so spit it out. Over."

"I'll get right to the point, captain, I'd like to offer you and the crew my share of the profit from the sale of this cargo to help me transport a Marnian off-world."

There was a long silence.

"Uh, over."

"Are you crazy, Arkovic? We can't just take one of those mermaids with us. This isn't some stray pet or zoo specimen you're talking about. You're talking about kidnapping a person. Over."

Devon smothered a laugh at how Doyle's views had changed.

"You misunderstand, sir. This is a person who wants to come with us. Over."

"Even so, Arkovic, I can't see how we could get an aquatic from down there in the ocean to up here on the ship. And if we could get it up here, where would we keep it? No, no, it's a tempting offer you're making, but the whole thing is just impractical. I'll have to say no, Arkovic. Over."

"But, sir, I have a few ideas about how to make the transfer work. And if you agree to my terms on behalf of the crew, then perhaps your men could begin converting a space in one of the cargo bays into an aquarium tank for her to live in. Over."

"Your whole share of the profit on this cargo to divide among us, eh? Well, I guess you can wait to cash in on your share of the future production down the road, can't you? You'll still come out of this a rich man. All right then, but I'll assume no liability for the health and safety of this passenger once she's in the tank. You'll have to personally monitor the habitat systems and replicate any needed minerals, food and what-have-you. Agreed?"

"Agreed. If you'll just advise chief Simmons that you've approved the Marnian coming aboard? Then I'll coordinate the actual transfer with the chief and Ted Hollander up on the surface platform. Over."

"Very well, Mr. Arkovic, but complete your preparations quickly. The harvester is on the surface, and we don't want to waste fuel hanging around waiting for you and this passenger once we're ready to leave. *Osprey* out."

Devon keenly missed his thrusters as the call ended. It would have been nice to take a moment to hang limp with relief. Instead, he kicked with his fins to head over and join Annika to share the good news.

Before he could reach her side, his earphones exploded with noise as Mary's voice shouted over the sound of an alarm blaring in the background.

"ALERT. ALL PERSONNEL. PIRATE VESSEL SPOTTED ENTERING THE SYSTEM. ALERT ..."

Chapter 40: Deal or No Deal

Ted Hollander was on the platform watching Chief Simmons and his crew extracting the cargo from the harvester. The sub bobbed on the surface nearby, its recovery being a much lower priority than the cargo. The strain of the dive mission was catching up to Ted, and he was just settling down to sit on the base of one of the cranes when the com in his left ear blasted him upright.

"ALERT. ALL PERSONNEL. PIRATE VESSEL SPOTTED ENTERING THE SYSTEM. ALERT ..."

He yanked the bud out of his ear as the message began to repeat. All the crewmen on the platform were frozen in place listening to the bulletin, and every man's eyes were wide.

"All right, you mangy scut suckers," chief Simmons yelled. "You heard Mary. We've got incoming and I have no plans to leave this Glaeon behind for those slimy bastards to cart off. Get your useless asses moving, do ya hear?"

Crewmen scurried back to work with increased speed while Ted fingered his com control looking up at the two shuttles hovering overhead.

I wish I knew how far out the pirates are and how fast they'll be on us.

The outline of an idea was percolating in his brain.

"Yes, captain, I think this is our best shot at getting us and the cargo out before they can disable *Osprey* with their weapons," he explained to captain Doyle. "Over."

"But that'll mean we'll have to use the Lagrange point behind the second moon for the jump out, Hollander," the captain objected. That's risky. Over."

"Less risky than trying to reach the exit at the rim of the system and having them catch *Osprey* before we get there. And my diversion should give you plenty of time to get behind the moon and make your calculations, don't worry about that. Over."

"So, we're all dependent on one flaming hot shot pilot to get us out of here in one piece, eh?"

"I can do it, captain. You know I can. And if I don't make it to the rendezvous, then you can still leave without me. Or if things go sideways, we use plan B like we talked about before. Over."

"Very well, Mr. Hollander, take command of Shuttle Two and … Wait a minute. We have the final figures on when the pirates will enter orbit coming in now. Alright. The computer says they'll experience a twenty-minute sensor blackout as they reverse thrust to enter high orbit. So, I want that cargo loaded and everyone on both shuttles standing by to lift in fifteen minutes. Understood? Over."

"Roger that, captain. It'll be tight, but we can do it. Hollander out."

***

Devon squeezed Annika's hand again as they drifted side by side twenty meters below the platform. The sub was in position to be hoisted onto the surface vessel prior to being loaded on the shuttle. All they needed now was for Suni to show up with Annika's jinks. A quick whispered conference had assured him that she was all in favor of his plan to evacuate her. Scylla continued to hover nearby, however. Ostensibly to observe the airbreathers at work. However, there was no doubt the Leader intended to reclaim Annika as his prisoner if the plan to move her up to the ship failed.

Given those circumstances Devon would have preferred that she wait inside the flooded airlock. It made him nervous the way Scylla kept casting smiling glances their way as the minutes ticked by. He wasn't sure what he could do to stop Scylla if the big Glad tried to grab Annika. Visions of borrowing a speargun from the crew on the platform and threatening to shoot the Leader danced in his head. As appealing as that scenario was, he wasn't sure if there were any weapons on the platform, or how to use them if he got one.

"I'm sure Suni will be back soon," Annika said.

Her voice, her eyes, those mesmerizing fins. Everything about her intoxicated him.

I'll tear Scylla's gills out with my bare hands if he tries anything.

It startled him as his earphones crackled and Ted's voice came through.

"Alright Devon, I'm going up to Shuttle Two now. The crew should be ready to lift the sub in about five minutes. Are you in position? Over."

"Not quite Ted, still waiting on … some important supplies. Is there any wiggle room on that timeline? Over."

"Chief Simmons says get your ass in that sub or get left behind. Over."

"Understood. We'll be ready. Good luck, Ted."

"See you on the other side, Dip Boy. Hollander out."

Annika turned an anxious gaze on him as he closed the channel.

"Devon, you have to go. You can't wait for me and get trapped here."

His determination to save her was hard and bright as steel now.

No way do I get this close and then end up failing her, again.

"Don't worry Annika, I have an idea how to get them to wait a little longer."

He held up a finger to silence any objections as he opened a com channel to the ship.

"This is Devon Arkovic calling *Osprey*. Come in *Osprey*. Over."

"*Osprey* here. Over."

Mary's voice sounded clipped and harried. Devon hoped she would still be inclined to help him.

"I need another quick conference with the captain, Mary. A private conference like before. Over."

"Very well, standby."

The wait seemed to take forever, and he strained his eyes for any glimpse of Suni that would make this unpleasant task unnecessary.

"Doyle, here. What is it now, Arkovic? Over."

"Er, captain, we've run into one last problem down here and may need a little more time. I wanted to make it clear that if we don't lift in the shuttle then I want my shares to go to my family, not you and crew. Over."

"Well, I can't very well ask the crewmen on the platform to dilly dally around waiting for you when we've got pirates in-system, now can I? Over."

"No, I can see that. But I was hoping you could make clear to the platform crew that they should load the cargo first, so we have as much time as possible before the sub lifts? Over."

"I suppose I can do that. But now I have work to do, Arkovic. Some of it for you and your fish friend. So, stay off this channel, can't you? *Osprey* out."

Devon sagged with relief.

"Ok, I think I bought us a few more minutes. I just hope it's enough."

"If anyone can get those jinks for me, it's Suni."

"I can believe—"

The com channel cut in again and Devon got an earful of chief Simmons' dulcet tones.

"You there, Arkovic? This is Chief Simmons. Over."

"I'm here chief. Did you speak to the captain? Over."

"I did. And what do you mean by interfering in my operation? Over."

"What's the problem, chief? All I'm asking is for you to load the cargo first, so we have a few extra minutes to get some critical supplies delivered. Over."

"And that would be just fine except we're going to have to put that sub in the hold first or the cargo pod won't fit. That would mean lifting without the Glaeon. Guess how many up here voted for that option? Over."

Chapter 41: Second Historian

She could see from Devon's expression that it wasn't good news. His face was ashen, and she had to reach out and keep him afloat when he forgot to kick with those over-sized paddles on his feet.

Annika thought about simply dashing away so that he would save himself and go.

Well, it was a beautiful dream, but there's no point in leaving Marna if I don't have the jinks. Maybe I can outswim Scylla's Glads and Goons if I dart away suddenly.

But the idea of sacrificing her last few minutes with Devon in a doomed bid for freedom had no appeal.

My place is here on Marna, anyway. Working for my people in whatever way I can. Maybe I can find a way to escape Scylla before any offspring are conceived. The only thing I can do for Devon is to make sure he's in that sub when it lifts.

Glancing over her shoulder, she gave a convincing little jump, crying out and pointing in the direction of the village.

"There he is! It's Suni. Quick, Devon, get in the sub so we can reset the lock for me."

"I don't see him," Devon said, squinting out the way she pointed.

"But *I* do. Now hurry and get in while we still have time."

He allowed her to hustle him inside the airlock. Then, before she could change her mind, she slammed the hatch and spun the wheel. The sub hummed as it forced the water out of the lock into the ocean. Annika willed herself to avoid the small window below the hatch where she knew he would be peering out at her.

Suddenly the sub bounced as the lines leading to the crane above began moving. She saw the light next to the airlock door change color and an irresistible force drew her around to look in the front viewport at him. Devon was standing by the control panels with a hand on the viewport yelling something she couldn't hear.

A strand of her hair floated in front of her blocking him from view, and she brushed it aside smiling sadly at him. Then the external loudspeaker on the sub cut in.

"I think I see them on the scan. He's coming. It has to be him. Go get the jinks and come back. Hurry."

As she glanced up it was clear that the sub had a way to go before it left the water.

There's still time.

With a burst of speed like she had never known before, she took off in the direction of the village.

A group of figures came into view almost at once and she circled them to blow off speed. Her heart almost broke when she didn't see Suni among the larger figures at first. Then she realized that he was actually riding on the shoulders of the Glad lieutenant.

Suni sprang away from his mount as she appeared waving a small container.

"I got two," he said. "It was all the Moddr had."

"It will be enough," she assured him.

All at once her throat was tight and her gills felt heavy as she looked into Suni's eyes.

Will I ever see him again?

"Say goodbye to Magda for me."

"Of course."

"And take care of your little Umiko."

"I will."

"Remember, you are Marna's First Historian now."

Suni shook his head. "Second Historian, mistress. And I will make sure you are always remembered as the First. The one who taught us the great value of the stories of our lives."

There was so much more to say, and no time left to say anything. She had never imagined leaving Marna. All her hopes and dreams for the future were here. Suni was nodding as if he understood.

"This is not the end, Dear One. We will never stop pursuing the goals of the revolution. I will continue the fight here, while you carry the story of our struggles to the stars."

"I promise I will share our stories wherever I go. Good-bye my dear Suni."

"Good-bye, Little One."

She embraced him quickly while the Glad and his Goons looked on open jawed. Then Suni raised his fist in their old rebel salute.

"The Change is Coming!" he cried out.

"Bring the Rain!" she replied, returning the salute.

Then she darted away almost as fast as she had come.

The sub was nearing the surface by the time she returned. She wasted no time speaking to Devon but concentrated all her effort on turning the wheel on the airlock one-handed. The container with the precious jinks was cuddled to her chest as she wriggled inside. Then the hatch clanged shut and she spun the wheel again.

The motion of the sub changed as it broke the surface. First it swung wildly, then banged down onto the deck of the platform.

Devon spoke to her on the COM, but she was too filled with emotion to do more than assure him that she was fine, and the jinks were safe. She dared not peek through the window at the over realm. The idea of all that cold horrible air scared her. But it was too late to change her mind and dive back down into her beloved ocean. A world she had always taken for granted until she had been plucked up beyond the sky.

Devon kept her apprised of what was happening as the sub swayed and bumped it's way aboard the shuttle. She squeezed her eyes shut as Devon counted down toward the launch of the shuttle into space. It was thrilling and terrifying, just the way Devon had described a carnival ride.

***

Devon sat strapped in his seat in the sub as the shuttle roared aloft. This time, it was his turn to distract Annika during the ride, so he kept up a running patter about where they were and what was happening. Shuttle One and Shuttle Two both lifted just as the pirate vessel went blind when it began its breaking maneuver to enter orbit. The *Osprey's* computers had calculated twenty minutes of sensor blackout for Shuttle One to make it to *Osprey* and be hidden inside the hangar bay. No time for a gentle ride. Gee forces pressed him into his seat and maneuvers tossed him about with no warning. The airlock stood in the center of the sub like a great silent monolith, and he could only wonder what this ride felt like in there.

But Annika is tough. She'll be alright.

He strained to follow the chatter in his headphones between the pilot and the techs on *Osprey* as they spoke in jargon and numbers. There was no com chat with Ted in Shuttle Two, but that was to be expected. The whole ascent seemed to go well at first, but then the voices took on an urgent edge. The pilot kept repeating numbers back, and no one sounded happy. According to the clock in the sub, Devon could see that the twenty-minute window was almost up. He was just about to give Annika a warning to expect some more bumps as they docked when he heard the captain cut into the com chatter.

"Belay that, Shuttle One. You're too damn slow and we're out of time. We'll have you dock on the starboard side so *Osprey* can provide cover. Maintain course and await my order for reverse thrust. Helm, come 20 degrees right, on heading 248.4. Hangar deck, prepare for emergency docking."

Devon could hear one of the bridge crew yelling in a panic over the open circuit. "Great Galaxies, they're coming out of blackout now, captain! We're not going to make it!"

"We will if I have anything to say about it," Doyle snarled. "Steady everyone. Shuttle One, reverse thrust now. Hangar deck, snatch and stash, boys."

The sub tilted all the way on its side and Devon clenched his teeth as a giant hand seemed to yank him sideways. Then a series of loud bangs echoed around him. It was like being inside a giant cathedral bell.

"Hangar deck, report," he heard the captain snap over the COM.

"Shuttle secure captain."

Devon unbuckled his harness and gingerly felt his head for bruises while he switched to the com channel for the airlock.

"Annika? How are you doing?"

He was almost sure he could hear a stream of bubbles hitting the com pickup before she answered.

"Your carnival rides can't be worse than that. Can they, Devon?"

Chapter 42: The Art of War

Ted kept glancing at the scan while Shuttle Two blasted upward. The gap between the two sister ships continued to widen and he could hear the techs on *Osprey* beginning to panic. The pirate ship was still in blackout but Shuttle One was rising so slowly he could tell it would never make it to *Osprey* in time. At this rate, Shuttle One would be in full view when the pirates finished their braking maneuver.

Damn it. Even if I lit my ass on fire and flew loops, there is no way I could keep them from noticing there are two shuttles in the sky.

Ted scrunched up his face as his whole clever plan fell apart. He was supposed to make the pirates think his ship was the only shuttle and then lead them away from *Osprey*.

Blast and damn, time for plan B.

***

On the bridge of the *Osprey*, Captain Doyle had reached a similar conclusion. Shuttle One was moving much slower than expected and the pirates were due to recover from sensor blackout any moment.

"Mary, get me Hollander on a narrow beam transmission."

"Aye, captain."

In seconds, Ted was replying to the hail.

"Shuttle Two here. Over."

"Hollander, this is Captain Doyle. It looks like our hostiles may see Shuttle One before we can grab her. I'm going to have to ask you to switch to plan B."

There was a brief pause before the pilot replied.

"Understood, captain. Plan B. Over."

"Any instructions for your shares of the profit, Hollander?"

There was another tiny pause from Ted.

"You can give my shares to Arkovic, captain," Ted replied with a trace of a chuckle. "Over."

"What about your family, Hollander? Over."

"Family? What family?" Ted sniffed. "Nah, give my shares to the Dip Boy. I still owe him for saving me from the Marnians. Over."

"Very well, Hollander, I'll see that he gets them. And I want to thank you for saving this ship and crew. Over."

"Just get your people home, captain. Shuttle Two out."

Doyle closed his eyes as the circuit went dead. He hated to ask Hollander to sacrifice himself, but even with Shuttle Two providing a distraction, they were far from out of the woods. com traffic with Shuttle One resumed as he lifted his chin and gripped the arms of his command chair.

"Reducing speed for docking in five seconds, *Osprey*. Over." the pilot on Shuttle One announced.

"Belay that, Shuttle One," Doyle cut in. "You're too damn slow and we're out of time. We'll have you dock on the starboard side so *Osprey* can provide cover. Maintain course and

363

await my order for reverse thrust. Helm, come twenty degrees right, on heading 248.4. Hangar deck, prepare for emergency docking."

"Great Galaxies, they're coming out of blackout now, captain!" the man on sensors cried out. "We're not going to make it!"

"We will if I have anything to say about it," Doyle snarled. "Steady everyone. Shuttle One, reverse thrust now. Hangar deck, snatch and stash, boys."

The captain winced as his ship shuddered and squealed in protest as Shuttle One was yanked aboard.

"Hangar deck, report," he snapped as the light on his panel showed the cargo bay doors closing.

"Shuttle One secure, captain," the breathless voice of first officer Chenoquen replied.

"Did those bastards have time to get a look at Shuttle One?" Doyle asked his sensor tech, Eaggi Burlocku.

"Not sure, captain," Burlocku replied. "That maneuver may have put *Osprey* between the shuttle and the pirates, but I can't be sure."

"Well then, all we can do is proceed with the plan," Doyle growled. "Helm, resume course for the Lagrange point."

"Aye, captain."

Doyle ground a knuckle into his forehead while seconds ticked by and *Osprey* gathered speed, heading for the safety of the far side of the moon.

If those bastards spotted Shuttle One, it won't matter if Hollander plays the wounded bird for us. They'll never buy it.

"Navigation," he snapped. "Begin calculations for the jump as soon as we're in range of the Lagrange point."

"Yes, sir."

Doyle kept his eyes on the schematic on the viewscreen, waiting to see the pirate vessel veer off in pursuit of Shuttle Two. His ears strained for any sound of Ted putting on his show on the com to draw the pirates' attention as planned. Course projections on the scan continued to show the pirate ship on an intercept course for *Osprey*. His teeth sank into his lip til he tasted blood.

Come on Hollander. What are you waiting for? Start squealing like a fat prize pig already.

The plot now showed the pirates closing the distance on *Osprey* while the Lagrange point was still out of reach.

"Captain!" Burlocku's voice climbed a full octave in a single word. "We've just been painted with targeting sensors."

"Mr. Ngrrfow," Doyle yelled at his helmsman, "evasive—"

"Missile launch. Missile launch." Burlocku screamed. "Forty-seven seconds to impact."

There was nothing left to do, so Doyle simply sat watching the weapon's approach on the plot on his main viewer. He knew *Osprey* was just a freighter, not a military vessel. Too slow for the nimble response time required to survive this attack.

Damn that flyboy, Hollander. He let us down.

Doyle considered making a ship wide announcement, then discarded the idea. There was no time for anyone to make it to escape pods or lifeboats.

And if they did bug out, what do they have to look forward to other than being captured by the pirates?

"Three, two, one," Burlocku counted down.

Everyone braced for impact, but there was no explosion and no decompression. Doyle watched as the tracking plot showed the missile continuing on its way past *Osprey*.

"It missed," Burlocku said, voice cracking. "They missed us."

"Be quiet, you fool," Doyle snapped, losing patience with the excitable sensor officer. "It was a shot across our bow."

Right on cue, Mary piped in the message she was receiving from the pirate ship.

"... and the next one will blow you out of the sky," a deep, angry voice snarled. "So, heave to and prepare to be boarded, you scum. You have one minute."

Captain Garvin Doyle bared his teeth, but there was nothing he could do.

***

Ted shut down his com channel and stared out the viewport at the expanse of stars.

The captain is probably right. If I don't sacrifice myself, then no one will get out alive.

He knew he ought to start broadcasting on an open channel as planned, but instead he punched up a scan to show all three ships. His own vessel was in a low orbit of Marna while *Osprey* was closing on the planet's moon. The pirates were between him and *Osprey* now, accelerating to prevent his mothership from escaping. He knew *Osprey* could never outrun the pirates. Their only hope was for him to carry out plan B and distract their enemies into pursuing Shuttle Two instead.

Which means that I'll get the honor of being the pirates' only captive.

He'd never longed for the adulation reserved for heroes. He preferred to be admired for his skill rather than reckless bravery. But plan B didn't rely on his skills. At least not his piloting skills.

All I have to do is make them think I have the Glaeon. Then they'll leave Osprey alone.

He reached out to open a channel, but something stayed his hand. There was the beginning of another idea tickling the back of his mind.

If I could take those murdering bastards out, would I still have time to rendezvous with Osprey?

Just as a smile lit his face, Ted saw the new track appear on the scan plot. A small object was racing toward *Osprey* at a speed that could only mean a missile.

***

Like all the others on the bridge, Mary Chenoquen sat watching the scan, showing the missile's approach. Burlocku was counting down, but the rest of the bridge crew sat back from their boards, hands resting in their laps. She wished her husband was here with her, but the first officer had been sent to oversee operations in the hangar bay. Everyone automatically braced themselves for the final moment as the count wound down, but when it ended, nothing happened. Mary shared a look of wonder with her crewmates. There was no time to enjoy their new lease on life, however, before she got a burst of static in her earphones and the harsh voice of a stranger began speaking.

She quickly piped in the signal she was receiving so the captain could hear the message from the pirate ship.

"... and the next one will blow you out of the sky," the voice snarled. "So, heave to and prepare to be boarded, you scum. You have one minute."

Before the captain had time to react, she heard Ted hailing on a coded frequency.

"Captain, I have Ted Hollander on a coded channel saying something about a new plan."

"Let's hear it," Doyle snapped.

Once Ted had shared the details of his idea with the captain, the pilot switched channels to send out a general broadcast. His voice poured from the bridge speaker with all the anguish of a spacer facing a cruel and inevitable death.

"*Osprey*, come in *Osprey*. This is Shuttle Two on approach. I'm having trouble with one of my engines and cannot match your speed for docking. *Osprey*, do you read? Over."

The tension in the air was thicker than mud as they all waited to see how the pirates would react to Ted's first salvo.

"*Osprey*? Come in *Osprey*," Ted repeated, "this is Shuttle Two declaring an emergency. I have engine failure and cannot maintain speed. You have to come back for me. Over."

"Mr. Burlocku, keep your eye out for any more missile launches," Doyle said as Ted continued to put on a show for the pirates.

The sensor officer only gulped and turned back to his board, forgetting to acknowledge the order.

"*Osprey*, do you read me? This is Shuttle Two, come in, please. You can't leave me behind like this. I have the cargo. Captain, do you hear me? I said I was able to finish loading the Glaeon and I'll give you every last one of my shares if you will just come back and get me. Over."

Then a new voice boomed out over the COM.

"This is Captain Resnick of the armed freighter Claw. Maintain current course and standby, Shuttle Two. We will match orbit with you and render assistance."

Captain Doyle was grinning now, and a small seed of hope took root in Mary's heart.

***

Ted was enjoying himself as he continued to squawk into the com circuit like the last chicken facing the ax. He could see the pirate ship losing speed now as it slowed to match orbits with him, allowing *Osprey* to pull ahead and gain shelter behind the moon. Ted chuckled to himself as unclipped his harness and headed for the cargo hold.

Time to rig up my little surprise.

Chapter 43: Frenemy

Devon straddled the airlock inside the sub, waiting for the light to turn green. The crew had rolled the sub on its side again in order to extract Annika from the lock, so he had perched on top while he waited his turn to exit the vehicle. Finally, the light turned green. He was careful not to disturb the sub's balance as he opened the airlock door and crawled inside. It took only seconds for him to eel his way to the open hatch and poke his head out into *Osprey's* hangar bay.

"Hi there," he said, waving to a group of crew and medical personnel below him. They were grouped around a medico capsule filled with water that rested on the deck. "How's she doing?" he asked.

One of the medical types dressed in yellow coveralls glanced up and shrugged. "How should I know?" he said. "She's awake and moving, but I have no way to assess her and no idea what's normal for this species, even if I could get some readings."

"Subspecies, actually," Devon corrected the man absently.

He could see Annika's fins moving, but a couple of burly deckhands and first officer Chenoquen blocked most of his view of her.

"Huh?" the medical fellow said, scratching his head.

"Marnians are not a different species. They are standard

humans modified to live as aquatics."

"If you say so." The man shrugged again.

All at once, a siren blared out a warning.

"What's happening?" Devon yelled over the noise.

"Five-minute jump warning," Chenoquen called back.

A crewman on the platform next to the hatch offered a hand to help Devon the rest of the way out.

He twisted and strained to escape the lock, then raced down the ladder. By the time he was on the deck, the medico capsule containing Annika was heading for the door on its antigravity units. Annika braced her hands on the sides of the narrow box as the water sloshed with the movement. He quickly stepped up to her side, and she spared him a nervous smile.

"So, what happened to Ted Hollander?" he asked officer Chenoquen. "I don't see Shuttle Two in the hangar. Is he going to make it back to *Osprey* before we jump?"

The man looked at him as if he was dense.

"Mary told me Hollander is staying behind, playing decoy to let us escape."

"But then he's supposed to speed up and rendezvous with us before we jump, right?"

"The captain had to change the plan when your shuttle was so slow to lift. Now Hollander is trying to sucker them into believing that he has the Glaeon on a disabled shuttle. I bet he'll have to stay behind to make that work, though. Mary said something about a plan C, but she didn't have a chance to tell me what it is."

"Maybe Ted knows how to fool the pirates and still get away."

"Too late now. There's no time for a pickup before we jump."

371

Devon set his jaw.

"If there's a chance Ted's alive, we can't just jump out and leave him here!"

Chenoquen only shrugged as if to say it was out of his hands.

Devon looked down at Annika in the capsule. Her face was only inches from the surface.

Probably closer than she's ever been before. And she's just had to endure being poured out of the airlock into this capsule. I can't just run off and leave her now. But Ted will die here if we proceed with the jump.

The jump siren sounded again, this time with a two-minute warning. There was no way to explain anything to Annika without a com setup. He raised a hand and held her eyes for a moment, hoping she would forgive him, then took off at a dead run, heading for the bridge.

***

Ted was swearing steadily as he worked. His brilliant new plan C had hit a major snag. He'd thought he was home free once he convinced the pirate captain to buy his story. Not only had he suckered the greedy bastard into believing the Glaeon was on his shuttle. His enemy was also convinced that Shuttle Two had a worsening engine problem that would prevent it from escaping a decaying orbit. Ted had made sure to emphasize to Captain Resnick that only quick work would prevent his little ship from plunging back down toward the planet and burning up in the atmosphere. It was that fixed timeline that succeeded in forcing Resnick to choose between pursuing *Osprey* or saving Shuttle Two. However, that same urgency meant that Ted was now short on time to fix a faulty detonator that was ruining everything.

"Blast you and the idiot who made you," Ted swore at the stubborn gadget.

He wiped the sweat out of his eyes and dried his fingers on his pants before making another effort to crack open the casing on the detonator. He was about ready to take a hammer to the thing.

Everything with his new plan had gone just perfect up until he tried to rig up a remote controller for this cursed detonator. Ted could hardly believe his eyes when the thing would only display an error message on its tiny screen.

"No!" he howled, smacking the little mechanism with the palm of his hand.

But it was no use. The light on the detonator remained red, and the error message blinked up at him from the controller.

I really am down a gravity well without a thruster this time.

Everything depended on him having the ability to detonate explosives at a distance. Without that capability, Ted knew he was a dead duck.

All during the time while the pirate ship was on approach, he'd crammed as many explosives as possible into the second submarine sitting in Shuttle Two's cargo hold.

Plan C involved him causing a sudden decompression of the cargo bay so the sub packed with explosives would blast across the gap between the ships and strike the pirate vessel. If he managed to hole the pirate ship with his improvised bomb-submarine, then he would be free to make his rendezvous with *Osprey*. But without remote control of the explosives, his scheme was in ruins.

So much for my brilliant plan. Damn this stupid, stupid piece of junk.

Ted dropped the offending detonator on the sub's control board and glanced at the feed from the shuttle's external camera. Once the enemy vessel had taken up station nearby, the pirate captain had announced that two crewmen in p-suits would be coming over to confirm whether the Glaeon was actually onboard.

The delay in setting up the detonator and its remote had cost Ted a precious ten minutes so far. Now, the scouts from the pirate ship were already leaving their airlock to make the crossing.

Ted was almost weeping with frustration. Not only might he have missed his window to catch up with *Osprey* but, very soon he'd have two pirates barging through his door looking for treasure. He was out of time and out of clever ideas.

So, Ted boy, you can either throw yourself on the mercy of a couple of very disappointed pirates or stay right here and set off these charges yourself when the time comes.

Chapter 44: Schrodinger's Ted

Devon charged through the corridors of the ship and straight onto the bridge. No one stopped him or even noticed that he was there. He could hear the computer counting down to jump on the ship-wide address system.

"Wait, captain," he cried out as he skidded to a stop. "We can't leave yet."

The captain turned to face him as Devon stood dripping onto the floor of the bridge, flapping his arms like a lunatic.

"Captain, you've got to stop the jump."

Doyle looked over at one of his officers and made a chopping motion with one hand. The man keyed in commands on his board and the computer voice halted its countdown.

"Alright, Mr. Arkovic," the captain growled. "What's this all about? Those pirates have already taken one shot at us. I don't intend to hand them a chance for another go."

"I understand, captain, but Shuttle Two is not on board. We can't leave without Ted."

The captain's eyebrows climbed his forehead in amazement.

"Is that why you had me stop the jump?" he said. "Don't you think I know Shuttle Two hasn't docked? Mr. Hollander is out there delaying those pirates so we can escape. Don't you think

375

we ought to repay that sacrifice by actually going?"

"But Ted was supposed to lure them away and then rendezvous with us. Can't we wait a little longer and see if he makes it?"

"I'm afraid there was a change of plans, Mr. Arkovic. All your delays plus the weight of the submarine on top of the cargo put your shuttle behind schedule. We couldn't be sure the pirates didn't see both shuttles. Hollander had to put on a song and dance to make sure they thought he had the Glaeon so they would drop their pursuit of *Osprey*."

Devon felt all the blood drain from his face. The chill from his wet clothing sank into his heart, and all he could think of was Ted's cocky smirk disappearing under the beam of a pirate's blaster.

"But ... but. Surely, they won't shoot the shuttle down if they think the Glaeon is onboard. They might leave him adrift once they find out he doesn't have it."

Everyone stared at him, but no one replied to that ridiculous suggestion. Now that he heard it out loud, even Devon thought it was stupid idea.

"Hollander did have some wild plan for holing the pirate vessel using explosives he had on the shuttle. But if he did succeed in disabling them, we ought to have heard from him by now. Face it, Arkovic, the kid is gone."

Devon set his jaw stubbornly. "I don't see how you can be so sure."

"Look man, Hollander's plan was always a long shot, and I think he knew that. In fact, he left instructions to transfer his shares to you if he didn't survive. So, congratulations you've gone from flat broke to filthy rich again in less than an hour."

Devon's head was pounding, trying to take it all in, but one fact stood out from the rest.

"So, it still seems to me that there's no way to know for sure whether Ted succeeded."

"We're as sure as I need to be," Doyle sniffed. "The safety of this ship and crew is my responsibility, Mr. Arkovic. Don't you see that if we wait around much longer, those pirates could come along and launch a missile right up our ass? Is that what you want?"

"What I want? What I want is to be sure Ted is really gone before we abandon him here."

He and Doyle glared at each other across the bridge.

"It seems to me, captain, that the pirates would have already shown up by now if they were still chasing us. Isn't that right? Ted must have at least drawn them away onto another vector. If he did that much, maybe he also succeeded in disabling them. I think we owe it to our crewmate to verify whether he is alive or not before we just write him off like this. It's like he's dead and not dead at the same time. How can you settle for that?"

The atmosphere on the bridge grew charged as one after another of the crew aimed hostile glances his way.

"Also, as Ted's designated heir, I'd like to go on record that I pushed for confirmation of death in these circumstances. It's too weird for us to leave without being sure. I'm no gold digger, and I'm not willing to profit from his shares if there's any chance we could rescue Ted. I vote we get all the facts before we make the jump."

It cheered him to hear mutters of agreement from all sides this time.

"First of all," Captain Doyle said, raising his voice to be heard, "this is a ship, not a democracy, Mr. Arkovic. We don't vote on what to do. I decide. That said, you do make a good point that if Ted didn't disable the pirates, then they would have been back after *Osprey* in a hot second."

Doyle chewed his lip as he frowned at the schematic showing the *Osprey*, Marna's moon and the planet beyond. No other ships or weapons were visible.

The navigator, Mr. Thomas, dared to interrupt the captain's thoughts with a diffident suggestion.

"We could always wait here behind the moon until we orbit far enough to get a look at where we last saw Shuttle Two," Thomas said. "And even if the pirates *are* still lurking around, as long as they don't get too close, I should be able to recalculate and jump out using the Lagrange jump point before they get off another shot."

Captain Doyle rubbed his chin in thought, then nodded at his navigator.

"Very well, Mr. Thomas, since you are confident that we can make the jump quickly enough, we'll wait and take a look. But, Mr. Nggrfow, I want to drop a sensor buoy behind *Osprey* to alert us and provide maximum time to make the jump if the pirates try to sneak up on our rear. Meanwhile, continue orbiting on this course until we can scan for Mr. Hollander."

"Aye, captain." The helmsman turned to his board and began punching in commands.

"Mary," the captain went on, "I want you monitoring all channels and I want to hear anything you pick up in real time."

"Aye, captain," Mary said. Her smile threatened to split her cheeks as she turned back to her station and resettled her headphones.

"And you, Arkovic." Captain Doyle pointed a finger at the puddle around his feet. "Move your drippy ass off my bridge and go get cleaned up. We'll handle things from here."

"Captain," Mary Chenoquen cried out with a hand to her ear. "I've got an automated distress call that could be from the pirate vessel and a weaker signal that sounds like Ted. Transferring Ted to main speaker."

"... *Osprey*, this is Shuttle Two requesting coordinates for rendezvous. Over."

Devon saw the captain gesture at Mary for an open channel.

"This is *Osprey*. Read you loud and clear, Shuttle Two. Hollander, is that you? Over."

"Yes, captain, it's me. Alive and well. Over."

Just then, the scene of Ted's skirmish with the pirates came in view around the curve of the planet.

"Holy black holes," the helmsman Burlocku swore. "Look at that ship."

They all took a moment to watch the pirate ship tumbling out of control, heading away from the planet. Captain Doyle recovered first.

"Well, don't keep us in suspense, Hollander. Give me a report, boy."

"Yes, sir. Well, I had a little trouble with some equipment. Chief Simmons owes me a big stiff drink for that. But I got the gear working just in time and my attack went off without a hitch. They never saw it coming. Anyway, the pirate ship is adrift and leaking atmosphere. I have no information on survivors and don't particularly care. Shuttle Two has damage to the cargo bay doors, so I wouldn't want to go far in her, but I believe I'll have enough control for docking if I use *Osprey's* port side hatch, sir. Over."

"Very well, Mr. Hollander. Since you are not in immediate distress and the unfriendlies seem neutralized, we'll rendezvous and collect you, then proceed to the normal jump point at the edge of the system. I'll look forward to hearing your full report once you're back aboard. Over."

"Thank you, sir, I'll be happy to tell that tale as often as asked. Please transmit instructions in text on channel ..."

Devon couldn't stop grinning as the chatter between ships got technical. All that mattered to him was that Ted had not been left behind to die alone. It was one more thing to celebrate on this amazing day.

Ted was alive, and Annika had escaped from her brutal rival. All the people he cared about had made it through this day in one piece.

We're all safe and we're going home.

Chapter 45: Aftermath

The soft clicking of machinery echoed from the recesses of the room as Devon entered the cargo bay. His footsteps alerted her to his presence, and Annika appeared on the other side of the glasteel to greet him. The sight of her floating there in a swirl of glowing fins and brilliant red hair still took his breath away. Her sea-green eyes seemed to swallow him as he gazed at her until an impish smile appeared to remind him that this was not some icon to be revered, but a real living woman.

"Is the crew, ok?" she asked.

Her voice emanated from a speaker mounted on the wall behind him, but he was used to that by now. That speaker on the wall, along with a microphone in her tank, were the only things that kept Annika from being completely isolated in the little six by six-meter tank the crew had built for her.

"Everyone is fast asleep and doing fine," he nodded.

Apart from necessary trips to the galley and the head, his daily check on the crew in the ship's hibernation chamber was the only time he left this cargo bay. He'd even brought in a cot to sleep on so Annika could alert him if anything went wrong with the systems that maintained her little world. At two months out from Marna they had covered only half the distance on their journey to the galactic center.

Although he'd caught her staring sadly into the distance a few times over the last eight weeks, she never complained. She voiced no regrets about choosing to subject herself to this limited existence, or about missing her home. Annika only mentioned Marna when she spoke of how she still hoped to find another way to help her people in the future.

But today she appeared to be her usual cheerful self.

"So, professor, what's on the agenda today?"

His habit of always bringing her something new from the ship's library after checking on the sleeping crew had earned him the nickname professor. Fortunately, *Osprey's* library contained more data files for uplink than even Annika's voracious appetite for knowledge could consume. While her favorite subject was history, of course, he'd guided her in exploring other subjects too. Information that would help prepare her for life in the greater galaxy. It was just bad luck that the depth of her curiosity on dry topics like economic theory or soil composition would have made any real professor proud. A few times, he patiently watched along with her so she could ask questions while she binged on documentaries about standard human environments on various worlds. After that, though, he was relieved to find she was more than willing to kick back with a few popular entertainment vids.

This time, however, Devon had something else in mind. He smiled and shook his head at her as she prepared to connect an uplink cable to her neural port.

"I think I'd like to declare a holiday from study, just for today," he said.

Moving closer to her tank, he placed a hand on his side of the thick, transparent barrier. Annika's smile widened as she drifted closer to press her own hand against the inside of the tank opposite his. Devon's breath caught in the back of his throat as the moment stretched like a kiss. It wasn't possible that he could really feel anything from that touch on the other side. Yet, the coiling, twining movements of her fins matched the growing urges deep in his chest.

Drawing his hand away, he moved toward the ladder that led to the small platform overlooking her tank. He could see her waiting for him as he looked down from that perch, a fuzzy shape suspended in a cloudy film of fins. He took one of the compact breather units down from a shelf and set it on the rim of the tank for later. Then, slipping off his ship suit, he tossed it aside. As he eased himself down onto the edge of the platform, he saw that she was also peeling away her own upper and lower coverings. His heart pounded as her fins brushed his toes while dappled reflections on the surface created tantalizing blurs across his view of her body below him. Once she had moved to the far side of the tank, he scooted forward right to edge of the platform. Then, taking in a deep breath, he dropped through the surface to immerse himself in her world.

Author Note

Please visit my website, FionaKolodzy.com, for information on forthcoming books in The LEAP Conspiracy series. You may also enjoy my Alternative Romance series, PLUMDELICIOUS.

Thank you for reading my book. I sincerely hope you enjoyed it, and I would greatly appreciate you providing a review. I am a new author, and this is my very first sci-fi book!

Leave a review to help this book reach new readers. Before you leave, please go to this book's page on Amazon and add your review of *Crack the Sky*. I appreciate your time and I look forward to reading your reviews.

Expose your friends to a new adventure. Get an extra eBook or paperback copy for someone you know or recommend this title to others.

Acknowledgements

I would like to thank my son Naren Kelso, narenkelso.com for another great job on the book cover for Crack the Sky and for his work on my website fionakolodzy.com. Some images for this cover were drawn from DALL-E (heavily modified) and the rest are Naren's own work.

As always, my beta readers, Kathleen Rios, Anaya Palay, and Mary Stanley have been invaluable for detecting those errors and typos that Kevin, the ProWritingAid software and my own eye miss. Also, my dear friend Donna Braswell and my other son, Anil Kelso, were great sounding boards for issues and ideas when I got stuck.

And of course, many thanks to my dear husband, Kevin Kolodzy. His meticulous work and high standards continue to result in books in which we can both take pride. Everyone has their strengths, but alas, it is not one of mine to slog through all the finicky work involved in final production. That is why I am so lucky to have someone like Kevin handling production issues for me. He takes care of all the final formatting of my manuscripts, ensuring that both e-book and paper book versions meet exact specifications. Next, he collects reviews and works on various elements like the cover, table of contents, ISBN, QR code, and copyright process before putting everything together into a final product. I don't know how other self-published authors do all that and still have time to write. Without Kevin doing the heavy lifting on those very painstaking tasks, my books would get written, yet never cross the finish line and make it into print.

The LEAP Conspiracy Books

Book 1: Crack the Sky (November 2023)

Alone and unprepared, diplomat Devon Arkovic descends to an underwater city on the water-bound planet of Marna. According to legend, an entire colony of aquatically-modified workers was abandoned here centuries ago, along with a cache of the precious, life-extending substance Glaeon. Devon and his airbreather companions hope to recover this sunken treasure for the LEAP Corporation. During negotiations, he meets the beautiful young rebel, Annika Sharone. Now, Devon must choose between completing his mission or helping Annika overthrow a ruthless tyrant who is ready to trade away the freedom of the Marnian aquatics to a galaxy full of greedy airbreathers.

Book 2: Thwart the Tide (2024)

Annika and Devon leave Marna and travel to the galactic Center to team up with Devon's old pal, Alistair, and revive the LEAP Corporation. LEAP must quickly establish its claim to the life-extension substance Glaeon before a rival corporation steals control. However, many airbreather groups oppose having a less-than-human aquatic like Annika involved in important decisions regarding this rare and valuable resource. Annika will have to stand up a whole galaxy full of airbreathers and ultimately decide whether to make a great personal sacrifice to protect the Marnian people's future.

Book 3: Summon the Storm (TBA)

Now that Annika has left Marna and is safe from any reprisals, her old nanny, Magda, succumbs to a nosy airbreather reporter and reveals the true story of the Marnian revolution. All Magda's secrets come out as she relives both her triumphs and regrets from that epic time. But, how will off-worlders as well as Marnians react when they finally learn all the terrible details of how young Annika Sharone first launched her bid to become the Leader of Marna?

Book 4: Bring the Rain (TBA)

Annika and Devon return to Marna to usher in a new era of peace and prosperity. They are eager to re-start production of Glaeon but first Annika must calm the anti-airbreather sentiment that has only intensified among the aquatics while she was off-world. Both airbreathers and aquatics must work together to re-establish production or Annika will lose control of the LEAP Corp to a rival corporation. There's no time to waste, yet she must confront her old enemy, Scylla, before she can take charge of her people's destiny.

Please visit my website, fionakolodzy.com

The Plumdelicious Series Books

Book 1: In Case of DESIRE (November 2022)

Gambling on a daring idea to save their marriage, good-girl Sarah and her husband, Nathan, embark on a journey of insight, determined to rekindle their own lost spark of passion.

Lured into joining the elite swinger group Plumdelicious, they ride the whirlwind of bizarre experiences and wild sexual encounters together, plunged into a new, secret life of attending glamorous parties, carousing at mansions, and cruising steamy tropical islands.

The two novices are in over their heads and have only each other to rely on during their adventure. But will this radical experiment deepen their bond as they hope? Or end up tearing them apart?

Book 2: In Case of DECEIT (June 2023)

Determined to add a little spice into their happily ever-after, Sarah and Nathan Wood re-immerse themselves in the swinger lifestyle. However, fitting in some flings for fun while juggling kids and running a successful swinger website takes a few adjustments this time around. The pair soon take the dangerous step of going on solo dates. Everyone knows swinging is never supposed to lead to falling in love for real. So what happens when a casual swinger finds romance with a second woman who captures his heart?

This second book in the Plumdelicious series stands alone and can be read as a single adventure.

Book 3: In Case of DARING (2024)

Their plates are full, running a swinger club and raising teens, but the urge to explore lives on. Sarah meets an exciting billionaire philanthropist as their circle widens to include displaced immigrants and LGBTQ staff.

Book 4: In Case of DISCOVERY (TBA)

The new generation come into their own. Sarah and Nathan's children experience sexual awakenings at college, while the young employees at the Plumdelicious Club navigate troubles of their own.

This is the QR code to link to The Plumdelicious Series, Book 1: **In Case of DESIRE**, on the Amazon site product page.

FIONAKOLODZY.com

Scan this code to visit Fiona's website, see new releases, Sign Up to receive newsletters, freebies, and more!

www.ingramcontent.com/pod-product-compliance
Lightning Source LLC
Chambersburg PA
CBHW030803260626
47169CB00001B/176